W9-CGO-887

THE STAR TREK READER III

Also published by E. P. Dutton

The Star Trek Reader by James Blish
The Star Trek Reader II by James Blish

THE STAR TREK READER III

adapted by
James Blish

Based on the Television Series
Created by
Gene Roddenberry

E. P. Dutton
New York

The nineteen episodes contained in *The Star Trek Reader III* first published in hardcover, 1977, by E. P. Dutton, a Division of Sequoia-Elsevier Publishing Company, Inc., New York

Library of Congress Catalog Card Number: 76-20260

ISBN: 0-525-20961-1

Published simultaneously in Canada by
Clarke, Irwin & Company Limited, Toronto and Vancouver

10 9 8 7 6 5 4 3 2 1

First Edition

CONTENTS

BOOK I—*Star Trek 5*

BOOK II—*Star Trek 6*

BOOK III—*Star Trek 7*

Book I

Star Trek 5

BOOK I—*Star Trek 5*

WHOM GODS DESTROY

(Lee Erwin and Jerry Sohl)

Dr. Donald Cory seemed almost effusively glad to see Captain Kirk and Spock, not very much to Kirk's surprise. There was ordinary reason enough: Kirk and Governor Cory were old friends, and in addition, Kirk's official reason for the visit was to ferry him a revolutionary new drug which might release him from his bondage. And what bondage! It would take the most dedicated of men to confine himself behind a force field, beneath the poisonous atmosphere of Ebla II, in order to tend the fourteen remaining incurably insane patients in the Galaxy.

"Fifteen, now," Cory said. He was a cheerful-looking man despite his duties, round-faced and white-haired. "You'll remember him, Jim: Garth of Izar."

"Of course I remember him," Kirk said, shocked. "He was one of the most brilliant cadets ever to attend the Academy The last I heard, he was a Starship Fleet Captain—and there were no bets against his becoming an admiral, either. What happened?"

"Something utterly bizarre. He was horribly maimed in an accident off Antos IV. The people there are master surgeons, as you've probably heard. They virtually rebuilt and restored him—and in gratitude, he offered to lead them in an attempt to conquer the Galaxy. They refused, and he then tried to destroy the entire planet with all its inhabitants. One of his officers queried the order with Starfleet Command and, naturally, he wound up here."

"How is he responding?" Spock asked.

"Nobody here responds to anything we try," Cory said. "That in fact is the ultimate reason why they're here at all. Perhaps your new drug will help, but frankly, I'm pessimistic; I can't afford not to be."

"That's understandable," Kirk said. "I'd like to see Garth, Donald. Is that possible?"

"Of course. The security section is this way."

The security cells offered evidence, were any needed, that rare though insanity now was, it was no respecter of races. Most of the inmates behind the individual force fields were humanoid, but among them was a blue Andorian and a pig-faced Tellarite. Perhaps the most pathetic was a young girl, scantily dressed and quite beautiful; her greenish skin suggested that someone of Vulcan-Romulan stock had been among her ancestors, though probably a long time back, for she showed none of the other physical characteristics of those peoples.

As the group passed her, she called out urgently, "Captain! Starship Captain! You're making a mistake! Please—get me out of here and let me tell you what has happened!"

"Poor child," Cory said. "Paranoia with delusions of reference—closer to a classic pattern than anybody else we have here, but all the same we can't break through it. Captain Kirk is pressed for time at the moment, Marta."

The girl ignored him. "There's nothing wrong with me. Can't you see just by looking at me? Can't you tell just by listening to me? Why won't you let me explain?"

"A rational enough question, that last," Spock observed.

"I *am* rational!"

Kirk stopped and turned toward her. "What is it you want to say to me?"

The girl shrank away from the invisible barrier and pointed. "I can't tell you, not in front of him."

"You're afraid to talk because of Governor Cory?"

Her expression became sly, her tone confidential. "He isn't *really* Governor Cory at all, you know."

Kirk looked at Cory, who spread his hands helplessly. "I don't mean to sound callous," he said, "but I hear it every day. Everyone is plotting against her, and naturally I'm the chief villain. Garth's cell is around the corner. He's been unusually disturbed and we've had to impose additional restraints."

He waved them forward. As Kirk turned the corner, he was stunned to discover what Cory had meant by "restraints." The man in the cell was shackled spread-eagled against the wall, his chin sunk upon his chest, a vision straight out of a medieval torture chamber. With a muffled exclamation, Kirk stepped forward. Surely no modern rehabilitation program could necessitate . . .

At the sound, the prisoner looked up. He was disheveled, haggard and wild-eyed, but there could be no doubt about his identity.

He was Governor Cory.

Kirk spun. The other Cory was not there. Standing at the bend of the corridor was a tall, hawk-nosed man with deep-set, glowing eyes, with a phaser trained on the two *Enterprise* officers. Behind him crowded most of the supposedly restrained inmates Kirk had previously seen, also armed.

"Garth!"

"No other," the tall man said pleasantly. "You said you wanted to see me, Captain. Well, here I am. But I suggest you step into the cell first. The screen's down—that's why we had the Governor shackled. Tlollu, put the Vulcan in the biggest empty cell. Captain, drop your weapons on the floor and join your old friend."

Kirk had no choice. As he entered, a faint hum behind him told him that the force field had gone up. He crossed quickly to Cory and tried to release him, but the shackles turned out to be servo-driven; the control was obviously outside somewhere. Cory said hoarsely, "Sorry he tricked you, Jim."

"Don't worry, we'll think of something."

"Our esteemed Governor," Garth's voice said, "reacts to pain quite stoically, doesn't he?"

Kirk turned. The green-skinned girl was also free, and clinging to Garth, who was fondling her absently.

"Garth, you've got me. What's the point in making Cory suffer like this . . ."

"You will address me by my proper title, Kirk!"

"Sorry. I should have said Captain Garth."

"Starship Fleet Captain is merely one of my minor titles," Garth said with haughty impatience. "I am Lord Garth of Izar—and future Emperor of the Galaxy."

Oho, this was going to be very tricky; Garth had described his own madness all too accurately. "My apologies, Lord Garth."

"We forgive you. Of course, you think I'm a madman, don't you, and are humoring me. But if so, why am I out here while you two are in there?" Garth roared with laughter at his own joke. Kirk, finding the girl, Marta, watching him intently, forced a smile. She whispered in Garth's ear. "Later, perhaps. Marta seems quite taken with you, Captain Fortunately for you, I have no weaknesses, not even jealousy."

"I tried to warn you, Captain," Marta said. "Remember?"

"She did, you know," Garth said affably. "But of course I had so arranged matters that you would not listen. Our Marta is indeed a little unstable."

"What," Kirk said, "do you expect to accomplish with a staff of fourteen mad creatures?"

"Now you try reason. That is better. The Izarians, Captain, are inherently a master race. Much more so than the Romulans and the Klingons, as their failures have shown. When I return triumphantly from exile, my people will rally to my cause."

"Then you have nothing to fear from Governor Cory. Why don't you release him?"

"I fear no one; the point is well taken. You see, we can also be magnanimous." He touched a device at his belt. Behind Kirk, Cory's shackles sprang open with a clang; Kirk only just managed to catch the tortured Governor before he fell to the floor.

"Thank you, Lord Garth," Kirk said. "What have you done with the medicine I brought?"

"That poison? I destroyed it, of course. Enough of this chatter; it is time I took command of the ship you brought me. You will help me, of course."

"Why should I?"

"Because I need the ship," Garth said, with surprised patience. "My crew mutinied. So did my Fleet Captains. The first use I will make of the *Enterprise* is to hunt them down and punish them for that."

"My crew won't obey any such lunatic orders," Kirk said, abandoning with disgust any attempt to be reasonable with the poor, dangerous creature. "You're stuck, Garth. Give it up."

"Your crew will obey you, Captain. And you forget how easily I convinced *you* that I was your old friend Governor Donald Cory. It's a helpful technique, as you will observe. Watch."

Garth's features, even his very skin, seemed to crawl. When the horrifying metamorphosis was over—and it took only a few seconds—the man inside the false Cory's clothes was no longer Garth, but a mirror-Kirk.

The duplicate grinned, gave a mock salute, and strode off. Marta remained for a moment, giving Kirk a look of peculiar intensity. Then she too left, murmuring something under her breath.

"I—was praying you wouldn't get here at all," Cory said. "A starship is all he needs—and now he's got one."

"Not quite. And even if he does gain command of the *Enterprise*, one of my officers is bound to appeal his first crazy order to Starfleet Command, just as his own officers did."

"Jim, are you sure of that?"

Kirk realized that he was not at all sure of it. In the past, acting under sealed orders had forced him to give what seemed to be irrational orders often enough so that, tit for tat, his crew assumed any irrationality on his part was bound to be explained eventually. He had, in fact, long been afraid that that would be the outcome.

"No—I'm far from sure. But one starship is not a fleet; even if my officers obey him implicitly, there's a limit to the harm he can do."

"Those limits are pretty wide," Cory said. "He says he has devised a simple, compact method for making even stable suns go nova. I think it quite likely that he has. Can you imagine what a blackmail weapon that would be? And if the Izarians do rally to him—which wouldn't surprise me either, they've always been rather edgy and recalcitrant members of the Federation—then he has his fleet, too. It won't do to underestimate him, Jim."

"I don't. He was a genius, that I remember very well. What a waste!"

Cory did not answer.

"How does he manage that shape-changing trick?"

"The people of Antos taught him the technique of cellular metamorphosis and rearrangement, so he could help them restore the destroyed parts of his body. It's not uncommon in nature; on Earth, even lowly animals like crabs and starfish have it. But Garth is a long way from being a lower animal. He can mimic any form he wishes to now. He used it to kill off my entire medical staff—and to trap me. And laughed. I can still hear that laugh. And to think I hoped to rehabilitate him!"

"There's still a chance. Even masquerading as me, Garth can't get aboard the *Enterprise* without a password—we made that standard procedure after some nasty encounters with hypnosis and other forms of deception."

"Where does that leave us, Jim? He's got us."

"Why," Kirk said slowly, "he will have to ask us for help. And when that time comes, he'll get it—and it will be, with any luck at all, not the help he thinks he wants, but the help he needs."

"If you can do that," Cory said, "you're a better doctor than I am."

"I'm not a doctor at all," Kirk said. "But if I can get him into McCoy's hands . . ."

"McCoy? If you mean Leonard McCoy, he's probably Chief Medical Director of Starfleet Command by now. Hopeless."

"No, Donald. Garth is not an admiral, and McCoy is not warming any bench on Earth, either. He's in orbit right above our heads. He's the Medical Officer of the *Enterprise*."

Cory was properly staggered, but he recovered quickly. "Then," he said, "all we have to do is get Garth onto the *Enterprise*—which is exactly what he wants. I can't say that you fill me with optimism, Jim."

Garth appeared outside the cell the next day, all smiles and solicitude. "I hope you haven't been too uncomfortable, Captain?"

"I've been in worse places."

"Still, I'm afraid I've been somewhat remiss in my duties as your host. In my *persona* as Cory, I invited you down to my planet for dinner—you and Mr. Spock. The invitation still stands."

"Where is Mr. Spock?"

In answer, Garth beckoned, and Spock was brought around the corner, surrounded by an armed guard of madmen. Among them was Marta, smiling, a phaser leveled at Spock's head.

"Nice to see you, Mr. Spock."

"Thank you, Captain."

Kirk turned back to Garth. "Isn't Governor Cory dining with us?"

"Governor Cory is undergoing an involuntary fast, necessitated by his resisting me. You will find, however, that for those who cooperate we set a handsome table."

Kirk was about to refuse when Cory said, "You can't help me by going hungry, Jim. Go along with them."

"Good advice, Governor," Garth said, beaming. "Well, Captain?"

"You're very persuasive."

Garth laughed and led the way.

The staff refectory of the Elba II station had evidently been once as drably utilitarian as such places always tend to be, but now it looked like the scene of a Roman banquet. Garth waved Kirk and Spock to places between himself and Marta. They sat down wordlessly, aware of the vigilant presence at their backs of the Tellarite and the Andorian. Kirk became aware, as well, that Marta was virtually fawning on him.

Garth glared at her. "Hands off, slut."

This only seemed to please the girl. "You're jealous, after all!" she said.

"Nonsense. I'm above that sort of thing. The Captain is annoyed by your attentions. That's all."

The girl looked sweetly at Kirk. "Am I annoying you, darling?"

This looked like a good opportunity to provoke a little

dissension in the ranks of the mad. "Not really," Kirk said.

"You see? He's fascinated by me and it bothers you. Admit it."

"He said nothing of the sort," Garth retorted. "Your antics will lead to nothing but your being beaten to death."

"No, they won't. You wouldn't. I'm the most beautiful woman on this planet."

"Necessarily, since you're the only one," Garth said.

The girl preened herself. "I'm the most beautiful woman in the Galaxy. And I'm intelligent, too, and I write poetry and I paint marvelous pictures and I'm a wonderful dancer."

"Lies. all lies! Let me hear one poem you've written."

"If you like," Marta said calmly. She got up and moved to the front of the table, striking an absurdly theatrical pose. At the same time, Spock leaned slightly closer to Kirk.

"Captain," he said almost inaudibly, through motionless lips, "if you could create a diversion, I might find my way to the control room to release the force field."

Kirk nodded. The notion was a good one; all they would need would be a few seconds if Scotty had a security detail alerted—as he probably did have if Garth had already tried to pass himself off as Kirk without the password.

Garth was glaring at Marta, who, however, was looking only at Kirk. She began:

> Shall I compare thee to a summer's day?
> Thou art more lovely and more temperate.
> Rough winds do shake the darling buds of May,
> And summer's lease hath all too . . .

"*You* wrote that?" Garth broke in, shouting.

"Yesterday, as a matter of fact."

"More lies. It was written by an Earthman named Shakespeare a long time ago."

"Which doesn't change the fact that I wrote it again yesterday. I think it's one of my best poems, don't you?"

Garth controlled his temper with an obvious effort. "Sit down, Marta, you waste everyone's time. Captain, if you really want her, you can have her."

"Most magnanimous," Kirk said drily.

"You will find that I *am* magnanimous to my friends

—and merciless to my enemies. I want you, both of you, to be my friends."

"Upon what, precisely," Spock said, "will our friendship be based?"

"Upon the firmest of foundations—enlightened self-interest. You, Captain, are second only to me as the finest military commander in the Galaxy."

"That's flattering, but at present I'm primarily an explorer."

"As I have been too. I have charted more new worlds than any man in history."

"Neither of these records can help a man who has lost his judgment," Spock said coldly. "How could you, a Starship Fleet Captain, have believed that a Federation squadron would blindly obey an order to destroy the entire Antos race? That people is as famous for its benevolence as for its skill—as your own survival proves."

"That was my only miscalculation," Garth said. "I had risen above this decadent weakness, but my officers had not. My new officers, the men in this room, will obey me without question. As for you, you both have eyes but cannot see. The Galaxy surrounds us—limitless vistas —and yet the Federation would have us grub away like ants in a somewhat larger than usual anthill. But I am not an insect. I am a master, and will claim my realm."

"I agree," Kirk said, "that war is not always avoidable and that you were a great warrior. I studied your victory at Axanar when I was a cadet. It's required reading at the Academy to this day."

"Which is as it should be."

"Quite so. But my first visit to Axanar was as a newfledged lieutenant with the peace mission."

"Politicians and weaklings," Garth said. "They threw away my victory."

"No, they capped it with another. They were statesmen and humanitarians, and they had a dream—a dream that has become a reality and has spread throughout the stars. A dream that has made Mr. Spock and me brothers."

Garth smiled tightly and turned to Spock. "Do you feel that Captain Kirk is your brother?"

"Captain Kirk," Spock said, "speaks figuratively. But

with due allowance for this, what he says is logical and I do, in fact, agree with it."

"Blind—truly blind. Captain Kirk is your commanding officer and you are his subordinate; the rest is sugar-coating. But you are a worthy commander in your own right, and in my fleet you will assuredly have a starship to command."

"Forgive me," Spock said, "but exactly where *is* your fleet?"

Garth made a sweeping gesture. "Out there—waiting for me; they will flock to my cause with good reason. Limitless wealth, limitless power, solar systems ruled by the elite. We, gentlemen, are that elite. We must take what is rightfully ours from the stultifying clutches of decadence."

Spock was studying Garth with the expression of a bacteriologist confronted by a germ he had thought long extinct. "You must be aware," he said, "that you are attempting to repeat the disaster that resulted in your becoming an inmate of this place."

"I was betrayed—and then treated barbarically."

"On the contrary, you were treated justly and with a compassion you displayed toward none of your intended victims. Logically, therefore, it would . . ."

Garth bounded to his feet with a strangled cry, pointing a trembling forefinger at Spock. All other sound in the hall stopped at once.

"Remove this—this walking computer!"

Spock was removed, none too gently. Kirk's abortive move to intervene was blocked by the smiling Marta, who had produced her phaser seemingly from nowhere.

Garth took the weapon from her, and instantly switched back to his parody of the affable host. "Won't you try some of this wine, Captain?"

"Thank you, but I prefer to join Mr. Spock."

"And I prefer that you remain here. We have many divertisements more diverting than Marta's poetry, I assure you. By the way, I assume you play chess?"

"Quite a lot. We have a running tournament aboard the *Enterprise*."

"Not unusual. How would you respond to Queen to Queen's Level Three?"

So—Garth had tried to fool Scotty and had been

stopped by the code challenge; now he was fishing for the countersign. "There are, as you know, thousands of possible responses, especially if the move is not an opening one."

"I'm interested in only one."

"I can't for the life of me imagine which."

"'For the life of me' is a well-chosen phrase," Garth said, smiling silkily. "It could literally come to that, Captain."

"I doubt it. Dead I'm of no use to you at all."

"I could make you beg for death."

Kirk laughed. "Torture? You were Academy-trained, Garth. Suppose *I* attempted to break *your* conditioning by such means; would it work?"

"No," Garth admitted. "But observe, Captain, that Governor Cory is not Academy-trained, and furthermore has been weakened by his recent, ah, reverses. And among his medical equipment is a curious chair which was used in the rehabilitation process. As such it was quite painless, and, I might add, also useless. It made men docile, and hence of no use to me. I have added certain refinements to it which make it no longer painless—yet the pain can be prolonged indefinitely because there is no actual destruction of tissue."

"In the midnights of November," Marta said suddenly, "when the dead man's fair is nigh, and danger in the valley, and anger in the sky—I wrote that this morning."

"Very appropriate," Kirk said grimly.

"Tell him what he wants. Then we'll go away together."

Kirk's lips thinned. It was the old double device of the carrot and the stick, and in a very crude form, at that. But it wouldn't do to reject the carrot out of hand; the girl was obviously too unstable for that.

"Torturing Governor Cory," he said, "would be quite useless. I would simply force you to kill me; if you didn't, I would intervene."

"Phasers can be set to stun."

"If I am unconscious, I can't be blackmailed by Governor Cory's pain, can I?"

Garth glared at him for a long moment with unwinking eyes. Then a spasm of pure rage twisted his face. Raising the phaser, he leveled it at Kirk and fired point-blank.

Kirk awoke to a sound of liquid gurgling quietly. Then it stopped, and Kirk felt a cup of some sort being pressed to his lips. He swallowed automatically. Wine. Pretty good, too.

"Slowly," said a woman's voice. "Slowly, my darling."

That was Marta. He opened his eyes. He was lying on a divan with the girl sitting beside him, a goblet in her hands; there was a carafe on a small table nearby.

"Rest," she said. "You're in my room." She took his hand and kissed it gently, then stroked his face.

Kirk studied her. "So he's decided to give the carrot another try?"

"I don't understand you," she said. "I was terrified that he would put you in the Chair. I told him I would discover your secret. I lied. I would have told him anything to save you from the torment."

After a moment Kirk said, "I think you mean that."

"I do." She leaned forward and embraced him, sighing and clinging. "This is where I've longed to be. I think I knew I loved you the first moment I saw you."

Kirk disengaged himself gently. "I want to help you, Marta. If I can get back to the *Enterprise,* I'll be able to."

"It's not possible."

"There's a way," Kirk said. "If I can get to the control room and cut off the force field, Garth is finished."

"Garth is my leader."

"And he'll lead you to your destruction. He has already destroyed the medicine that might have helped you. But I think my Ship's Surgeon has a sample he might be able to duplicate."

"I will help you in a little while," Marta said thoughtfully. "Your friend Spock will soon be here, and then we will see. I've arranged that much, at any rate."

Was there no predicting this girl? "How did you do it?"

"A convincing lie," she said, shrugging, "told to a guard who finds me desirable."

"Marta, let me help you, too. If I can get away from Garth, back aboard . . ."

She silenced him with a kiss, which he did not fight. When they separated, she was breathing hard and her eyes were glittering.

"There is a way," she said. "A way in which we can

be together always. Where Garth cannot harm us. Trust me and believe in me, darling."

She kissed him again, clutching at him with almost animal intensity. At the same time, he became aware that her left hand was burrowing between the cushions of the divan. He pulled away, to discover a long, thin, wicked-looking knife which she had been about to drive into his back.

He shoved her away, hard. Almost at the same instant, Spock stepped into sight and seized her upper arms from behind.

She looked back over her shoulder. "You mustn't stop me," she said reasonably, reproachfully. "He is my love and so I must kill him. It is the only way to save him from Lord Garth."

Spock pinched her neck. The knife clattered to the floor as she slumped.

"Apparently," Spock said expressionlessly, "she has worked out an infallible method for ensuring male fidelity. An interesting aberration."

"I'm glad to see you, Mr. Spock."

"Thank you, Captain. I am now armed, and I assume we will try to reach the control room. Would you like the weapon?"

"No, I'm still a littly shaky; you handle it. The room will be guarded."

"Then we will blast our way in."

That was surprisingly ferocious of Spock; perhaps the attempted murder of his Captain had shaken him momentarily? "Only if it's absolutely necessary, Mr. Spock. Meanwhile, set your phaser on 'stun.' "

"I have already done so, Captain."

They stepped cautiously out of the room, then were forced to duck back in again as footsteps approached. Once the inmates had passed, they stole out into the corridor.

The guard before the control room was the Tellarite. He seemed to be in some sort of trance; Spock stunned him as easily as shooting a sitting duck. Kirk scooped up the fallen man's phaser, and they stuffed the limp body into a nearby closet.

Kirk cautiously tried the door. "Unlocked," he whispered. "I'll kick it open; you go in ready to shoot."

"Yes, Captain."

They burst in; but the place was deserted. Spock strode to the master switch and threw it. "Force field now off, Captain."

Kirk stationed himself at the console and activated the communicator. "Kirk to *Enterprise*. Kirk to *Enterprise*."

"Here, Captain," Uhura's voice said. "Mr. Scott, it's Captain Kirk!"

The view screen lit to show Scotty's face. "Scott here, Captain. You had us worried."

"Have Dr. McCoy synthesize a new supply of drug as fast as possible."

"Aye aye, sir."

"And I want a fully armed security detail here, Scotty, on the double."

"They're already in the Transporter Room."

"It would be better," Spock said, "if you were to return to the *Enterprise* at once."

"Why?" Kirk asked in astonishment.

"Your safety is vital to the ship. I can take charge of the security detail."

"I see," Kirk said. "Very well, Mr. Spock. Mr. Scott, beam me aboard on receipt of countersign."

"Aye, sir," the engineer said. "Queen to Queen's Level Three."

"Mr. Spock will give the countersign." Kirk leveled his phaser. "Go ahead, Spock—if that's who you are. Give him the countersign. You're supposed to know it."

"Security guard ready," Scott's voice said. "Mr. Sulu, lock into beamdown coordinates. Ensign Wyatt, ready to energize."

Spock reached for the master switch, his lineaments already changing into the less familiar ones of Garth. Kirk pulled his trigger. Nothing happened. The switch clicked home; the force field was reactivated.

"Blast away, Captain," Garth said. "I would not be fool enough to let you capture a charged phaser."

"Where is Spock? What have you done to him?"

"He is in his cell. And I have done nothing to him yet. But anything that does happen henceforth will be on your conscience—unless you give me the countersign."

"Captain Garth . . ."

"Lord Garth."

"No, sir. Captain—Starship Fleet Captain—is an honored title, and it was once yours."

"Quite true," Garth said, but his own phaser did not waver. "And I was the greatest of them all, wasn't I?"

"You were. But now you're a sick man."

Garth bristled. "I've never been more healthy."

"Think," Kirk said. "Think back. Try to remember what you were like before the accident that sent you to Antos IV."

"I—I can't remember," Garth said. "It's—almost as if I died and was reborn."

"But I remember you. You were always the finest of the Fleet Captains. You were the prototype, and a model for the rest of us."

"Yesss—I do remember that. It was a great responsibility—but one I was proud to bear."

"And you bore it well. Captain Garth, the disease that changed you is not your fault. Nor are you truly responsible for the things you've done since then—no matter how terrible they may seem to you, or to us."

"I don't want to hear any more of this," Garth said, but his voice was less decisive than his words. "You—you're weak, and you're trying to drain me of my strength."

"No! I want you to regain what you once had. I want you to go back to the greatness you lost."

For a moment Kirk thought he had been winning, but this was all too evidently the wrong tack. Garth stiffened, and the wavering phaser came back into line.

"I have never lost greatness! It was taken from me! But I shall be greater still. I am Lord Garth, Master of the Galaxy."

"Listen to me, dammit . . ."

"The others failed, but I will not. Alexander, Lee Kuan, Napoleon, Hitler, Krotus—all of them are dust, but I will triumph."

"Triumph or fail," Kirk said levelly, "you too will be dust."

"Not yet. Back to your cell, ex-Captain Kirk. Soon your doubts will be laid to rest. Out!"

The Tellarite and the Andorian came back for him the next day and hauled him out into the corridor, leaving

Governor Cory behind. They brought him back to the refectory, where all the rest of Garth's followers—except Marta, who was not to be seen—were working to transform the hall from a banquet scene into some sort of ceremonial chamber. Garth was there, seemingly childishly happy, dividing his attention between Kirk and his minions.

"The throne must be higher—higher than anything else. Use that table as a pedestal. Welcome back, Captain. You will be needed for our coronation."

"Coronation?" Kirk said, a little dazed.

"I know that even a real throne is merely a chair, but the symbolism is important, don't you agree? And the crown will be only a token in itself; but it will serve as a standard around which our followers will rally."

"You have only a handful of men."

Garth smiled. "Others have begun with less, but none will have reached so far as we. Good, very good. Now we will want a royal carpet for our feet. That cloth will do nicely. The tread of our feet will sanctify it."

"And it will still be a tablecloth, stained by food and wine," Kirk said. "That's all."

"My dear Captain, you do refuse to enter into the spirit of the thing, don't you? Would you prefer a larger role in the ceremony? You could serve as a human sacrifice, for example."

"I'm sure I wouldn't enjoy the rest of it. And you seem to need me alive."

"That's true. All right. How about Crown Prince?"

"I'm not part of the family. Who were they again? Krotus, Alexander, Hitler, Genghis Khan and so forth?"

"Genghis Khan," Garth said reflectively. "I'd forgotten about him. Heir apparent, I believe, that's the proper role for you. Now we think we are ready. Excuse us for the moment, Captain."

Garth bowed grandly and went out. The guards remained alert; the Tellarite, who had been stunned in Garth's earlier attempt to trick the countersign out of Kirk, was regarding the Captain with especial vigilance—and no little animosity. Evidently he had forgotten, if he had ever known, that the whole charade had been arranged by Garth himself.

Suddenly the air shook with a blast of recorded music.

Kirk did not have to be an expert to recognize it: it was, ironically, *Ich bete an die Macht der Liebe*, by somebody named Bortniansky, to which all Academy classes marched to their graduation.

The refectory doors were drawn aside, and Garth, not very resplendent in a cast-off uniform, entered solemnly, chin up, eyes hooded. Beneath his right arm was tucked a crown which looked as if it had been hastily cut from a piece of sheet metal. On his right arm was Marta, swathed in trailing bedsheets and looking decidedly subdued.

The other madmen dropped to their knees, and the cold nose of a phaser against the back of his neck reminded Kirk not to remain standing alone. It came just in time—he had been almost about to laugh.

Stepping slowly in time to the processional, the "royal" couple proceeded along the "carpet" to the "throne," which they mounted. Garth turned and signaled his followers to rise. The music stopped.

"Since there is no one here, or elsewhere in the known universe, mighty enough to perform such a ceremony," he said grandly, "we will perform it ourselves. Therefore, we hereby proclaim that we are Lord Garth, formerly of Izar, now Master-that-is-to-come of the Galaxy."

He settled the metal crown upon his own head. "And now, we designate our beloved Marta to be our consort."

Garth kissed her chastely on the forehead. She shrank away from him, but stood her ground. Carefully, he fastened around her throat what appeared to be a necklace with a diamond pendant; conceivably it held the diamond from Garth's own Fleet Captain clasp, but somehow Kirk doubted that.

Garth seated himself upon the throne. "And now, guards, remove our beloved consort and our heir apparent, so that they may conclude their vital roles in this ritual."

They took Marta out first. As she was surrounded, she she began to keen—an eerie, wailing dirge that chilled Kirk's blood. They had her hands pinned behind her back.

Then the Tellarite and the Andorian were prodding

him out of the refectory, through a different door. He saw at once where he was being driven: back to the control room. Behind him, the music crashed out again, and the guards marched him along in step.

"Listen to me," he said urgently, under cover of the noise. "This may be your only chance."

They poked him with their phasers. The door to the control room loomed ahead.

"Garth will destroy all of us if you don't help me stop him," Kirk continued to the air before him. "He's using you. All he wants is power for himself. I brought you something that might have cured you, but he destroyed it."

There was no answer. Why did he continue to try reasoning with these madmen anyhow? But at the moment there seemed to be nothing else to try.

The control room was empty. The closing of the door cut the music off. The blades of the force-field switch gleamed invitingly only a few yards away.

"If I can get a patrol in here, they'll bring more of the medicine. Garth will be finished and all of us will be safe again. Safe, and well."

Stolidly, one of the guards waved him to a chair. Kirk shrugged and sat down. There was what seemed to be an immensely long wait.

Then Garth came in, still in uniform but no longer wearing the crown. In one hand he was carrying a small flask packed with glittering crystals.

"Well done," he said to the guards. "Kirk, your resistance has now reached the point of outright stupidity, and is a considerable inconvenience to us. We propose to take sterner measures."

"If it's any further inconvenience to you, I'll be happy to cooperate."

"We shall see. Let us first introduce you to our latest invention." He tossed the flask into the air and caught it with the other hand. "This is an explosive, Captain, the most powerful one in history. Or, let us be accurate, the most powerful of all chemical explosives This flask can vaporize the entire station; in fact, the crater it would leave would crack the crust of the planet. We trust you do not doubt our word."

"You were quite capable of such a discovery in the

past," Kirk said. "I have every reason to believe you still are."

"Good. Here!" Suddenly, Garth tossed the flask to one of the guards. Since the man had only one hand free to catch it, he very nearly dropped it. He was in great haste to throw it back to Garth, who resumed juggling it, laughing.

"How are your nerves, Captain?"

"Excellent, thank you. If it happens to me, it happens to you. That's all I need to know."

"Then we are halfway toward a solution already," Garth said. "Actually, dropping the flask would not so much as break it; the explosive must be set off electrically, from the board. But in fact, I am quite prepared to do so. Do you see why?"

"I can see that you're bluffing."

"Then your logic is deficient. Perhaps we need your friend Spock to help you reason. He is a logical man. Yes, a very logical man." Garth looked briefly at the guards. "Go and bring the Vulcan here to us."

The guards went out. Kirk felt the first surge of real hope in days. To the best of his knowledge, Spock—the real Spock—had not been taken out of his cell since his first imprisonment, when he had been confronted with impossible odds; and, being logical, had allowed himself to be taken. But in hand-to-hand combat, he was also a machine of outright inhuman efficiency. Sending only two guards to fetch him—and on top of that, aliens who probably had no experience with either the human or the Vulcan styles of infighting—was folly; or so he had to hope.

"In the meantime, Captain, let us expose the logic of the situation to you. It is your responsibility to preserve Federation lives and property—not only your life, Mr. Spock's, Governor Cory's, but that of everyone here, even including our own. You need not confirm this; as a sometime officer of the Federation—as our uniform should remind you—this was once our responsibility as well."

"It still is," Kirk said stonily.

"We have higher responsibilities now. Above all, a responsibility to our destiny. To this, you hold the key. We cannot advance further until we are in command of the *Enterprise*. Nor can we expect another such opportunity to arise in the practicable future. It might be said, in short, that if you remain stubborn, we no longer have a future, and are under no further responsibility toward it. Do you follow us so far?"

Kirk was a good distance ahead of him by now, and not at all liking what he found there. Even Spock, he suspected, would have to concede that the trap was indeed logical, however insane.

There was a buzz from the console. Moving sidewise, Garth activated a screen. Kirk could not see what it showed, but Garth obligingly told him.

"Your Vulcan friend is a most ingenious fellow. He has somehow disposed of my associates—who will suffer for their inefficiency—and is coming this way, armed. This could be most amusing."

"The joke is entirely on you," Kirk said. "You'll have no chance to play logic games now. Whichever one of us you shoot first, the other one will have you."

"Our training was as good as yours; the outcome is by no means so inevitable. Indeed, it suggests an even better scheme."

Garth moved behind Kirk, out of sight. This moved him away from the console, which he evidently reconsidered, for a moment later he went back to it—changed.

There were now two Captain Kirks. Even the uniforms were in a nearly identical state of wear and tear now. Smiling, Garth threw in all his previous cards; he even put his phaser out of reach.

Kirk tensed to spring. At the same instant, the door shot open and Spock crouched in it, phaser ready. He seemed prepared for anything except, possibly, what he found; he actually blinked in surprise.

"That's Garth," Garth said urgently, pointing. "Blast him!"

"Hold it, Spock! The madman *wants* you to shoot me!"

"Look at us carefully, Spock. Can't you tell I'm your Captain?"

"Queen to Queen Three," Spock said.

"I won't answer that. It's the one thing he wants to know."

"Very clever, Garth. I was about to say the same thing."

Spock, keeping both Kirks under the gun, crossed to the master switch.

"What are you doing?"

"Arranging to beam down a patrol," Spock said. "I should be interested to hear any objections."

"They'll walk into a trap."

"That's true, Spock. Garth can destroy the whole station instantly if he wants."

The double agreement halted the Science Officer. After a moment he said, "What maneuver did we use to defeat the Romulan torchship off Tau Centi?"

"Conchrane deceleration."

"A standard maneuver with an enemy faster than one's self. Every Starship Captain knows that."

"Agreed, Captain," Spock said to both. "Or Captains. Gentlemen, whichever one of you is Captain Garth must at this moment be expending a great deal of energy to maintain the image of Captain Kirk. That energy level cannot be maintained indefinitely. Since I am half Vulcan, I can outwait you; I have time."

"I propose a simpler solution. Shoot us both."

"Wait, Spock! I agree, he's quite right. But you must *shoot to kill*. It's the only way to ensure the safety of the *Enterprise*."

Instantly, Spock whirled on Garth and fired. Kirk sprang to the console.

"Kirk to *Enterprise* . . ."

"Scott here. Queen to Queen's Level Three."

"Queen to King's Level One."

"Aye aye, sir. Orders?"

"Beam down Dr. McCoy with the new drug supply—and the security guards with him."

"Aye, sir. Scott out."

Kirk turned. "Well done, Mr. Spock. Did you damage either of the guards seriously?"

"I fear I broke the Tellarite's arm."

"A trifle. Help me haul this hulk to the treatment room."

Garth, still unconscious, was in the same chair he had once proposed to use as an instrument of torture; Cory had stripped it of his modifications.

"Dr. McCoy, how long does this drug need to take effect?"

"Reversal of arterial and brain damage begins at once, but the rate depends on the individual. I'd say you could start as soon as—great looping comets!"

Garth had still been mimicking Kirk, even while stunned, a further evidence of his enormous personal drive. But now the change back was beginning; Kirk had forgotten that McCoy hadn't seen the process before.

"All right," McCoy said, swallowing. "Start now."

The chair whined, almost inaudibly. Then Cory cut it off. "That's all I dare give him for a starter."

Garth's eyes opened. They were peaceful but vacant, as though he had no mind left at all. They passed from one captor to another, without recognition. He began to whimper.

Kirk leaned toward him. "Captain."

Garth's moans stopped. He looked pleadingly up at Kirk.

"Captain Garth—I'm James Kirk. Perhaps you remember me."

Garth's expression, or lack of it, did not change. He looked toward Spock, and frowned slightly.

"I am a Federation Science Officer, Captain," Spock said.

"We are from the Starship *Enterprise*," Kirk said. "I am her Captain."

Garth looked back at Kirk, long and hard. Something was awakening in him, after all. He struggled to speak. Finally the mumbled words became clear.

"Federation—Starship . . ."

"Yes, sir. The *Enterprise*."

Cory was watching closely. Garth slowly reached out his hand. Kirk took it.

"A—privilege, sir. My ship is—no, cancel that. I have no ship. I am a Fleet Captain."

"My honor, Captain."

"That's enough," Cory said. He put his arms under Garth's and helped him from the chair. "Thank you, gentlemen. I can manage him now, and the rest of them, I'm sure."

As they moved off, Garth turned for a last look at

Kirk. It was now alarmingly penetrating, but still puzzled. "Should I know you, sir?" he asked.

Time for a new beginning. "No, Captain—no."

He was led out. Looking after him, Kirk said, Tell me something, Mr. Spock."

"Yes, Captain."

"Why was it so impossible to tell the difference between us?"

"It was not impossible, Captain. Our presence here is proof of that."

"Yes, and congratulations. But what took you so *long?*"

"The interval of uncertainty was actually fairly brief, Captain. It only seemed long—to you. As I threatened then, I could have waited you both out, but you made that unnecessary by proposing that I kill both of you. It was not a decision Garth could have made."

Kirk felt a faint chill. "Excuse me, Mr. Spock, but I think that's wrong. He had only just finished readying himself to destroy not only both of us, but the whole station."

"Yes, Captain, I believe he was capable of that. It would have been a grand immolation of his whole scheme. But to die by himself, ignominiously, leaving followers behind to see his defeat—no, I do not believe megalomaniacs think like that."

"I see. Well, there's no doubt about how you think."

"Indeed, sir?"

"Yes, indeed—fast. *Very* fast." Kirk raised his communicator. "Kirk to *Enterprise*. Three to beam up, Scotty."

"King," Spock added without a trace of a smile, "to King's Level One."

THE THOLIAN WEB

(Judy Burns and Chet Richards)

The bridge was at full muster—Kirk, Scott, Spock, Uhura, Chekov, Sulu—and extremely tense. The *Enterprise* was in unsurveyed territory, approaching the last reported position of the Starship *Defiant,* which had vanished without a trace three weeks ago.

"Captain," Spock said, "I have lost the use of all sensors. Were I to believe these readings, space itself is breaking up around us."

"A major failure?"

"Not in the sensors, sir; I have run a complete systems check. The failure is mine; I simply do not know how to interpret these reports."

"Captain," Scott added, "there may be no connection, but we're losing power in the warp engines."

"How bad is it?"

"We can hardly feel it now, but it's richt abnormal all the same. I canna find the cause."

Now it was Chekov's turn. "Captain, we have visual detection of an object dead ahead. It *looks* like a starship."

It did, at that, but not a starship in any condition to which they were accustomed. It was visibly shimmering.

"Mr. Spock, what's wrong with it?"

"Nonexistence, to put the matter in a word, Captain. There is virtually no radar return, mass analysis, radiation traces. We see it, but the sensors indicate it isn't there."

"Mr. Chekov, narrow the field and see if you can bring up the identification numbers. It's the *Defiant*, all right. Mr. Sulu, impulse engines only. Close to Transporter range. Lieutenant Uhura, open a hailing channel."

"I've been trying to raise them, sir, but there's no response."

Chekov shifted the viewing angle again. The other ship showed no gaping holes or other signs of damage. It was just ghostly—and silent.

"Within Transporter range, sir."

"Thanks, Mr. Sulu. Lieutenant, order Dr. McCoy to the Transporter Room. Mr. Spock, Mr. Chekov, I'll want you as well. Environment suits all around; O'Neil to handle the Transporter. Take over, Mr. Scott."

The Transporter was locked onto the bridge of the *Defiant*. The lighting there turned out to be extremely subdued; even some monitor lights were not functioning. But the situation was all too visible, nonetheless.

A man somewhat older than Kirk, wearing a captain's stripes, lay dead in his command chair, a number one phaser clutched in one hand. The other hand was twisted in the hair of a junior officer. The junior was also dead, with both his hands locked around the Captain's neck.

Chekov was the first to speak. "Has there ever been a mutiny on a starship before?"

"Technically," Spock said, "the refusal of Captain Garth's fleet to follow his orders when he became insane was a mutiny. But there has never been any record of an occurrence like this."

McCoy stopped to examine the bodies. "The Captain's neck is broken, Jim."

"This ship is still functioning," Spock said after a quick check of the communications console. "It is logical to assume that the mutineers are somewhere aboard. Yet the sensors show no sign of life anywhere in the vessel."

"Odd," Kirk said reflectively. "Very odd. Spock, you

stay here with me. Chekov, get down to Life Support and Engineering. Dr. McCoy, check out sickbay. I want some answers."

The two men moved off. As they did so, Scott's voice sounded in Kirk's helmet. "Captain, Mr. Sulu reports that he can't get an accurate fix on the *Defiant*, but it seems to be drifting away. Should he correct for range?"

Still odder. How could one ship be moving relative to the other when neither was under power? "Keep us within beaming range, but not too close."

"Chekov reporting, Captain. All dead in Life Support and in Engineering as well."

"Right. Get back up here. Bones?"

"More bodies, Jim. Proximate cause of deaths, various forms of violence. In short, I'd say they killed each other."

"Could a mental disease possibly have inflicted all of the crew at once?"

"It may still be here, sir," Chekov said, reappearing. "I feel pretty funny myself—headachy, dizzy."

"I can't answer the question," McCoy's voice said. "According to the medical log, even the ship's surgeon here didn't really know what was going on. The best I can do for you is take all the readings I can get and analyze them later. Now what the devil . . . ?"

"Bones! What's happening?"

There was a brief silence. Then: "Jim, this ship's beginning to dissolve! I just put my hand right *through* a corpse—and then through the wall next to him."

"Get back up here on the double. Kirk to *Enterprise*. Mr. Scott, stand by to beam us back."

"Captain, I can't. Not all at once, at least."

"What do you mean? What's going on over there?"

"Nothing we can understand," Scott's voice said grimly. "The *Defiant* is fading out, and it's—well, something is ripping the innards out of our own ship. It's jamming our Transporter frequencies. We've got only three working, and I can't be sure about those. One of you has got to wait."

"Request permission to remain," Spock said. "I could be completing the data."

"It's more important to get what you already have into analysis on the *Enterprise*. Don't argue. I'll probably be right after you."

But he was not. Within moments after Spock, Chekov and McCoy materialized aboard the *Enterprise*, the *Defiant* had vanished.

Scott was at the consoles with the Transporter officer. Spock joined them, removing his helmet, and scanned the board.

"See anything I don't?" Scott said.

"Apparently not. Everything is negative."

McCoy took off his own helment. "But he's got to be out there somewhere. If the Transporter won't grab him, what about the shuttlecraft? There must be some way to pick him up."

"There is no present trace of the Captain, Doctor," Spock said evenly. "The only next possible action is to feed the computer our data and see what conclusions can be drawn."

The computer was the fastest of its kind, but the wait seemed frustratingly long all the same. At last its pleasantly feminine voice said: "Integrated."

"Compute the next period of spatial interphase," Spock told it.

"Two hours, twelve minutes."

Spock shut the machine off. Scott was staring at him, aghast. "Is that how long we have to wait before we can pick up the Captain? But, Spock, I don't think I can hold the ship in place that long. The power leak is unbalanced and I haven't been able to trace it, let alone stop it."

"You will have to keep trying," Spock said. "The fabric of space is very weak here. If we disturb it, there will be no chance of retrieving the Captain alive."

Chekov was looking baffled; worse, he was looking positively ill. "I don't understand," he said. "What's so special about this region of space?"

"I can only speculate," Spock said. "We exist in a universe which coexists with a multitude of others in the same physical space, but displaced in time. For certain brief periods, one area of such a space overlaps an area of ours. That is the time of interphase when we connect with the *Defiant*'s universe."

"And retrieve the Captain," Uhura added.

"Perhaps. But the dimensional structure of each universe is totally dissimilar to the others. Any use of power would disturb what can at best be only a tenuous and brief connection. It might also result in our being trapped ourselves . . ."

"And die like them?" Chekov said raggedly. Suddenly his voice rose to a yell. "Damn you, Spock . . ."

He sprang. Spock, surprised, was knocked backward, Chekov's hands around his neck. Sulu attempted to drag Chekov off; the enraged man struck out at him. Scott promptly grabbed him by that arm. It was all that they could do to handle him, but the distraction enabled Spock to get in a neck pinch.

"Security guards to the bridge," Spock said to the intercom. "Dr. McCoy, will you also please report?"

McCoy appeared almost at once, taking in the scene at a glance. "He jumped you? My fault, I should have checked him the minute he said he was feeling funny, but there was so much else going on. Anybody notice any spasms of pain? Ah. What about his behavior? Hysterical? Frightened?"

"He looked more angry than frightened to me," Uhura said. "But there was nothing to be angry about."

"Nevertheless," Spock said, "there were all the signs of a murderous fury. After what we have seen aboard the *Defiant,* the episode is doubly disturbing."

"I'll say it is," McCoy said. "Guards, take him to sickbay. I'll see what I can find out from seeing the thing in its first stages. Spock, on the other subject, what makes you think Captain Kirk is still alive?"

"The Captain was locked in the Transporter beam when the *Defiant* phased out, Doctor. It is possible that he was saved the shock of transition. If we do not catch him again at the precise corresponding instant in the next interphase, he will die. There is no margin for error; his environmental unit can supply breathable air for no more than another three point twenty-six hours."

"Mr. Spock," Sulu called from the helm. "A vessel is approaching on an intercept vector."

Spock walked quickly to the command chair, and Scott went back to his post. "Status, Mr. Sulu," Spock said.

"Range, two hundred thousand kilometers and closing. Relative velocity, zero point five one C."

"Red alert," Spock said. The klaxon began to sound

throughout the ship. At the same instant, Uhura captured the intruder on the main viewing screen.

The stranger was crystalline in appearance, blue-green in coloration, and shaped like a tetrahedron within which a soft light seemed to pulsate. As the scene materialized, Sulu gasped.

"Stopped dead, Mr. Spock. Now, how do they do that? Range, ninety thousand kilometers and holding."

"Mr. Spock," Uhura said. "I'm getting a visual signal from them."

"Transfer it to the main viewer."

The scene dissolved into what might have been the command bridge of the alien vessel. Most of the frame, however, was occupied by the upper half of an unknown creature. Like its vessel, the alien was almost jewel-like in appearance, multifaceted, crystalline, though it was humanoid in build. A light pulsated rapidly but irregularly inside what seemed to be its head.

"I am Commander Loskene," the creature said at once in good Federation Interlingua. "You are trespassing in a territorial annex of the Tholian Assembly. You must leave this area immediately."

Spock studied Loskene. The pulsating light did not seem to be in synch with the voice. He said formally, "Spock, in command of the Federation Starship *Enterprise*. Commander, the Federation regards this area as free space."

"We have claimed it. And we are prepared to use force, if necessary, to hold it."

"We are not interested in a show of force. The *Enterprise* has responded to a distress call from one of our ships and is currently engaged in rescue operations. Do you wish to assist us?"

"I find no evidence of a disabled ship. My instruments indicate that ours are the only two vessels in this area."

"The other ship is trapped in an interspatial sink. It should reappear in one hour and fifty minutes. We request that you stand by until then."

"Very well, *Enterprise*. In the interest of interstellar amity, we will wait. But we will not tolerate deceit."

The view wavered, and then the screen once more

showed the Tholian ship. Now there was nothing to do but wait—and hope.

The moment of interphase approached at last. As before, Scott personally took over the Transporter console. In the command chair, Spock watched the clock intently.

"Transporter Room."

"Aye, Mr. Spock. I'm locked onto the Captain's coordinates."

"Interphase in twenty seconds . . . ten seconds . . . five, four, three, two, one, energize!"

There was a tense silence. Then Scott's voice said, "The platform's empty, Mr. Spock. There's naught at all at those coordinates."

"Any abnormality to report, Mr. Sulu?"

"The sensor readings don't correspond to those we received the last time we saw the *Defiant*. Insofar as I can tell, the Tholian entry into the area has disturbed the interphase."

"McCoy to bridge," said the intercom. "Has the Captain been beamed aboard, Mr. Spock?"

"No, Doctor. And the interphase period has been passed. We will have to wait for the next one."

"But he hasn't got enough air for that! And there's been another case like Chekov's. I have had to confine my orderly to sickbay."

"Have you still no clues as to the cause, Doctor?"

"I know exactly what the cause is," McCoy's voice said grimly. "And there's nothing I can do to stop it. The molecular structure of the central nervous system, including the brain, is being distorted by the space we are in. Sooner or later the whole crew will be affected—unless you get the *Enterprise* out of here."

"Mr. Spock!" Sulu broke in. "We're being fired upon!"

The announcement came only seconds before the bolt itself struck. The *Enterprise* lurched, but did not roll.

"Damage control, report," Spock said.

"Minor structural damage to sections A-4 and C-13."

"Engineering, hold power steady. Mr. Sulu, divert all but emergency maintenance power into the shields."

"Sir," Sulu said, "that will reduce phaser power by fifty percent."

Almost as if it had heard him, the Tholian ship darted

forward. It seemed to be almost within touching distance before it fired again. This time, the shock threw everybody who was not seated to the floor.

"Engineering to bridge. Mr. Spock, we can't take another like that. We'll either have to fight or run."

"Mr. Sulu, lock in phaser tracking controls. Divert power to the phaser banks and fire at the next close approach. Lieutenant Uhura, open a channel to the Tholians."

McCoy came onto the bridge, his face masklike. On the main viewing screen, the pyramidal ship looped around and began another run.

"Spock, what's the use of this battle?" McCoy demanded. "You've already lost the Captain. Take the ship out of here."

Spock, intent upon the screen, did not answer. The pyramid zigzagged in. Then both vessels fired at once. The *Enterprise* rang like a gong and the lights flickered, but the screen showed that the Tholian, too, had sustained a direct hit. There was no visible damage, but the pyramid had again stopped dead, and then began to retreat.

"A standoff," Spock said. "Mr. Scott, status?"

"Convertors burned out," Scott's voice said. "We've lost drive and hence the ability to correct drift. I estimate four hours in replacement time."

"By that time," Sulu said, "we'll have drifted right through that—that gateway out there."

"Are you satisfied?" McCoy said, picking himself up off the deck. "Spock, why did you do it?"

"To stay in the area for the next interphase," Spock said, "required for disabling the Tholian ship."

"But you're ignoring the mental effects! How can you risk your whole crew on the dim chance of rescuing one officer—one presumed dead, at that? The Captain wouldn't have done that!"

"Doctor, I hardly believe that now is the time for such comparisons. Get down to your laboratory at once and search for an antidote to the mental effects. Since we must remain here, that is your immediate task. Mine is to command the *Enterprise*."

McCoy left, though not without an angry glare.

"Mr. Spock, something has just entered sensor range,"

Sulu said. "Yes, it's another Tholian ship. Loskene must have contacted them at the same time they intercepted us. Loskene is moving back out of phaser range."

"Lieutenant, attempt contact again."

"No response, sir."

On the screen, the two Tholian ships joined—literally joined, base to base, making what seemed to be a single vessel like a six-sided diamond. Then they began to separate again. Between their previously common bases a multicolored strand stretched out across space.

Spock rose and went to the library computer station. The Tholians met again, separated, spinning another thread. Then another. Gradually, a latticework of energy seemed to be growing.

"Switch scanners, Mr. Sulu."

The screen angle changed. The tempo of the Tholian activity was speeding up rapidly. From this point of view, it seemed that the *Enterprise* was already almost a third surrounded by the web and it kept on growing.

Spock pulled his head out of the hooded viewer. "Fascinating," he said. "And very efficient. If they succeed in completing that structure before we are repaired, we shall not be able to run even if we wished to."

Nobody replied. There seemed to be nothing to say.

There was a service for Kirk. It was brief and military. Spock, as the next in command, spoke the eulogy. The speech was not long, but it was interrupted all the same, by another seizure of madness striking down a crewman in the congregation. Afterward, the tension seemed much greater.

As the rest filed out, McCoy stopped Spock at the doorway. "There is a duty to be performed in the Captain's cabin," he said. "It requires both of us."

"Then it will have to wait. My duties require my immediate return to the bridge."

"The Captain left a message tape," the surgeon said. "It was his order that it be reviewed by both of us should he ever be declared dead—as you have just done."

"It will have to wait for a more suitable moment," Spock said, putting his hand on the corridor rail.

"Why? Are you afraid it will change your present status?"

Spock turned sharply. "The mental and physical state of this crew are your responsibility, Doctor. As I have observed before, command is mine."

"Not while a last order remains to be obeyed."

For a moment Spock did not reply. Then he said, "Very well. To the Captain's quarters, then."

McCoy had evidently visited Kirk's quarters before the service, for laid out on a table was the black velvet case which contained Kirk's medals, and it was open. The surgeon looked down at them for a long moment.

"He was a hero in every sense of the word," he said. "Yet his life was sacrificed for nothing. The one thing that would have given his death meaning is the survival of the *Enterprise*. You have made that impossible."

Spock said glacially, "We came here for a specific purpose."

"Maybe not the same one. I came to find out, among other things, really why you stayed and fought."

Spock closed the box. "The Captain would have remained to recover a man at the risk of his own life, other things being equal. I do not consider the question closed."

"He wouldn't have risked the ship. And what do you mean, the question isn't closed? Do you think he may be still alive after all? Then why did you declare him dead—to assure your own captaincy?"

"Unnecessary. I am already in command of the *Enterprise*."

"It's a situation I wish I could remedy."

"If you believe," Spock said, "that I remained just to fire that phaser and kill James Kirk or this crew, it is your prerogative as Medical Officer of this ship to relieve me of duty. In the meantime, I suggest that we play the tape you referred to, so I can get back to the bridge and you can resume looking for an antidote for the madness."

"All right." McCoy turned to Kirk's viewer and flipped a switch. The screen lit; in it, Kirk was seated at his desk.

"Spock. Bones," Kirk's voice said. "Since you are playing this tape, we will assume that I am dead, the tactical situation is critical and you two are locked in mortal combat.

"It means also, Spock, that you have control of my ship and are probably making the most difficut decisions of your career. I can offer only one small piece of advice, for what it's worth. Use every scrap of knowledge and logic you've got to save the ship, but temper your judgment with intuitive insight. I believe you have that quality. But if you can't find it in yourself, then seek out McCoy. Ask his advice. And if you find it sound, take it.

"Bones, you heard what I just told Spock. Help him if you can, but remember that *he* is the Captain. His decisions, when he reaches them, are to be obeyed without further question. You might find that he is capable of both human insight and human error, and they are the most difficult to defend. But you will find that Spock is deserving of the same loyalty and confidence that you all have given me.

"As to the disposal of my personal effects . . ."

McCoy snapped the switch, and turned. For a moment the two men studied each other, less guardedly than before. Then McCoy said, "Spock, I'm sorry. It hurts, doesn't it?"

Spock closed his eyes for a moment. Then he turned and left. McCoy remained for a moment longer, thoughtful, and then stepped out into the corridor.

He was greeted by a stifled scream. Turning, he saw Uhura running toward him, half out of uniform, her normally unshakable calm dissolved in something very close to panic. She saw McCoy and stopped, gasping, trying to get words out; but before they could form, a stab of pain seemed to go through her and her knees buckled. She grabbed the rail for support.

The signs were all too clear. McCoy surreptitiously got out his hypospray, and then went to steady her.

"Lieutenant!" he said sharply. "What is it?"

"I—Doctor, I've just seen the Captain!"

"Yes, he just left a moment ago."

"No, I don't mean Mr. Spock. The captain. He's alive!"

"I'm afraid not. But of course you saw him. We would all like to see him."

Her legs were still shaking, but she seemed somewhat calmer now. "I know what you're thinking. But it isn't that. I was looking into my mirror in my quarters, and there he was. He was—sort of shimmering, like the *Defiant* was when we first saw it. He looked puzzled —and like he was trying to tell me something."

McCoy brought the hypospray up. Uhura saw it and tried to fight free, but she was too wobbly to resist. "I did see him. Tell Mr. Spock. He's alive, he's alive . . ."

The hypospray hissed. "I'll tell him," McCoy said gently. "But in the meantime, you're going to sickbay."

One of Scott's crewmen attacked him within the same hour. The effect was spreading faster through the ship. The Tholian web was now two-thirds complete, and the *Enterprise* was still without impulse drive, let alone the thrust to achieve interstellar velocity.

The crewman's attack failed; but a shaken Scott was on the bridge not ten minutes later.

"Mr. Spock—I've just seen the Captain."

"Spock to McCoy; please come to the bridge. Go on, Mr. Scott."

"He was on the upper engineering level—sparkling, rather like a Transporter effect. He seemed to be almost floating. And I think he saw us. He seemed to be breathing pretty heavily—and then, hey presto! he winked right out."

The elevator doors snapped open and McCoy came out, fast enough to pick up most of Scott's account. He said, "Scotty, are you feeling all right?"

"Och, I think so. Tired, maybe."

"So are we all, of course. Don't fail to see me if you have any other symptoms."

"Right."

"Lieutenant Uhura told a similar story before she went under," Spock said. "Perhaps we ought not to discount it entirely. Yet in critical moments, men sometimes see exactly what they want to see, even when they are not ill."

"Are you suggesting," McCoy said, "that the men are seeing the Captain because they've lost confidence in you?"

"I am making no suggestions, but merely stating a fact."

"Well, the situation is critical, all right. And there have

been more assaults on the lower decks. And if Scottie here's being affected, that will finish whatever chance we have to get the *Enterprise* out of here."

"Have you any further leads on a remedy?"

"A small one," McCoy said. "I've been toying with the idea of trying a chlortheragen derivative. But I'm not ready to try anything so drastic, yet."

"Why not?"

"Well, for one thing . . ."

"Gentlemen," Scott said quietly. "Mr. Spock. Look behind you."

At the same moment, there was a chorus of gasps from the rest of the personnel on the bridge. Spock turned.

Floating behind him was an image of Captain Kirk, full length but soapily iridescent. He seemed to recognize Spock, but to be unable to move. Kirk's hand rose to his throat, and his lips moved. There was no sound.

Spock—hurry!

The figure vanished.

The Tholian web continued to go up around the *Enterprise*, section by section. The pace had slowed somewhat; Loskene and his compatriots seemed to have concluded that the *Enterprise* would not or could not leave the area.

Aboard the ship, too, the tension seemed to have abated, if only slightly. It was now tacitly accepted that the apparition of the Captain on the bridge had not been a part of the lurking madness, and that he had been, therefore, alive then.

Spock and Scott were having another computer session.

"So your reluctance to use the phasers now stands endorsed," the Engineering Officer said. "They blasted a hole right through this crazy space fabric and sent the *Defiant* heaven only knows where."

"And would have sent the Captain with it, if we had not had a Transporter lock on him during the first fade-out. As of now, only the overlap time has changed; the next interphase will be early, in exactly twenty minutes. Can you be ready?"

"Aye," Scott said, "she'll be back together, but we'll have only eighty percent power built up."

"It will have to do."

McCoy came up behind them, carrying a tray bearing a flask and three glasses. "Compliments of the house, gentlemen," he said. "To your good health and the health of your crew. Drink it down!"

"What is it?" Spock said.

"Generally, it's an antidote-cum-preventive for the paranoid reaction. Specifically, a derivative of chlortheragen."

"If I remember aright," Scott said, "that's a nerve gas used by the Klingons. Are you trying to kill us all, McCoy?"

"I said it was a derivative, not the pure stuff. In this form it simply deadens certain nerve inputs to the brain."

"Any good brand of Scotch will do that for you."

"As a matter of fact," McCoy said, "it works best mixed with alcohol. But it does work. It even brought Chekov around, and he's been affected the longest of any of us."

Scott knocked his drink back, and made a face. "It'll nae become a regular tipple with me," he said. "I'll be getting back to my machines."

Spock nodded after him and crossed to the command chair. A moment later Chekov himself entered, beaming, and took his regular position. Uhura was already at her post, as was Sulu.

"Your absence was keenly felt, Ensign," Spock said. "To begin with, give me an estimated time for completion of the Tholian tractor field."

"At the enemy's present pace, two minutes, sir."

"Mr. Sulu, I have the computers programmed to move us through the interspatial gateway. Stand ready to resume the helm as soon as we emerge on the other side—wherever that may be."

"Transporter Room."

"Scott here."

"Ready for interphase in seventy-five seconds."

"Aye, sir, standing by."

"Mr. Spock," Sulu said, "the Tholians are getting ready to close the web. It seems to be contracting to fit the ship."

"Counting down to interphase," Chekov said. He now had an open line to the Transporter Room. "One minute."

"Mr. Scott, have we full power?"

"Only seventy-six percent, Mr. Spock."

"Can the computer call on it all at once?"

"Aye, I think she'll stand it."

"Thirty seconds."

Suddenly, on the viewing screen, between the *Enterprise*, a tiny figure in an environmental suit popped into being.

"I see him!"

"He's early!"

"It's the Captain!"

The webbing began to slide across the screen in a heavy mesh. Behind it, stars slid past as well.

"Tractor field activated," Sulu said. "We're being pulled out of here."

"Try to maintain position, Mr. Sulu."

The ship throbbed to the sudden application of power at the computer's command. Heavy tremors shook the deck.

The web vanished.

"We broke it!" Chekov cheered.

"No, Ensign, we went out through the interdimensional gateway. Since we went through shortly after interphase, we should still be in some part of normal space. Compute the distance from our original position."

"Umm—two point seventy-two parsecs." Chekov looked aghast. "But that's beyond Transporter range!"

"You forget, Mr. Chekov, that we have a shortcut. Mr. Scott, are you still locked on the Captain?"

"Aye, sir, though I dinna understand how."

"You can beam him in now—we have broken free."

"Aye, sir—got him! But he's unconscious. McCoy, this is your department."

"I will be down directly," Spock said. "Mr. Sulu, take over."

As it turned out, no elaborate treatment was needed; taking Kirk's helmet off to let him breathe ship's air removed the source of the difficulty, and once he had been moved to his quarters, an epinephrine hypospray brought him quickly to consciousness. For a moment he looked up at Spock and McCoy in silence. Then McCoy said, "Welcome home, Jim."

"Thanks, Bones. You know, I had a whole universe to myself after the *Defiant* was thrown out. There was absolutely no one else in it. Somehow I could sense it."

"That must have been disorienting," McCoy observed.

"Very. I kept trying to get through to the ship. I think I did at least three times, but it never lasted. I must say I like a crowded universe much better. How did you two get along without me?"

"We managed," McCoy said. "Spock gave the orders. I found the answers."

Spock gave McCoy a curious glance, but nodded confirmation.

"You mean you didn't have any problems?" Kirk said, with slight but visible incredulity.

"None worth reporting, Captain," Spock said.

"Let me be the judge of that."

"Only such minor disturbances, Captain, as are inevitable when humans are involved."

"Or are involved with Vulcans," McCoy added.

"Understood, gentlemen. I hope my last orders were helpful in solving the problems not worth reporting."

"Orders, Captain?" Spock said.

"The orders I left for you—for both of you—on tape."

"Oh, those orders!" said McCoy. "There wasn't time, Captain. We never got a chance to listen to them."

"The crisis was upon us and then passed so quickly, Captain, that . . ."

"I see," Kirk said, smiling. "Nothing worth reporting happened, and it all happened so quickly. Good. Well, let's hope there will be no similar opportunity to test those orders that you never heard. Let's get to work."

LET THAT BE YOUR LAST BATTLEFIELD

(Oliver Crawford and Lee Cronin)

An airborne epidemic was raging on Ariannus; the *Enterprise* was three hours and four minutes out from the stricken planet on a decontamination mission when her sensors picked up, of all unexpected objects, a Starfleet shuttlecraft. Furthermore, its identification numbers showed it to be the one reported stolen from Starbase 4 two weeks earlier.

Its course was very erratic, and it was leaking air. There was a humanoid creature aboard, either injured or ill. Kirk had the machine brought aboard by tractor, and then came the second surprise. The unconscious creature aboard it was, on his left side, a very black man—while his right-hand side was completely white.

Kirk and Spock, curious, watched the entity, now on the surgery's examination table, while McCoy and Nurse Chapel did what seemed indicated. This, in due course, included an injection.

"Doctor," Spock said, "is this pigmentation a natural condition of this—individual?"

"So it would seem. The black side is plain ordinary melanin."

"I never heard of such a race," Kirk said. "Spock? No? I thought not. How do you explain it, Bones?"

"At the moment, I don't."

"He looks like the outcome of a drastic argument."

"I would think not," Spock said seriously. "True, he would be difficult to account for by standard Mendelian evolution, but unaccountable rarities do occur."

"A mutation?" McCoy said. "Tenable, anyhow."

"Your prognosis, Bones?"

"Again, I can't give one. He's a novelty to me, too."

"Yet," Spock said, "you are pumping him full of your noxious potions as if he were human."

"When in doubt, the book prevails. I've run tests. Blood is blood—even when it's green like yours. The usual organs are there, somewhat rearranged, plus a few I don't recognize. But—well, judge the treatment by its fruits; he's coming around." The alien's eyes blinked open. He looked as though he were frightened, but trying not to show it.

"Touch and go there for a bit," McCoy said. "But you're no longer in danger."

"You are aboard the Starship *Enterprise*," Kirk added.

"I have heard of it," the alien said, relieved. "It is in the fleet of the United Federation of Planets?"

"Correct," Kirk said. "And so is that shuttlecraft in which you were flying."

"It was?"

"Don't you usually know whose property you're stealing?"

"I am not a thief!"

"You're certainly no ordinary thief," Kirk said, "considering what it is you appropriated."

"You are being very loose with your accusations and drawing conclusions without any facts."

"I know you made off with a ship that didn't belong to you."

"I do not 'make off' with things," the alien said, biting off the words. "My need gave me the right to its use—and note the word well, sir—the use of the ship."

Kirk shrugged. "You can try those technical evasions with Starfleet Command. You'll face your charges there."

"I am grateful that you rescued me," the alien said with sudden dignity.

"Don't mention it. We're glad we caught you. Who are you?"

"My name is Lokai."

"Go on."

"I am from the planet Cheron."

"If I remember correctly," Spock said, "that is located in the southernmost part of the Galaxy, in a quarter that is still uncharted."

"What are you doing so far from your home?" Kirk asked. Lokai did not answer. "You know that upon completion of our mission, you will be returned to Starbase to face a very serious charge."

"The charge is trifling. I would have returned the ship as soon as I had—" Lokai stopped abruptly.

"Had what? What were you planning to do?"

"You monotoned humans are all alike," Lokai said in a sudden burst of fury. "First condemn and then attack!" Struggling to get a rein on his temper, he sank back. "I will answer no more questions."

"However we view him, Captain," Spock said, "he is certainly no ordinary specimen."

Lokai looked at the First Officer as though seeing him for the first time. "A Vulcan!"

"Don't think he'll be any easier on you," McCoy said. "He's half human."

"That's a strange combination."

Spock raised one eyebrow. "Fascinating that you should think so."

"You're not like any being we've ever encountered," Kirk added. "We'd like to know more about you and your planet."

"I—I'm very tired."

"I think that's an evasion. Surely you owe your rescuers some candor."

"I insist," Lokai said, deliberately closing his eyes. "I am extremely tired. Your vindictive cross-examination has exhausted me."

Kirk looked down at the self-righteous thief for a moment. Then Chekov's voice said from the intercom, "Contact with alien ship, Captain. They request permission to beam a passenger aboard. They say it's a police matter."

"Very well. I'll see him on the bridge. Let's go, Mr. Spock."

Still another surprise awaited them there. The newcomer was almost a double for Lokai—except that he was black on his right side and white on his left.

"I am Bele," he said. His manner was assured and ingratiating.

Kirk eyed him warily. "Of the planet Cheron, no doubt. What brings you to us?"

"You bear precious cargo. Lokai. He has taken refuge aboard this ship. I am here to claim him."

"All personnel on this vessel are subject to my command. No one 'claims' anyone without due process."

"My apologies," Bele said readily. "I overstepped my powers. 'Claim' was undoubtedly an unfortunate word."

"What authorization do you have and from what source?"

"I am Chief Officer of the Commission on Political Traitors. Lokai was tried for and convicted of treason, but escaped. May I see him, please?"

"He's in sickbay. Understand that since you are now aboard the *Enterprise,* you are bound by its regulations."

Bele smiled, a little cryptically. "With your permission, Captain."

There were two guards at the door of Sickbay when Kirk, Spock and Bele arrived; McCoy was inside. Lokai glared up at them.

"Well, Lokai, it's a pleasure to see you again," Bele said. "This time I'm sure our 'joining' will be of a permanent nature. Captain, you are to be congratulated. Lokai has never before been rendered so—quiescent."

Lokai made a sound remarkably like a panther snarling, which brought in the two guards in a hurry. "I'm not going back to Cheron," he said with savage anger. "It's a world of murdering oppressors."

"I told you where you were going," Kirk said. "We brought your compatriot here simply as a courtesy. He wanted to identify you."

"And you see how this killer responds," Bele said. "As he repays all his benefactors . . ."

"Benefactors?" Lokai said. "You hypocrite. Tell him how you raided our homes, tore us from our families, herded us like cattle and sold us as slaves!"

"They were savages, Captain," Bele said. "We took them into our hearts and homes and educated them."

"Yes! Just enough education to serve the Master Race."

"You were the product of our love and you repaid us with murder."

"Why should a slave have mercy on the enslaver?"

"Slave? That was changed millennia ago. You were freed."

"Freed? Were we free to be men—free to be husbands and fathers—free to live our lives in dignity and equality?"

"Yes, you were free, if you knew how to use your freedom. You were free enough to slaughter and burn all that had been built."

Lokai turned to Kirk. "I tried to break the chains of a hundred million people. My only crime is that I failed. Of that I plead guilty."

"There is an order in things," Bele said. "He asked for Utopia in a day. It can't be done."

"Not in a day. And not in ten times ten thousand years by your thinking. To you we are a loathsome breed who will never be ready. I know you and all those with whom you are plotting to take power permanently. Genocide for my people is the Utopia you plan."

Bele, his eyes wide with fury, sprang at Lokai. The guards grabbed him. "You insane, filthy little plotter of ruin! You vicious subverter of every decent thought! You're coming back to stand trial for your crimes."

"When I return to Cheron, you will understand power. I will have armies of followers."

"You were brought here to identify this man," Kirk told Bele. "It is now clear, *gentlemen,* that you know each other very well. Bringing you together is the only service this ship has to offer. It is not a battlefield."

"Captain," Lokai said, "I led revolutionaries, not criminals. I demand political asylum. Your ship is a sanctuary."

"I'll say it just once more. For you this ship is a prison."

"Captain, it is imperative that you return him for judgment."

"Cheron is not a member of the Federation. No treaties have ever been signed. Your demand to be given possession of this prisoner is impossible to honor. There are no extradition procedures to accomplish it. Is that clear, Commissioner Bele?"

"Captain," Bele said, "I hope you will be sensible."

"I'm not interested in taking sides."

"Since my vessel has left the area—I was only a paid passenger—I urge you to take us to Cheron immediately."

Kirk felt himself beginning to bristle. "This ship has a mission to perform. Millions of lives are at stake. When that is completed, I'll return to Starbase 4. You will both be turned over to the authorities. You can each make your case to them."

"I'm sorry, Captain, but that is not acceptable. Not at all!"

"As a dignitary of a far planet," Kirk said, seething, "I offer you every hospitality of the ship while you are aboard. Choose any other course, and . . ."

"You're the Captain," Bele said with sudden mildness.

"And as for you, Lokai, I suggest you rest as much as possible. Especially your vocal chords. It seems you will have a double opportunity to practice your oratory at Starbase . . ."

He was interrupted by the buzz of the intercom. "Chekov to Captain Kirk. Urgent. Will you come to the bridge, sir?"

It was urgent, all right. The ship was off course; it seemed to have taken a new heading all by itself; it was moving away from Ariannus on a tack that would wind it up in the Coal Sack if it kept up. A check with all departments failed to turn up the nature of the malfunction.

"Mr. Spock, give me the coordinates for Cheron."

"Roughly, sir, between 403 Mark 7 and Mark 9."

"Which is the way we're heading. Get Bele up here. I assigned him to the guest quarters on Deck 6."

Bele, once arrived, did not wait to be asked any questions. "Yes," he said, "we are on the way to Cheron.

I should tell you that we are not only a very old race but a very long-lived one; and we have developed special powers which you could not hope to understand. Suffice it to say that this ship is now under my direction. For a thousand of your terrestrial years I have been pursuing Lokai through the Galaxy. I haven't come this far and this long to give him up now."

The elevator doors snapped open and Lokai ran out, followed by the two security guards.

"I will not return to Cheron!" he cried despairingly. "You guaranteed me sanctuary! Captain Kirk . . ."

"He cannnot help you," Bele said. "You have lost, Lokai. You are on your way to final punishment."

"Stop him!"

"Not this time, you evil mound of filth. Not this time."

"My cause is just. You must help me—all of you . . ."

"The old cry. Pity me! Wherever he's gone, he has been helped to escape. On every planet he has found fools who bleed for him and shed tears for the oppressed one. But there is no escape from this ship. This is your last refuge."

With a cry of rage, Lokai leaped at him. Kirk pulled him off. "Security," he said, "take both of these men to the brig."

The guards stepped forward. In an instant, a visible wall of heat formed around both the aliens.

Bele laughed. "You are helpless, Captain."

"What a fool I am," Lokai said bitterly, "expecting help from such as you."

"This ship," Kirk said, "is going to Ariannus. The lives of millions of people make no other choice possible."

"You are being obtuse, Captain. I am permitting no choice. My will now controls this ship and nothing can break it." Every cord in Bele's body and every vein in his head stood out with the ferocity of his determination.

"Bele, I am Captain of this ship. It will follow whatever course I set for it—or I will order it destroyed."

Bele stared at him. "You're bluffing. You could no more destroy this ship than I could change colors."

Kirk turned sharply toward Uhura. "Lieutenant, tie bridge audio into master computer."

"Aye aye, sir."

Kirk sat down and hit a button on his chair. "Destruct Sequence. Computer, are you ready to copy?"

"Working," said the computer's voice.

"Stand by to verify Destruct Sequence Code One."

"Ready."

"This is Captain James T. Kirk of the Starship USS *Enterprise*. Destruct Sequence One—Code One One A."

There was a rapid run of lights over the face of the computer, accompanied by the usual beeping. Then on the upper left of the panel a yellow square lit up, with a black figure 1 in its center.

"Voice and Code One One A verified and correct. Sequence One complete."

"Mr. Spock, please continue."

"This is Commander Spock, Science Officer. Destruct Sequence Number Two—Code One One A Two B."

"Voice and code verified and correct. Sequence Two complete."

"Mr. Scott."

The sweat was standing out on Scott's brow. Perhaps no one aboard loved the *Enterprise* as much as he did. Looking straight into Kirk's eyes, he said mechanically, "This is Lieutenant Commander Scott, Chief Engineering Officer. Destruct Sequence Number Three—Code One B Two B Three."

"Voice and code verified and correct. Destruct Sequence engaged. Awaiting final code for thirty-second countdown."

"Mr. Spock, has this ship returned to the course set for it by my orders?"

"No, Captain. We are still headed for Cheron."

Bele said nothing. Kirk turned quietly back to the computer. "Begin thirty-second countdown. Code Zero-Zero-Destruct-Zero."

"Count beginning. Thirty. Twenty-nine."

"Now," Kirk said, "let us see you prevent the computer from fulfilling my commands."

"Twenty-five."

"You can use your will to drag this ship toward Cheron. But I control this computer. The final command is mine."

"Fifteen."

"From five to zero," Kirk said, "no command in the

universe can stop the computer from completing its Destruct order."

"Seven."

"Waiting," Kirk said relentlessly.

"Five."

The lights stopped blinking and became a steady glare, and the beeping became a continuous whine. Chekov hunched tensely over his board. Sulu's hand was white on the helm, as though he might put the ship back on course through sheer muscle power. Uhura looked at Kirk for a moment, and then her eyes closed peacefully. Spock and Scott were tensely impassive.

"Awaiting code for irrevocable five seconds," the computer's voice said.

Kirk and Bele stared at each other. Then Kirk turned back to the computer for the last time.

"Wait!" Bele said. It was a cry of despair. "I agree! I agree!"

Kirk's expression did not change. He said, "Captain James Kirk. Code One Two Three Continuity. Abort Destruct order."

"Destruct order aborted." The computer went silent.

"Mr. Spock, Are we heading for Ariannus?"

"No, sir. The *Enterprise* is now describing a circular course."

"And at Warp Seven, Captain," Scott added. "We are going nowhere mighty fast."

"I warned you of his treachery," Lokai said. "You have weapons. Kill him!"

"We are waiting, Commissioner," Kirk said, "for you to honor your commitment."

"I have an alternative solution to offer, Captain. Simple, expedient, and, I am sure, agreeable. Captain—I am happy to have you complete your mission of mercy to Ariannus. It was madness to interfere with such a worthwhile endeavor."

Kirk listened stonily.

"Please, sir. You may proceed to Ariannus. Just guarantee me that, upon completion, you will take me and my traitorous captive to Cheron."

"Sir," Kirk said, "he is not your captive—and I make no deals about control of this ship."

Bele's shoulders sagged. He closed his eyes for a

moment, his face curiously distorted, and then opened them again. "The ship's course is now in your control."

"Mr. Sulu?"

"She responds, sir. I'm resetting course for Ariannus."

"And as for you two—let me reaffirm my position. I should put both of you in the brig for what you have done. As Lokai observed, we have weapons, from which no heat shield will protect you. But I won't do it, since you are new to this part of the Galaxy, which is governed by the laws of the United Federation of Planets. We live in peace with the fullest exercise of individual rights. The need to resort to force and violence has long since passed. It will not be tolerated on this ship."

"You are both free to move about the ship. An armed guard will accompany each of you. I hope you will take the opportunity to get to know the ways of the Federation through some of its best representatives, my crew. But make no mistake. Any interference with the *function* of this ship will be severely punished. That's all."

Bele, his face inscrutable, nodded and went out, followed by a guard.

Lokai said, "You speak very well, Captain Kirk. Your words promise justice for all."

"We try, sir."

"But I have learned to wait for actions. After Ariannus —what is your justice? I shall wait to see it dispensed."

He too went out followed by a guard. Spock looked after him.

"Fascinating," the First Officer said. "Two totally hostile humanoids."

"Disgusting is what I call them," Scott said.

"That is not a scientifically accurate description," Spock said.

"Fascinating isn't one, either. And disgusting describes exactly what I feel about those two."

"Your feelings, as usual, shed no light on the matter."

"Enough for one day," Kirk said. "Those two are beginning to affect you."

Lokai settled upon Uhura as his next hope, perhaps feeling that since he had made no headway with the white members of the crew, a black one might be more sympathetic. He was talking eagerly to her in the rec room, with Chekov and Spock as bystanders. Racially, the four made a colorful mixture, though probably none of them was aware of it.

". . . and I know from my actions you must all think me a volcanic hothead—erupting lava from my nostrils at danger signals that are only figments of my imagination. But believe me, my friends, there can be no moment when I can have my guard down where such as Bele are present. And so what happens? I act the madman out of the anger and frustration he forces upon me and thereby prove his point that I *am* a madman."

"We all act incorrectly when we're angry," Uhura said.

"After all," Chekov added cheerfully, "we're only human."

"Ah, Mr. Chekov, you have used the phrase which puts my impatience into perspective—which focuses on my lack of ability to convey to your captain, and to you, yes you here in this room, my lack of ability to alert you to the real threat of someone like Bele. There is no persecution on your planet. How can you understand my fear, my apprehension, my degradation, my suffering?"

"There was persecution on Earth once," Chekov said.

"Yes," said Uhura. "But to us, Chekov, that's only something we were taught in history class."

"Yes, that's right. It was long ago."

"Then," said Lokai, "how can I make your flesh know how it feels to see all those who are like you—and only because they are like you—despised, slaughtered and, even worse, denied the simplest bit of decency that is a living being's right. Do you know what it would be like to be dragged out of your hovel into a war on another planet? A battle that will serve your oppressor and bring death to you and your brothers?"

There seemed to be no answer to that.

Bele, for reasons not to be guessed at, continued to work on Kirk—perhaps because he had developed a grudging respect for the man who had faced him down, or perhaps not. He visited the Captain's quarters whenever asked, though Kirk took care on each occasion to see that Spock was present as well.

"Putting the matter in the hands of your Starfleet

Command is of course the proper procedure," Bele said on one such occasion. "Will it be long before we hear from them, Captain?"

"I expect the reply is already on the way, Commissioner."

"But Command may not arrive at the solution you anticipate," Spock added. "There is the matter of the shuttlecraft Lokai appropriated."

"Gentlemen," Bele said, almost airily, "we are discussing a matter of degree. Surely, stealing a shuttlecraft cannot be equated with the murder of thousands of people?"

"We don't know that Lokai has done that," Spock said.

"Well, the one thing we're agreed on is that Lokai is a criminal."

"We are agreed," Kirk said, "that he took a shuttlecraft—excuse me. Kirk here."

"Captain," Uhura's voice said, "I have your communication from Starfleet Command."

"Fine, Lieutenant. Read it out."

"Starfleet Command extends greetings to Commissioner Bele of the planet Cheron. His urgent request to be transported to his planet with the man he claims prisoner has been taken under serious consideration. It is with great regret that we report we cannot honor that request. Intragalactic treaty clearly specifies that no being can be extradited without due process. In view of the circumstances we have no doubt that after a hearing at Starbase, Commissioner Bele will be provided transportation, but whether with or without his prisoner remains to be determined. End of message."

Bele's face was a study in the attempt to retain a bland mask over anger. "As always," he said, "Lokai has managed to gain allies, even when they don't recognize themselves as such. He will evade, delay and escape again, and in the process put innocent beings at each other's throats—for a cause they have no stake in, but which he will force them to espouse violently by twisting their minds with his lies, his loathsome accusations, his foul threats."

"I assure you, Commissioner," Kirk said, "our minds will not be twisted by Lokai—or by you."

"And you're a leader of men—a judge of character?" Bele said contemptuously. "It is obvious to the most simpleminded that Lokai is of an inferior breed . . ."

"The evidence of our eyes, Commissioner," Spock said, "is that he is of the same breed as yourself."

"Are you blind, Commander Spock?"

"Obviously not; but I see no significance in which side of either of you is white. Perhaps the experience of my own planet may help you to see why. Vulcan was almost destroyed by the same conditions and characteristics that threaten to destroy Cheron. We were a people like you—wildly emotional, often committed to irrationally opposing points of view, to the point of death and destruction. Only the discipline of logic saved our people from self-extinction."

"I am delighted Vulcan was saved, Commander, but expecting Lokai and his kind to act with self-discipline is like expecting a planet to stop orbiting its sun."

"Maybe you're not a sun, and Lokai isn't a planet," Kirk said. "Give him a chance to state his grievances—listen to him—hear him out. Maybe he can change; maybe he *wants* to change."

"He cannot."

"Change is the essential process of all existence," Spock said. "For instance: The people of Cheron must have once been monocolored."

"Eh? You mean like both of you?"

"Yes, Commissioner," Kirk said. "There was a time—long ago, no doubt—when that must have been true."

Bele stared at them incredulously for a moment, and then burst into uproarious laughter.

While he was still recovering, the intercom sounded. "Scott here, Captain. We are orbiting Ariannus. We're ready with the decontamination procedure and Ariannus reports all ground precautions complete."

"Very good, Scotty, let her rip. Kirk out."

"I once heard," Bele said, still smiling, "that on some of your planets the people believe that they are descended from apes."

"Not quite," Spock said. "The apes are humanity's cousins, not their grandfathers. They evolved from common stock, in different directions. But in point of fact, all advanced forms of life have evolved from more primitive stages. Mutation produces changes, and the fittest of these survives. We have no reason to believe that we are at the end of the process—although no doubt the development of intelligence, which enables us to change our environment at will, has slowed down the action of selection."

"I am aware of the process," Bele said, somewhat ironically, "and I stand corrected on the detail. But I have told you that we are a very old race and a long-lived one. We have every reason to believe that we *are* the end of the process. The change is lost in antiquity, but it seems sensible to assume that creatures like Lokai, of generally low intelligence and virtually no moral fiber, represent an earlier stage."

"Lokai has sufficient intelligence to have evaded you for a thousand years," Kirk said. "And from what I've seen of you, that can't have been easy to do."

"Nevertheless, regardless of occasional clever individuals, whom we all applaud, his people are as I have described them. To suggest that behind both of us is a monochrome ancestor . . ."

The buzzer sounded again. "Captain, Scott here again. We have completed the decontamination orbit. Orders?"

"Program for Starbase 4. We'll be right with you."

Bele was showing signs of his strained and intense look of concentration which Kirk had no reason to recall with confidence. Kirk said, in the tone of an order, "Join us on the bridge, Commissioner?"

"Nothing I would like better."

But when they arrived, the bridge personnel were in turmoil. They were clustered around the computer, at which Scott was stationed.

"What's wrong?" Spock asked.

"I don't rightly know, Mr. Spock. I was trying to program for Starbase 4—as ordered—but I can't get a response."

Spock made a quick examination. "Captain, some of the memory banks are burned out."

"See if you can determine which ones."

"I will save you that trouble, Mr. Spock," Bele said. "They are in Directional Control and in the Self-Destruct circuit. You caught me by surprise with that Destruct procedure before." As he spoke, the fire sheath began to form around him. "Now can we go on to Cheron without any more discussion?"

"Stand clear of him," Kirk said. "Guard, shoot to stun."

The heat promptly increased. "I cannot block your weapon," Bele said, "but my heat shield will go out of control if I am rendered unconscious. This will destroy not only everyone here, but much of the ship's bridge itself."

The Cheronian was certainly a virtuoso at producing impasses. As he and Kirk glared at each other, the elevator doors parted and Lokai came storming out to the Captain.

"So this is the justice you promised after Ariannus! You have signed my death warrant! What do you do—carry justice on your tongues? Or will you fight and die for it?"

"After so many years of leading the fight," Kirk observed, "you seem very much alive."

"I doubt that the same can be said for many of his followers," Spock said.

Bele laughed contemptuously. At once, a fiery sheath grew also around Lokai.

"You're finished, Lokai. We've got your kind penned in their districts in Cheron. And they'll stay that way. You've combed the Galaxy and come up with nothing but monocolored primitives who snivel that they've outgrown fighting."

"I have given up on these useless pieces of bland flesh," Lokai raged. "But as for you, you—you half of a tyrant . . ."

"You image in a cheap mirror . . ."

They rushed together. Their heat shields fused into a single, almost solid mass as they struggled. Its edges drove the crew back, and wavered perilously near to the control boards.

"Bele!" Kirk shouted. "Keep this up and you'll never get to Cheron, you'll have wrecked the bridge! This will be your last battlefield—your thousand years of pursuit wasted!"

The combatants froze. Then Bele threw Lokai away from him, hard. Lokai promptly started back.

"And Lokai, you'll die here in space," Kirk continued.

"You'll inspire no more disciples. Your cause will be lost."

Lokai stopped. Then his heat shield went down, and so, a moment later, did Bele's.

"Captain," Spock said, "I believe I have found something which may influence the decision. I can myself compute with moderate rapidity when deprived of the machine . . ."

"Yes, and beat the machine at chess, too. Go on."

"Because of our first involuntary venture in the direction of Cheron, our orbit around Ariannus was not the one originally planned. I believe we can leave it for Starbase 4 in a curve which will pass us within scanning range of Cheron. With extreme magnification, we might get a visual readout. I can feed Mr. Sulu the coordinates; he will have to do the rest of the piloting by inspection, as it were, but after the piloting he did for us behind the Klingon lines* I am convinced he could fly his way out of the Cretan labyrinth if the need arose."

"I believe that too," Kirk said. "But what I don't see is what good you think will come out of the maneuver."

"Observing these strangers and their irreconcilable hatreds," Spock said, "has given me material to draw certain logical conclusions. At present it is only a hypothesis, but I think there would be value in testing it."

Anything Spock said was a possibly valid hypothesis was very likely to turn out to be what another man would have called a law of nature. Kirk said, "It is so ordered."

The visual readout of Cheron was wobbly, but growing clearer; Sulu had sufficiently improved upon Spock's rather indefinite course corrections so that the moment of closest approach would be not much over 15,000 miles. It was an Earthlike planet, but somewhat larger, by perhaps a thousand miles of diameter. Both Bele and Lokai were visibly moved by the sight. Well, a thousand years is a long time, Kirk thought, even for a long-lived race.

"There is your home, gentlemen," he said. "Not many details yet, but if you represent the opposing factions there typically, we must be picking up a raging battle."

"No, sir," Spock said from his console. The words

*See *Spock Must Die!*

could not have been simpler, but there was something in his tone—could it possibly have been sadness?—that riveted Kirk's attention, and that of the Cheronians as well. "No conflicts at all."

"What are you picking up?" Kirk said.

"Several very large cities. All uninhabited. Extensive traffic systems barren of traffic. Vegetation and lower animals encroaching on the cities. No sapient life forms registering at all, Captain."

"You mean the people are *all* dead?"

"Yes, Captain—all dead. This was what I had deduced when I suggested this course. They have annihilated each other—totally."

"My people," Bele said. "All dead."

"Yes, Commissioner," Spock said. "All of them."

"And—mine?" Lokai said.

"No one is left. No one."

The two survivors faced each other with ready rage. "Your bands of murderers . . ."

"Your genocidal maniacs . . ."

"Gentlemen!" Kirk said in his command voice. Then, more softly, "The cause you fought for no longer exists. Give up your hate, and we welcome you to live with us."

Neither seemed to hear him; the exchange of glares went on.

"You have lost, Bele. I have won."

"You always think you win when you destroy."

"What's the matter with you two?" Kirk demanded, his own temper at last beginning to fray. "Didn't you hear my First Officer? Your planet is dead. Nobody is alive on Cheron just because of this kind of hate! Give it up, in heaven's name!"

"You have lost the planet," Lokai said. "I have won. I have won because I am free."

Suddenly, he made a tremendous leap for the elevator. The doors opened for him, and then, with a wild laugh, he was gone. Bele made as if to rush after him; Kirk stopped him.

"Bele—listen! The chase is finished."

"No, no! He must not escape me!"

"Where can he go?" Spock said.

"I think I know the answer to that," Uhura said. "Someone has just activated the Transporter."

"Oh," Kirk said. "Are we in Transporter range of Cheron?"

"Just coming into it," Spock said. "And a sentient life form is beginning to come through on the planet."

"It is he!" Bele cried. "Now I'll get him!"

He sprang for the elevator in turn. The guards, now belatedly alert, moved to stop him, but Kirk held up his hands.

"Let him go. Bele, there's no one there to punish him. His judges are dead."

"I," Bele said, "am his punisher." Then he too was gone.

There was a brief silence. Then Uhura said, "Captain, the Transporter has been activated again."

"Of course," Kirk said wearily. He felt utterly washed out. "Is he showing up on Cheron on the scanners now, Mr. Spock?"

"Some second sapient life form is registering. I see no other possible conclusion."

"But," Uhura said, "it doesn't make any sense."

"To expect sense from two mentalities of such extreme viewpoints is not logical," Spock said. "They are playing out the drama of which they have become the captives, just as their compatriots did."

"But their people are dead," Sulu said slowly. "How can it matter to them now which one is right?"

"It does to them," said Spock. "And at the same time, in a sense it does not. A thousand years of hating and running have become all of life."

"Spock," said McCoy's voice behind them, "may I remind you that I'm supposed to be the psychologist aboard this ship?"

"Spock's human half," Kirk said, turning, "is perhaps better equipped to perceive half measures taking over the whole man than the rest of us, Bones. And his Vulcan side quite accurately predicted the outcome. Hate wasn't all Lokai and Bele had at first, but by allowing it to run them, that's all they ended up with. This is their last battlefield—and let us hope that we never see its like again. Mr. Sulu, Warp Two for Starbase 4."

THIS SIDE OF PARADISE

(Nathan Butler and D. C. Fontana)

There was no answer from the Sandoval colony on Omicron Ceti III to the *Enterprise's* signals, but that was hardly surprising; the colonists, all one hundred and fifty of them, had probably been dead for the better part of three years, as two previous colonies had died, for reasons then mysterious. Elias Sandoval had known this past history and had determined to settle on the planet anyhow; it was in all other respects a tempting place.

It was not until after his group had settled in—and had stopped communicating—that the Berthold emission of the planet's sun had been discovered. Little enough was known about Berthold radiation even now, but it had been shown that direct exposure to it under laboratory conditions distintegrated living animal tissue in as little as seventy-two hours. A planet's atmosphere would cut down some of the effect, to the point where a week's exposure might be safe, but certainly not three years. And there was no preventive, and no cure.

The settlement proper, however, was still there and was easy to spot. Kirk made up a landing party of six, including himself, Spock, McCoy, Lieutenant Timothy Fletcher (a biologist), Sulu and a crewman named

Dimont. The settlement proved to consist of a surprisingly small cluster of buildings, with fields beyond it. Kirk looked around.

"It took these people a year to make the trip from Earth," he said. "They came all that way—and died."

"Hardly that, sir," said a man's voice. The party snapped around toward it.

A big, bluff, genial-looking man clad in sturdy work clothes had come around a corner of a building, with two others behind him, similarly dressed and carrying tools. The first man came forward, holding out his hand.

"Welcome to Omicron Ceti III," he said. "I am Elias Sandoval."

Kirk took the hand, but could think of nothing to say but a mumble of thanks.

"We've seen no one outside our group since we left Earth four years ago," the man went on. "We've expected someone for quite some time. Our subspace radio has never worked properly and we, I'm afraid, had no one among us who could master its intricacies. But we were sure when we were not heard from, a ship would come."

"Actually, Mr. Sandoval, we didn't come because of your radio silence . . ."

"It makes little difference, Captain. You are here, and we are happy to have you. Come, let me show you our settlement."

He began to walk away, not bothering to look back, as if certain that they would follow. The other colonists had already left.

"On pure speculation," McCoy said drily, "just as an educated guess, I'd say that man isn't dead."

Spock checked his tricorder. "The intensity of Berthold radiation is at the predicted level. At this intensity, we will be safe for a week, if necessary. But . . ."

"But these people shouldn't be alive," Kirk said. "Well, there's no point in debating it in a vacuum. Let's get some answers."

He started after Sandoval. From closer range, the buildings could be seen to be not deserted, only quiet. Nearby, a woman was hanging out some wash; in another structure, a woman placed a fresh-baked pie in a window to cool. It might have been a tranquil Earthly farm community of centuries ago, except for a scattering of peculiar plants with bulbous pods, apparently indigenous, which revealed that it was on another planet.

Sandoval led the landing party into his own quarters. "There are two other settlements," he said, "but we have forty-five colonists here."

"What was the reason for the dispersal?" Kirk asked.

"We felt three separate groups might have a better opportunity for growth. And, if some disease should strike one group, the other two would be less likely to be endangered. Omicron is an ideal agricultural planet, Captain, and we determined that we would not suffer the fate of expeditions that had gone before us."

A woman came from an inner door and stopped, seeing the strangers. She looked Eurasian, and was strikingly beautiful.

"Ah, Leila," Sandoval said, turning to her. "Come and meet our guests. This is Leila Kalomi, our botanist. Captain Kirk, Dr. McCoy, Mr. Spock . . ."

"Mr. Spock and I have met," she said, holding out a hand to him. "It has been a long time."

He took the hand gently but awkwardly. "The years have seemed twice as long," he said.

She bowed her head, silently accepting the compliment. Then she looked up, as if searching his face for something more; but there was nothing but his usual calm. He released her hand slowly.

"Mr. Sandoval," Kirk said, "we do have a mission here. A number of examinations, tests . . ."

"By all means, please attend to them, Captain. I think you'll find our settlement interesting. Our philosophy is a simple one: that men should return to the less complicated life. We have very few mechanical things here—no vehicles, no weapons—" He smiled. "As I said, even the radio has never worked properly. We have harmony here—complete peace."

"We'll try not to disturb your work. Gentlemen, if you'll come outside now . . ."

On the porch, he flipped open his communicator. "Kirk to *Enterprise*."

"*Enterprise*. Lieutenant Uhura here."

"Lieutenant, we've found the colony apparently well and healthy. We're beginning an investigation. Relay that information to Starfleet, and then beam down to me all the information we have on this last Omicron expedition."

"Yes, sir. *Enterprise* out."

"Gentlemen, carry out your previous instructions. If you find anything out of the ordinary, report to me at once."

The party scattered.

Dimont was the first to find the next anomaly. He had been raised in the farm country of the Mojave, and was leading cows to pasture when he was six, up at dawn and then working all day in the fields. It was his opinion, expressed to Sulu, that "they could use a little of that spirit here."

But there was no place for it. There were no cows here; the one barn hadn't even been built for them, but only for storage. Nor were there any horses, pigs, even dogs. A broader check disclosed that the same was true of the whole planet: there was nothing on it but people and vegetation. The records showed that the expedition had carried some animals for breeding and food, but none seemed to have survived. Well, that was perhaps not an anomaly in the true sense, for they couldn't have survived. In theory, neither could the people.

But they had. "I've examined nine men so far," McCoy reported, "ages varying from twenty-three to fifty-nine. Every one of them is in perfect physical shape—textbook responses. If everybody was like them, I could throw away my shingle. But there's something even stranger."

"What is it?" Kirk asked.

"I've got Sandoval's medical record as of four years ago when he left Earth. There was scar tissue on his lungs from lobar penumonia suffered when he was a child. No major operations, but he did have an appendectomy. But when I examined the man not an hour ago, he was as perfect as the rest of them."

"Instrument malfunction?"

"No. I thought of that and tested it on myself. It accurately recorded my lack of tonsils and those two broken ribs I had once. But it *didn't* record any scar tissue on Sandoval's lungs—and it *did* record a healthy appendix where one was supposedly removed."

Fletcher's report also turned up an anomaly. "The soil here is rich, the rainfall moderate, the climate temperate the year round. You could grow anything here, and they've got a variety of crops in—grains, potatoes, beans. But for an agricultural colony they actually have very little acreage planted. There's enough to sustain the colony, but very little more. And another thing, they're not bothering to rotate crops in their fields—haven't for three years. That's poor practice for a group like this, even if the soil is good."

It was like a jigsaw puzzle all one color—a lot of pieces but no key to where they fitted.

Then came the order to evacuate, direct from Admiral Komack of Starfleet. Despite the apparent well-being of the colonists, they were to be moved immediately to Starbase 27, where arrangements were being made for complete examinations of all of them. Exposed Starship personnel were also to be held in quarantine until cleared at the Starbase. Apparently somebody up the line thought radiation disease was infectious. Well, with Berthold rays, anything seemed to be possible, as McCoy observed wrily.

"You'll have to inform your people of Starfleet's decision," Kirk told Sandoval. "Meanwhile we can begin to prepare accommodations for them aboard ship . . ."

"No," said Sandoval pleasantly.

"Mr. Sandoval, this is not an arbitrary decision on my part. It is a Starfleet order."

"This is completely unnecessary. We are in no danger here."

"We've explained the Berthold radiation and its effect," McCoy said. "Can't you understand . . ."

"How can I make *you* understand, Doctor? Your own instruments tell you we are in excellent health, and our records show we have not had one death among us."

"What about the animals?" Kirk said.

"We are vegetarians."

"That doesn't answer my question. Why did all the animals die?"

"Captain, you stress unimportant things," Sandoval said, as calmly as before. "We will not leave. Your arguments have some validity, but they do not apply to us."

"Sandoval, I've been ordered to evacuate this colony,

and that's exactly what I intend to do, with or without your help."

"And how will you do that?" Sandoval said, turning away. "With a butterfly net?"

It was Spock who was finally given the key. He was standing with Leila looking out over a small garden, checking his tricorder.

"Nothing," he said, "not even insects. Yet your plants grow, and you have survived exposure to Berthold radiation."

"It can be explained," Leila said.

"Please do."

"Later."

"I have never understood the female capacity to avoid a direct answer on any subject."

She put a hand on his arm. "And I never understood you, until now." She tapped his chest. "There was always a place in here where no one could come. There was only the face you allow people to see. Only one side you allow them to know."

"I would like to know how your people have managed to survive here."

"I missed you."

"You should be dead."

She took her hand from his arm and stepped back. "If I show you how we survived, will you try to understand how we feel about our life here? About each other?"

"Emotions are alien to me . . ."

"No. Someone else might believe that—your shipmates, your Captain. But not me. Come this way."

She led him to an open field, uncultivated, with pod plants growing amid grass and low brush. They rustled gently in a little breeze.

"This is the place," she said.

"It looks like any other such area. What is the nature of this thing, if you please?"

"The specific elements and properties are not important. What is important is that it gives life—peace—love."

"What you describe was once called in the vernacular 'a happiness pill.' And you, as a scientist, should know that is impossible."

"No. And I was one of the first to find them."

"Them?"

"The spores." She pointed to the pod plants.

Spock bent to examine them. At the same moment, one of the pods flew apart, like a powdery dandelion broken by the wind. Spock dropped his tricorder to shield his face as the powder flew up about him. Then he screamed.

Leila, frightened, moved forward a step, reaching out a hand to him.

"I—can't," he moaned, almost inaudibly. "Please—don't—don't . . ."

"It shouldn't hurt, not like this! It didn't hurt us!"

"I'm not—like you."

Then, slowly, his face began to change, becoming less rigid, more at peace. Seeing the change, Leila reached up to touch his cheek with gentle fingers. He reached out to gather her into his arms, very gently, as though afraid this woman and this feeling were so fragile that he might break them.

After the kiss, she sat down, and he lay down beside her, his head in her lap. "See the clouds," he said after a while. "That one looks like a dragon—you see the tail and the dorsal spines?"

"I have never seen a dragon."

"I have, on Berengaria VII. But I never saw one in a cloud before." His communicator abruptly shrilled, but he ignored it. "Or rainbows. Do you know I can tell you exactly why one appears in the sky—but considering its beauty was always out of the question."

"Not here," Leila said. The communicator shrilled again, insistently. "Perhaps you should answer?"

"It will only be the Captain."

But finally he lifted the communicator and snapped up the screen. Kirk's anxious voice sounded instantly. "Mr. Spock!"

"What do you want?" Spock asked lazily.

"Spock, is that you?"

"Yes, Captain. What do you want?"

"Where are you?"

Spock considered the question calmly. "I don't believe I want to tell you."

"Spock, I don't know what you think you're doing, but

this is an order. Report back to me at the settlement in ten minutes. We're evacuating the colony to Starbase 27 . . ."

"No, I don't think so."

"You don't think so *what?*"

"I don't think so, *sir.*"

"Spock, report to the settlement immediately. Acknowledge. Spock!"

The First Officer tossed the communicator away among the plants.

It seemed to be their fruiting time; they were bursting all over the area now. Fletcher was caught next, then McCoy, then Sulu and Dimont—and finally Kirk himself.

But Kirk alone was unaffected. As peace and love and tranquillity settled around him like a soggy blanket, he was blazing. His temper was not improved by the discovery that McCoy was arranging for transportation to the ship not of colonists or their effects, but of pod plants. Evidently a couple of hundred were already aboard. Hotter than ever, Kirk ordered himself to be beamed aboard.

He found the bridge deserted except for Uhura, who was busy at her communications board. All other instruments were on automatic.

"Lieutenant, put me through to Admiral Komack at Starfleet."

As she turned from the board, Kirk was shocked to see that she, too, wore the same sweet, placid expression as the others. She said, "Oh—I'm afraid I can't do that, Captain."

"I don't suppose," Kirk said tightly, "it would do any good to say that was an order."

"I know it was, Captain. But all communications are out."

"All?" Kirk reached past her and began to flick switches on the board.

"All except for ship to surface; we'll need that for a while. I short-circuited all the rest." She patted his arm. "It's really for the best."

She arose, and strolled away from him to the elevator, which swallowed her up. Kirk tried her board again, but to no effect. He slammed his fist down in aggravation.

Then he noticed a light pulsing steadily on Spock's library-computer. Moving to that station, he pushed the related button.

"Transporter Room."

There was no answer, but clearly the room was in use. He made for it in a hurry.

He found a line of crew personnel in the corridor leading to the Transporter Room. All waited patiently. Every so often the line moved forward a few steps.

"Report to your stations!"

The crewmen stared at him quietly, benevolently—almost pityingly.

"I'm sorry, sir," one of them said. "We're transporting down to join the colony."

"I said, get back to your stations."

"No, sir."

"Do you know what you're saying?"

"You've been down there," the crewman said earnestly. "You know how beautiful it is—how perfect. We're going."

"This is mutiny!"

"Yes, sir," the crewman said calmly. "It is."

Kirk went back to the bridge and to the communications board. As Uhura had said, ship to ground was still operative. He called McCoy, and was rather surprised to get an answer.

"Bones, the spores of your damnable plants have evidently been carried throughout the ship by the ventilation system. The crew is deserting to join the Omicron colony, and I can't stop them."

"Why, that's fine," McCoy said; his accent had moved considerably south of the Mason-Dixon line, almost to his Georgia boyhood. "Y'all come right down."

"Never mind that. At least you can give me some information. I haven't been affected. Why not?"

"You always were a stubborn cuss, Jimmy. But you'll see the light."

Kirk fumed in silence for a moment. "Can't you tell me anything about the physical-psychological aspects of this thing?"

"*I'm* not concerned with any physical-psychological aspects, Jim boy. We're all perfectly healthy."

"I've been hearing that word a lot lately. Perfect. Everything is perfect."

"Yup. That it is."

"I'll bet you've even grown your tonsils back."

"Uh-huh," McCoy said dreamily. "Jim, have you ever had a real, cold, Georgia-style mint julep?"

"Bones, Bones, I need your help. Can you run tests, blood samples, anything at all to give us some kind of lead on what these things are? How to counteract them?"

"Who wants to counteract Paradise, Jim?"

"Bones—" But the contact had been broken at the other end. Then he headed back for the Transporter Room. He was going to get some cooperation from his ship's surgeon if he had to take the madman by the ears.

He found Spock in Sandoval's office, both looking languidly pleased with themselves.

"Where's McCoy?"

"He said he was going to create something called a mint julep," Spock said, then added helpfully, "That's a drink."

"Captain," Sandoval said. "Listen to me. Why don't you join us?"

"In your own private paradise?"

Sandoval nodded. "The spores have made it that. You see, Captain, we *would* have died three years ago. We didn't know what was happening then, but the Berthold rays you spoke of affected us within two or three weeks of our landing here. We were sick and dying when Leila found the plants."

"The spores themselves are alien, Captain," Spock added. "They weren't on the planet when the other two expeditions were attempted. That's why the colonists died."

"How do you know all this?"

"The spores—tell us. They aren't really spores, but a kind of group organism made up of billions of submicroscopic cells. They act directly on the central nervous system."

"Where did they come from?"

"Impossible to tell. It was so long ago and so far away. Perhaps the planet does not even exist any longer. They drifted in space until finally drawn here by the Berthold radiation, on which they thrive. The plants are native, but they are only a repository for the spores until they find an animal host."

"What do they need us for?"

"Bodies. They do no harm. In return they give the host complete health and peace of mind . . ."

"Paradise, in short."

"Why not?" Spock said. "There is no want or need here. It's a true Eden. There is belonging—and love."

"No wants or needs? We weren't meant for that, any of us. A man stagnates and goes sour if he has no ambition, no desire to be more than he is."

"We have what we need," said Sandoval.

"Except a challenge! You haven't made an inch of progress here. You're not creating or learning, Sandoval. You're backsliding—rotting away in your paradise."

Spock shook his head sadly. "You don't understand. But you'll come around, sooner or later."

"Be damned to that. I'm going back to the ship."

He could not remember any time before when he had been so furious for so long a time.

The *Enterprise* was utterly deserted now. Without anybody aboard her, Kirk had a new and lonely realization of how big she was. And yet for all her immense resources, he was helpless. It was amazing how quickly all her entire complement had surrendered to the Lethe of the spores, leaving him and no one else raging futilely . . .

Raging?

Futilely?

Wait a minute.

There were pod plants all over the ship, so there was no problem about getting a sample. He took it down to McCoy's laboratory, located a slide, and then McCoy's microscope. A drop of water on the slide—right; now, mix some of the spores into the drop. Put the slide under the microscope. It had been decades since he had done anything like this, but he remembered from schooldays that one must run the objective lens down to the object, and then focus *up*, never down. Good; the spores came into register, tiny, and spined like pollen grains.

Getting up again, he went through McCoy's hypospray rack until he found one of a dozen all labeled *adrenaline*. He sprayed the slide, and then looked again.

There was nothing there. The spores were adrenalin-soluble. He had found the answer. It was almost incredibly dangerous, but there was no other way. He went back to the bridge and called Spock. If Spock didn't answer . . .

"Spock here. What is it now?"

"I've joined you," Kirk said quietly. "I understand now, Spock."

"That's wonderful, Captain. When will you beam down?"

"I've been packing some things, and I realized there's equipment aboard we should have down at the settlement. You know we can't come back aboard once the last of us has left."

"Do you want a party beamed up?"

"No, I think you and I can handle it. Why don't I beam you up now?"

"All right. Ready in ten minutes."

Kirk was waiting in the Transporter Room, necessarily, when the First Officer materialized, and was holding a metal bar in both hands, like a quarter-staff. Spock took a step toward him, smiling a greeting. Kirk did not smile back.

"*Now*," he said harshly, "you mutinous, disloyal, computerized half-breed—we'll see about you deserting my ship!"

Spock stared. He seemed mildly surprised, but unflustered. "Your use of the term half-breed is perfectly applicable, Captain, but 'computerized' is inaccurate. A machine can be computerized, but not a man."

"What makes you think you're a man? You're an overgrown jackrabbit. You're an elf with an overactive thyroid."

"Captain, I don't understand . . ."

"Of course you don't! You don't have brains enough to understand! All you've got is printed circuits!"

"Captain, if you'll . . ."

"But what can you expect from a freak whose father was a computer and whose mother was an encyclopedia!"

"My mother," Spock said, his expression not quite so bland now, "was a teacher, my father an ambassador."

"He was a freak like his son! Ambassador from a planet

of freaks! The Vulcan never lived who had an ounce of integrity!"

"Captain—please—don't . . ."

"You're a traitor from a race of traitors! Disloyal to the core! Rotten—like all the rest of your subhuman race! And you've got the gall to make love to that girl! A human girl!"

"No more," Spock said stonily.

"I haven't even got started! Does she know what she's getting, Spock? A carcass full of memory banks that ought to be squatting on a mushroom instead of passing himself off as a man. You belong in a circus, Spock, not a starship! Right next to the dog-faced boy!"

With this, Kirk stepped forward and slapped the livid Spock twice, hard. With a roar, Spock swung out at him. Kirk leaped back out of his way, raising the bar of metal between his hands to parry the blow.

It was not much of a fight. Kirk was solely concerned with getting and keeping out of the way, while Spock was striking out with killing force, and with all the science of his once-warrior race. There could be only one ending. Kirk was deprived of the metal bar at the third onslaught, and finally took a backhand which knocked him to the floor against the far wall. Spock, his face contorted, snatched up a stool and lifted it over his head.

Kirk looked up at him and grinned ruefully. "All right, Mr. Spock. Had enough?"

Spock stared down at him, looking confused. Finally he lowered the chair.

"I never realized what it took to get under that thick hide of yours. Anyhow, I don't know what you're mad about. It isn't every First Officer who gets to belt his Captain—several times." He felt his jaw tenderly.

"You—you deliberately did that to me."

"Yes. The spores, Mr. Spock. Tell me about the spores."

Spock seemed to reach inside himself. "They're—gone. I don't belong any more."

"That was my intention. You said they were benevolent and peaceful. Violent emotions overwhelm and destroy them. I had to get you angry enough to shake off their influence. That's the answer, Spock."

"That may be correct, Captain, but we could hardly

initiate a brawl with over five hundred crewmen and colonists. It is not logical."

Kirk grinned. "I was thinking of something you told me once about certain subsonic frequencies affecting the emotions."

"Yes, Captain. A certain low organ tone induces a feeling of awe. There is another frequency that affects the digestion."

"None of those will do. I want one that irritates people—something that we could hook into the communications station and broadcast over the communicators."

"That would of course also have to involve a bypass signal." Spock thought a moment. "It can be done."

"Then let's get to work."

"Captain—striking a fellow officer is a court-martial offense."

"If we're both in the brig, who's going to build the subsonic transmitter?"

"That's quite logical, Captain. To work, then."

The signal generated by the modified Feinbergers and rebroadcast from the bypassed communicators went unheard in the settlement, but it was felt almost at once, almost as though the victims had had itching powder put under their skins. Within a few minutes, everyone's nerves were exacerbated; within a few more, fights were breaking out all over the colony. The fights did not last long; as the spores dissolved in the wash of adrenalin in the bloodstream, the tumult died back to an almost aghast silence. Not long after that, contrite calls began to come in aboard the *Enterprise.*

The rest was anticlimax. The crew came back, the colonists and their effects were loaded aboard, the plants were cleaned out of the ship except for one specimen that went to Lieutenant Fletcher's laboratory. Finally, Omicron Ceti III was dwindling rapidly on the main viewing screen, watched by Kirk, Spock and McCoy.

"That's the second time," McCoy said, nodding toward the screen, "that Man has been thrown out of Paradise."

"No—this time we walked away on our own. Maybe we don't belong in Paradise, Bones," Kirk said thoughtfully. "Maybe we're meant to fight our way through. Struggle. Claw our way up, fighting every inch of the way. Maybe we can't stroll to the music of lutes, Bones—we must march to the sound of drums."

"Poetry, Captain," Spock said. "Nonregulation."

"We haven't heard much from you about the Omicron Ceti III experience, Mr. Spock."

"I have little to say about it, Captain," Spock said, slowly and quietly, "except that—for the first time in my life—I was happy."

Both the others turned and looked at him; but there was nothing to be seen now but the Mr. Spock they had long known, controlled, efficient, and emotionless.

TURNABOUT INTRUDER

(Gene Roddenberry and Arthur H. Singer)

The *Enterprise* had been proceeding to a carefully timed rendezvous when she received a distress call from a group of archaeologists who had been exploring the ruins on Camus Two. Their situation was apparently desperate, and Kirk interrupted the mission to beam down to their assistance, together with Spock and McCoy.

In the group's headquarters they found two of the survivors, one of whom Kirk knew: Dr. Janice Lester, the leader of the expedition. She was lying on a cot, semi-conscious. Her companion, Dr. Howard Coleman, looked healthy enough but rather insecure.

"What's wrong with her?" Kirk asked.

"Radiation sickness," said Coleman.

"I'd like to put the ship's complete medical facilities to work to save her. Can we get her aboard the *Enterprise*?"

"Exposing her to the shock of Transportation would be very dangerous. The radiation affects the nervous system."

McCoy looked up from his examination of the woman. "I can find no detectable signs of conventional radiation injury, Dr. Coleman," he said.

"Dr. Lester was farthest from the source. Fortunately for me, I was here at headquarters."

"Then the symptoms may not have completely developed."

"What happened to those who were closest to the point of exposure?" Kirk asked.

"They became delirious from the multiplying internal lesions and ran off mad with pain. They are probably dead."

"What form of radiation was it?" McCoy asked.

"Nothing I have ever encountered."

Janice Lester stirred and moaned, and her eyes fluttered open. Kirk came to her side and took her hand, smiling.

"You are to be absolutely quiet. Those are the doctor's orders, Janice, not mine."

Spock had been scanning with his tricorder. "Captain, I am picking up very faint life readings seven hundred meters from here. Help will have to be immediate."

Kirk turned to McCoy, who said, "There is nothing more to be done for her, Captain. Your presence should help quiet her."

As McCoy and Spock went out, Janice released Kirk's hand, and she said with great effort, "I hoped I would never see you again."

"I don't blame you."

Her eyes closed. "Why don't you kill me? It would be easy for you now. No one would know."

"I never wanted to hurt you," Kirk said, startled.

"You did."

"Only so I could survive as myself."

"I died. When you left me, I died."

"You still exaggerate," Kirk said, trying for the light touch. "I have heard reports of your work."

"Digging in the ruins of dead civilizations."

"You lead in your field."

She opened her eyes and stared directly into his. "The year we were together at Starfleet is the only time in my life I was alive."

"I didn't stop you from going on with space work."

"I had to! Where would it lead? Your world of Starship captains doesn't admit women."

"You've always blamed me for that," Kirk said.

"You accepted it."

"I couldn't have changed it," he pointed out.

"You believed they were right. I know you did."

"And you hated me for it. How you hated. Every minute we were together became an agony."

"It isn't fair . . ."

"No, it isn't. And I was the one you punished and tortured because of it."

"I loved you," she said. "We could have roamed among the stars."

"We would have killed each other."

"It might have been better."

"Why do you say that?" he demanded. "You're still young."

"A woman should not be alone."

"Don't you see now, we shouldn't be together? We never should have—I'm sorry. Forgive me. You must be quiet now."

"Yes." Her eyes closed and her head sank back on the cot.

"Janice—please let me help you this time."

In a deadly quiet voice, she said, "You are helping me, James."

He looked at her sadly for a moment and then turned away. The rest of the room, he noticed for the first time, was a litter of objects the group had collected from the ruins. The largest piece seemed to be an inscribed slab of metal, big enough to have been part of a wall. Kirk crossed to it. On its sides, he now saw, were what seemed to be control elements; some kind of machine, then. He wondered what sort of people had used it, and for what.

"A very remarkable object," Janice's voice said behind him.

"Really? What is it for, do you know?"

"Mentally superior people who were dying would exchange bodies with the physically strong. Immortality could be had by those who deserved it."

"And who chose the deserving?"

"In this case," she said, "I do."

The wall flared brilliantly in Kirk's face, and he felt a fearful internal wrench, as though something were trying to turn him inside out. When he could see again . . .

. . . he was looking at himself, through the eyes of Janice Lester.

Kirk/J left the wall, and coming over to the cot, found a scarf, which he began to fold. Then he bent and pressed it over the woman's mouth and nose.

"You had your chance, Captain Kirk. You could have smothered the life in me and they would have said Dr. Janice Lester died of radiation sickness acquired in the line of duty. Why didn't you? You've always wanted to!"

Janice/K's head moved feebly in denial. The scarf pressed down harder.

"You had the strength to carry it out. But you were afraid, always afraid. Now Janice Lester will take Captain Kirk's place. I already possess your physical strength. But *this* Captain Kirk is not afraid to kill." Kirk/J was almost crooning now, a song of self-hatred. "Now you know the indignity of being a woman. But you will not suffer long. For you the agony will soon pass—as it did for me."

The woman's hand tried to pull his away.

"Quiet. Believe me, it is better to be dead than to live alone in the body of a woman."

The struggling ceased, but Kirk/J did not release his hand until he heard footsteps outside. Then he replaced the scarf and went back to examining the wall. The search party entered only a moment later, looking grim.

"Your report, Dr. McCoy."

"We were too late. There was no way to help them."

"Was it radiation as reported?"

McCoy nodded. "I believe it was celebium. Dr. Coleman does not agree. It's essential to be specific."

"Why? Radioactivity is radioactivity, whatever the source."

"Yes, but in this case there was chemical poisoning involved as well. All the heavy elements are chemically virulent."

"Evidently," Spock added, "the field team broke through a newly exposed crust to a hidden cache of the radioactive element, whatever it was. The damage was instantaneous. They could not get away."

"That," Kirk/J said angrily, "will reflect on Dr. Lester's reputation for thorough preparedness."

"I don't think Dr. Lester can be blamed," McCoy said. "It was a most unfortunate accident, Captain."

"It was careless field work. Dr. Lester will be held responsible—unfair as it may be."

Dr. Coleman looked somewhat fearfully at Kirk/J and went quickly to Janice, bending to examine her. "Dr. McCoy!"

McCoy was there in an instant, tricorder out. "Jim, did you notice any unusual symptoms while we were gone?"

"Nothing at all. She has remained unconscious all the time."

"Dr. Lester is near death," Coleman said.

"Perhaps the shock of knowing what happened to her staff is part of the problem."

"I'm sure it is."

"Beaming her up to the *Enterprise*," McCoy said, "would be less harmful than waiting."

Kirk/J looked questioningly at Coleman, who now seemed frightened. "I don't know," the man said.

"Then we'll go."

At Kirk/J's orders, two medical aides were ready with a stretcher when the party materialized in the Transporter Room. Coleman accompanied the patient to sickbay.

"Mr. Spock, take the ship out of orbit and resume designated course. Dr. McCoy, a word with you, please. You and Dr. Coleman disagree in your diagnosis. Please try to come to an agreement as fast as possible. The matter is especially disturbing—for personal reasons."

"I didn't realize you knew her so well," McCoy said.

"It has been a long time since I saw her. I walked out when it became serious."

"You must have been very young at the time."

"Youth doesn't excuse everything. It's a very unhappy memory."

"Everything possible will be done, Jim."

"Good. Thank you—Bones."

Kirk/J went to the bridge. Uhura, Chekov and Scott were all at their posts, as was Sulu. Spock was intent over his console. Kirk/J looked searchingly at the new faces, and Uhura and Sulu smiled back.

He came slowly to the Captain's position and touched the chair lightly, testing its maneuverability, almost as if with awe. Then he sat down in it and looked up at the viewing screen.

"Course, Mr. Chekov?"

"One twenty-seven, Mark eight."

"Mr. Sulu, set speed at Warp Factor Two."

"Warp Factor Two, sir."

"Mr. Spock, would you come here a moment, please? Thank you. We have a problem with our patient. The two doctors disagree on their diagnosis."

"That is hardly unusual in the medical fraternity, sir."

"Too bad it doesn't help cure their patients," Kirk/J said with an edgy smile.

"I think you can rely on Dr. McCoy's advice."

The edginess grew. "Do you have any specific evidence that confirms his opinion?"

"Not precisely, Captain. It is not my function."

"Then don't add to the confusion, Mr. Spock." Kirk/J arose and strode angrily to the elevator.

In sickbay, he found that Janice/K was regaining consciousness. Moments of quiet were interspersed with sudden flailing movements, which were restrained by straps, and moaning. A very frightened Dr. Coleman was pacing beside her.

"How long has this been going on?" Kirk/J asked.

"It just began."

"You must put a stop to it. If you let Dr. Lester become fully conscious, she will know what has happened."

"Probably no one will believe it," Coleman said.

"Probably?"

"That's all we can hope for. How could death be explained now?"

Kirk/J went to the head of the cot, Coleman following on the other side. "I tell you, it can't continue!"

"You killed every one of the staff. You sent them where you knew the celebium shielding was weak. Why didn't you kill *him*? You had the perfect opportunity."

"You didn't give me enough time."

"You had every minute you asked for."

"He hung onto life too hard. I couldn't . . ."

"You couldn't because you love him," Coleman said, his voice beginning to rise. "You want *me* to be his murderer."

"Love *him*?" Kirk/J said, his voice also rising. "I loved the life he led—the power of the Starship Commander. It's my life now."

"I won't become a murderer." Coleman turned and walked quickly toward the door. Kirk/J leaped to block his way.

"You *are* a murderer. You knew it was celebium. You could have treated them for that. You are a murderer many times."

The moaning grew louder. The doors to the medical lab opened and McCoy and Nurse Chapel came to the cot.

"I thought I could quiet Dr. Lester by my presence," Kirk/J said smoothly. "It seems to have had the opposite effect."

"It has nothing to do with you," Coleman said, with ill-concealed agitation. "It's a symptom of the developing radiation sickness."

"Tests with the ship's equipment," McCoy said, "show no sign of internal radiation damage."

"Dr. Coleman," Kirk/J said, "didn't Dr. Lester's staff become delirious before they went off to die?"

"Yes, Captain."

"But, Jim," said McCoy, "Dr. Lester could as easily be suffering from a phaser stun from all the symptoms I detect."

"Dr. Lester and her staff have been under my supervision for two years now," Coleman said stiffly. "If you do not accept my recommendations, responsibility for her health—or her death—will be yours."

Kirk/J looked toward the bed. Janice/K's movements were growing stronger. Then they stopped as her eyes opened; she looked about as if struggling to see and recognize the faces.

"Dr. McCoy," Kirk/J said, "I'm sorry, but I shall have to remove you from the case and turn it over to Dr. Coleman."

"You can't do that! On this ship, my medical authority is final."

"Dr. Coleman wishes to assume full responsibility. Let him do so."

"I will not allow it."

"It has been done." Kirk/J turned to Coleman. "Dr.

Lester is your patient. I believe you were about to administer a sedative when I came in."

"No!" the woman cried. "No sedative!" But the job was done.

Starting with the considerable advantage of her year in Starfleet with Kirk, Janice Lester had spent more years studying every single detail of a starship's operation—a knowledge which was now to be put to the test. With a little experience, she could probably become invulnerable to suspicion. But the presence aboard of the personality of James Kirk, even under sedation, was a constant threat to her position. It would be better to leave Janice/K among strangers, who would probably consider her insane.

"Plot a course for the Benecia Colony, Mr. Chekov. How long would it take to reach the colony at present speed?"

"Forty-eight hours, Captain."

"Captain," Spock said, "it will delay our work at Beta Aurigae. It means reversing course."

"It can't be helped. We must take Dr. Lester where she can be treated."

"May I point out, Captain, that Starbase Two is on the direct route to our destination?"

"How long to Starbase Two, Mr. Chekov?" Kirk/J asked.

"Seventy-two hours, sir."

"That's twenty-four hours too long. Dr. Lester's condition is increasingly serious. Continue present course."

"Captain, if the diagnosis of Dr. Lester's illness is the critical problem, the Benecia Colony is definitely not the place for her," Spock said. "Its medical facilities are the most primitive."

"They will have to serve the purpose."

"Starbase Two is fully equipped and staffed with the necessary specialists to determine exactly what is wrong with the Doctor. Isn't that crucial to your decision, Captain?"

"Thank you, Mr. Spock. But the facilities will be of no use if Dr. Lester is dead. Time is of the essence. Continue on course, Mr. Sulu."

"Captain," Uhura said, "shall I advise Starfleet Command of the change of plans?"

"No *change* of plan has been ordered, Lieutenant. Our arrival at Beta Aurigae will be *delayed*. Our gravitational studies of that binary system will not suffer, and we may save a life. That is not unusual procedure for the *Enterprise*." Kirk/J arose and went toward the elevator.

"I believe," Spock said, "Starfleet will have to know that our rendezvous with the Starship *Potemkin* will not be kept as scheduled."

"Mr. Spock—if you would concentrate on the areas for which you are responsible, Starfleet would have been informed already."

"Sir, the Captain deals directly with Starfleet on these matters. I assumed that action on my part would be deemed interference."

"Advise Starfleet of the delay, Lieutenant Uhura. Mr. Sulu, maintain course. Increase speed to Warp Six."

Kirk/J escaped from the bridge to the Captain's quarters, but there was no respite there; McCoy was waiting for him.

"Dr. McCoy, are we about to have another fruitless argument about diagnosis?"

McCoy's fist slammed on the top of Kirk's desk. "No, dammit—sir. I'll let my record speak for me."

"Why are you so defensive? There was no implied criticism of you in my order to remove you from the case."

"That's not why I'm here. I'm here because Dr. Coleman's record says he is incompetent."

"That's the opinion of an individual."

"No, sir. It's the considered opinion of Starfleet Command. I checked with them. Dr. Coleman was removed from his post as Chief Medical Officer of his ship for administrative incompetence . . ."

"Administrative duties are not required of him here."

"As well as for flagrant medical blunders."

"Promotions and demotions are sometimes politically motivated," Kirk/J said. "You know that, Doc."

"Not in Starfleet headquarters, *Captain*. At least, not in the Surgeon General's office."

Kirk/J paced for a moment. "I'm afraid the order will have to stand. Dr. Coleman's experience with what happened on the planet had to be the deciding factor. I'm sure you appreciate that."

"I appreciate that you had to make a decision. I, too, have that responsibility, Jim. So I'm asking you to report for a complete checkup."

"Why? What do you base it on?"

"Developing emotional instability and erratic behaviour since returning from the planet."

"You'll never make that charge stick!" Kirk/J said furiously. "Any fool can see why you're doing this!"

"Starfleet Command will be the judge of my motive."

"I won't submit to this petty search for revenge."

"You will submit to Starfleet regulations," McCoy said. "They state that the ship's surgeon will require a full examination of any member of the crew about whom he has doubts—including the Captain. I am ordering you to report for that examination . . ."

He was interrupted by the intercom buzzer.

"Captain Kirk here."

"Lieutenant Uhura, sir. Starfleet Command is requesting additional details of the delay. Shall I handle it?"

"I'll be right there."

The examination could not be postponed indefinitely, however. Knowledge of the Captain's aberrant behaviour was spreading throughout the ship; the crew was becoming increasingly tense. To McCoy's apparent surprise, however, Kirk/J satisfied every test completely.

This stroke of luck was followed by another. Struggling out from under sedation in Dr. Coleman's absence, Janice /K had avoided another injection by persuading Nurse Chapel of her docility—and then had sawed through her restraining straps with a broken medicine glass. Running wildly through the ship holding the glass like a weapon, calling for help and denouncing the Captain as a strutting pretender, she presented the perfect picture of a dangerous madwoman—giving Kirk/J all the pretext he needed to have her put in isolation in a detention cell, with around-the-clock security.

In this, however, he underestimated Spock, of whose sharp observation and penetrating logic the bogus Captain had had only the briefest of experience. The Science Officer knew the limitations of his discipline; he knew, in particular, that the essence of a man's being, his selfhood, was inherently impossible of access to any objective medical test—McCoy himself had often made just this point. Janice/K's denunciation planted a seed in his own mind.

Something had happened to the Captain while he was on the planet. Whatever it was could have taken place only in the short time while he was alone with Dr. Lester. A talk with her might be the only way to shed light on it.

There were two strapping guards outside her detention cell. Spock said to the first, "How is Dr. Lester?"

"Conscious and quiet, Mr. Spock."

"Good. I have a few questions to ask her."

"Did the Captain order it, sir?"

"Why should he?" Spock said. "They are my questions. Therefore I am ordering it, Ensign."

"But the Captain said no one was to speak to Dr. Lester."

"Has such an order ever included his senior officers?"

"Well, no, sir." The ensign activated the door and Spock started in. "But, Mr. Spock, I believe the Captain meant a guard was to be present."

"By all means."

Janice/K's first words on seeing them were "Thank God! Spock, you've got to listen to me."

"That is why I came," Spock said. "Apparently something happened while you and the Captain were alone. What was it?"

"She changed bodies with me, with the aid of an ancient machine she'd unearthed. Spock, *I am Captain Kirk.* I know how unbelievable it sounds. But that's how it happened."

"It is a possibility I had not considered."

"Unless I can convince you, I have no hope at all of ever getting out of this body."

"Complete life-entity transfer with the aid of a mechanical device?"

"Yes. Dr. Lester's description of its function is the last moment I remember as myself."

"To my knowledge," Spock said, "such total transfer has never been accomplished with complete success anywhere in the Galaxy."

"It was accomplished and forgotten long ago on Camus II. I am a living example."

"That is your claim. As yet, it is unsubstantiated."

"I know, Spock. Nevertheless I'm speaking the truth. Listen—when I was caught in the interspace of the Tholian sector, you risked your life and even the *Enterprise* to get me back. Help me get back now. And, when the Vians of Minara demanded that we let McCoy die, we didn't permit it. How would I know those things if I were not James Kirk?"

"Such incidents may have been recorded. They could have become known to you."

"You are closer to the Captain than anyone in the universe. You know his thoughts. What does your telepathic sense tell you?"

Spock touched her face and closed his eyes, his own face a study in concentration as he established a mind meld. Then he withdrew his hand and looked at her with new determination.

"I believe you," he said. "My belief is not acceptable evidence. But I will make every effort to make it so. Only Dr. McCoy can help us. Come with me."

"I'm sorry, sir," the guard said. "But Dr. Lester can *not* leave here. You're asking me to violate the Captain's order."

"He is not the Captain."

"Sir, you must be as mad as she is. You're to leave here at once. I follow orders."

"Certainly, Ensign," Spock said. "We must all do our duty."

While he was still talking, he lashed out. The scuffle was brief, but the guard outside the cell was alert—he could be heard calling, "Security to Captain Kirk! The detention cell has been broken into!"

When they emerged, the guard was standing with his back to the opposite wall, phaser leveled. Kirk/J and two more guards were already coming down the corridor, followed by McCoy.

Spock stopped. "Violence is not called for, sir," he said. "No *physical* resistance will be offered."

Kirk/J hit the intercom button. "Security detail to Detention at once. Attention all personnel. First Officer Spock is being placed under arrest on a charge of mutiny. He has conspired with Dr. Lester to take over the ship from your Captain. A hearing will be immediately convened to consider the charges and specifications for a general court-martial." He turned to McCoy. "The board will consist of Scott, you and myself."

"I will not be made party to a court-martial of Spock," McCoy said. "There are better ways to handle it."

"You are not forced to condemn anyone. You are asked —no, you are ordered—to vote your honest convictions. Two out of three carries the final verdict. Convene the board. Guard, return Dr. Lester to isolation. She will be held for sanity tests."

The hearing was held in the briefing room. Kirk/J sat at the head of the table, gavel in hand; McCoy sat quietly to one side. Uhura was making a tape of the proceedings, and Chekov, Sulu and Nurse Chapel were listening intently as Scott began cross-examining Spock.

"Mr. Spock, you are a scientist—a leading scientist of the Galaxy."

"That's very pleasant to hear, Mr. Scott. But it is an exaggeration. I have long since sacrificed basic theoretical investigation for the more immediate excitement of life on the *Enterprise*."

"I meant, your approach to every problem is completely scientific."

"I hope so," Spock said.

"Therefore your statement that you believe this fantastic tale about transference of life entities between the Captain and Dr. Lester is intended to be taken seriously by this court."

"Completely seriously."

"Yet you have no evidence on which to base it."

"I have stated my evidence: telepathic communication with the mind of Captain James T. Kirk."

"You are a reasonable man, Spock," Scott said, exasperated. "But that is not a reasonable statement. Far from it. Far from it. Surely you must have had more than that to go on."

"It was sufficient for me."

"Well, it's not sufficient for a court. Your evidence is completely subjective. You know that, laddie. What has happened to you? We must have evidence we can examine out in the open."

Spock threw a challenging look toward Kirk/J. "You have heard a great deal of testimony—except that of the chief witness. The one who should be the real subject of this inquiry is kept locked away in isolation. Why, *Captain?*"

"She is dangerously insane," Kirk/J said. "We have seen evidence of that."

"She is dangerous only to your authority, *sir.*"

"Mr. Spock, my authority was granted to me by Starfleet Command. Only that high authority can take it away."

"Then why be afraid of the testimony of a poor insane woman?"

"This clumsy effort does not threaten my position, Mr. Spock. It does endanger your whole future."

"The witness, sir! Bring on the witness! Let your officers put the questions!"

Kirk/J hesitated a moment. Then he banged his gavel and nodded to a guard, who went out.

"Dr. McCoy."

"Yes, Captain."

"You were at one time disturbed by my orders and reactions, is that not true?"

"Yes, sir."

"But instead of trying to destroy me, you were searching for a way to help me. For the record, tell the court your findings."

"Physically the Captain is in the best of condition. His emotional and mental states are comparable to the time he assumed command of the *Enterprise.*"

"Mr. Spock, did you know the results of Dr. McCoy's examination?"

"I know them now," Spock said.

"And what have you to say now?"

"I am disappointed and deeply concerned that there is no objective evidence to support my position—so far."

"Since there is no evidence, will you give up your belief in the insane story of a woman driven mad by a tragic experience?"

Before Spock could reply, the door opened and the woman in question herself was brought in by two guards. Kirk/J pointed to a chair, and she sat down.

"Dr. Lester," he said, "I appreciate your being here. Everyone is deeply aware that you have already been subjected to inordinate emotional stress. Unfortunately, I have had to add to it in the interest of the safety of this crew. I had hoped that any further stress could be avoided. Mr. Spock disagrees. He is of the opinion that your testimony is important in determining the merits of his case. Since we are solely interested in arriving at a just decision, we must ask you a few questions. We shall all try not to upset you." At this, she nodded. "Now. You claim you are James T. Kirk."

"No, I am not Captain Kirk," Janice/K said composedly. "That is very apparent. I doubt that Mr. Spock would have put it that way. I claim that whatever it is that makes James Kirk a living being special to himself is held here in this body."

"I stand corrected. However—as I understand it—I am Dr. Janice Lester."

There was a snicker from the guards.

"That's very clever," she responded. "But I didn't say it. I said the body of James Kirk is being used by Dr. Janice Lester."

"A subtle difference that happens to escape me," Kirk/J said with a smile. "However, I assume that this—this switch was brought about by mutual agreement."

"No. It was brought about by a violent attack by Dr. Lester, with the use of equipment she discovered on Camus II."

"Violence by the lady perpetrated on Captain Kirk? Tsk, tsk. I ask the assembled personnel to look at Dr. Lester and visualize that historic moment."

This time the laughter was general. Kirk/J waited until it had ridden itself out, then continued, "And do you know any reason why Dr. Janice Lester would want this ludicrous exchange?"

"Yes! To achieve a power her peers would not accord her. To attain a position she does not merit by training or temperament. And most of all she wanted to murder the man who might have loved her—had her intense hatred of her own womanhood not made life with her impossible."

Spock rose angrily. "Sir, this line of questioning is self-serving. There is only one issue: Is the story of life-entity transfer believable? This crew has been to many places in the Galaxy. *You have not.* They are familiar with many strange events. They are trained to recognize that what seems completely unbelievable on the surface is scientifically possible if you understand the basic theory of the event."

"Mr. Spock, do you know of any other case like the one Dr. Lester describes?"

"Not precisely. No."

"Assuming you are correct in your belief, do you expect Starfleet Command to place that person"—his finger stabbed at Janice/K—"in command of this ship?"

"I expect only to reveal the truth."

"Of course you do. And with the truth revealed that I am not really the Captain—and knowing that she will not be appointed Captain—then of course *you* will become the Captain." Kirk/J looked at Spock with apparent compassion. "Give it up, Spock. Return to the *Enterprise* family. All charges will be dropped. The madness that temporarily overcame us all on Camus II will pass and be forgotten."

"And what will happen to Dr. Lester?"

"Dr. Lester will be properly cared for. Always. That is a debt and a responsibility I owe her from the past."

"No, sir!" Spock said emphatically. "I will not withdraw a single charge I have made. You are not Captain Kirk. You have ruthlessly appropriated his body. But the life entity within you is not that of Captain Kirk. You do not belong in command of the *Enterprise*. I will do everything in my power against you."

"Lieutenant Uhura," Kirk/J said with dangerous quietness, "play back the last two sentences of Mr. Spock's tirade."

Spock's voice rang out from the speaker of the recorder: "You do not belong in command of the *Enterprise*. I will do everything in my power against you."

"Mr. Spock, you have heard the statement you put into the record. Do you understand the nature of it?"

"I do. And I stand by it."

"And that is mutiny!" Kirk/J shouted, his face livid. "Deliberate—vindictive—insane at its base—but it is mutiny as charged and incitement to mutiny. Dr. McCoy, Mr. Scott, you have heard it. On the basis of these statements, I call for an immediate summary court-martial by powers granted to me as Captain of the *Enterprise*."

"Just a moment, Captain," Scott said. "I'm not ready to

vote Mr. Spock into oblivion so fast. Mr. Spock is a serious man. What he says is to be taken seriously, no matter how wild."

"Come to the point."

"I'm right at the nub of it, Captain. You don't put a man like Mr. Spock out of the service because of a condition akin to temporary insanity. Dr. McCoy, you said the woman may have become mentally deranged due to the radiation she was exposed to."

"Yes, Scotty."

"Couldn't the same thing have happened to Mr. Spock? He was a sight closer to the source of the radiation."

"It's possible."

"Then the mutiny is qualified by the temporary insanity due to the . . ."

"Thank you, my friend," Spock interrupted. "A noble try. But I was not exposed to the celebium. I took every precaution. And I have been given precautionary treatment since then by Dr. McCoy. I am completely sound in body and mind."

"Mutiny," said Kirk/J, pounding with the gavel. "A summary court-martial on the evidence and the charges is immediately invoked. A recess will be followed by a vote."

"Yes," Spock said. "An immediate vote. This matter must be cleared up at once, before . . ."

The gavel pounded a loud tattoo. "Silence!"

"Before our chief witness," Spock shouted above the din, "is left to die on an obscure little colony with the truth locked away inside her!"

Kirk/J rose, his face red with hysteria, almost to the point of apoplexy. "Silence, silence! A recess is declared. The summary court will then be in session. There will be no cross-discussion. No conferences. No collusion. I order the judges to be absolutely silent as they arrive at a decision on the charge of mutiny. When I return we will vote. The evidence presented here can be the only basis for your decision."

He stormed out of the room, leaving everyone stunned. McCoy began to pace. The silence stretched out. At last Scott said, "Who ever heard of a jury being forbidden to deliberate?"

He went out into the corridor, followed by the others,

leaving behind Janice/K, Spock and the guards, as well as Uhura.

"What's there to say?" McCoy said.

"Doctor, I've seen the Captain feverish, sick, drunk, delirious, terrified, overjoyed, boiling mad. Until now I've never seen him beet-red with hysteria. I know how I'm going to vote."

"I've been through this with Spock. He is not being scientific. And neither are you."

"It may not be scientific," Scott said, "but if Spock thinks it happened, it must be logical."

"Don't you think I know that? My tests show nothing wrong with the Captain. That's the only fact that will interest Starfleet."

"Headquarters has its problems—and we've got ours. Right now the Captain of the *Enterprise* is our problem."

McCoy frowned. He started to pace again, but was halted by Nurse Chapel.

"Doctor," she said, whispering, "I didn't notice it at the time. But in her first lucid moment, Dr. Lester asked why we were going to miss our rendezvous with the *Potemkin*. How could she know that?"

"Hmm. Especially since the Captain *didn't*. Scotty, the vote is going to be called in a few minutes."

"Let me put one last question. Suppose you voted with me in favor of Spock. That's two to one and Spock is free. What do you think the Captain will do?"

"I don't know."

"You know, all right. The vote will stick in his craw. He'll never accept it."

McCoy angrily walked away a few steps and then turned back and looked hard at Scott. "We don't know that."

"I tell you, he won't. Then, Doctor, that's the time to move against him. We'll have to take over the ship."

"We're talking mutiny, Scotty."

"Yes. Are you ready for the vote?"

"I'm ready for the vote."

Kirk/J was already back in the briefing room when they reentered. When they were all seated, he stood up. "Lieutenant Uhura, play back the tapes of the conversation in the corridor."

Uhura, looking both grief-stricken and guilt-ridden, moved a switch. Recorded voices said:

"Then, Doctor, that's the time to move against him. We'll have to take over the ship."

"We're talking mutiny, Scotty."

"Yes. Are you ready for the vote?"

"That's enough," McCoy said angrily. "We know what was said."

"Enough to convict you for conspiracy with mutineers," Kirk/J said, drawing his phaser. The guards followed suit. "You are so charged. The penalty is death."

Chekov and Sulu both jumped forward, talking almost at once.

"Starfleet expressly forbids the death penalty . . ."

"There is only one exception . . ."

"General Order Four has not been violated by any officer of the *Enterprise* . . ."

"All my senior officers have turned against me," Kirk/J said. "I am responsible. Execution will be immediate. Go to your posts. Guards, take them to the brig."

Only Uhura, Sulu and Chekov were at their posts on the bridge, a sadly depleted corporal's guard. They were working, but their expressions were listless, abstracted. Sulu said at last, "The Captain really must be cracking up if he thinks he can get away with an execution."

"Captain Kirk wouldn't order an execution even if he did crack up," Chekov said. "Spock's right, that can't be the Captain."

"What difference does it make who he is?" said Uhura. "Are we going to allow an execution to take place?"

Chekov clenched his fists. "If Security backs him up, how will we fight them?"

Sulu said, "I'll fight them every way and any way I can . . ."

The conversation was choked off as Kirk/J came onto the bridge, highly elated. When he spoke, the sentences seemed almost to tumble over one another in their haste to get out. "Lieutenant Uhura, inform all sections of the decision. Have each section send a representative to the place of execution on the hangar deck. Mr. Chekov, how far to the Benecia Colony?"

"Coming within scanning range."

"Plot coordinates for orbit. Mr. Sulu, lock into coordinates as soon as orbit is accomplished. Interment will take place on Benecia."

There were no "Ayes," and nobody moved. Kirk/J stared at his officers. "You have received your orders."

Still no response.

"You have received your orders. You will obey at once or be charged with mutiny." His voice began to rise in pitch, losing its male timbre. "Obey my orders or—or . . ."

Then, suddenly, he reeled, staggered, and fell into his chair, seemingly almost in a faint. His body contorted for a moment and then became rigid, his eyes staring wider, but sightlessly.

The others rose in alarm, but the seizure lasted only a moment. Then Kirk/J was out of the chair and leaped for the elevator.

Dr. Coleman was alone in the medical lab when Kirk/J burst in. "Coleman—the transference is weakening."

"What happened?"

"For a moment I was with the prisoners. I won't go back to being Janice Lester. Help me prevent it."

"The only way to prevent it is by the death of Janice Lester. You'll have to carry out the execution."

"I can't," Kirk/J said. "The crew is in mutiny. You must kill him for me."

"I have done everything else for you. But I tell you I will not commit murder for you."

"You can do it for yourself," Kirk/J said urgently. "If I am the Captain of the *Enterprise*, you will regain your position as a Ship's Surgeon. I will see to that."

"I would have been content with you, as you were. I did not need a starship."

"Unless Kirk dies, we will both be exposed as murderers. Does that leave you any choice?"

Reluctantly, Coleman picked up an air hypo, selected a cartridge and snapped it into place.

"The dose must be doubly lethal."

"It is," Coleman said impassively.

Kirk/J led the way to the brig. Judging by the woman's tense expression and the way the others were grouped around her, she too had felt that moment of transitory retransference, and was ready to fight to prolong it should it occur again.

"I have demanded the sentence of execution," Kirk/J said. "However, to prevent any further conspiracy, you will be placed in separate cells. If there is any resistance, a sedative will be administered until you learn cooperation. Dr. Lester is first. Follow Dr. Coleman."

Coleman went back out through the force field. Janice/K held back suspiciously, but then also stepped out into the corridor, Kirk/J behind her. After only a few steps he said loudly, "This woman obviously doesn't know what it means to obey an order."

The hypo flashed in Coleman's hand, but not quickly enough. Janice/K saw it and grabbed that arm with both hands, struggling with all her poor strength to deflect it.

Again the look of dizziness and complete terror overwhelmed Kirk/J; once more his body contorted and grew taut.

The same paralysis gripped Janice/K, its rigidity immobilizing Coleman's arm as her conscious efforts could never have done. Then she screamed.

"Don't! Don't! I have lost to the Captain! I have lost to James Kirk!" And then, in a cry of pure madness, "Kill him! Kill *him!*"

Kirk, whose first move had been to shut off the brig's force field, met Coleman's rush easily; a quick chop and it was over. He turned to Janice, whose face was contorted with hatred and agony. "Kill him! I want James Kirk dead! Kill him!" Then, sobbing painfully like a child, "I will never be the Captain—never—never—kill him . . ."

Coleman, who had been only momentarily stunned, tossed aside the hypo, clambered to his feet and came over to her. She began to collapse, and Coleman took her in his arms.

"You are," he said, "as I have loved you."

"Kill him," Janice said quietly, her eyes vacant. "Please."

Spock, McCoy and Scott were all out in the corridor. Kirk seized each of them in turn by the hand. "Bones, is there anything you can do for her?"

"I would like to take care of her," Coleman said pleadingly.

"Of course," said McCoy. "Come with me." He led them away toward sickbay.

Kirk looked after them. "I didn't want to destroy her," he said.

"You had to," Spock said. "How else could you have survived, Captain? To say nothing of the rest of us."

"Her life could have been as rich as any woman's, if only—" He paused and sighed. "If only . . ."

"If only," Spock said, "she had ever been able to take any pride in *being* a woman."

REQUIEM FOR METHUSELAH

(Jerome Bixby)

Rigellian fever struck aboard the *Enterprise* with startling suddenness, its origin unknown. Permission was asked, and received, of Starfleet Command to abort the current routine mission in order to search for a planet with large deposits of ryetalyn, the only known cure for the disease. By the time they found such a planet, one yeoman had died and four more were seriously ill.

Kirk, McCoy and Spock beamed down at once, leaving Scott at the con. McCoy scanned about him with his tricorder.

"There's a large deposit at bearing two seven three—about a mile away," he reported, his voice grim. "We've got four hours to get it processed, or the epidemic will be irreversible. Everybody on the *Enterprise* . . ."

As he started off with Kirk, Spock's voice stopped them.

"Most strange," he said. "Readings indicate a life form in the vicinity. Yet our ship's sensors indicated that this planet was uninhabited."

"Human?" Kirk said. "But we've got no time for that. Let's get to that ryetalyn deposit."

Again they started off, and again they were halted by a

sound—this time a steady whirring behind them. As they turned, they saw floating from behind a rock what could only be a robot: metallic, spherical, about the size of a beachball, studded with protuberances with functions which could only be guessed at. It came toward them at about chest height, flickering menacingly.

The three drew their phasers. A light blinked brightly on the robot's skin, and a bush next to Kirk went up in a burst of flame.

First Kirk and then the other two fired back—or tried to. All three phasers were inoperative. The robot continued to advance.

"Do not kill," a man's voice said. The robot stopped in midair. The owner of the voice came around from behind the same rock: a muscular man of about forty, whose bearing suggested immense dignity, assurance, authority.

"Thanks," said Kirk with relief. "I am Captain James Kirk, of the . . ."

"I know who you are. I have monitored your ship since it entered this system."

"Then you know why we're here, Mr. . . ."

"Flint. You will leave my planet."

"*Your* planet, sir?" Spock said.

"My retreat—from the unpleasantness of life on Earth—and the company of other people."

"Mr. Flint, I've got a sick crew up there," Kirk said. "We can't possibly reach another planet in time. We're sorry to intrude. We'll be happy to leave your little private world as soon as possible, but without that ryetalyn, you'd be condemning four hundred and thirty people to death!"

"You are trespassing, Captain."

"We're in *need*. We'll pay you for the ryetalyn—trade for it—work for it."

"You have nothing I want," Flint said.

"Nevertheless, we've got to have the ryetalyn. If necessary, we'll take it."

"If you do not leave voluntarily, I have the power to force you to leave—or kill you where you stand."

Kirk whipped out his communicator and snapped it open. "Kirk to *Enterprise*. Mr. Scott, lock phasers on landing party coordinates."

"Aye, Captain. All phasers locked on."

"If anything happens to us, there'll be *four* deaths," Kirk told Flint. "And my crew will come down and get the ryetalyn anyhow."

"It would be an interesting test of power," Flint said. "Your enormous forces—against mine. Who would win?"

"If you are not certain," Spock said, "I suggest you refrain from a most useless experiment."

"We need only a few hours," Kirk added.

"Have you ever seen a victim of Rigellian fever?" McCoy said. "It kills in one day. Its effects resemble bubonic plague."

Flint's expression turned remote. "Constantinople, Summer, 1334. It marched through the streets—the sewers. It left the city, by oxcart, by sea—to kill half of Europe. The rats—rustling and squealing in the night, as they, too, died . . ."

"You are a student of history, Mr. Flint?" Spock asked.

"I am." He seemed to rouse himself. "The *Enterprise*—a plague ship. Well, you have two hours. At the end of that time, you will leave."

"With all due gratitude," Kirk said, rather drily. "Mr. Spock, Bones . . ."

"No need," Flint said, indicating the robot. "M-4 will gather the ryetalyn you need. In the meantime, permit me to offer more comfortable surroundings."

"More comfortable" turned out to be a vast understatement. The central room of Flint's underground home was both huge and luxurious. Most impressive were the artworks—framed paintings, dozens of them, hung on the walls, except for one wall which was entirely taken up by books. There were statuary, busts, tapestries, illuminated glass cases containing open books and manuscripts of obvious antiquity, and even a concert grand piano. The place was warm, comfortable, masculine despite all these riches—at once both museum and home.

"Our ship's sensors did not reveal your presence here, Mr. Flint," Spock said.

"My planet is surrounded by screens which create the impression of lifelessness. A protection against the curious—the uninvited."

"Such a home must be difficult to maintain."

"M-4 serves as butler, housekeeper, gardener—ana guardian."

McCoy was looking into the illuminated cases with obvious awe. "A Shakespeare First Folio—a Gutenberg Bible—the 'Creation' lithographs by Taranullus of Centaurus VII—some of the rarest books in the Galaxy—spanning centuries!"

"Make yourselves comfortable," Flint said. "Help yourselves to some brandy, gentlemen." He went out, calmly.

"Do we trust him?" McCoy asked.

"It would seem logical to do so—for the moment."

"I'll need two hours," McCoy said worriedly, "to process that ryetalyn into antitoxin."

"If the ryetalyn doesn't show up in one hour, we go prospecting," Kirk said. "Right over Mr. Flint, if necessary."

Spock was now looking at the paintings. "This is the most splendid private art collection I have ever seen," he said. "And unique. The majority are works of three men: Leonardo da Vinci of the sixteenth century, Reginald Pollock of the twentieth century, and even a Sten from Marcus II."

"And this," said McCoy, going over to the bar and picking up a bottle, "is Sirian brandy, a hundred years old. Now where are the glasses? Ah. Jim? I know you won't have any, Spock. Heaven forbid that your mathematically perfect brainwaves be corrupted by this all too human vice."

"Thank you, Doctor. I will have brandy."

"Can the two of us handle a drunk Vulcan?" McCoy asked Kirk. "Once alcohol nits that green blood . . ."

"Nothing happens that I cannot control much more efficiently than you," Spock said, after a sip. "If I appear distracted, it is because of what I have seen. I am close to feeling an unaccustomed emotion."

"Let's drink to *that*," McCoy said. "What emotion?"

"Envy. None of these da Vinci paintings has ever been catalogued or reproduced. They are *unknown* works. All are apparently authentic—to the last brushstroke and use of materials. As undiscovered da Vincis, they would be priceless."

"Would be?" Kirk said. "You think they might be fakes?"

"Most strange. A man of Flint's obvious wealth and impeccable taste would scarcely hang fakes. Yet my tricorder analysis indicates that the canvas and the pigments used are of contemporary origin."

"This could be what it seems to be," Kirk said thoughtfully. "Or it could be a cover—a setup—even an illusion."

"That could explain the paintings," McCoy said. "*Similar* to the real thing . . ."

"One of you, get a full tricorder scan of our host," Kirk said. "See if he's human."

"The minute he turns his back," McCoy agreed.

Kirk got out his communicator. "Kirk to *Enterprise*. Mr. Scott, run a library check on this Mr. Flint we've encountered here—and on this planet, Holberg 917-G. Stand by with results; I'll contact."

"Aye, sir."

"Kirk out. Now let's enjoy his brandy. It *tastes* real."

But as he lifted the glass to his lips, he once again heard the whirring of the robot, M-4. The men froze warily as the machine entered and moved toward them, stopping to hover over a large, low table. A front panel opened, and out came cubes of a whitish material onto the table. The robot closed the panel and floated back a pace.

McCoy snatched up one of the cubes. "This looks like —it is! Ryetalyn! Refined—ready to be processed into antitoxin!"

"Whatever our host may be, he's come through," Kirk said. "McCoy, beam up to the ship and start processing."

"That will not be necessary," Flint said, appearing at the top of a ramp. "M-4 can prepare the ryetalyn for inoculation more quickly in my laboratory than you could aboard your ship."

"I'd like to supervise that, of course," McCoy said.

"And when you are satisfied as to procedures, I hope you will do me the honor of being my guests at dinner."

"Thank you, Mr. Flint," Kirk said. "I'm afraid we don't have time."

Flint came a step down the ramp. "I regret my earlier inhospitality. Let me make amends." He half turned, extending a hand.

At the top of the ramp appeared a staggeringly beautiful girl in loosely flowing robes. She looked down at the three strangers with a mixture of innocence and awe.

The two descended the ramp. The girl was graceful as well as lovely, yet she seemed quite unaware of the charm she radiated.

"I thought you lived alone, Mr. Flint," Kirk said when he could get his voice back.

"No, this is the other member of the family. Gentlemen, may I present Rayna."

The courtesies were exchanged. Then Rayna said, "Mr. Spock, I do hope we can find time to discuss inter-universal field densities, and their relationship to gravity vortex phenomena."

If Spock was as staggered as Kirk was by this speech, he did not show it. "Indeed? I should enjoy such a talk. It is an interest of mine."

"Her parents were killed in an accident, while in my employ," Flint explained. "Before dying, they placed their infant, Rayna Kapec, in my custody. I have raised and educated her."

"With impressive results, sir," McCoy said. "Rayna, what else interests you besides gravity vortex phenomena?"

"Everything. Less than that is betrayal of the intellect."

"The totality of the universe?" McCoy said gently. "All knowledge? Remember, there's more to life than knowing."

"Rayna possesses the equivalent of seventeen university degrees, in the sciences and arts," Flint said. "She is aware that the intellect is not all—but its development must come first, or the individual makes errors, wastes time in unprofitable pursuits."

"At her age, I rather enjoyed my errors," said McCoy. "But, no damage done, obviously, Rayna. You're the farthest thing from a bookworm I've ever seen."

"Flint is my teacher. You are the first other humans I have ever seen."

Kirk stared at her, not sure he liked what he had heard. But it was none of his business.

"The misfortune of men everywhere," McCoy was saying, "is our privilege."

Flint said, "If you would accompany my robot to the

laboratory, Doctor, you can be assured that the processing of the ryetalyn is well in hand."

McCoy picked up the ryetalyn cubes and looked uncertainly at M-4. The robot turned silently in midair and glided out, the surgeon in tow.

"Your pleasure, gentlemen?" Flint said. "Chess? Billiards? Conversation?"

Kirk was still staring at Rayna. "Why not all three?" he said absently.

Kirk was no pool shark, and found Rayna far better at it than he was. He lined up a shot, intent. Flint and Spock watched.

Flint said, "I have surrounded Rayna with the beautiful and the good of human culture—its artistic riches and scientific wisdom."

Kirk muffed the shot.

"I have protected her from its venality—its savagery," Flint went on. "You see the result, Captain."

Rayna had lined up a three-cushion shot, which paid off brilliantly. Kirk straightened, feeling resigned.

"Did you teach her *that?*" he asked.

"We play often."

"May I show you, Captain?" Rayna said. She stepped close to him, correcting his grip on the cue.

"You said savagery, Mr. Flint," Kirk said. "How long is it since you visited Earth?"

"You would tell me that it is no longer cruel. But it is, Captain. Look at your Starship—bristling with weapons . . ."

Kirk and Rayna were bending, close together, their arms intertwined on the cue as she set him up for the shot. He found that not much of his mind was on Flint.

". . . its mission to colonize, exploit, destroy if necessary, to advance Federation causes."

Kirk made the shot. This time it was a pretty good one.

"Our missions are peaceful," he said, "our weapons defensive. If we were such barbarians, we would not have *asked* for the ryetalyn. Your greeting, not ours, lacked a certain benevolence."

"The result of pressures that are not your concern."

Spock had wandered over to the piano and sat down, studying the manuscript on the music rack.

"Such pressures are everywhere," Kirk said, "in every man, urging him to what you call savagery. The private hells—the inner needs and mysteries—the beast of instinct. As humans, we'll always be that way." He turned to Rayna, who seemed surprised that anyone would dare to argue with Flint. "To be human is to be complex. You can't escape a little ugliness, inside yourself and from without. It's part of the game."

Spock began casually to pick out the melody of the music manuscript. Flint looked toward him, seemingly struck by a sudden notion, "Why not play the waltz, Mr. Spock?" He turned to Kirk. "To be human is also to seek pleasure. To laugh—to dance; Rayna is a most accomplished dancer."

Sight-reading, Spock began to play. Kirk looked at Rayna. "May I have the pleasure?"

She went into his arms. The first few steps were clumsy, for Kirk was somewhat out of practice, but she was easy to lead. She was wearing a half smile of seeming curiosity. Flint watched them both, outwardly paternal, but also speculatively.

Spock was doing very well, considering that the manuscript looked hastily written; but there was something in his intentness that suggested more than mere concentration on the problems of reading the notation.

As Kirk and Rayna whirled past Flint, she gave Flint a bright, pleased smile, more animated than any expression she had shown before. Flint returned the smile with apparent affection—but there was still that intent speculation underneath.

Then McCoy entered, looking very grim indeed. Spock stopped playing, and the dancing couple broke apart.

"Something wrong?" Kirk asked.

"Nothing to dance about. The ryetalyn is no good! We can't use it. It contains irillium—nearly one part per thousand."

"Irillium would make the antitoxin inert?" Spock said.

"Right. Useless."

"Most unfortunate that it was not detected," Flint said. "I shall go with M-4 to gather more ryetalyn and screen it myself. You are welcome to join me, Doctor." He went out, evidently to summon the robot.

"Time factor, McCoy?" Kirk said. "The epidemic?"

"A little over two hours and a half. I guess we can get in under the wire. I've never seen anything like the robot's speed, Jim. It would take us twice as long to process the stuff."

"Would we have made the error?" Kirk asked grimly.

"*I* made the error, just as much as the robot. I didn't suspect the contaminant until scanning the completed antitoxin showed it up. What if all the ryetalyn on this planet contains irillium?"

"Go with Flint. Keep an eye on procedures."

"Like a hawk," McCoy said, turning away. "That lab's an extraordinary place, Jim. You and Spock should have a look."

He went up the ramp after Flint. Spock got up from the piano bench, picking up the manuscript.

"Something else which is extraordinary," he said. "This waltz I played is by Johannes Brahms. But it is in manuscript, Captain—written in Brahms' own hand, which I recognize. It is an unknown waltz—absolutely the work of Brahms—but unknown."

"Later, Mr. Spock," Kirk said, preoccupied. "I think I will take a look at that laboratory. All our lives depend upon it. If we could get the irillium out of the existing antitoxin . . . Where did Rayna go?"

"I did not see her leave, Captain. I was intent upon . . ."

"All right. Stay here. Let me know when McCoy and Flint return."

Spock nodded and sat down again at the piano. As Kirk went up the ramp, the strains of the waltz began to sound again behind him.

He found the laboratory without difficulty, and it was indeed a wonder, an orderly mass of devices only a few of which looked even vaguely familiar. What use did Flint ordinarily have for such an installation? It implied research work of a high order and constantly pursued. Was there no limit to the man's intellectual resources?

Then Kirk realized that he was not alone. Rayna was standing on the other side of the lab, before another door. Her hands were clasped before her and her eyes were raised in an attitude of meditation, or of questioning for which she could not find the words. But she seemed also to be trembling slightly.

Kirk went to her, and she turned her head. Yes, she was shivering.

"You left us," Kirk said. "The room became lonely."

"Lonely? I do not know the word."

"It is a condition of wanting someone else. It is like a thirst—like a flower dying in a desert." Kirk halted, surprised at his own outburst of imagery. His eyes looked past her to the door. "What's in there?"

"I do not know. Flint has told me I must never enter. He denies me nothing else."

"Then—why are you here?"

"I—do not know. I come to this place when I am troubled—when I would search myself."

"Are you troubled now?"

"Yes."

"By what?" She looked intently and searchingly into his eyes, but did not answer. "Are you happy here, with Flint?"

"He is the greatest, kindest, wisest man in the Galaxy."

"Then why are you afraid? You *are* afraid; I can see it." He put his arms around her protectively. The trembling did not stop. "Rayna, this place is cold. Think of something far away. A perfect, safe, idyllic world—your presence would make it so. A world that children dream of . . ."

"Did I dream? My childhood—I remember this year—last year . . ."

What had Flint done to this innocent? He felt his expression hardening. She looked bewildered. "Don't be afraid," he said gently. He kissed her. It was meant to be only a brotherly kiss, but when he drew back, he found that he was profoundly shaken. He bent his head to kiss her more thoroughly.

As he did, her gaze flashed over his shoulder, and her eyes widened with horror. "No!" she cried. "No, no!"

Kirk whirled, belatedly aware of the whirring of the robot. The machine was floating toward him, lights flashing ominously. He put himself between the robot and the girl. It advanced inexorably, and he backed a step, trying to lead it away from Rayna.

"Stop!" Rayna cried. "*Stop!*"

M-4 did not stop. Kirk, backtracking, ducked beind a

large machine and pulled out his phaser; when the robot appeared, he fired point-blank. As he had more than half expected, the weapon failed to work.

"Stop! Command! *Command!*"

Steadily, the robot backed Kirk into a corner. He braced himself to rush it—futile, without doubt, but there was no other choice.

Then there was the hissing snap of a phaser, and the robot vanished.

Spock appeared from around the corner of the massive machine where Kirk had tried to ambush M-4, stowing his phaser.

"Whew," Kirk said. "Thank you, Mr. Spock."

"Fortunately the robot was too intent on you to deactivate my phaser," Spock said. "Dr. McCoy and Mr. Flint have returned with the ryetalyn."

Was Rayna all right? Kirk went to her. She seemed unharmed. Suddenly she lifted a hand to touch his lips. Then she turned away, wide-eyed, deep in troubled thoughts.

They were back in the central room—Spock, Rayna, and a very angry Kirk. Flint was quite calm. Behind his back, Spock had his tricorder out and aimed at him.

"M-4 was programmed to defend this household, and its members," Flint said calmly. "No doubt I should have altered its instructions, to allow for unauthorized but predictable actions on your part. It thought you were attacking Rayna. A misinterpretation."

Kirk was far from sure he bought that explanation. He took a step toward Flint.

"If it was around now, it might interpret quite correctly . . ."

Whirrrr.

The machine was back—or an exact duplicate of it, floating watchfully near Flint.

"Too useful a device to be without, really," Flint said. "I created another. Go to the laboratory, M-5."

Spock stowed his tricorder over his shoulder. "Matter from energy," he said. "An almost instantaneous manufacture, no doubt, in which your robot was duplicated from an existing matrix."

Flint nodded, but he did not take his eyes from Kirk.

"Be thankful that you did not attack me, Captain. I might have accepted battle—and I have twice your physical strength."

"In your own words, that might be an interesting test of power."

"How childish he is, Rayna. Would you call him brave —or a fool?"

"I am glad he did not die," Rayna said in a low voice.

"Of course. Death, when unnecessary, is tragic. Captain, Dr. McCoy is in the laboratory with the new ryetalyn. He is satisfied as to its purity. I suggest that you wait here, patiently—safely. You have seen that my defense systems operate automatically—and not always in accordance with my wishes."

Kirk felt a certain lack of conviction about this last clause.

Flint put his hand on Rayna's arm. "Come, Rayna."

After a last, long look at Kirk, she allowed herself to be led up the ramp. Scowling, Kirk took a stubborn step after them, but Spock held him back.

"I don't like the way he orders her around," Kirk said.

"Since we are dependent upon Mr. Flint for the ryetalyn, I might respectfully suggest, Captain, that you pay less attention to the young lady, should you encounter her again. Our host's interests do not appear to be confined to art and science."

"He loves her?" Kirk said.

"Strongly indicated."

"Jealousy! That could explain the attack. But still—he seemed to *want* us to be together; the billiards game —*he* suggested that we dance . . ."

"It would seem to defy the logic of the human male, as I understand it."

After an uneasy moment, Kirk brought out his communicator. "Kirk to *Enterprise*. Mr. Scott, report on the Rigellian fever."

"Nearly everybody aboard has got it, sir. We're working a skeleton crew, and waiting for the antitoxin."

"A little while longer, Scotty. Report on computer search."

"No record of Mr. Flint. He simply seems to have no past. The planet was purchased thirty years ago by a Mr. Nova, a wealthy financier and recluse."

"Run a check on Rayna Kapec. Status: legal ward, after death of parents."

"Aye, Captain."

As Kirk slowly put the communicator away, Spock said, "There is still a greater mystery. I was able to secure a tricorder scan of Mr. Flint, while you and he were involved in belligerence. He is human. But there are biophysical peculiarities. Certain body-function readings are disproportionate. For one thing, extreme age is indicated—on the order of six thousand years."

"Six thousand! He doesn't look it, not by a couple of decimal places. Can you confirm that, Mr. Spock?"

"I shall program the readings into Dr. McCoy's medical computer when we return to the ship."

"Time factor?"

"We must commence antitoxin injections within two hours and eighteen minutes, or the epidemic will prove fatal to us all."

Kirk frowned. "Why is the processing taking so long this time?"

"The delay would seem to be possibly deliberate."

"Yes," Kirk said grimly. "As if he were keeping us here for some reason."

"Most strange. While Mr. Flint seems to wish us to linger, he is apprehensive. It is logical to assume that he knows our every move—that he has us monitored."

The communicator beeped. "Kirk here."

"Scott, sir. There's no record of a Rayna Kapec in the Federation legal banks."

"No award of custody?"

"No background on her at all, in any computer bank. Like Flint."

"Thanks, Scotty. Kirk out. Like Flint. People without a past. By what authority is she here, then? What hold does he have over her?"

"I would suggest," Spock said, "that our immediate concern is the ryetalyn."

"Let's find McCoy."

As they headed for the door, Rayna entered. She seemed to be agitated. "Captain!" she called.

"Go ahead, Spock, I'll meet you in the laboratory."

When they were alone, Rayna said, "I have come to say goodbye."

"I don't want to say goodbye."

"I am glad that you will live."

Kirk studied her. She seemed innocent, uncertain, yet underneath there was a kind of urgency. She stood motionless, as if in the grip of forces she did not understand.

He went to her. "I know now *why* I have lived." He put his arms around her and kissed her. This second kiss was much longer than the first, and her response suddenly lost its innocence.

"Come with us," Kirk said hoarsely.

"My place . . ."

"Is where you want to be. Where do you want to be?"

"With you."

"Always."

"Here," she said.

"No, come with me. I promise you happiness."

"I have known security here."

"Childhood ends. You love *me*, not Flint."

For a long moment she was absolutely silent, hardly even seemed to breathe. Then she broke free of his arms and ran off. Kirk stared after her, and then started off to the laboratory, his heart still pounding.

The moment Kirk entered, McCoy said, "Flint lied to us. The ryetalyn isn't here."

"But I am picking up readings on the tricorder, Captain," Spock said. "The ryetalin is apparently behind that door."

The door toward which the tricorder was aimed was the same one Rayna had said Flint had forbidden her to enter.

"Why is Flint playing tricks on us?" Kirk demanded, suddenly furious at the constant multiplication of mysteries. "Apparently we're supposed to go in and get it—if we can! Let's not disappoint the chessmaster. Phasers on full!"

But as the weapons came out, the door began to rumble open of its own accord. A constant, low hum of power was audible from inside it.

Kirk lead the way. The ryetalyn cubes were conspicuously visible on a table. Kirk went toward them in triumph, but his attention was caught by a draped body encased on a slab. The slab carried a sign which read: "RAYNA 16."

The body was the supine form of a woman. The face was not quite human; it resembled dead white clay, beautifully sculptured and somehow unfinished. Nevertheless, it was clearly Rayna's.

Hung on the other side of the case was a clipboard with notes attached. Most of the scribbles seemed to be mathematical.

As if in a dream, Kirk moved on to a similar case. The figure in it was less finished than the first. Its face seemed to show marks of sculpture; the features were more crudely defined. Still, it too was Rayna's—Rayna 17.

"Physically human," McCoy said in a low voice, "yet not human. These are earlier versions. Jim—she's an android!"

"Created here, by my hand," Flint's voice said from the doorway. "Here, the centuries of loneliness were to end."

"Centuries?" Kirk said.

"Your collection of Leonardo da Vinci masterpieces, Mr. Flint," Spock said. "Many appear to have been recently painted—on contemporary canvas, with contemporary materials. And on your piano, a waltz by Johannes Brahms, an unknown work, in manuscript, written with modern ink—yet absolutely authentic, as are the paintings . . ."

"I am Brahms," Flint said.

"And da Vinci."

"Yes."

"How many other names shall we call you?" Spock asked.

"Solomon, Alexander, Lazarus, Methuselah, Merlin, Abramson—a hundred other names you do not know."

"You were born . . . ?"

"In that region of Earth later called Mesopotamia—in the year 3034 B.C., as the millennia are now reckoned. I was Akharin—a soldier, a bully and a fool. I fell in battle, pierced to the heart—and did not die."

"A mutation," McCoy said, fascinated. "Instant tissue regeneration—and apparently a perfect, unchanging balance between anabolism and katabolism. You learned you were immortal . . ."

"And to conceal it: to settle and live some portion of a life; to pretend to age—and then move on, before my nature was suspected. One night I would vanish, or fake my demise."

"Your wealth, your intellect, the product of centuries of study and acquisition," Spock said. "You knew the greatest minds of history . . ."

"Galileo," Flint said. "Moses. Socrates. Jesus. And I have married a hundred times. Selected, loved, cherished —caressed a smoothness, inhaled a brief fragrance—then age, death, the taste of dust. Do you understand?"

"You wanted a perfect woman," Spock said. "An ultimate woman, as brilliant, as immortal, as yourself. Your mate for all time."

"Designed by my heart," Flint said. "I could not love her more."

"Spock," Kirk whispered, "you knew."

"Readings were not decisive. However, Mr. Flint's choice of a planet rich in ryetalyn—I had hoped I was wrong."

"Why didn't you tell me?" Kirk asked harshly.

"What would you have said?"

"That you were wrong," Kirk said, "*wrong*. Yes, I see."

"You met perfection," Flint said. "Helplessly, you loved it. But you cannot love an android, Captain. *I* love her; she is my handiwork—my property—she is what I desire."

"And you put the ryetalyn in here to teach me this," Kirk said. "Does she know?"

"She will never know."

Kirk said tiredly, "Let's go, Mr. Spock."

"You will stay," Flint said.

"Why?"

"We have also learned what *he* is, Captain."

"Yes," said Flint. "If you leave, the curious would follow—the foolish, the meddlers, the officials, the seekers. My privacy was my own; its invasion be on your head."

"We can remain silent," Spock suggested.

"The disaster of intervention, Mr. Spock. I've known it—I will not risk it again." Flint's hand went to a small control box on his belt.

Kirk whipped out his communicator. Flint smiled, almost sadly. "They cannot answer, Captain. See."

A column of swirling light began to form slowly in a clear area of the life chamber. As it brightened, the form of the *Enterprise* was revealed, floating a few feet above the floor, tiny familiar lights blinking.

"No!" Kirk cried.

"The test of power," Flint said. "You had no chance."

"My crew . . ."

"It is time for you to join them."

Kirk felt sick. "You'd—wipe out—four hundred lives? Why?"

"I have seen a hundred million fall. I know Death better than any man; I have tossed enemies into his grasp. But I know mercy. Your crew is not dead, but suspended."

"Worse than dead," Kirk said savagely. "Restore them! Restore my ship!"

"In time. A thousand—two thousand years. You will see the future, Captain Kirk." Flint looked at the *Enterprise*. "A fine instrument. Perhaps I may learn something from it."

"You have been such men?" Kirk said. "Known and created such beauty? Watched your race evolve from cruelty and barbarism, throughout your enormous life! Yet now, you would do *this* to us?"

"The flowers of my past. I hold the nettles of the present. I am Flint—with my needs."

"What needs?"

"Tonight I have seen—something wondrous. Something I have waited for—labored for. Nothing must endanger it. At last, Rayna's emotions have stirred to life. Now they will turn to me, in this solitude which I preserve."

"No," said Rayna's voice. They all spun around.

"Rayna!" Flint said in astonishment. "How much have you heard?"

"You must not do this to them!"

"I must." Flint's hand moved implacably back to the belt device.

"Rayna," Spock said. *"What will you feel for him—when we are gone?"*

She did not reply, but the expression of betrayal, tragedy, and bitter hatred which she turned on Flint was answer enough.

All emotions are engaged, Mr. Flint," Spock said. "Harm us, and she hates you."

"Give me my ship," Kirk said coldly. "Your secret is safe with us."

Flint looked at Kirk levelly. Then there was the slightest suggestion of a shrug; here was a man who had lost battles before. He touched the belt control again.

The column of light with the toy *Enterprise* in it faded and vanished.

"That's why you delayed processing the ryetalyn," Kirk said, in a low, bitter voice. "You realized what was happening. You kept us together—me, Rayna—because I could make her emotions come alive. Now you're going to just take over!"

"I shall take what is mine—when she comes to me," Flint said. "We are mated, Captain. Alike immortal. You must forget your feelings in this matter, which is quite impossible for you."

"Impossible from the beginning," Kirk said in growing fury. "Yet you used me. I can't love her—but I do love her! And *she loves me!*"

Flint sprang. He was quick, but Kirk evaded him. The two combatants began circling like animals. As Kirk passed Spock, the First Officer seized his arm.

"Your primitive impulses cannot alter the situation."

"*You* wouldn't understand! We're fighting over a woman!"

"You are *not*," Spock said, "for *she* is not."

Kirk stepped back, turning his palms out toward his adversary. "Pointless, Mr. Flint."

"I will not be the cause of all this," Rayna said, in a voice both fiery and shaken. "I will not! I choose! I choose! Where I want to go—what I want to do! *I choose!*"

"I choose for you," Flint said.

"No longer!"

"Rayna . . ."

"*No*. Don't order me! *No* one can order me!"

Kirk looked at her in awe, and it seemed as though Flint was feeling the same sensation. He extended a hand toward her, and she turned from it. He dropped the hand slowly, staring at her.

"She's human," Kirk said. "Down to the last blood cell, she's human. Down to the last thought, hope, aspiration, emotion. You and I have created human life—and the human spirit is free. You have no power of ownership. She can do as she wishes."

"No man beats me," Flint said coldly.

"I don't want to beat you," Kirk said wearily. "There's no test of power here. Rayna belongs to herself now. She claims her human right of choice—to do as she will, think as she will, *be* as she will."

Finally Flint gave a tired nod. "I have fought for that also. What does she choose?"

"Come with me," Kirk said to her.

"Stay," said Flint.

There were tears in her eyes. "I was not human," she whispered. "Now, I love—I love . . ."

She moved slowly forward toward the two waiting men. She seemed exhausted. She stumbled once, and then, suddenly, fell.

McCoy was at her side in an instant, feeling for her pulse. Flint also knelt. Slowly, McCoy shook his head.

It hit Kirk like a blow in the stomach. "What—happened?" he asked.

"She loved you, Captain," Spock said gently, "and also Flint, as a mentor, even a father. There was not time enough to adjust to the awful powers and contradictions of her newfound emotions. She could not bear to hurt either of you. The joy of love made her human; its agony destroyed her." In his voice there was a note of calm accusation. "The hand of God was duplicated. A life was created. But then—you demanded ideal response—for which God still waits."

Flint bowed his head, a broken man. "You can't die, we will live forever—together." He sobbed. "Rayna—*child* . . ."

Kirk's hand moved, almost blindly, to his shoulder.

Kirk sat at his desk in his own cabin, in half light, exhausted, brooding. The door opened and Spock came in.

"Spock," Kirk said, and looked away.

"The epidemic is reduced and no longer a threat. The *Enterprise* is on course 513 mark seven, as you ordered."

"The very young and lonely man—the very old and lonely man—we put on a pretty poor show, didn't we?" He bowed his head. "If only I could forget . . ."

His head went down on his arms. He was asleep.

McCoy entered in full cry. "Jim, those tricorder readings of Mr. Flint are finally correlated. Methuselah is dying . . ."

Then he noticed Kirk's position, and added in a low voice, "Thank Heaven—sleeping at last."

"Your report, Doctor?" Spock said.

"Flint. In leaving Earth, with its complex of fields in which he was formed and with which he was in perfect balance, he sacrificed immortality. He'll live the remainder of a normal life-span—and die."

"That day, I shall mourn. Does he know?"

"I told him myself. He intends to devote his last years, and his gigantic abilities, to improving the human condition. Who knows what he might come up with?"

"Indeed," Spock said.

"That's all, I guess. I'll tell Jim when he wakes up, or you can." He looked at Kirk with deep sympathy. "Considering his opponent's longevity—truly an eternal triangle. You wouldn't understand, would you, Spock? I'm sorrier for you than I am for him. You'll never know the things love can drive a man to—the ecstasies, the miseries, the broken rules, the desperate chances—the glorious failures, and the glorious victories—because the word love isn't written in your book."

Spock was silent.

"I wish he could forget her." Still silence. "Good night, Spock."

"Good night, Doctor."

Spock regarded Kirk for another silent moment, and then moved deliberately to lock the door behind McCoy. Then he returned to Kirk. His hands floated to Kirk's dropped head, fingertips touching. He said, very gently, "*Forget . . .*"

THE WAY TO EDEN

(Arthur Heinemann and Michael Richards)

Under Federation orders to observe extreme delicacy, the *Enterprise* had beamed aboard the six people who had stolen the cruiser *Aurora*. The son of the Catullan Ambassador was one of them, and treaty negotiations between the Federation and the Ambassador were at a crucial phase. Clearly, none of the six had known much about operating a cruiser; in the attempt to escape, they had managed to destroy the cruiser, and had only been rescued by Scott's pinpoint skill with the Transporter.

"Scotty, are they aboard?" Kirk asked his control chair intercom.

"Aye, Captain, they are. And a nice lot, too."

"Escort them to the briefing room for interview."

There were other voices in the background, rising in an increasing hubbub. Suddenly a woman's voice became clearly audible above the others. "Why should we?"

At that, Chekov's head jerked up sharply, his expression one of recognition struggling with incredulity. Then a man's voice said, "Tell Herbert it's no go."

All the voices chimed in with a ragged chant: "No go no go no go no go . . ."

"What's going on?" Kirk asked.

"They refuse, sir," Scott called over the chant.

"Why?"

"I don't know. They're just sitting on the floor, the lot of them. You can hear them yourself. Shall I send for Security?"

"No, I'll come down. Sulu, take the con."

He and Spock could hear the chanting continuing long before he reached the Transporter Room. The six were, indeed, "a nice lot." One wore a simple robe, the others were nearly naked or in primitive costumes, with flowers worn as ornaments and painted on their bodies. There were three girls and three men, all but the one in the robe in their early twenties. They were squatting on the floor with a clutter of musical instruments around them.

"We are not in the mood, Herbert," one of the girls said; it was the same voice he had heard before. The others resumed the "No go" chant.

"Which one of you is Tongo Rad?" Kirk shouted.

The chant died down raggedly, and the newcomers looked curiously from Kirk to one of their number, a handsome humanoid who despite his costume had that intangible air which often goes with wealth and privilege. He got up and lunged forward, not answering, not quite insolent.

"You can thank your father's influence for the fact that you're not under arrest," Kirk snapped. "In addition to piracy, you're open to charges of violating flight regulations, entering hostile space and endangering the lives of others as well as your own."

"Hostile space?" Rad said.

"You were in Romulan territory when we yanked you out."

"Oh," said Rad. "I'm bleeding."

"On top of which you've caused an interstellar incident that could destroy everything that has been negotiated between your planet and the Federation."

"You got a hard lip, Herbert."

"If you have an explanation, I'm prepared to hear it."

Rad looked down at the older man in the robe, but there was no response. Rad sat down with the others and folded his arms.

Kirk turned to Spock. "Take them to sickbay for medical check. There may be radiation injury from the *Aurora* explosion."

The "No go" chant started up again immediately. Kirk started to shout, but Spock intervened.

"With your permission, Captain." He put his hands together, index finger to index finger, thumb to thumb, forming an egg shape. "One."

The group seemed to be surprised. The man in the robe rose. "We are one."

"One is the beginning," Spock said.

One of the boys, a rather puckish youth, said, "You One, Herbert?"

"I am not Herbert."

"He's not Herbert. We reach."

Kirk was wholly bewildered. Evidently all this meant something, however, and had almost miraculously achieved calm and accord.

"Sir," Spock said to the older man, "if you will state your purpose and objectives, perhaps we can arrive at mutual understanding."

"If you understand One, you know our purpose."

"I should prefer that you state it."

The older man smiled faintly. "We turn our backs on confusion and seek the beginning."

"Your destination?"

"The planet Eden."

"Ridiculous," Kirk said. "That planet's a myth."

Still smiling, the older man said, "And we protest against being harassed, pursued, attacked, seized, and Transported here against our wishes and against human law."

"Right, brother," said the puckish youth.

"We do not recognize Federation regulations nor the existence of hostilities. We recognize no authority but that within ourselves."

"Whether you recognize authority or not, I am it on this ship," Kirk said, restraining himself with difficulty. "I am under orders to take you back to Starbase peaceably. From there you will be ferried back to your various planets. Because of my orders you are not prisoners, but my guests. I expect you to behave as such."

"Oh, Herbert," said the puckish youth, "you are *stiff*."

"Mr. Spock, since you seem to understand these people, you will deal with them."

"We respectfully request that you take us to Eden," the robed man said. Despite the politeness of the words, and the softness of his voice, his insolence was obvious.

Kirk ignored him. "When they're finished in sickbay, see that they are escorted to the proper quarters and given whatever care they need."

"Yes, Captain."

"We respectfully request that you take us to Eden."

"I have orders to the contrary. And this is not a passenger ship."

"Herbert," said the girl who had first spoken. The others picked it up and another ragged chant followed Kirk as he went out: "Herbert Herbert Herbert Herbert . . ."

He was in a simmering rage by the time he returned to the bridge. Taking his seat, he said, "Lieutenant Uhura. Alert Starbase we have aboard the six who took the space cruiser *Aurora*. And that the cruiser itself was regrettably destroyed."

"Aye, sir."

"Personal note to the Catullan Ambassador. His son is safe."

"Captain, sir," Chekov said hesitantly. "I believe I know one of them. At least I think I recognized her voice. Her name is Irina Galliulin. We were in Starfleet Academy together."

"One of those went to the *Academy*?" Kirk said incredulously.

"Yes, sir. She dropped out. She—" Chekov stopped. Under his accent and his stiffness, it was apparent that he still felt a painful emotion about this girl.

Kirk looked away as Spock entered, and then back to Chekov. "Do you wish to see her? Permission granted to leave your post."

"Thank you, sir." He got up fast and left; another crewman took his post.

Kirk turned to Spock. "Are they in sickbay?"

"Yes, Captain."

"Do they seriously believe that Eden exists?"

"Many myths are founded on some truth, Captain. And they are not unintelligent. Dr. Sevrin . . ."

"Their leader? The man in the robe?"

Spock nodded. "Dr. Sevrin was a brilliant research engineer in acoustics, communications and electronics on Tiburon. When he started the movement, he was dismissed from his post. Young Rad inherits his father's extraordinary abilities in the field of space studies."

"But they reject that—everything this technology provides—and look for the primitive."

"There are many who are uncomfortable with what we have created," Spock said. "It is almost a biological rebellion. A profound revulsion against the planned communities, the programming, the sterilized, artfully balanced atmospheres. They hunger for an Eden, where Spring comes."

"We all do, sometimes," Kirk said thoughtfully. "The cave is deep in our ancestral memories."

"Yes, sir."

"But we don't steal cruisers and act like irresponsible children. What makes you so sympathetic toward them?"

"It is not so much sympathy as curiosity, Captain. A wish to understand. And they regard themselves as aliens in their worlds. It is a feeling I am familiar with."

"Hmm. What does Herbert mean?"

"It is somewhat uncomplimentary, sir. Herbert was a minor official notorious for his rigid and limited pattern of thought."

"I get the point," Kirk said drily. "I shall endeavor to be less limited in my thinking. But they make it difficult."

There were only five of the six in the examining room when Chekov came in. Four were sprawled about listening to the puckish youth, who was tuning something that looked like a zither. Apparently satisfied, he hit a progression of chords and began to sing softly.*

Looking for the new land—
Losing my way—
Looking for the good land—
Going astray—
Don't cry.
Don't cry.
Oh I can't have honey and I can't have cream

---

*I much regret that I cannot reproduce the music which went with this script; it was of very high quality. The script I have does not name the composer.—J.B.

But the dream that's in me, it isn't a dream.
It'll live, not die.
It'll live, not die.
I'll stand in the middle of it all one day,
I'll look at it shining all around me and say
I'm here!
I'm here!
In the new land,
In the good land,
I'm here!

"Great, Adam," one of the others said. There was a murmur of applause.

Chekov cleared his throat. "Excuse me. Is Irina Galliulin with you?"

"Getting her physical," Adam said. He hit a chord and sang:

I'll crack my knuckles and jump for joy—
Got a clean bill of health from Dr. McCoy.

"You know Irina?" someone else said. Chekov nodded.

"Say, tell me," said Tongo Rad. "Why do you people wear all those clothes? How do you breathe?"

Nurse Chapel came out of the sickbay with two medics. She looked over the group and pointed to Sevrin. "You're next."

Sevrin sprawled, oblivious. Chapel nodded to the two medics, who stepped forward and, picking up the limp form, dragged it into sickbay. A moment later, Irina came out.

"Irina," Chekov said.

She did not seem to be surprised. She smiled, her strange, habitual smile, which rarely left her—but there was watchfulness behind it.

"Pavel Andreievich," she said calmly. "I had thought we might encounter each other."

"You knew I was on the *Enterprise*?"

"I had heard."

"Irina—why—" He stopped, all eyes upon him. "Come."

He led her out into the corridor, which was empty. He stared at her for a moment, taking in the bizarre, brief costume, the long hair, the not-quite-untidiness. When he spoke, it was almost with rage.

"How could you do this to yourself? You were a scientist. You were a—a decent human being. And now look at you!"

"Look at yourself, Pavel," she said calmly.

"Why did you do it?"

"Why did you?"

"I am proud of what I am. I believe in what I do. Can you say that?"

"Yes." Momentarily her voice was sharp; then the smile returned. Chekov took her arm and they walked toward the lounge. "We should not tear at each other so. We should meet again in joy. Today, when I first knew it was your ship that followed us, I thought of you, I wondered what I would find in you. And I remembered so much. In spite of that uniform, I still see the Pavel I used to know. Are you happy in what you do?"

"Yes."

"Then I accept what you do."

"You even talk like them."

Yeomen passed them, turning to look at the odd couple. Chekov led Irina into the lounge. "Why did you go away?" he asked.

"It was you who went."

"I came back to look for you. I looked. I looked. Where did you go?"

"I stayed in the city. With friends."

"You never felt as I did. Never."

"I did."

"You don't have it in you to feel so much. Even when we were close you weren't with me. You were off thinking of something else." She shook her head, the smile still there. "Then why did you stay away?"

"Because you disapproved of me. Just as you do now. Oh, Pavel, you have always been like this. So correct. And inside, the struggle not to be. Give in to yourself. You will be happier. You'll see."

"Go to your friends," Chekov said grayly.

After a moment she left, still with that maddening smile. There seemed to be another hubbub starting in the corridor. Chekov went after her, quickly.

The noise was coming from outside sickbay, where there was something very like a melee going on. The group from the *Aurora* was trying to get in, over the opposition of Nurse Chapel and two security guards. The group was shouting noisily, angrily, demanding entrance, demanding to see Sevrin.

Kirk came out of the elevator and forced his way through the crowd, not without a what-the-hell glance toward Chekov.

"Herbert Herbert Herbert Herbert Herbert . . ."

The sickbay doors shut automatically behind Kirk and Nurse Chapel, mercifully deadening the sound. "I thought all those animals were in their cages," she said.

Sevrin was sitting on a bed, defiant, the two medics standing ready to grab him. McCoy was finishing what had evidently been a strenuous examination.

"What's going on, Bones?"

"Trouble. Your friend here didn't want a checkup. Turns out there was a reason."

"I refuse to accept your findings," Sevrin said.

"You don't have the choice."

"They are the product of prejudice, not science."

"I don't know what this man was planning to do on a primitive planet," McCoy continued. "Assuming it existed. But I can tell you what would happen if he'd settled there. Within a month there wouldn't be enough of those primitives left to bury their dead."

"Fantasy," Sevrin said. "Fantasy."

"I wish it were. There's a nasty little bug evolved in the last few years, Jim. Our aseptic, sterilized civilizations produced it. *Synthococcus novae*. It's deadly. We can immunize against it but we haven't licked all its problems yet."

"Does he have it?" Kirk asked. "What about the others?"

"The others are clear. And he doesn't have it. He's a carrier. Remember your ancient history? Typhoid Mary? He's immune to it, as she was. But he carries the disease, spreads it to others."

"Is the crew in danger?"

"Probably not. They all had full spectrum immunizations before boarding. My guess is that his friends had their shots too. But a regular program of booster shots is necessary. I'll have to check on everyone aboard. There may have been some skips. Until that's done, this fellow should be kept in total isolation."

"This is outrageous," Sevrin said. "There is nothing wrong with me. You're not isolating me, you're imprisoning me. You invent the crime, find me guilty, sentence me . . ."

"Would you like to run the tests yourself, Doctor?" There was no answer. "You knew you were a carrier before you started out, didn't you?"

"No!"

"Then why did you fight the examination?"

"It was an infringement on my rights as a human being . . ."

"Oh, stop ranting."

"Put him in isolation," Kirk said.

"Be ready for his friends' objections. They're a vocal lot."

"I'm ready."

There was still a crowd in the corridor; four of the *Aurora* group (one girl was missing) were sitting or sprawling on the deck; among them stood Sulu, Chekov and several crewmen. The protesters were chanting, but this time each of them had a different slogan.

"Eden now!"

"Free Ton Sevrin!"

"James T. Kirk is a brachycephalic jerk!"

"McCoy is a doctor of veterinary medicine!"

Sulu was talking to one of the girls, between slogans. He seemed confused but fascinated. Thus far no one had noticed Kirk's arrival.

"You don't belong with them," the girl was telling Sulu. "You know what we want. You want it yourself. Come, join us."

"How do you know what I want, Mavig?"

"You're young. Think young, brother." Lifting a hand to him, she gave him an egg.

"Mr. Sulu," Kirk said sharply. Sulu started, stiffened with embarrassment, and hastily gave the egg back to Mavig. "Explain, Mr. Sulu."

"No explanation, sir."

Kirk turned to the group, which had gotten even noisier upon seeing him. "Dr. Sevrin will be released as soon as we determine it is medically safe."

"Herbert Herbert Herbert Herbert . . ."

Ignoring them, Kirk strode toward the elevator with

Sulu, stepping over the bodies. Chekov followed. As he approached Irina, she lay back provocatively.

"Don't stay with Herbert. Join us. You'll be happier. Come, Pavel."

"Link up, Pavel," Adam said.

"Join us."

"Link up, Pavel. Link up, Pavel."

Adam struck a chord on his instrument and began to sing:

> Stiff man putting my mind in jail—
> Judge bangs the gavel, and says
> No bail—
> So I'll lick his hand and wag my tail . . .

Blessedly the elevator doors opened at this point, and Kirk, Sulu and Chekov made their escape.

The bridge was a haven of routine activity, with Spock in charge. Chekov and Sulu went to their posts. But before Kirk could settle, the intercom cut in with its signal.

"Engineering to bridge," Scott's voice said.

"Kirk here."

"Captain, I just had to give one of those barefooted what-do-you-call-ems the boot out of here. She came in bold as brass, tried to incite my crew to disaffect."

"All right, Scotty." He shut the intercom off and turned to Spock, his irritation finally breaking out. "Mr. Spock, I don't seem to communicate with these people. Do you think you can persuade them to behave?"

"I shall endeavor, sir."

"If it weren't for that Ambassador's son, they'd be in the brig."

"Yes, sir." Spock went out.

He found Sevrin sitting cross-legged in the isolation ward, in a yoga-like position, a cold, hostile figure. There was one security guard in the corridor outside. Spock stood on the other side of the isolation shield.

"Doctor, can you not keep your people from interfering with the running of the ship?"

"I have no influence over what they do."

"They respect you. They will listen to your reasoning. For their sake, Doctor, you must stop them."

The baleful eyes lifted to Spock's face, answer enough in themselves.

"Dr. Sevrin, I can assist you and your group. I can use the resources of the *Enterprise* to establish whether or not Eden exists, and to plot its exact location. I can present a case to Federation that would allow your group to colonize that planet." There was no answer. "Neither you nor they are at present charged with any crime worse than theft, plus a few lesser matters. The charges may be waived. But incitement to mutiny would tip the balance. And Federation would never allow the colonization of a planet by criminals. If they persist, they will be so charged, and forever barred from Eden."

"As I have been barred," Sevrin said softly. The voice was low, but the gleaming eyes were those of a fanatic.

Spock hesitated a moment. "Then you knew you were a carrier?"

"Of course I knew. You have researched my life. You have read the orders restricting me to travel only in areas of advanced technology, because of what my body carries."

"I fail to understand why you should disobey them."

"Because this is poison to me!" Sevrin looked around, as if seeing all the technology of the ship, representing all the technology of space. "This stuff you breathe, this stuff you live on. The shields of artificial atmosphere we have layered about every planet. The programs in those computers that run your ship and your lives for you. Those bred what my body carries! This is what your sciences have done for me! You have infected me!"

He shook his fist at the ceiling; his "you" was obviously not Spock but the whole Galaxy. He began to pace.

"Only the primitives can cleanse me. I cannot purge myself until I am among them. Only their way of living is right. I must go to them."

"Your very presence will destroy the people you seek out! Surely you know that."

"I shall go to them and be one of them. Together we will make a world such as this Galaxy has never seen. A world, a life. A life!" His passion spent, Sevrin sat down, and after a moment lifted his head to look at Spock, a faint smile on his lips. "And now you are about to assure me that your technologies will find a cure for me. And I will be free to go."

"Yes, Doctor."

"And for that reason I must persuade my friends to behave, so they too will be allowed."

"Yes."

"Send them in," Sevrin said, smiling still. "I'll talk to them."

It was an uneasy victory, whose outcome was uncertain. Spock went back to the bridge.

"They've been a lot quieter," Kirk reported. "How did you accomplish it?"

"It had nothing to do with me. Could I speak to you a moment, sir?"

Kirk rose and both went to Spock's console. "What is it?"

"Dr. Sevrin is insane. I did not consult Dr. McCoy. But I have no doubt of it."

"I'll have Bones check him again," Kirk said, stunned. "You had great respect for him. I'm sorry, Mr. Spock. But it explains some of what they've done."

"His collapse does not affect my sympathy with the moevment, sir. There is no insanity in what they seek—I made a promise which I should like to keep. With your permission, I must locate Eden. I shall work in my quarters. May I have the assistance of Mr. Chekov in the auxiliary control room?"

"Mr. Chekov, assist Mr. Spock."

The auxiliary control room was deserted except for Chekov, who was at the plotting console, bent over the computer, studying.

Spock's voice came over the intercom. "Ready for your plottings, Mr. Chekov."

Chekov fed a tape into the computer. The door opened, and Irina entered, hesitantly. "Am I allowed in?" she asked.

He concentrated stiffly on his work. "Yes."

"I have been looking for you, Pavel. What room is this?"

"Auxiliary control."

"What's it for?"

"Should the main control room break down or suffer damage, we can navigate the ship from here."

"Oh."

"What do you want?"

"To apologize. I should not have teased you. It was cruel."

"It doesn't matter," Chekov said.

"But it does. It is against everything I believe in."

"Let us not discuss your beliefs."

"And I do not like having you angry with me," she said softly. "Or disapproving."

"Then why do you do such things?"

She began to wander about the room, examining the panels in seeming childlike curiosity. Chekov continued working, but his eyes followed her when she was not looking in his direction. Then she came back to him. "What are you working on?"

"I am assisting Mr. Spock in locating your Eden."

"Now you are teasing me," she said in sudden sharpness.

"I am not. These tapes contain star charts, and we project the orbits of the various known planetary systems here, determining by a mathematical process whether or not they are affected by other bodies not yet charted."

"Do you know all these things?"

"What I do not know I find out from the computer banks. If I knew nothing at all, I could navigate this ship simply by studying what is stored in there. They contain the sum of all human knowledge. They solve our problems of navigation, of control, of life support . . ."

She bent over the computer, close to him. "They tell you what do do. And you do what they tell you."

"No. We use our own judgment also."

She came still closer. "I could never obey a computer."

"You could never listen to anyone. You always had to be different."

"Not different. What I wanted to be. There is nothing wrong in doing what you want."

She faced him, smiling still. Abruptly Chekov arose, took her in his arms, and kissed her hungrily.

"I am not receiving, Mr. Chekov," said the intercom. "Spock to Mr. Chekov. Repeat. I am not receiving."

Chekov broke free and opened his intercom. "I am sorry, Mr. Spock. I was momentarily delayed."

With permission, the *Aurora* group had stored its gear and bedded down in the Recreation Room. Adam and Mavig were relaxing when Rad entered.

"His name is Sulu," Rad said. "Specialist in weapons and navigation. His hobby is botany."

"Can?" said Adam.

"Can. I reach botany. It's my favorite of studies. What's yours?"

"Vulcan. Spock is practically One now."

Irina came in; the others were instantly alert.

"Everything can be handled from auxiliary control. The computers contain all the information we need. We can do it."

"It starts to chime," Adam said.

"When will it?" Rad wanted to know.

"Soonest. Like Sevrin said, now, we should go out, swing as many over as we can."

"You suggest any special ways to swing them?"

"Just be friendly. You know how to be friendly, then they'll be friendly and we'll all be one. All right? Scatter. Remember, it's a party we're inviting them to and we're providing the entertainment."

"I like parties," Rad said.

"I like the entertainment we've planned. All hit numbers."

Adam and Rad grinned at each other. Then everyone went off, in different directions. Adam headed directly for Spock's quarters.

Spock said "Come in" absently. He was at his computer, studying the images, making notes. Adam approached him diffidently.

"Am I crossing you?" he asked. Spock shook his head. "I was wondering if—" He stopped, noting the lute hanging on the wall behind Spock. "Hey, brother. You play?"

Spock nodded.

"Is it Vulcan? Can I try it?"

Spock took the lute down and gave it to Adam, who tried several chords. "Oh, that's now. That's real now. I reach that, brother, I really do. Give."

He passed the lute back to Spock, who amusedly played a few runs.

"Hey. How about a session, you and us. It would *sound.* That's what I came for. I wanted to ask, you know, great white captain up there he don't reach us, but would he shake on a session? I mean, we want to cooperate like you asked, so I'm asking."

"If I understand you correctly," Spock said, "I believe the answer might be yes."

"I'll spread the word."

The Recreation Hall was jammed. Lights had been dimmed, with the effect of spotlighting the group. They were singing; for those crew members who could not be present, intercoms carried the music throughout the ship. The words went like this:

I'm talking about you.
I'm talking about me.
Long time back when the Galaxy was new,
Man found out what he had to do.
Found he had to eat and found he had to drink,
And a long time later he found he had to think.

(spoken)

I'm standing here wondering.

(sung)

If a man tells another man, 'Out of my way'
He piles up trouble for himself all day.
But all kinds of trouble come to an end
When a man tells another man, 'Be my friend.'

(spoken)

What's going to be?

(sung)

There's a mile wide emptiness between you and me,
Can't reach across it, hardly even see—
Someone ought to take a step one way or other.
Let's say goodbye—or let's say brother.
Hey out there
Hey out there
I see you
I see you
Let's get together and have some fun.
Don't know how to do it but it's got to be done.

There was enthusiastic applause. The three girls took up the song. The boys faded back, clapping rhythmically. The clapping soon spread throughout the audience.

On the bridge, Uhura, Sulu and Scott were at their

posts, listening. When Kirk came in, Uhura turned the intercom off.

"Thank you."

"At least we know where they are and what they're doing," Scott said. "I don't know why a young head has to be an undisciplined one. Troublemakers."

"I made a bit of trouble at that age, Scotty. I think you may have."

The intercom buzzed. "Spock to bridge."

"Go ahead."

"Captain, something strange is taking place. Two of the boys slipped out of the group somewhere during the last five minutes, and now the girls are beginning to go. And it is not Haydn's Farewell Symphony they are staging, either."

"Come to the bridge."

"Something strange here too," Sulu said. "I have no response on controls. We're going off course."

Scott crossed to Sulu's console and checked it. "It's shorted—no, it's channeled over somewhere—yes, to auxiliary control."

As Spock entered, Kirk began calling. "Bridge to auxiliary control. Bridge to auxiliary control."

"Captain," Spock said, "in my opinion someone else is running the ship."

"That's right, Captain," said Sevrin's voice from the intercom. "Someone else is running the ship. I am. All functions, Captain. Life support as well. I suggest that you do not attempt to regain control. I do not intend to return the helm to you until and unless we reach Eden. If I am in any way prevented from reaching that destination, I shall destroy the ship and all aboard."

Scott and Sulu had been frantically checking circuits. Now Scott said, "He can do it, Captain. He has got everything channeled over."

"Start a traceback on all circuits. See if you can bypass."

"Do that," Sevrin's voice said, "and I shall retaliate. I shall not warn you again."

"We are leaving the neutral zone now, Captain," Sulu said. "Bearing into Romulan space."

"Do you read any patrols, Mr. Spock?"

"No, sir."

"They'll be on us soon enough. Dr. Sevrin! You are violating Romulan space and endangering the peace of the Galaxy. They will see this as a military intrusion and attack. Bring her about. Now. If you bring her about and return to Starbase, nothing will be said about this."

"Like you said, brother Sevrin," said Adam's voice.

"If you do not, you will never reach Eden. You and this ship will be destroyed. We would be no match for a Romulan flotilla."

"He's got jelly in the belly," said Adam. "Real scared."

"Adam, Rad—you are being led by a man who is insane. You are being used by him. Spock, tell them."

"Adam," Spock said. "There is a file in the computer banks on Dr. Sevrin. You will find in it a report attesting to the fact that he is a carrier of a bacillus strain known as *Synthococcus novae*."

"Ain't that just awful?"

"You will also find a report from the same hospital giving a full psychiatric profile of him, projecting these actions of his."

"Yeah, brother."

"You know I reach you," Spock said. "I believe in what you seek. But there is a tragic difference between what you want and what he wants."

"You're making me cry," Adam said. Then he began to sing:

> Heading out to Eden—
> Yeah, brother!
> Heading out to Eden—
> Yeah, brother!
> No more trouble in my body or my mind—
> I'll live like a king on whatever I find—
> Eat all the fruit and throw away the rind—
> Yeah, brother!"

Kirk shut off the intercom; it was impossible even to try to determine a course of action through that noise. He got up and looked at Spock, who nodded.

"We are within sensor range of Eden and continuing to approach," he said.

"Whatever they're going to do, they'll do it now," Kirk said. "We have no choice left. Mr. Spock, Mr. Scott, come with me. And let's make it fast."

He led them down the corridors to auxiliary control.

"Phasers out and on full. We'll cut through the door. If Sevrin stops Life Function, we should be able to get through and start it again before any serious consequences follow—I hope. We'll take shortcuts in turn, so as not to risk killing somebody and damaging equipment when we hole through. I'll go first, then Spock, then Scott."

His phaser spat, followed by Spock's. Then another sound started, like the whine of an oscillator, going higher and higher. Spock, with his sensitive hearing, reacted first. He dropped his phaser and clapped his hands to his ears.

"Mr. Spock!" As Kirk went to him the sound stopped. "It has stopped. It's all right, Mr. Spock."

"It—hasn't stopped—Captain. It is beyond—no! Captain—they are using . . ."

Kirk's head suddenly swam. If there was an end to Spock's sentence, he never heard it.

An unknown time later, Kirk came to, finding the corridor just as before, Spock and Scott stirring to consciousness. No, not just as before; the door to auxiliary control was open, and there was no one in there.

The three of them got to their feet and staggered in. Spock pointed. "There it is. An ultrasonic generator, feeding into the ventilation system . . ."

The First Officer suddenly leaped forward and smashed the device with an iron first.

"Why did you do that?" Kirk said. "The parts could have . . ."

"It was set to go off again in a few seconds, Captain—and this time on a killing frequency. It must have been Sevrin's work; I doubt that the youngsters would have let him do it had they known the device could be made lethal. Clearly he didn't intend us to get back to make any reports."

Kirk grabbed the intercom and began calling. "Kirk to bridge. Come in, do you read me? Engineering. Hangar deck. Transporter Room. Do you read me? Kirk to bridge."

"Captain?" Scott's voice said.

"Sulu here, Captain. What happened to us? I heard a whistle and then . . ."

"Never mind, Sulu," Kirk said. "Do we have control of the ship?"

"It's still all in auxiliary, sir," said Chekov's voice. "Some of the gear is jammed."

"Can we break orbit if we have to?"

"I think so, sir."

"Hangar deck to Captain."

"Kirk here."

"Sir, one of the shuttlecrafts has been taken. We were all knocked out . . ."

"Stand by. Mr. Spock, do you read any Romulans?"

"Negative, Captain. I am picking up the shuttlecraft, however."

"Where?"

"It has landed. Sir, except for those aboard the shuttlecraft, I read no sign of life at all. Neither animal nor humanoid. And there are only five life forms aboard the craft."

"Auxiliary control to McCoy. Bones, are you all right?"

"Yes, Jim."

"Stand by the Transporter Room. Full medical gear."

"Bridge to Captain Kirk," said Uhura's voice. "Do you wish hailing frequency, sir?"

"No. They tried to destroy us. Let them think they succeeded. I want coordinates zeroed in so that when we beam down we are not visible to them. Mr. Scott, the con is yours. If a Romulan patrol appears, hold in orbit; Lieutenant Uhura is to try to make them understand. I don't want to provoke combat. Mr. Chekov, join us in the Transporter Room. Mr. Spock, you too."

The garden was brilliant with sunshine, dazzling with flower color, opulent with heavy-laden fruit trees, one of them a giant. But it was utterly silent. The landing party looked about in awe.

"The legends were true, sir," Spock said in a low voice. "A fantastically beautiful planet."

"Eden," said Chekov.

Kirk said, "It almost—was this what they believed they'd find?" Spock nodded. "I can understand now. But why have they remained in their ship? Well, spread out and approach with caution."

The other three moved away. Kirk remained where he

was, flipping open his communicator. "Dr. Sevrin, this is Captain Kirk. You are under arrest. You will debark from your ship."

The shuttlecraft remained silent, its doors shut. Then there came a whimpering little sound, in Irina's voice. "No . . ."

"You will come out at once."

"No! No!" This time it was a scream of pure terror. Kirk went after McCoy.

"Bones, you heard that? What do you make of it?"

"She sounds terrified."

"Of what?"

McCoy took out his tricorder. "I don't know, Jim. I don't read anything abnormal. Wait a minute . . ."

There was a yell of pain from Chekov. He was standing by a flowering plant, his right fist clenched to his chest, his face contorted. They got to him fast.

"What is it, Chekov?"

"The flower, sir. I touched it. It's like fire."

McCoy forced him to unclench the fist. Fingers and palm were stained and seared. The surgeon aimed the tricorder at it, then at the flower, the plant proper, the grasses.

"The sap in it is pure acid," McCoy said. "All the plant life. The grass, too." He took out his medical kit and smeared ointment over Chekov's hand.

"Their feet!" Kirk said. "They were barefoot! Don't touch a thing. Bones, will our clothing protect us?"

"For a short time."

"Captain," Spock called. "Come over here, please." He was standing under the largest fruit tree. Kirk joined him and looked down. Adam lay dead on the ground, twisted, a half-eaten piece of fruit from the tree still clutched in his hand.

"Bones," said Kirk.

McCoy took readings. "Poison. The fruit is deadly." Spock bent and picked up the body, his enormous strength holding it easily. He looked at Kirk. "His name was Adam."

Understanding now, Kirk walked to the shuttlecraft openly, Spock beside him. Kirk pushed a button, and the doors opened. He called in gently, "You will be cared for."

The girls and Rad came limping out, murmuring in pain.

"It hurts," Irina said.

"I know," Spock said. "It hurts us all."

Chekov went at once to Irina and held her comfortingly as McCoy began to treat her. Kirk went on inside the craft.

Dr. Sevrin sat on the deck in the yoga position, immobile, heedless of his blistered, naked feet. His injuries were shockingly worse than those of the others.

"Bones, in here, please! Dr. Sevrin—Dr. Sevrin. Look at him, Bones. How can he stand it?"

"He should be beamed aboard. He needs more attention than I can give him here."

"No!" Sevrin said suddenly. "No. We are not leaving."

"We'll take care of you aboard the ship," Kirk said.

"We are not leaving Eden. None of us."

"Be sensible, Sevrin."

"We're not leaving!" As Kirk bent to help him, Sevrin thrust him savagely aside, lunged for the door and ran, despite the agony it must have cost him. He plunged straight toward the huge fruit tree. There was no chance of stopping him; by the time Kirk and McCoy were out of the craft, he had reached the tree, seized a fruit and bitten into it.

"No! I have found my Eden!"

Then he moaned, doubled, and fell.

The group by the shuttlecraft were for a moment paralyzed by shock. Then Chekov turned to Irina. "He too is dead, Irina."

She looked at him in a daze. "And the dream is dead. He sacrificed so much for it. When we landed, and he saw Eden finally, he cried, all of us felt the same. It was so beautiful. And we ran out into it—and . . ."

"Spock to *Enterprise*. Mr. Scott, stand by to beam the injured aboard. Medical team to the Transporter Room."

Everything was normal again on the bridge. Uhura said, "I have Starbase now, Captain."

"Alert them that we have the four and will be beaming them down. And mark the incident closed."

"Yes, sir."

"Bridge to Transporter Room. Scotty, are they there?"

"Three of them, sir."

"Stand by. Mr. Chekov, do you wish to attend?"

Chekov stood hesitantly. "Captain, sir, I wish first to apologize for my conduct during this time. I—did not maintain myself under proper discipline. I endangered the ship and its personnel by my conduct. I respectfully submit myself for disciplinary action."

"Mr. Chekov," Kirk said with a faint smile. "You did what you had to. As all of us did. Even your friends. You may go."

"Thank you, sir."

He started for the elevator. but as he did so, the doors opened and Irina stepped out. For a moment they looked at each other in silence.

"I was coming to say goodbye," Chekov said.

"And I was coming to say goodbye to you."

They kissed, gently, sadly. Irina said, "Be incorrect, occasionally."

"And you be correct."

"Occasionally."

She turned back to the elevator, but was intercepted by Spock. "Miss Galliulin, it is my sincere wish that you do not give up your search for Eden," he said. "I do not doubt but that you will find it—or make it yourselves."

She bowed her head, entered the elevator and was gone. Chekov and Spock went back to their posts. Chekov still seemed to be caught in the moment; then he became aware of the silence about him, the awareness of the others. He looked around.

Kirk was smiling faintly; he turned to Spock, whose face was expressionless, but who was nodding.

Kirk said, "We reach, Mr. Chekov."

Book II

Star Trek 6

BOOK II—*Star Trek 6*

THE SAVAGE CURTAIN
(Gene Roddenberry and Arthur Heinemann)

The planet, newly discovered in an uncharted area of space, was clearly not a Class M world. The atmosphere boiled with poisonous reds and greens; the surface was molten lava.

And yet, from one small area Spock picked up persistent readings of carbon cycle life forms—and artificial power being generated in quantities great enough to support a considerable civilization. Hailing on all frequencies at first produced nothing . . . and then, suddenly, the *Enterprise* was being scanned, an incredibly swift and deep probe.

Kirk barely had time to call for alert status when the probing was over. Almost immediately afterward, the image of the planet on the main viewing screen dissolved into a swirling jumble of colors. These slowly gathered together into a face and figure, entirely human, dressed in clothing like those worn in the mid-1800's on Earth. He was sitting on nothing and with nothing visible behind him, as though in limbo. His expression was benign and calm.

"Captain Kirk, I believe?" the figure said. "A pleasure to make your acquaintance, sir."

Kirk, Spock and McCoy stared incredulously at the familiar figure. Finally, Kirk motioned to Uhura.

"Your voice-telegraph device is quite unnecessary,

Captain," the figure said. "Do I gather that you recognize me?"

"I . . . recognize what you appear to be."

"And appearances can be quite deceiving." The figure smiled. "But not in this case, James Kirk. I am Abraham Lincoln."

Kirk considered this incredible claim and apparition, and then turned to his First Officer. "Spock?"

"Fascinating, Captain."

"I've been described in many ways, Mr. Spock," the smiling man said, "but never with that word."

"I was requesting your analysis of this, Mr. Spock."

"They did scan us and our vessel," Spock said, "and doubtless obtained sufficient information to present this illusion."

"Illusion?" the figure said. "Captain, will you permit me to come aboard your vessel? No doubt you have devices which can test my reality."

After a moment's hesitation, Kirk said, "We'd be honored to have you aboard, Mr. President."

The figure reached into its vest pocket, pulled out a large watch on a heavy gold chain and snapped the lid open. "Do you still measure time in minutes?"

"Yes, sir."

"Then you should be over my position in . . . twelve and a half minutes. Until then, Captain . . ." The image on the screen rippled, dissolved and re-formed itself as the planet. Amid the hot reds and poisonous greens of the atmosphere there was now a spot of soft blue. Spock leaned into his hooded viewer.

"An area of approximately a thousand square kilometers, sir," he said. "It's completely Earthlike, including an oxygen-nitrogen atmosphere."

"He called it to the second, sir," Chekov added. "We'll be over it in exactly twelve minutes now."

Kirk touched the intercom button. "Security. Send a detachment to the Transport Room immediately. Phaser side arms—but be prepared also to give presidential honors. Captain out."

"Jim," McCoy said, "you don't really believe he's Abraham Lincoln?"

"It's obvious he believes it, Bones." Kirk stood up. "Mr. Spock, Doctor, full dress uniforms, please. Mr. Sulu, the con is yours."

In the Transporter Room, Security Chief Dickenson had assembled two security guards, phasers at port. Dickenson himself sported white boots and belt, plus a traditional bos'n's whistle on a gold chain.

Engineering Officer Scott, in full kilt, entered and moved to the Transporter console, fuming. "Full dress! Presidential honors! What's all this nonsense, Mr. Dickenson?"

"I understand President Lincoln is coming aboard, sir."

Scott whirled. "Are you daft, man?"

"All I know, sir, is what the Captain tells me, sir," Dickenson said uncomfortably. "And he said he'd have the hide of the first man who so much as smiles."

McCoy entered, also in full dress, with his tricorder over his shoulder. Scott eyed him dourly; McCoy gave back stare for stare.

"I'd have expected sanity from the ship's surgeon, at least." Scott irritably punched controls on the console. "President Lincoln, indeed! No doubt followed by Louis of France and Robert the Bruce."

Kirk and Spock had come in in time to catch this last remark.

"And if so, Mr. Scott, we'll execute appropriate honors to each," Kirk said. "Gentlemen, I don't believe for a moment that Abraham Lincoln is actually coming aboard. But we are dealing with an unknown and apparently quite advanced life form. Until we know ... well, when in Rome, we do as the Romans do."

"Bridge to Transporter Room," Chekov's voice said over the intercom. "One minute to overhead position."

"Locking onto something," Scott said. He looked closer, and then gestured at the panel. "Does that appear human to you, Mr. Spock?"

Spock joined him and inspected the console. "Fascinating! . . . For a moment it appeared almost mineral. Like living rock, with heavy fore-claws . . . Settling down into completely human readings now."

"We can beam it aboard any time now, Captain," Scott said.

"Set for traditional ruffles and flourishes. Security, stand ready."

"Phaser team, set for heavy stun," Dickenson said. "Honor guard, ready."

The two security men posted themselves on opposite sides of the Transporter chamber, weapons set, raised and aimed. The four men comprising the honor guard snapped into parade rest. Dickenson raised his whistle to his lips.

"Energize."

The sparkling column appeared, solidified, vanished. The figure left standing there seemed to be inarguably Abraham Lincoln, dressed in the well-remembered 19th century suit, bearded, his face registering the sad wisdom of his presidential years.

Dickenson blew his whistle. Spock pushed a panel button and everyone came to attention. Ruffles and flourishes filled the air.

"Salute!" Kirk said. Everyone did except the two guards, whose phasers remained ready. Lincoln, too, stood gravely at attention through the music. Then Kirk said, "Two!," broke the salute and stepped forward.

"The USS *Enterprise* is honored to have you aboard, Mr. President."

"Strange," Lincoln said, stepping down. "Where are the musicians?"

"Taped music, sir. Starships on detached service do not carry full honor detachments."

"Taped music? Perhaps Mr. Spock will be good enough to explain that to me later." Lincoln extended a hand to Kirk. "A most interesting way to come aboard, Captain. What was the device used?"

"A matter-energy scrambler sir. The molecules of your body were converted to energy, and beamed to this chamber where they were reconverted to their original pattern."

Lincoln hesitated. "Well, since I am obviously here and quite whole, whatever you mean apparently works very well indeed." He looked at the two guards. "If those are weapons, gentlemen, you may lower them. At my age, I'm afraid I'm not very dangerous."

"Readings, fully human, sir," McCoy said.

Kirk signaled the guards to holster their weapons, and then introduced everyone present.

"Please stand at ease, gentlemen," Lincoln said. "I hope to talk to each of you, but meanwhile, your Captain is consumed with questions and I shall do my utmost to answer them. And I trust your duties will permit time to answer some of mine. At your service, Captain."

"Mr. Spock." Kirk led his First Officer and his guest off toward the Briefing Room.

"A marvel," Lincoln said. "A total marvel. I can hardly credit my eyes. We thought our *Monitor* the most formidable vessel imaginable—an iron ship that floated on water! You can imagine my amazement at an iron ship that floats on air."

"Mr. President—"

"Yes, Captain. Forgive my excitement at the novelty of all this."

"Sir ... I find some of your comments hard to equate with other statements. For example, you are not at all surprised at the existence of this vessel. But you then exhibit only a 19th century knowledge about it—for example, stating that this vessel 'floats on air.'"

"I don't understand. What *does* your vessel float on, captain?"

Kirk exchanged a look with Spock and said patiently, "Sir, the atmosphere surrounding any planet is a relatively thin envelope."

Lincoln appeared genuinely puzzled. Spock went on: "Given our present altitude, sir, and a present speed converting to 19,271 Earth miles per Earth hour, our velocity counterbalances the pull of this planet's gravity, creating equal but opposite forces which maintain us in orbit."

This was quite a distance away from the real physical situation, but Spock had evidently decided to choose terms which might be familiar to a 19th century educated man, rather than having to explain what was meant by free fall through a matter-distorted space-time matrix. But even the simplification did not work.

"When the choice is between honesty and disguising ignorance," Lincoln said, "a wise man chooses the former. I haven't the faintest idea what you said."

"With all respect, sir, that still does not answer my question," Kirk said. "For example, you knew my name. How is it you know some things about us but not others?"

"Bless me! Yes, I do see the contradiction," Lincoln said, frowning. "Please believe I have neither desire nor intention to deceive you, gentlemen. I must have been told these things, but I . . . I cannot recall when or where."

"Can you guess who it might have been, sir?" Spock said. "What others exist on the planet's surface with you?"

"Others? What others do you mean?"

"That's clearly not Earth down there, Mr. President," Kirk said. "Or do you believe that it is?"

"Strange," Lincoln said thoughtfully, "I never considered that before. No, I do not claim it to be Earth."

"Less than thirty minutes ago, the temperature and atmosphere at any point down there would have made your existence in this form impossible."

"You don't say! I can only assure you that I am what I appear to be, gentlemen: an all too common variety of *Homo sapiens*. Either way, I am too ordinary, James. I am surprised you've always thought so highly of me. The errors, the unforgivable errors I made. McClellan at first appeared to me a veritable Napoleon; Grant seemed a whisky-befuddled barbarian . . ." He shook his head. "There were so many things I could have done to end the war earlier, to save so many lives, so much suffering . . ."

"I'm sure you did all you could—"

"Why do you stop, James? Afraid of showing compassion? It is the noblest of qualities . . . I am certain there is an answer to these contradictions you point up so well." His frown suddenly dissolved. "Yes, that's it, of course. You are both invited to disembark with me. You will receive the answers down there. There is no need to hurry your decision, Captain. I am most anxious to inspect a vessel which at least *appears* to float on air."

"We shall be honored," Kirk said. "Mr. Spock, inform the others. We'll consider this in the Briefing Room in one hour."

Lincoln looked around again. "Fascinating!" he said to Spock, smiling. "If I may borrow your favorite word."

"I'm flattered, sir."

"The smile lends attraction to your features, Mr. Spock."

Kirk turned, but Spock's face was as stony as always. "I'm afraid you're mistaken, sir," Kirk said. "Mr. Spock never smiles."

"Indeed?" Lincoln offered no further comment. Had he seen something behind Spock's expression? It would be in character.

They went up to the bridge, where the main viewing screen still showed a segment of the planet below them. Lincoln stared at it in awe, while Sulu and Chekov stared at him.

"Good Lord!"

"As I recall," Kirk said, "your Union Army observation balloons were tethered six hundred or so feet high, sir. We're six hundred forty-three miles above this planet."

"You can measure great distances that closely?"

"We do, sir," Spock said, moving to his station and checking his instruments. "Six hundred forty-three miles, two thousand twenty-one feet, two point zero four inches at this moment, in your old-style measurement."

"Bless me."

Uhura came onto the bridge. "Excuse me, Captain—"

"What a charming Negress," Lincoln said, then added quickly, "Oh, forgive me, my dear. I know that in my day some used that term as a description of property."

"Why should I object to the term, sir?" Uhura said, smiling. "In our century, we've learned not to fear words."

Kirk said, "May I present our communications officer Lt. Uhura."

Lincoln shook hands with her, returning the smile. "The foolishness of my own century had me apologizing where no offense was given."

"Actually," she said, "I feel my color much lovelier and superior to yours and the Captain's."

"Superior? Then some of the old problems still exist?"

"No, sir," Kirk said. "It's just that we've learned to each be delighted in what we are. The Vulcans learned that centuries before we did."

"It's basic to the Vulcan philosophy, sir," Spock said. "How an infinite variety of things combine to make existence worthwhile."

"Yes, of course," Lincoln said. "The philosophy of 'nome'—meaning 'all.'" He paused, his frown returning. "Now, how did I know that? Just as I seem to know that on the planet's surface you will meet one of the greatest Vulcans in all the long history of your planet. My mind does not hold the name. But I know that he will be there."

"Excuse me, Captain," Uhura said, "but Mr. Scott is waiting for you in the Briefing Room."

"Oh, yes. Mr. President, with your permission I should like to make Lt. Uhura your guide at this point; I have a meeting."

"I would be delighted."

"Then we'll rejoin you shortly, sir. Mr. Sulu, the con is yours until Mr. Scott returns to the bridge."

In the Briefing Room, as Kirk and Spock entered, McCoy was saying to Spock: "Where the devil are they?"

"Perhaps looking up a plate of haggis in the galley? They've been everywhere else."

"Sorry, gentlemen," Kirk said, crossing to the table. "We were delayed."

"Jim, I'd be the last to advise you on your command image—"

"I doubt that, Bones, but continue."

"Do I have to lay it out for you? Practically the entire crew has seen you treating this imposter like the real thing—when he can't possibly be the real article, Captain!"

"Lincoln died three centuries ago and more, on a planet hundreds of light years away." Scott jerked a thumb over his shoulder.

"More in that direction, Engineer," Spock said, pointing down and to the left.

"The exact direction doesn't matter, you pointed-eared hobgoblin! You're the Science Officer," added McCoy, "why aren't you—well, doing whatever Science Officers do at a time like this?"

"I am, Doctor. I am observing the alien."

"At last. At least someone agrees with us he's an alien."

"Yes, he's an alien, of course," Kirk said after a moment's hesitation.

"And potentially dangerous," McCoy pressed on.

"Mad!" said Scott. "Loony as an Arcturian dog-bird."

"Spock and I have been invited to beam down to the planet's surface with him. Comments on that?"

"A big one," McCoy said. "Suddenly, miraculously, we see a small spot of Earth-type environment appear down there. Is it really there or do we just think we see it there?"

"You could beam down into a sea of molten lava," Scott said. "At the moment it's a raftlike mineral crust several hundred meters thick, over a molten iron core. It looks stable, but it was notably unstable in its formative phase."

"And there are transient images of life forms," McCoy said. "Minerallike themselves. Jim, that patch of Earth was created after our ship was scanned. Whoever they are, they examined us, determined our needs and supplied them down there. It smells, Captain. It's a trap."

"But why would they want to destroy only two of us?" Kirk said.

"It would be illogical of them, with such abilities," Spock said "They could as easily trick us into destroying the entire vessel."

"Spock are you implying that it's probably safe to beam down?"

"I am not Doctor. There's no doubt that they want us down there for some hidden purpose Otherwise they would have revealed some logical reason for all of this"

"Why Lincoln, Spock?" Kirk said. "Any speculation on that?"

"I need not speculate when the reason is obvious, Captain President Lincoln has always been a very personal hero to you. What better way to titillate your curiosity than to make him come alive for you?"

"Not only to me, Spock."

"Agreed I felt his charm, too. He is a magnificent work of duplication."

"But he has a *special* emotional involvement for you," McCoy said. "Interesting, since you're the one who will make the decision whether or not to beam down."

"Don't do it, Captain," Scott said.

Kirk thought about it. Finally he said, "The very reason for the existence of our starships is contact with other life. Although the method is beyond our comprehension, we *have* been offered contact. I'm beaming down. As for you, however, Mr. Spock—"

Spock stood. "Since I was included in their invitation to make contact, I must beam down with you, Captain."

McCoy exploded. "You're both out of your heads!"

"And you're on the edge of insubordination, Doctor," Kirk said.

"Would I be insubordinate to remind the Captain that this has the smell of things happening to him which I may not be able to patch back together this time?"

"Aye," Scott growled.

"Your concern noted and appreciated, gentlemen," Kirk said. "Mr. Spock, standard uniform, phasers and tricorder. Mr. Scott, have President Lincoln guided to the Transporter Room; we'll beam down immediately."

The three materialized in what seemed to be a wild canyon. The slopes were steep and boulder-strewn; on the floors there were shrubbery and trees. Kirk looked around.

"Captain!" Spock said. "Our weapons and tricorders did not beam down."

Kirk reached under his shirt and found his communicator still there, although his phaser and tricorder had indeed vanished. "Captain to *Enterprise*, come in ... *Enterprise*, come in ..."

Spock was also trying, but quickly gave over in favor of a careful examination of his communicator. "Undamaged," he reported. "Yet something prevents them from functioning."

Kirk swung angrily to Lincoln. "Your explanation, sir."

"I have none, Captain. To me this seems quite as it should be."

"Why have our weapons been taken? Why can't we communicate with our ship?"

"Please believe me. I know nothing other than what I have already told you—"

"The game's over! We've treated you with courtesy, we've gone along with who and what you think you are—"

"Despite the seeming contradictions, all is as it appears to be. I *am* Abraham Lincoln—"

"Just," another voice entered, "as I am who I appear to be."

Another man was approaching them: a tall, distinguished Vulcan. It was obvious that he was old, but as erect and strong as was usual with Vulcans even in age. The dignity and wisdom apparent in his features and bearing matched those of Lincoln's.

"Surak!" Spock said, in outright open astonishment.

"Who?" Kirk said.

"The greatest who ever lived on our planet, Captain. The father of all we became."

Surak stopped and made the Vulcan hand sign. "Live long and prosper, Spock. May you also, Captain Kirk."

"It is not logical that you are Surak," Spock said. "There is no fact, extrapolation from fact, or theory which would make it possible—"

"Whatever I am, Spock, would it harm you to give response?"

Spock slowly lifted his hand and returned the sign. "Live long and prosper, image of Surak, father of all we now hold true."

The newcomer almost smiled. "The image of Surak read in your face what was in your mind, Spock."

"As I turned and beheld you, I displayed emotion. I beg forgiveness."

Surak nodded gravely. "The cause was more than sufficient. We need speak no further of it. Captain, in my time, we knew not of Earthmen. And I am pleased to see we have differences. May we together become greater than the sum of both of us."

"Spock," Kirk said in an iron voice, "we will not go along with these charades any longer!"

He was answered by still another new voice, seemingly out of the air—an oddly reverberating voice. "You will have the answer soon, Captain."

A strange, shrilling sound, a little like the chiming of bells, followed the voice, and then, directly before the four, there was a rainbow flashing which congealed slowly into a bizarre shape. It was a creature made seemingly of rock, about the size and shape of a man but with clawlike appendages and a mouth which, like a cave, seemed to be permanently open. It was seated in a rock chair carved to fit its body.

"I am Yarnek," the voice reverberated from the open maw. "Our world is called Excalbia. Countless who live on that planet are watching. Before this drama unfolds, we give welcome to the ones named Kirk and Spock."

"We know nothing of your world or customs," Kirk said. "What do you mean by a drama about to unfold?"

"You are intelligent life forms. I am surprised you do not perceive the honor we do you." A claw gestured. "Have we not created in this place on our planet a stage identical to your own world?"

"We perceive only that we were invited down here and came in friendship. You have deprived us of our instruments for examining your world, of our means of defending ourselves and of communicating with our vessel."

"Your objection is well taken. We shall communicate with your vessel so that your fellow life forms may also enjoy and profit from the play. Behold . . . we begin."

At these words, four figures came into view at the edge of the glade, and approached cautiously. One was a squat human in a Mongol costume of about the 13th century; another, also human, in the uniform of a 21st century Colonel; one was a Klingon, and the last a female Tiburon. Except for the Colonel, who was dapper and not unhandsome, they were an ugly-looking lot.

"Some of these you may know through history," Yarnek said. "Genghis Khan, for one. And Colonel Green, who led a genocidal war in the 21st century on Earth. Kahless the Unforgettable, the Klingon who set the pattern for his planet's tyrannies. Zora, who experimented with the body chemistry of subject tribes on Tiburon.

"We welcome the vessel *Enterprise* to our solar system and our spectacle. We ask you to observe with us the confrontation of the two opposing philosophies you term 'good' and 'evil.' Since this is our first experiment with Earthlings our theme is a simple one: survival. Life and death. Your philosophies are alien to us and we wish to understand them and discover which is the stronger. We learn by observing such spectacles."

"What do you mean, survival?" Kirk said.

"The word is explicit. If you and Spock survive, you may return to your vessel. If you do not, your existence is ended. Your choice of action is unlimited, as is your choice of weapons, should you wish to use any—you may fabricate anything you desire out of what you find around you. Let the spectacle begin."

"Mr. Spock and I refuse to participate."

"You will decide otherwise," Yarnek said, and then dissolved into that same mist of rainbows from which he had emerged.

"Analysis, Spock. Why do they want us to fight?"

"It may be exactly as explained, Captain. Our concept of good and evil would be strange to them. They wish to see which is strongest."

"And they'll have the answer if it kills us. Do you recall the exact location where we beamed down?"

"We have strayed from it somewhat, Captain. It was in that area beyond those boulders."

"Ship's coordinates may still be locked in there." He started toward the spot, ignoring the others, Spock following. Lincoln and Surak were soon lost from view; but after a moment, rounding a large boulder, Kirk found himself face to face with them again. After staring at them, Kirk tried again, taking another path—with the same result.

"Mr. Spock?"

"I have no explanation, sir. Unless the creature is compelling us to circle. Quite obviously it is preventing us from reaching that area."

"I'm afraid, Captain," Lincoln said, "that none of us may leave until we do what it demands of us."

From the group of potentional antagonists, Colonel Green stepped forward, his hand extended in a gesture of peace. His manner seemed friendly, even intended to charm. "Captain Kirk. May I? I'm Colonel Green. I quite agree with your attitude toward this charade. It's ridiculous to expect us to take part in it."

Kirk looked at him with open suspicion, and Green stopped while he was still a few steps away. "What do you want?"

"Exactly what you do. To get out of here. I have no quarrel with you, any more than you have with me."

"You're somewhat different from the way history paints you, Colonel."

"History tends to exaggerate," Green said with a small laugh. "I suggest we call a halt to this at once, and see if we can't find a way out of our difficulties. My associates are in full agreement with me."

Kirk looked beyond him at the "associates." Zora bowed gravely. Khan was hunkered down on the ground; apparently he was bored. Well, he had never been much of a man for talk. Kahless looked around curiously at the slopes.

"You were tricked into coming here, weren't you?" Green said. "So were we all."

"Where did you come from?"

"I don't remember ... Isn't that strange? My memory used to be quite remarkable." He came closer, took Kirk's elbow confidentially, drawing him to one side. "But wherever it was, I want to get back. So it seems to me, Captain, that we have common cause, and that our enemy is that creature."

"What do you propose?"

"That we combine forces and reason out some way to overcome it. Are we in agreement?"

Kirk hesitated, studying him. "As I recall, Colonel, you were notorious for striking out at your enemies in the midst of negotiating with them."

"But that was centuries ago, Captain!" Green said, with a louder laugh. "And not altogether true! There is much that I'd change now if I could. Don't let prejudice and rumor sway you."

"Captain!" Spock shouted.

Suddenly everything seemed to be happening at once. Swinging, Kirk saw in a flash that Khan had somehow gotten to higher ground and was holding a boulder over his head in both hands. Then Green's arm was locked around Kirk's neck and he was thrown halfway to the ground. Kirk lashed out, staggering Green, and as he sprang to his feet saw Lincoln wrestling with Khan, who seemed to have missed whomever he had been aiming the boulder at.

Then the brawl was over as suddenly as it had begun, the four antagonists vanished among the boulders and trees of the canyon. Total silence swept over them. Breathing hard, Kirk joined the other three. All had been battered, Spock severely.

"Is anyone hurt?" Kirk said.

"I fear my clothing is somewhat damaged," Lincoln said. "But how delightful to discover at my age that I can still wrestle."

"Mr. Spock?"

"Quite all right, Captain. However, I suggest that we prepare ourselves for another attack."

"No," Kirk said. "Green was right. That rocklike thing, Yarnek, is the enemy. Not those illusions."

"For an illusion, my opponent had a remarkable grip," Lincoln said, "But I forgot. You consider me an illusion, too."

"The Captain speaks wisely," Surak said. "These four are not our enemy. We should arrive together at a peaceful settlement."

The bell-like trilling began once more, and with it the rainbow swirling. Yarnek was back.

"I am disappointed," the creature said. "You display no interest in the honor we do you. We offer you an opportunity to become our teachers. By demonstrating whether good or evil is more powerful—"

Kirk lunged at the creature. It did not move—but when Kirk seized it, it was as though he had tried to grab a red-hot stove. With a yell he snatched his hands back.

"You find my body heat distressing?" Yarnek said.

"You forget the nature of this planet ... I must conclude that your species requires a cause to fight for. You may now communicate with your ship."

Kirk fumbled for his communicator, and despite the pain of his seared hands, managed to flip it open. "Kirk to *Enterprise*. Come in. Kirk to *Enterprise*, Do you read me?"

"Be patient, Captain," Yarnek said. "They read you."

Suddenly the communicator came alive in a bedlam of shouting voices, backed up by the sound of the ship's alarm. The bridge was obviously in turmoil.

"Mr. Scott!" Uhura called. "The Captain is trying to reach us."

"Engineering!" Scout was shouting. "Give me that again, man I canna hear you."

"Deterioration has just started, sir."

"What is it Lieutenant?" Kirk demanded.

"Where?" Scott shouted.

"Red Alert, Captain," Uhura said. "Mr. Scott is standing by."

"In the shielding between matter and antimatter. I don't know what started it."

"What caused the alert?"

"I don't know, sir. Mr. Scott, I have the Captain."

"Check for radiation. Get a repair crew on it at once."

"I have already, sir. We can't seem to stop it."

"Is there danger of detonation?"

"Estimate four hours, sir."

"Mr. Scott sir, I have the Captain!"

"What? Oh—Captain, Scott here."

"Beam us aboard fast, Scotty."

"I canna, sir. There's a complete power failure. We're on emergency battery power only."

"What's happening?"

"I can't explain it, sir. Matter and antimatter are in Red Zone proximity. No knowing how it started and no stopping it either. The shielding is breaking down. Estimate four hours before it goes completely. That'll blow us up for fair!"

"The estimate is quite correct," Yarnek's hollow voice said. "Your ship will blow itself to atoms within four hours, Captain—unless you defeat the others before then. Is that cause enough to fight for?"

"What if they defeat us?"

"To save your ship and your crew, you have to win."

"Scotty, alert Starfleet Command. Disengage nacelles and jettison if possible. Scotty, do you read me?"

"Your communicators once more no longer function," Yarnek said. "You may proceed with the spectacle." With a chime and a shimmer, the creature was gone.

"The war is forced upon us, Captain," Lincoln said. "History repeats itself."

"Well," Kirk said, "I see nothing immoral in fighting illusions. It's play their game, fight, or lose the ship and every crewman aboard."

Spock looked toward Surak. "And if they're real, Captain?"

Kirk chose to let that go by. "We'll use the top of the defile as a base. It's defensible. They can't approach without our seeing them."

"Are we fighting a defensive war, James?" Lincoln said.

"We don't have the time. But if it goes against us I want a place to retreat to. Right now I want to scout them out, find their weaknesses and attack."

Lincoln smiled. "Do you drink whisky?"

"Occasionally," Kirk said, startled. "Why?"

"Because you have qualities very much like those of another man I admired greatly. One I mentioned before—General Grant."

The reminder of the possible illusory nature of all this was jarring, distracting. "Thank you. We'll need weapons. Spock, I believe the primitive Vulcans made something like a boomerang."

"Yes, Captain. However—"

"Spears, too. Slings. Mr. President, you used slings as a boy—"

"Indeed I did." Lincoln stripped off his coat, pulled

out his shirttail and ripped from it a long strip. Again that conflict of realism and illusion.

"Captain," Spock said, "logic dictates that we consider another course." He looked deferentially toward Surak, who thus far had remained a profoundly troubled nonparticipant in the discussion.

"In my time on Vulcan we too faced these alternatives," Surak said. "We had suffered devastating wars that nearly destroyed our planet and another was about to begin. We were torn. And out of our suffering some of us found the discipline to act. We sent emissaries to our opponents to propose peace. The first were killed. Others followed. Ultimately, we achieved peace, which has lasted since then."

"The circumstances were different, Surak."

"The face of war never changes. Look at us, Captain. We have been hurt. So have they. Surely it is more logical to heal than kill."

"I'm afraid that kind of logic doesn't apply here," Kirk said.

"That is precisely why we should not fight—"

"My ship is at stake!"

Surak said, "I will not harm others, Captain."

"Sir," Spock said, "his convictions are most profound on this matter—"

"So are mine, Spock! If I believed there was a peaceful way out of this—"

"The risk would be mine alone, Captain," Surak said. "And if I fail, you would lose nothing. I am no warrior."

There was a moment of silence, while Kirk looked from one Vulcan to the other.

"The Captain knows that I have fought at his side before," Spock said. "And I will now if need be. But I too am Vulcan, bred to peace. Let us attempt it."

"You saw how treacherously they acted," Kirk said.

"Yes, Captain," Surak said. "But perhaps it is our belief in peace which is actually being tested."

"Wellll . . . I have no authority over you. Do as you think best."

"Thank you. May you live long and prosper." Surak

gave the Vulcan sign and went off. Kirk watched him depart, doubtful, but also with some awe. Then he shook the mood off.

"The weapons, gentlemen—in case he fails."

Time went past. The three fashioned crude spears, bolos, slings, boomerangs, and gathered rocks for throwing. Spock was visibly on edge; he kept looking after the vanished Surak.

"A brave man," Kirk said.

"Men of peace usually are, sir. On Vulcan he is revered as the Father of Civilization. The father-image has much meaning for us."

"You show emotion, Mr. Spock," Kirk said, and then was instantly sorry he had said it; this was surely no time for needling. But Spock replied only:

"I deeply respect what he accomplished."

"Let's hope he accomplishes something here."

As if on cue, the air was rent by a harrowing scream of agony.

"Surak!" Spock cried.

"Yes," Kirk said grimly. "I would guess that they're torturing him."

"Mr. Spock!" Colonel Green's voice called, from no very great distance off. "Your friend wants you. He seems to be hurt."

"Help me, Spock!" Surak's voice called, raw with pain.

"You can't let him suffer," Green said.

"Sir," Spock said, his face like stone. "They are trying to goad us into attacking rashly."

"I know that."

"And he was aware that this might happen when he went—" Spock was interrupted by another scream.

"I should not have let him go," Kirk said.

"You had no choice, Captain—" Another scream. It cut Kirk like a knife, but Spock went on through it. "You could not have stopped him."

"How can you ignore it?"

"I suspect it, sir. A Vulcan would not cry out so."

"So his suffering doesn't matter?"

"I am not insensitive to it, sir, nor am I ignoring it."

"I don't care whether he is Vulcan or not. He is in agony."

"The fact that he might not be Vulcan does not blind me to the fact."

The cry came again. "But you can listen to that and chop logic about it?" Kirk said. "Well, I can't!"

Kirk strode off toward the antagonists' camp. Spock was after him in one bound, grasping his arm.

"Captain, that is what they want of us. They are waiting for us to attempt a rescue."

"Perhaps we can rescue him, Mr. Spock," Lincoln said. "I suggest that we do exactly what they want."

"Do what they want?"

"Not the way they want it, however. We must first convince them that they have provoked us to recklessness. James? You seem taken aback. I do not mean to presume upon your authority—"

"It isn't that."

"What I propose to do is that I circle around to their rear while you two provide a frontal distraction. It should be sufficiently violent to cover what I do."

"Which is—?"

"Slip into their camp and free him."

"No," Kirk said.

"I was something of a backwoodsman, James. I doubt that you could do what I was bred to."

"I won't have you risk it."

"I am no longer President," Lincoln said, with a slight smile. "Mr. Spock, any comment?"

"No, sir."

"Then," Lincoln said, "one matter further, gentlemen. We fight on their level. With trickery, brutality, finality. We match their evil ... You forget James. I know I am reputed a gentle man. Kindly I believe the word is. But I was Commander in Chief during the four bloodiest years of my country's history. I gave orders that sent a hundred thousand men to death by the hands of their brothers. There is no honorable way to kill, no gentle way to destroy. There is nothing good in war—except its ending. And you are fighting for the lives of your crew."

"Mr. President," Kirk said, "your campaign."

The scream came again. It was markedly weaker.

Khan and Green were on watch as Kirk and Spock worked their way among the boulders to the enemy camp. Kirk made no particular effort at concealment, "accidentally" showing himself several times. By the time they were in range, Zora and Kahless had appeared, weapons at the ready.

Kirk and Spock rose as one, threw spears, and ducked again. One of the spears narrowly missed Khan, who with a wild yell retaliated with a boulder that came equally close.

When Kirk looked again, Green was gone, and a moment later, so were Kahless and Zora. Then Green came back. What did that maneuver mean? But Kirk was left no time to see more; Green threw a spear at him with murderous accuracy, and he was forced to duck again.

Lincoln, creeping up at the rear, almost tripped a man-trap made of a tied-down sapling. Backing off, he deliberately tripped it, and then resumed crawling.

Ahead he could see Surak, bound to a tree, head slumped. No one else seemed to be around.

"Surak!" he called in a low voice. "I will have you free in a minute." Racing forward, he began to cut the thongs binding the Vulcan. "The others have drawn them away. We will circle around. It was a worthy effort, Surak. No need to blame yourself for its failure."

The thongs parted. As Lincoln put out a hand to help Surak, the Vulcan collapsed at his feet. He was dead.

"Help me, Lincoln!"

Lincoln spun. The voice had been Surak's, but it was coming from Kahless. He and Green were standing in the direction from which Lincoln had just come, grinning, spears ready.

It was only afterward that Kirk was able to sort the battle out. Their four antagonists had charged them, leaping with spears raised. Hit by a rock, Kirk stumbled and fell, and Zora was upon him at once; but whatever expertise she may have had in body chemistry, she was no fighter. Kirk rolled and threw her aside, hard. She was hurt and lay watching him in terror.

Nearby, Spock and Khan were fighting hand to hand. They seemed to be evenly matched, but Kirk had no chance to help—Kahless was upon him. The struggle was a violent, kaleidoscopic, head-banging eternity. When it stopped, very suddenly, it took Kirk several seconds to realize that he had killed the Klingon. Snatching up a spear, he ran at Khan, who broke free of Spock and fled, looking wildly behind him. Green was running now, too. Kirk snatched up a spear and threw it. He did not miss.

Then it was all over. Inside the enemy camp, they found the bodies of Lincoln and of Surak. They looked down with rage and grief. Neither could find anything to say.

Then, once more, the bell-like chiming sounded, and the seated, stony figure of Yarnek emerged from its cocoon of rainbows.

"You are the survivors," the echoing voice said. "The others have run off. It would appear that evil retreats when forcibly confronted. However, you have failed to demonstrate to me any other difference between your philosophies. Your good and your evil use the same methods, achieve the same results. Do you have an explanation?"

"You established the methods and the goals," Kirk said.

"For you to use as you chose."

"What did you offer them if they won?"

"What they wanted most—power."

"You offered me the lives of my crew."

"I perceive," Yarnak said. "You have won their lives."

Kirk boiled over. "How many others have you done

this to? What gives you the right to hand out life and death?"

"The same right that brought you here: the need to know new things."

"We came in peace—"

"And you may go in peace." Yarnak faded from view.

Kirk took out his communicator. "Kirk to *Enterprise* . . . Mr. Sulu, beam us aboard."

On the bridge everything seemed to be functioning normally, as though nothing had ever gone wrong.

"Mr. Spock," Kirk said. "Explanation?"

"Conjecture, sir, rather than explanation."

"Well?"

"It would seem that we were held in the power of creatures able to control matter, to rearrange molecules in whatever fashion they desired. So Yarnak was able to create the images of Surak and Lincoln and the others, after scanning our minds, by making use of its fellow creatures as source matter."

"They seemed so real, Spock. To me, especially, Mr. Lincoln. I feel I actually met Lincoln."

Spock nodded. "And Surak. In a sense, perhaps they were, Captain. Created out of our own thoughts, how could they be anything but what we expected them to be?"

"It was so hard to see him die once again. I begin to understand what Earth endured to achieve final peace." Kirk paused. "Mr. Spock . . . is there a memorial to Surak on Vulcan?"

"Yes, sir. A monument of great beauty. However, it is held generally that the true memorial to him is the peace and the friendship that have endured among Vulcans since his time with them."

"The same with Lincoln. I think of all our heroes on Earth, he is the most loved today. We see his dreams around us. We have the brotherhood and equality of men that he hoped for, and we're still learning what he knew instinctively."

"Men of such stature live beyond their years."

"They were alive today, Spock. Those were more than rearranged molecules we saw."

"We projected into them our own concepts of them, sir."

"Did we?" After a moment, Kirk shook his head. "There is still much of their work to be done in the galaxy, Spock . . . Mr. Sulu, break orbit for our next assignment."

THE LIGHTS OF ZETAR
(Jeremy Tarcher and Shari Lewis)

The *Enterprise* was enroute to Memory Alpha when the storm first appeared. Memory Alpha was a planetoid set up by the Federation solely as a central library containing the total cultural history and scientific knowledge of all planetary Federation members. The ship had a passenger, Lt. Mira Romaine, an attractive woman of about thirty. She was on board to supervise the transfer of newly designed equipment which the *Enterprise* was also carrying. At the moment, she was on the bridge talking to Scott at his position.

"Mr. Scott, I hope I haven't been too much trouble to you with all the questions I've asked."

"Well, I'm sorry the trip is coming to an end," Scott said. "I'm going to miss your questions."

Kirk watched them amusedly. "Present position, Mr. Chekov?"

"On course—one seventy-two mark four."

"Mr. Scott, as soon as we are within viewing range of Memory Alpha, you and Lt. Romaine will go to your stations in the emergency manual monitor. Prepare for direct transfer of equipment."

"Yes, Captain."

"We're ready, sir," Mira added.

"Lieutenant," Spock said, "may I offer my congratulations on what will be a first in the Federation."

"And good luck," Kirk added.

"Thank you, Mr. Spock, Captain."

"I didn't think Mr. Scott would go for the brainy type," Chekov said, almost too softly for Kirk to overhear.

"I don't think he's even noticed she has a brain. Has she?" Sulu said. A red light came up on his panel. "Captain, I am picking up a high intensity reading. Shall I display it?"

"Yes." Kirk looked at the main viewing screen. In the blackness of space there was a faint light source. "Is that Memory Alpha?"

"No, sir."

"Magnification eight."

The light now showed as a cloud of vaguely organic shape, almost like a brain. It sparked and flashed intermittently in varied hues, like a series of inspired thoughts.

"Is that some kind of storm?" Kirk said.

"Quite possible, Captain," Spock said. "I've never seen one of such great intensity and strange conformation."

"Captain," Sulu added, "it is approaching at warp two point six and accelerating."

"Recheck your readings, Mr. Sulu. It is impossible for a natural phenomenon to move faster than the speed of light."

"It is definitely doing so," Spock confirmed—and indeed the thing was visibly growing on the screen. "It therefore cannot be a phenomenon of nature."

"Deflector on. Condition yellow."

The light source filled the screen. The glare was almost unbearable. Then the screen went blank.

Kirk tried to snap out an order and found that he could not. The whole bridge was suddenly deathly silent. No one moved.

Then, just as abruptly, it was over. "Mr. Sulu, full scan on that turbulence or whatever it was!" Kirk noticed Scott staring uncertainly over Kirk's own shoulder. Turning to see what he was looking at, he was just in time to see Mira crumple out of sight behind the command chair.

"Mira!" Scott leapt from his post, knelt beside her and lifted her head off the floor. "Mira!"

She murmured unintelligibly. It was not that the sounds were indistinct, but as though they were in an unknown language.

"What's that you're saying?" Scott said. Kirk and Spock were now also bending close. The strange murmuring went on.

McCoy came onto the bridge and crossed at once to the group, his tricorder already out and in use. He said, "Was she hurt by the fall or by the action of that . . . disturbance?"

"I don't know," Kirk said. "You were closest, Scotty. Did you notice?"

"She collapsed when it was over."

McCoy gave her a shot. The murmuring died away. Her expression changed from a curiously rapt look to one of relaxation. Then her eyes opened and she looked around in confusion.

"Easy now," Scott said. "You took quite a fall."

"I'm fine now," she said.

"Let me be the judge," McCoy said. "Can you walk to Sickbay?"

"Doctor, I'm fine, really I am." Again she looked around the bridge, obviously still puzzled. "Is everyone else—all right?"

"Aye, they are," Scott said. "You do just as Dr. McCoy says."

"Why? I never felt better in my—"

"Lieutenant, report to Sickbay," Kirk said. "That's an order."

"Yes, sir." She followed McCoy resignedly toward the elevator.

Scott said, "Would it be all right for me to go to Sickbay?"

"You will stay at your post, Mr. Scott. Lt. Uhura, damage report, all stations."

"All stations are operative."

"Mr. Spock?"

"Some equipment was temporarily out of order. My sensors were inoperative."

"Any damage to the warp engines?"

"None, Captain."

"Good. From the action of that—that storm, we may need all the speed we can get."

"It was not a storm, Captain," Spock said.

"Mr. Chekov, get a fix on whatever it was and try to project its path . . . That was a novel experience for the *Enterprise*. Would you agree, Mr. Spock?"

"Unforgettable, Captain."

"Yes? I was hoping you had an explanation."

"None at the moment, Captain. Only a sharply etched memory of what I felt during the onslaught."

"Memory Alpha was hailing us a moment before," Uhura said. "I wanted to respond, but I couldn't make my hand move."

"It was not hands that were paralyzed, it was eyes," Chekov said. "I couldn't force my eyes to look down to set a new course."

"No," Sulu said, "speech was affected. I couldn't utter a sound."

"Nor could I," Kirk said. "You seemed to be having the same trouble, Mr. Spock."

"Yes, Captain, I was."

"Any explanation yet?"

"Only of the result," Spock said, "none of the cause. In each case, different areas of the brain were affected. Our voluntary nerve functions were under some form of pressure."

"Or of attack?"

"Attack might be a more precise formulation, Captain."

"Lt. Romaine seems most susceptible. Mr. Scott, perhaps you'd better go down to Sickbay after all. If she was the only one of four hundred and thirty people who passed out, we'd better find out why."

"Aye, sir," Scott said, heading for the elevators with alacrity.

"I have plotted the storm's path, Captain," Chekov

said. "On its present course it will hit the Memory Alpha planetoid as it did us."

"Uhura, warn them of the proximity of the phenomenon. Can you give us an ETA for it, Chekov?"

"It's impossible, Captain. It has the ability to change speed."

"Sorry, Captain," Uhura said, "But I'm unable to establish contact with the planetoid. Am hailing on all frequencies. No response."

"It does not matter, Captain," Spock said. "Memory Alpha has no protective shields. When the library complex was assembled, shielding was regarded as inappropriate to its totally academic purpose. Since the information on the memory planet is freely available to everyone, special protection was deemed unnecessary."

"Wonderful," Kirk said sarcastically. "I hope the 'storm' is aware of that rationale."

"We're completing approach to the planetoid," Sulu said. "But the storm's gotten there first."

"Uhura, get through to—"

"I cannot," Uhura said. "I cannot get past the interference, sir."

"Mr. Spock, how many people are there on Memory Alpha?"

"It varies with the number of scholars, researchers, scientists, from various Federation planets who are using the computer complex."

"Mr. Chekov, maintain standard orbit."

"The storm is now leaving Memory Alpha," Sulu reported.

"And," Spock added, "the sensors give no readings of energy being generated on the planetoid."

"Any life readings?"

"None, sir."

"Check for malfunction."

Spock did so. "Sensors inoperative again."

"We'd better find out what's going on down there." Kirk turned to the intercom. "Kirk to Sickbay. Is Mr. Scott there?"

"Scott here. I was checking on the lass. She's going to be fine though. Nothing wrong with her."

"I'm relieved to hear your prognosis. Is the doctor there with you?"

"McCoy here Jim."

"How's the girl?"

"I think she's in good shape."

"Apparently Scotty thinks so, too. Both of you, meet me in the Transporter Room, on the double. Mr. Spock, come with me. The con is yours, Mr. Sulu."

The four materialized in a computer room on Memory Alpha. The room was utterly silent, and there was no light at all.

"Somehow," McCoy grumbled, "I find transporting into the darkness unnerving."

"Scotty," Kirk said, "can you give us some light in here?"

Scott checked the boards nearby; they could hear him fumbling. Then a small glow appeared, a safelight of some sort. "This will have to do. The generator is inoperative. The alternative is to go back to the ship for hand torches."

Spock moved to the face of the largest computer cabinet with his tricorder, but for several moments simply stood there, doing nothing. Kirk guessed he was waiting for his eyes to become dark-adapted, a gift far better developed in Vulcans than in humans. Then he lifted the tricorder.

"Damage report, Mr. Spock?"

"It's a disaster for the galaxy, Captain. The central brain damaged—all memory cores burned out. The loss might be irretrievable."

Kirk took a step and stumbled over something large and soft. He put a hand down to it, but he too could see better now.

"Mr. Spock. I've just encountered a body. Look around the floor."

There was a long silence. Then Spock said: "There are dead men and creatures from other planets sprawled all around us. Move very carefully until you can see better. I'm scanning for a life reading . . . Yes, I have one, very faint."

"Location, Mr. Spock?"

"It is too weak to get an exact bearing, but . . ." He moved away.

"We'd better find him while he's still alive. We have to get more knowledge of this . . . enemy."

"Over here, Captain," Spock's voice called.

The other three carefully moved toward the sound of his voice. At his feet a girl, evidently a technician, was on her knees, struggling to get up. An already dead man nearby had evidently tried to help her. She was murmuring.

Spock listened intently. "The same garbled sounds," he said, "that Lt. Romaine was making when she fainted after the disturbance."

"Are you sure, Spock?"

"Absolutely sure."

Kirk flipped open his communicator. "Kirk to *Enterprise* . . . Mr. Sulu. Beam down Lt. Romaine immediately—and have her bring five hand torches."

"Yes, sir."

The technician's voice murmured on, but it was becoming steadily weaker. Then she pitched forward on her face.

McCoy took a reading, and then silently shook his head. Kirk said: "Can you tell what she died of?"

"Severe brain hemorrhaging due to distortion of all neural centers. Dissolution of all basic personality patterns. Even the autonomic nervous system."

"The attack, Captain, was thorough," Spock said.

"What did the others die of?"

"Each had a different brain center destroyed," McCoy said. "Just how, I can't tell you. Maybe when I get back to the ship's computer—"

The shimmer of the Transporter effect briefly illumated the charnel chamber and Mira materialized. The beam of a flashlight leapt from her hand, but Scott moved swiftly to step into it, blocking her view of the bodies.

"Mira—the Captain has some questions. Give me the rest of the torches."

"Here you are . . . Yes, Captain?"

Kirk said gently: "Mira, while you were unconscious you were, uh, speaking."

"What did I say?" She seemed genuinely surprised.

"We don't know. You talked in a strange language we didn't understand. We found one person barely alive in here, and she was speaking in the same way—"

"Was speaking?" Before anyone could move to prevent her, she darted around the central computer and swept the beam of her flash over the floor. When she spoke again, it was in a frightened whisper. "All dead . . . just like I saw them. Captain, we must get back to the ship."

"Why?"

Her hands went to her brow. She seemed unable to answer.

"Tell me why!"

"Captain—that . . . that . . . it's returning!"

"How do you know?"

"I know. You'll be killed if we stay."

"I assure you, lieutenant," Spock said, "that unexplained phenomenon was headed away from the planetoid before we came here. It is probably seeking other victims."

"I tell you, it will kill us!" Her panic was genuine, that was clear.

Kirk's communicator beeped. "Bridge to Captain Kirk. The storm has reappeared on the long-range scanner."

"I told him it is not a storm," Spock said.

"Course, Mr. Sulu?"

"Coming back in this direction, and closing fast."

"Beam us up."

The minute he saw the Transporter Room coming into being around him, Kirk headed for the intercom, but Scott's voice stopped him.

"Captain, wait! We've lost Mira."

Kirk turned and saw that Lt. Romaine was indeed

not there. Lt. Kyle was at the Transporter controls. Scott leaped to his side.

"Where is she? Stabilize her!"

"Something's interfering with the transporter signal," Kyle said. "I have her coordinates, but she's suspended in transit."

"Let me." Together the two men struggled with the controls. Suddenly, Kyle said, "Aha, it's cleared," and at the same moment Mira materialized on the Transporter platform. She stepped off, dazed but smiling.

"Mr. Scott, Lt. Romaine, you'd best go to the emergency manual monitor and see if enough new equipment is in inventory to repair at least some of Memory Alpha." Kirk hit the intercom. "Mr. Sulu, get us out of here. Mr. Spock, to the bridge, please."

In the emergency manual monitor, Mira and Scott were working side by side. The inventory had proceeded for some time in silence. Then Scott said:

"When I—thought we lost you, back there in the Transporter Room—well, you're not to do that again."

"It was so frightening," she said. "I felt pulled apart."

"You almost were. There was interference with the Transporter mechanism."

"And that's more than you can say about me," she said. What she meant by this, Scott had no idea.

"I'll tell you something. You are the sanest—the smartest—the nicest—and the most beautiful woman that has ever been aboard this ship."

"And what else?"

"Anything else, I'm keeping to myself for the moment."

"But I'm so much trouble to you."

"Trouble? What trouble? Of course, you could drive a man daft, but that's not what I call trouble."

She smiled. "Do I drive you daft, Scotty?"

"Well now—if it was me, you might have to work at it."

"I'd be willing—" Then, as if embarrassed, she turned away and resumed being busy.

"The *Enterprise* has been my life," Scott said. "I love this ship, and I love every day I've spent on it. But, until you came aboard, I didn't know how lonely it is to be free in the galaxy ... So, don't you talk of trouble." He took her in his arms. "Now I want to forget about Memory Alpha."

It was the wrong thing to say. She pushed against his chest, her hands trembling. "Scotty ... before that ... I saw it—exactly as it happened."

"What of it? That happens to lots of people. There's a French term for it. They think they're seeing something before it actually occurs. But actually one eye picked it up without realizing—"

"My eyes weren't playing tricks!"

He smoothed her brow. "Then I'm sure there is some other perfectly reasonable explanation that will erase that worried frown."

"But Scotty, I saw the men dead in their exact positions—before I ever left the ship."

He put his hands on her shoulders. "Listen to me. I told you in Sickbay what strange tricks a first trip in space can play on your mind. That's all it is."

"No, Scotty."

"Have you ever had visions of future events before this?"

"Never."

"And if you ask me, *nobody* ever has," Scott said firmly. "That seeing the future is pure bunk. You know that, don't you?"

"I always believed it."

"And you're absolutely right."

"But what is it, Scotty? What is frightening me? Ever since we've been near that—that storm, I've had such strange thoughts ... feelings of such terror."

"Space space, space, that's all it is."

"Then I don't have to report it?"

"If you want to spend the trip in Sickbay," Scott said. "But what good would it do? McCoy can no more cure it than he can cure a cold. It'll pass."

"When I get my permanent assignment ... I hope it will be to the *Enterprise*."

"You just better make sure of it."

"Captain," Sulu said. "It's changing course."

"Plot it, Mr. Chekov."

"Present course will bring it across our starboard bow."

"Mr. Spock, you made a statement that that phenomenon was not a storm."

"Yes, Captain. No known conditions in space would support it as a natural phenomenon. But the sensors seem to be in working order at the moment. Perhaps this time the elusive creature will reveal something about itself." He bent into his hooded viewer. "It seems to be maintaining its distance, but matching course with us. I am receiving increasing magnitudes of energy. Yes—undoubtedly a life form. Fascinating!"

"Control your fascination, Mr. Spock. Pragmatically, what are the implications?"

"We saw the results of full contact in the deaths on Memory Alpha. The humanoid neurological system is destroyed when fully exposed to these peculiar wave patterns."

"But what *is* it, Spock?"

"Not what is it, sir. What are they. There are ten distinct life units within it, Captain. They are powerfully alive and vital."

"Who are they? Where are they from?"

"Impossible to determine without programming for computer analysis."

"Not now." Kirk shot a glance at the main viewer. "It's clear we can't outrun them. Can we shield against them?"

"I do not think so, sir."

"There must be some defensive action we can take."

"Captain, it is a community of life units. Their attack is in the form of brain waves directed against the brain that is most compatible."

"A living brain!" Kirk said. "Perhaps we can avoid a

next time. Lt. Uhura, open all channels and tie in the universal translator. Maybe I can talk to them."

Uhura got to work. Indicators began to light up. "All channels open," she said finally. "Translator tied in."

Kirk looked up at the form of lights on the viewer. Incongruously, he felt wryly amused at the notion of trying to talk to an electrical cloud. "This is Captain James Kirk of the USS *Enterprise.* We wish you no harm. Physical contact between us is fatal to our life form. Please do not come any closer to this ship."

There was no response; only a faint wash of static. Spock said, "Perhaps it did not understand."

"Captain, change in velocity recorded," Sulu said. "It has accelerated its approach."

"Perhaps it will understand another language," Kirk said, beginning to feel angry. "Condition Red Alert. Prepare for phaser firing."

The Red Alert began flashing, and the distant alarm echoed throughout the ship.

"Mr. Sulu, lock in phasers for firing across their course. Do not hit them."

"Locked in, sir."

"Fire."

The phaser shot lanced to one side of the lights and on off into deep space.

"Reaction, Mr. Sulu?"

"None, sir. They are still approaching."

Apparently a shot across the bow was insufficiently convincing. "Lock to target."

"Locked on, sir."

"Fire."

The shot seemed to score a direct hit. The community of life units dispersed in apparent confusion, and then began to reform. So they *could* be hurt—

"Captain, Captain," Scott's voice shouted from the intercom, without even waiting for an acknowledgment. "Scott here. The phaser shots—they're killing Mira."

"Killing Lt. Romaine? How—"

"When you fired, she was stunned, she crumpled. Another shot and you'll kill her."

"Get her to Sickbay at once . . . Mr. Spock, we appear to be at an impasse. Any suggestions?"

"Only one, Captain," the Science Officer said. "There seems to be only one possible defense. If we can find an environment that is deadly to the life form—and at the same time, isolate the girl from the deadly effects of it—"

"It sounds like asking the impossible." Kirk turned to the intercom. "Kirk to Dr. McCoy . . . Bones, is Lt. Romaine well enough to be talked to?"

"I think so," McCoy's voice said. "I can have her ready in a few minutes."

"Bring her and Mr. Scott to the Briefing Room as soon as possible. Bring all available biographical data on the lieutenant. . . . Mr. Spock, come with me."

In the Briefing Room, Spock went immediately to his slave console; Kirk sat at the center of the table, McCoy next to him.

"Go easy on her, Jim. She's in a bad state."

"I'll try. But this can't be postponed."

"I know. I was pretty hard on her myself the first time this happened. I needn't have been. We might know more."

"I'll be careful."

The door opened to admit Scott and Mira. He was holding her by the arm. She seemed pale and distraught. After she was seated, Scott went to his chair at the opposite end of the table.

Kirk leaned toward her and said gently: "This is not a trial, Lt. Romaine. You are not being accused of anything."

"I know," Mira said, almost in a whisper. She glanced toward McCoy. "I didn't mean to be uncooperative, Doctor."

"Of course you didn't," McCoy said. "I told the Captain that."

"I'll tell you everything I know. I trust all of you implicitly. I want to help."

"Good," Kirk said. "This investigation is prompted by two events that may be connected. The first time was when you passed out on the bridge. The second is when we fired the ship's phasers into the force that is attacking us, and we seriously injured you."

"It wasn't serious, Captain. You mustn't worry about hurting me."

"We're glad we didn't. Nevertheless, we won't take that particular defense measure again. Now, this is how we will proceed. Spock will provide everything we know about our attackers. Dr. McCoy has access to Starfleet's exhaustive file on you. A comparison of the two may turn up some unsuspected connection that will protect you—and ourselves. All right, gentlemen? Dr. McCoy, you begin. Does Lt. Romaine have any history of psychosomatic illness?"

"Occasional and routine teen-age incidence."

"Any evidence of any involuntary or unconscious telepathatic abilities?"

"None."

"Any pathological or unusual empathic responses?"

"No, Captain. Not empathic. However, an exceptionally flexible and pliant response to new learning situations."

At this Spock leaned forward, but made no comment.

"There's one other thing, Captain," McCoy said. "Right after our phasers hit that thing, I gave Lt. Romaine the Steinman Standard Analysis. I don't have the results here but Nurse Chapel is having it sent down. In the meantime, I see nothing else very illuminating in the psychological file. Lt. Romaine has developed strong defenses to guard against her extreme competitiveness. Marked scientific and mathematical abilities set up an early competition with her distinguished father. It appears that the problem is still not completely resolved."

"That's not true," Mira said, tears coming to her eyes. "It was over long ago. I'm not like that—not any more."

"Everybody's record has much worse comments

from the psychology majors," Kirk said. "Luckily for us, nobody ever reads ours. Pretend you didn't hear. Mr. Spock, any functional and motivating data on the life force?"

"I have asked the computer why these beings pursue the *Enterprise*. The first answer was 'Completion.' When I requested an alternate formulation, it gave me 'Fulfillment' instead. I find both responses unclear, but the machine has insufficient data to give us anything better, thus far."

The door opened and a yeoman entered with a cartridge which he handed to McCoy. The surgeon inserted it into his viewer. Almost at once, he cast a disturbed look at Mira.

"What is it, Doctor?"

"A comparison of our Steinman with Starfleet records shows that Lt. Romaine's fingerprints, voice analysis, reintal patterns, all external factors are the same as before. But according to the two encephalograms, her brain wave pattern has been altered."

"Isn't that impossible?" Kirk asked.

"That's what I was taught. The BCP is as consistent as fingerprints."

"Let's see it."

McCoy put the tape deck into the slot on the desk, and the tri-screen lit up. They all looked at it for a moment. Then Spock said, "Doctor, I believe that's the wrong slide."

"No it isn't, Spock. It's from tape deck D—brain circuitry pattern of Lt. Mira Romaine."

"No, Doctor. It happens tc be tape deck H—the impulse tracking we obtained on the alien life units."

"Nurse Chapel followed this every step of the way. There can't be an error."

Mira was staring in tense horror at the screen.

"According to your records, Dr. McCoy," Spock said, "Lt. Romaine did not show abnormal telepathatic ability."

"That's right, Spock. Exceptional pliancy *was* indicated. It might be a factor."

"It must be. There is an identity of pattern between

these alien life forms and the mind of Lt. Romaine. Their thoughts are becoming her thoughts."

Scott said: "Mira's tried to tell me all along that she was seeing things happen in advance—"

"Why didn't you report it?" Kirk said.

"You don't report space sickness. That's all I ever thought it was."

"What else did she see?"

Scott thought a moment. "The first attack on the ship ... the attack on Memory Alpha ... and—the time we almost lost her."

"Those were all acts carried out by our attacker. Anything else?"

Scott got up and went over to Mira, who was still staring at the screen. "I thought there was another time. I guess I was wrong."

"Was he wrong, Lieutenant?" Kirk said.

Mira finally looked up at Scotty, who sank to one knee beside her. In a trancelike voice, she said, "Yes. There was one other time."

"What did you see?"

"I saw Scotty," she said, still looking at him intently.

"Where?"

"I don't know."

"What was he doing?"

"He was dying." Her hand went to Scott's face. "Now I understand what's been happening. I've been seeing through another mind. I have been flooded by thoughts that are not my own ... by desires and drives that control me—" Suddenly she broke completely and was in Scott's arms. "Scotty—I would rather die than hurt you. I would rather die!"

"What's all this talk of dying?" Scott demanded. "They've called the turn on us three out of four times. That's a better average than anybody deserves. It's our turn now. We'll fight them. So let's not hear anything more about dying."

It was a bold speech, but Kirk could think of no way that the *Enterprise* could back it up. He punched the intercom. "Ensign Chekov, what success have you had with the evasive tactics?"

"Useless, sir. They'll probably be through the shields again in a minute or so."

Kirk turned to Mira. "They may destroy you and us as they did Memory Alpha. You are especially susceptible to their will. There is one way we might survive. Do not resist. Let them begin to function through you. If we can control that moment, we have a chance. Will you try?"

"Tell me what to do," she said, her voice shaky.

"Everybody down to the antigrav test unit. Follow me."

"Attention all personnel!" Sulu's voice barked from the intercom. "Clear all decks! Alien being has penetrated ship!"

The door to the gravity chamber opened off the interior of the medical lab. As the group from the Briefing Room entered at a run, Kirk said, "As soon as she enters the chamber, secure all ports."

But as Mira started for the chamber, the swirling colors of the life force pervaded the lab. She stopped and spun around, her hand going to her brow, her eyes blazing, her face contorted with struggle. Scott started toward her.

"Don't touch me!" It was a piercing scream. "Scotty—stay away—"

The multicolored flashes slowly and finally were gone, leaving Mira standing as if frozen. Then her lips parted, and from them came once more the sound of the unknown language.

"We've lost her to them," Scott said desperately, starting toward her once more.

"Stay where you are!" Kirk said.

McCoy added, "She could kill us all in this state."

"She will," Spock said, "unless we are able to complete what the Captain is planning."

Scott was looking at Mira in agony. "Stay with us, Mira. Stay with us, Mira Romaine!"

"I am trying," she said. It was her own voice, but

coming out in smothered gasps. "I want to be . . . with you . . . They are too strong."

"Fight them now, Mira," Kirk said. "Don't lose yourself to them. Hold on."

The girl sank against the door to the gravity chamber. Her eyes closed, her body became taut with the effort at control.

"I am Mira Romaine," she said, and this time her voice was angry. "I will be who I choose to be. Let me go!"

But the struggle was too much for her. Her body went limp, and her eyes opened, inexpressibly sad. In a voice like a lost soul, utterly unlike anything she had ever sounded before, she said:

"She cannot prevent us. You cannot stop us."

Scott lunged forward, but Kirk grabbed him. "Mira! Mira!"

"That's not Mira talking," McCoy said.

"Captain, we must deal with them directly," Spock said. "Now, while she retains partial identity, we can speak to them. Her voice will answer for them."

"I am the commander of this vessel," Kirk said to the entranced girl. "Do you understand me?"

"We understand you. We have searched for a millennium to find the One through whom we can see and hear and speak and live out our lives."

"Who are you?"

"We are of Zetar."

"All humanoid life on Zetar," Spock said, "was destroyed long ago."

"Yes. All corporeal life was destroyed."

"Then what are you?" Kirk demanded.

"The desires, the hopes, the thoughts and the will of the last hundred from Zetar. The force of life in us could not be wiped out."

"All things die."

"At the proper time. Our planet was dying. We were determined to live on. At the peak of our plans to go elsewhere, a sudden final disaster struck us down. But the force of our lives survived. And now at last we have found the One through whom we can live it out."

"The body you inhabit has its own life to lead."

"She will accept ours."

"She does not wish it. She is fighting to retain her own identity."

"Her mind will accept our thoughts. Our lives will be fulfilled."

"Will she learn like the people on Memory Alpha learned?"

"We did not wish to kill."

"You did kill!"

"No! Resisting us killed those on Memory Alpha. We did not kill. We wanted only the technician, but she fought back."

"The price of your survival is too high."

"We wish only the girl."

"You cannot have her," Kirk said fiercely. "You are entitled to your own lives. But you cannot have another's!"

Mira herself seemed to hear this, and her eyes to respond. When she spoke again, the voice was her own. "Life was given to *me*. It is mine. I will live it out—I will . . ."

Her voice weakened, and she sank back. McCoy took a tricorder reading. "The girl's life reading is becoming a match to the—Zetarians," he said. "She is losing."

"Do not fight us."

"They will not accept their own deaths," Spock said.

"They will be forced to accept it," Kirk said.

"You will all die," said the Mira/Zetar voice.

"Captain," Spock said, "unless we can complete the plan at once, they will carry out their threat."

McCoy said, "Jim, you realize that the pressure you need to kill the Zetarians might kill her, too?"

"At least, our way she has a chance. We must get her into the antigrav chamber."

They all moved in about her, in a close circle. Scott

forced himself to the front and said, "Mira will not kill me."

He stooped and quickly picked her up in his arms. He faced the opening to the gravity chamber, and his head snapped back, his face contorted in agony. Nevertheless he got her into the chamber, and the doors closed behind her. Then he crumpled to the floor. His face now, however, was relaxed. As McCoy bent over him, his eyes opened.

"I knew she wouldn't kill me," he said, with a faint smile.

Kirk and Spock went to the chamber's console, joined after a moment by McCoy. After a sweeping glance, Kirk then crossed to the bull's-eye port which gave visual access to the chamber.

"Neutralize gravity, Mr. Spock."

Mira's body lay on the floor of the chamber where Scott had put it for what seemed to be a long time. Then she moved feebly, and the motion set her to drifting weightlessly.

"The Zetarians are growing stronger," McCoy said. "The weightless state is their natural condition, after all."

"Begin pressurizing," Kirk said. "Bring it up to two atmospheres."

Spock turned a rheostat slowly. There seemed to be no change in Mira. Theoretically, there should begin to be some sort of feedback system going into operation between Mira's nervous system, as it responded to pressures on her body not natural to her, and the occupying wave patterns of the Zetarian brain; but no such effect was evident yet.

"Two atmospheres, Captain."

"Increase at the rate of one atmosphere a minute."

"Wait a minute, Jim," McCoy said. "Not even a deep-sea diver experiences pressure increases at that rate. They take it slowly, a few atmospheres at a time."

"That's just what I'm counting on, Bones. If it's something Mira can adapt to, there'll be no adverse effect on her, and hence none on them. Run it up as ordered, Mr. Spock."

His hands darting, Spock tied the pressure rheostat into circuit with a timer. "Rising now as ordered, Captain."

A quick glance at the big bourdon gauge showed this. Kirk glued his face back to the glass.

Still nothing seemed to be happening, except that Mira's head was now lolling from side to side.

"Jim, you're going to kill her at this rate!"

Kirk did not respond. The chamber was beginning to look hazy, as though water were beginning to condense out of the atmosphere inside it—but that couldn't be, because water vapor didn't condense except to a *decrease* in pressure—

The fogginess increased, and became luminescent. In a moment more, the chamber was pulsating with the multiple lights of the Zetar life force. It grew brighter and brighter for several seconds.

"Jim, you can't—"

Kirk silenced the surgeon with a savage gesture. Almost at the same moment, the lights vanished, and with them the fog.

"Cut, Spock!"

There was the snap of a toggle. Mira's eyes were now open. She looked entirely normal, though a little bewildered at finding herself floating in midair. Scott snatched up the microphone which fed the intercom in the tank.

"Don't move, Mira! It's going to be all right! They're gone—they're gone!"

Kirk turned away and gestured to McCoy to take over.

"Reduce pressure very *very* gradually, Mr. Spock," the surgeon said.

"It will tax Mr. Scott's patience, Doctor."

"We have all the time in the world, now," Scott said, his eyes glowing.

"Precisely," McCoy said. "And after all this, we don't want to lose the subject to a simple case of the bends. Lieutenant, lie perfectly still; you're in free fall and the slightest movement may bounce you off the chamber walls—and I don't want even the slightest bruise. Don't move at all, just take deep regular breaths . . . that's it . . . Mr. Spock, restore gravity very gradually. I want her to ground without even a jar . . . Mira, don't hold your breath. Breathe deeply and continuously . . . That's it—in, out, in, out, keep it steady . . . Fine. You won't be out of there for another two hours, so you might as well relax. The battle's over, anyhow."

There was a deep sigh all around. Perhaps Mira had given up holding her breath, but it was evident that she had not been alone.

"Spock," Kirk said, "is it possible for you to judge the long-range mental effects on the Lieutenant?"

"I am not an expert, Captain, and bear in mind that Lt. Romaine's mind was invaded by something quite inhuman. However, despite Starfleet's judgment of her pliancy, she put up a valiant struggle to retain her identity. I would propose that that augurs well."

"Spock is right, Jim," McCoy said, to Kirk's surprise. "While the truth was hard for her to take, when it was brought out, the girl reacted well. The struggle she put up in this experience, I would say, will strengthen her whole ego structure."

"Would either of you credit Scotty's steadfast belief in her as a factor?"

Spock's eyebrow arched suspiciously. "You mean 'love' as a motivation? Humans claim a great deal for that particular emotion. It is possible, but—"

"No 'buts' at all," McCoy said. "It was a deciding factor—and will be, in the girl's recovery."

"Then, do I understand you both agree that Lt. Romaine need not return to Starbase for further treatment?"

"I would say," Spock said, "that work is the better therapy."

"Absolutely, Jim."

"Scotty, unsmash your nose from that port and give us a sober opinion. How is Lt. Romaine now?"

"Beautiful, Captain."

"Ready to return to work?"

"Positively, Captain."

There was an exchange of grins all around. Then Kirk turned to the intercom. "Kirk to bridge."

"Sulu here, Captain."

"Set course for Memory Alpha. Lt. Romaine has lots of work to do there."

THE APPLE
(Max Ehrlich and Gene L. Coon)

Even from orbit, Gamma Trianguli VI seemed both beautiful and harmless, as close to an earthly paradise as the *Enterprise* had ever encountered. Such planets were more than rare, and Kirk thought for a few moments that he might have happened upon a colonizable world—until the sensors indicated that there was already native humanoid life there.

He duly reported the facts to Starfleet Command, who seemed to be as impressed as he was. Their orders were to investigate the planet and its culture. Under the circumstances, Kirk ordered a landing party of six: himself, Spock, Chekov, Yeoman Martha Landon, and two security guards, Marple and Kaplan.

Carrying tricorders and specimen bags, the party materialized in what might almost have been a garden. Large exotic flowers grew in profusion, and there were heavily laden fruit trees. Here and there, outcroppings of rainbow-colored rock competed with the floral hues, and over it all stretched a brilliant, cloudless day. Feeling a sudden impulse to share all this beauty as widely as possible, Kirk called down McCoy and two more security guards—Mallory and Hendorf, as it turned out.

McCoy looked around appreciatively. "I might just put in a claim for all this and settle down."

"I doubt that the natives would approve, Bones," Kirk said. "But it is pretty spectacular."

"A shame we have to intrude."

"We do what Starfleet tells us."

Spock, who had knelt to inspect the soil, arose. "Remarkably rich and fertile, Captain. Husbandry would be quite efficacious here."

"You're sure about that?" Kirk said, amused without quite knowing why.

"Quite sure. Our preliminary readings indicate the entire planet is covered by growth like this. Quite curious. Even at the poles there is only a slight variation in temperature, which maintains a planet-wide average of seventy-six degrees."

"I know," Kirk said. "Meteorologically, that's almost impossible."

"It makes me homesick, Captain," Chekov said. "Just like Russia."

"It's a lot more like the Garden of Eden, Ensign," McCoy said.

"Of course, Doctor. The Garden of Eden was just outside Moscow. A very nice place. It must have made Adam and Eve very sad to leave."

Kirk stared at him; Chekov seemed completely straight-faced and earnest. Was this just another of his outbreaks of Russian patriotism, or some side effect of his developing romance with Yeoman Landon? "All right. There's a village about seventeen kilometers away on bearing two thirty-two. We'll head that way."

"Captain!" The call had come from Hendorf, who was examining one of the plants: a small bush with large pods, at the center of each of which was a cluster of sharp, thick thorns. "Take a look at—"

With only a slight puff of noise, one of the pods exploded. Hendorf staggered and looked down at his chest. Perhaps a dozen thorns were sticking in a neat group near his heart. He opened his mouth in an attempt to speak, and then collapsed.

McCoy was there first, but only a quick examination was needed. "He's dead."

"What was all that about Paradise?" Kirk said grimly. He took out his communicator. "Kirk to *Enterprise* . . . Mr. Scott, we've already had a casualty. Hendorf has been killed by a poisonous plant at these coordinates. As soon as we've moved out of the way, beam up his body."

"Aye, Captain. That's a shame about Hendorf." Scott paused a moment. "We seem to have a little problem up here, too. We're losing potency in the antimatter banks. I don't think it's serious, but we're looking into it."

"What's causing it?"

"We're not sure. We've run measurements of the electromagnetic field of the planet, and they're a wee bit abnormal. Could have something to do with it."

"Well, stay on top of it. Kirk out."

"I find that odd, Captain," Spock said.

"So do I. But Scotty'll find the problem. Turn up anything with your tricorder?"

"Indeed, sir. Most puzzling. There are strong vibrations under the surface, for miles in every direction."

"Subsurface water?"

"I don't believe so. They are quite strong and reasonably regular. Though I have no evidence to support it, I feel that they are artificially produced. I will, of course, continue to investigate."

"Of course. It may tie in with Scotty's trouble. Ensign Mallory, we'll be heading for the village. Go ahead and scout it out. Avoid contact with the humanoids, but get us a complete picture. And be careful. There may be other dangers besides poisonous plants. Keep in constant communicator touch."

"Aye aye, sir."

Spock held up a hand and froze. "Captain," he said, very softly. "I hear something . . ." He swung his tricorder. "Humanoid . . . a few feet away . . . moving with remarkable agility . . . bearing eighteen."

Kirk made a quick, surreptitious gesture to the two remaining security guards, who nodded and disappeared in opposite directions in the brush. Kirk moved cautiously forward along the bearing. But there was nobody there. Puzzled, he turned back.

"What is it?" Chekov said.

"A visitor," Spock said. "One wanting to retain his anonymity, I would say."

Martha Landon, who had been sticking close to Chekov throughout, shivered.

"What's the matter?"

"Oh, nothing, I suppose," the girl said. "But . . . all this beauty . . . and now Mr. Hendorf dead, somebody watching us. It's frightening."

"If you insist on worrying, worry about me," Chekov said. "I've been wanting to get you in a place like this for a long time."

She beamed at him; obviously nothing could make her happier. Kirk said sharply: "Mr. Chekov, Yeoman Landon, I know you find each other fascinating, but we did not come here to carry out a field experiment in human biology. If you please—"

"Of course, Captain," Chekov said, hurriedly breaking out his tricorder. "I was just about to take some readings."

Kirk rejoined Spock and McCoy, shaking his head. "Nothing. Whoever it is, it moves like a cat."

"Jim, I don't like this."

"Neither do I, Bones, but we have an assignment to carry out. All hands. We've been watched, and we'll probably be watched. Move out—formation D—no stragglers."

The start of the maneuver brought Spock to an outcropping of the rainbow-colored rock. He picked up a piece, studied it, and applied slight pressure. The lump broke into two unequal parts.

"Most interesting. Extremely low specific gravity. Some uraninite, hornblende, quartz—but a number of other compounds I cannot immediately identify. An analysis should be interesting."

He tucked the smaller portion into his specimen bag, and tossed the larger piece away. When it hit the ground, there was a small but violent explosion.

Kirk, shaken, looked around, but no one had been

hurt. "You wouldn't mind being a little more careful where you throw rocks, Mr. Spock?"

Spock stared at the outcropping. "Fascinating. Obviously highly unstable. Captain, if indeed this material is as abundant elsewhere as it is here, this is a find of some importance. A considerable source of power."

"Humph. A Garden of Eden—with land mines." His communicator buzzed. "Kirk here. What is it, Scotty?"

"Our antimatter banks are completely inert. I couldn't stop it. But I found out why. There's a transmission of some sort, a beam, from the surface. It affects antimatter like a pail of water on a fire. We're trying to analyze it, but it pinpoints in the area of the village you're approaching, so maybe you could act more effectively from down there."

"We'll try. Kirk out . . . Mr. Spock, could this correlate with the vibrations you detected? A generator of some kind?"

"Possibly. If so, an immense one. And undoubtably subterranean—*Jim!*"

With a shout, Spock leapt forward and knocked Kirk to the ground. When Kirk got back to his feet, more astonished than angry, Spock was staring at a dozen thorns neatly imbedded in his chest. Then the Vulcan slowly crumpled and fell.

"Spock! McCoy, do something!"

McCoy was already there. "Still alive." He dipped into his kit, came up with his air hypo, inserted a cartridge and gave Spock a shot, seemingly all in one smooth motion. Then, after a moment, he looked up at Kirk. "Not responding, Jim. We'll have to get him to the ship."

"And not just him. We're overextended." Kirk took out his communicator. "Scotty? We're beaming back up, all of us. Notify the Transporter Room. And make arrangements to pick up Ensign Mallory; he's scouting ahead of us."

"Aye aye, sir . . . Transporter Room, stand by to beam up landing party . . . Standing by, Captain."

"Energize."

The sparkle of the Transporter effect began around them. The surroundings started to fade out . . . and then wavered, reappeared, faded, reappeared and stabilized.

"Mr. Scott! What's wrong?"

"No Transporter contact, Captain. The entire system seems to be inhibited. The way it is now, we couldna beam up a fly."

"Any connection with the warp drive malfunction?"

"I dinna ken, skipper, but I'll check on it, and get back to you. Scott out."

Kirk started to turn back to McCoy, then halted with astonishment as he saw Spock stirring. The Vulcan sat up weakly, looking distinctly off his normal complexion.

"Spock!"

"I am quite all right, Captain . . . A trifle dizzy . . ."

"Bones?"

"It must be hard to poison that green Vulcan blood. And then there was the shot. I guess he just took a while bouncing back."

"Just what did you think you were doing?" Kirk demanded, helping Spock up.

"I saw that you were unaware of that plant, so I—"

"So you took the thorns yourself!"

"I assure you I had no intention of doing so. My own clumsiness prevented me from moving out of the way."

"I can jump out of the way as well as the next man. Next time you're not to get yourself killed. Do you know how much money Starfleet has invested in you?"

"Certainly. In training, fifteen thousand, eight hundred a year; in pay up to last month—"

"Never mind, Spock. But . . . thanks."

"Jim," McCoy said, "the more I think about this place, the more I get an idea that . . . Well, it's kind of far out, but . . ."

"Go on, Bones."

"Well, when bacteria invade a human body, the

white corpuscles hurry to the invasion point and try to destroy the invader. The mind isn't conscious of it. The body just does it."

"You might be right, Bones. Not only is something after us, but I think it's also after the ship."

Spock shook his head. "To affect the ship at this extreme range, Captain, would require something like a highly sophisticated planetary defense system. It would hardly seem possible—"

He stopped as the group was suddenly enveloped in shadow. They turned as one and stared at the sky. Great towering masses of storm clouds were gathering there. It was impossible; thirty seconds ago the sky had been cloudless. An ominous rumble confirmed that the impossible was indeed happening.

With a deafening clap of thunder, a jagged, blue-white stab of lightning flashed in their midst, tumbling them all like ninepins.

Then the shadow lifted. Kirk got up cautiously. At the spot where the security guard named Kaplan had been standing, there was now only a spot of charred, smoking earth. Helpless, at a loss for words, furious, Kirk stared at it, and then back at the sky as Spock joined him.

"A beautiful day, Mr. Spock," Kirk said bitterly. "Not a cloud in the sky. Just like Paradise."

His communicator beeped. "Mallory here, Captain. I'm near the village. Coordinates one-eighteen by two-twenty. The village is—" Mallory's voice was interrupted by a blast of static.

"What was that, Mallory? I don't read you."

"I'm getting static too. I said it's primitive—strictly tribal from the looks of it. But there's something else—"

Another tearing squeal of static. Mallory's voice stopped. Kirk could not get him back.

"Captain," Spock said, "those coordinates were only a few thousand meters off that way."

"Let's go! On the double!"

They crashed off. As they broke out of the other side of the undergrowth, Kirk saw Mallory running toward them over a field littered with rainbow-colored rocks.

"Over there, Captain," the security guard shouted. "It's—"

He had turned his head as he ran, to point. It was impossible to tell exactly what happened next. Perhaps he stubbed his toe. A rock exploded directly under him.

By the time they reached him, no check by McCoy was needed. His body lay unmoving, bloody, broken.

Kirk, shaken, closed his eyes for a moment. First Hendorf, then Kaplan. He had known Kaplan's family. And Mallory ... Mallory's father had helped Kirk into the Academy ...

Spock took his arm, waving the others off.

"Captain ... in each case, it was unavoidable."

"You're wrong, Spock. I should have beamed us all up the minute things started to go wrong."

"You were under orders. You had no choice."

"I could have saved two men at least. Beamed up. Made further investigations from the ship. Done something! This ... blundering along down here ... cut off from the ship ... the ship's in trouble itself ... unable to help it ..."

"We can help it, Captain. The source of the interference with the ship must be here on the planet. Indeed, this may be the only place the difficulty can be solved."

"And how many more lives will I lose?"

"No one has ever stated Starfleet duty was particularly safe. You have done everything a commander could do. I believe—" He broke off, listening. "Captain ... I think our visitor is back again."

Reluctantly, Kirk turned to Marple, the last of the security guards of the landing party. "Ensign, go ahead fifty yards, swing to your left, cut back, and make a lot of noise. Mr. Spock, Mr. Chekov, make a distraction, a loud one."

He moved quietly away from them toward the brush. Behind him, Chekov's voice rose: "What kind of a tricorder setting do you call that?"

"I will not have you speaking to me in that tone of voice, Ensign!"

"Well, what do you want, violins? That's the stupidest setting I've ever seen—and you a Science Officer!"

Kirk crept stealthily forward.

"It's time you paid more attention to your own duties," Spock's voice shouted uncharacteristically. "Furthermore, you are down here to work, not to hold hands with a pretty yeoman!"

There was somebody, or something, ahead now. Kirk parted the brush. Directly in front of him, his back turned, was a small humanoid, his skin copper red, his hair platinum blond. There seemed to be two tiny silver studs behind his ears. Kirk tensed himself to spring.

At the same time, Marple came crashing toward them from the opposite side. The alien sprang up and ran directly into Kirk's arms. The alien struggled. Measuring him coolly, Kirk struck him squarely on the jaw, and he went down. Clutching his face, he began to cry like a child.

Kirk stood over him, slowly relaxing. Obviously, this creature was no threat. "I'm not going to hurt you," he said. "Do you understand? I won't hurt you."

He spoke, without much hope, in Interstellar. To his surprise, the alien responded in the same tongue, though much slurred and distorted.

"You struck me with your hand."

"I won't strike you again. Here." Kirk extended his hand to help the being up. After a moment, the hand was taken. "You've been following us, watching us. Why?"

"I am the Eyes of Vaal. He must see."

"Who is Vaal?"

"Vaal is Vaal. He is everything."

"You have a name?"

"I am Akuta. I lead the Feeders of Vaal."

The rest of the party began to gather around them. Akuta tried to flinch in all directions at once.

"They won't hurt you either. I promise. Akuta, we

have come here in peace. We would like to speak to your Vaal."

"Akuta alone speaks to Vaal. I am the eyes and the voice of Vaal. It is his wish."

"This is fascinating," Spock said. He stepped forward and put his hands gently to Akuta's head, turning it slightly for a closer look at the two small metal studs. "If you will permit me, sir ... Captain, observe."

"Antennae?" Kirk said.

Akuta had suffered the examination without protest. "They are my ears for Vaal. They were given to me in the dim time, so the people could understand his commands, and obey."

"The people," Kirk said. "Are they nearby?"

"We are close to Vaal, so we may serve him. I shall take you there."

Kirk's communicator shrilled. "Kirk here."

It was Scott: "Captain, something's grabbed us from the planet's surface! Like a giant tractor beam! We can't break loose—we can't even hold our own."

"Warp drive still out?"

"Yes, Captain. All we have is impulse power, and that on maximum. Even with that, we'll only be able to maintain power for sixteen hours. Then we'll burn up for sure."

"Mr. Scott, you are my Chief Engineer. You know everything about that ship there is to know ... more than the men who designed it. If you can't get those warp engines going again—you're fired."

"I'll try everything there is to try, sir. Scott out."

Kirk turned to Akuta. "Tell me about Vaal."

"All the world knows about Vaal. He makes the rains fall, and the sun to shine. All good comes from Vaal."

"Take us to him. We want to speak with him."

"I will take you, but Vaal will not speak with you. He speaks only to me."

"We'll take our chances."

Nodding, Akuta led the way.

Vaal became visible from a clearing some distance away. He was a great serpentlike head, seeming to have been cut out of a cliff. His mouth was open. In color it was greenish bronze, except for its red tongue, which extended from its open mouth. There were steps cut in the tongue, so that a man could walk right up and into the mouth. Two huge fangs extended down, white and polished. Vaal's eyes were open, and they glowed dimly red, pulsating regularly. Even from here, they could hear that the pulsation was timed with a faint but powerful-sounding low-pitched hum.

They drew closer, both Spock and Chekov taking tricorder readings. "Of a high order of workmanship, and very ancient," the First Officer said.

"But this isn't the center, Spock," Kirk said.

"No, Captain. The center is deep beneath it. This would seem to be an access point. In addition there is an energy field extending some thirty feet beyond the head in all directions. Conventional in composition, but most formidable."

"Akuta, how do you talk to Vaal?"

"Vaal calls me. Only then."

Kirk turned to the rest of the party, scowling. "Well, we can't get to it, and we can't talk to it until it's ready to talk."

"Vaal sleeps now," Akuta said. "When he is hungry, you may be able to talk with him—if he desires it."

"When does he get hungry?"

"Soon. Come. We will give you food and drink. If you are tired, you may rest."

He led them down the hill and back into the jungle. It was not very long before they emerged in a tiny village, which looked part Polynesian, part American Indian, part exotic in its own way. There were small thatched huts with hanging batik tapestries, simply made and mostly repeating the totem image of Vaal. At one end of the village area were neatly stacked piles of the explosive rainbow-colored rock. About a dozen aliens were there, men and women, all very handsome, all younger than Akuta. They seemed to be doing nothing at all.

"Akuta," Kirk said, "where are the others?"

"There are no others."

"But . . . where are the children?"

"Children? You speak unknown words to me."

"Little people," Kirk explained. "Like yourselves. But they grow."

"Ah," said Akuta. "Replacements. None are necessary. They are forbidden by Vaal."

"But," said Martha Landon, "when people fall in love—" Chekov was standing next to her, and at these words he smiled and slipped his hand around her waist. She pressed it to her.

"Strange words," said Akuta. "Children . . . love. What is love?"

"Well . . . when a man and a woman are . . . attracted . . ." She did not seem to be able to go any farther. Akuta stared at her and at Chekov's arm.

"Ah. The holding. The touching. Vaal has forbidden this."

"There goes Paradise," said Chekov.

During the questioning, the People of Vaal had been drawing closer and closer, not menacingly, but in simple curiosity. Akuta turned to them.

"These are strangers from another place. They have come among us. Welcome them."

A young man stepped forward, beaming. "Welcome to Vaal."

A girl, beautiful as a goddess, though wearing slightly less, stepped out with a lei of flowers in her hands, smiling warmly. She went to Kirk and put the lei over his head. "Our homes are open to you."

Thus encouraged, the others came over, giggling, touching, exploring, examining the clothing and the gadgets of the strangers. Another young woman put a necklace of shells around Spock's neck.

"It does something for you, Mr. Spock," Kirk said.

"Indeed, Captain. It makes me most uncomfortable."

"I am Sayana," the girl said. "You have a name?"

"I am Spock."

Sayana repeated the name, pointing to him, and so did the rest of the natives, with a wave of laughter.

"I fail to see," Spock said, "what they find so amusing."

"Come," said Akuta. He led the landing party off to one of the huts. The rest of the People of Vaal continued to crowd around, laughing and probing gently.

The interior of the hut was simple, indeed primitive. There were a few baskets, a few wooden vessels, some hangings with the totem image on them, sleeping mats on the floor.

"This house is your house," Akuta said. "I will send food and drink. You are welcome in the place of Vaal."

He went out. Chekov stared after him. "Now we're welcome. A while ago this whole planet was trying to kill us. It doesn't make sense."

"Nothing does down here," McCoy agreed. "I'm going to run a physiological reading on some of those villagers."

He went out after Akuta. Kirk took out his communicator. "Kirk to *Enterprise*. Come in."

"Scott here, sir."

"Status report, Scotty."

"No change, Captain. The orbit is decaying along the computed lines. No success with the warp drive. We're going down and we can't stop it."

"I'm sick of hearing that word 'can't,' Scott," Kirk said harshly. "Get my ship out of there."

"But, sir—we've tried everything within engineering reason—"

"Then use your imagination! Tie every dyne of power the ship has into the impulse engines. Discard the warp drive nacelles if you have to and crack out of there with just the main section—but get out!"

"Well, we could switch over all but the life support circuits and boost the impulse power—black the ship out otherwise—"

"Do it. Kirk out."

McCoy reentered, frowning. "Incredible," he said. "I

ran a complete check on the natives. There's a complete absence of harmful bacteria in their systems. No tissue degeneration, no calcification, no arteriosclerosis. In simple terms, they're not growing old. I can't begin to tell you how old any of them are. Twenty years—or twenty thousand."

"Quite possible," Spock said. "It checks with my atmosphere analysis. The atmosphere completely screens out all dangerous radiation from their sun."

"Add to that a simple diet," Kirk said, "perfectly controlled temperature ... apparently no vices at all ... no natural enemies ... and no 'replacements' needed. Maybe it is Paradise, after all—for them."

Outside, there was a curious vibrating sound, not loud, but penetrating, like the striking of an electronic gong. Kirk went out, beckoning to Spock.

The People of Vaal were no longer lounging around. They were moving off toward the cliff, picking up rocks from the stockpiles as they left. Kirk and Spock followed.

At the cliff, the people entered the mouth of Vaal with the rocks, and came out without them. The red eyes were flashing, brightly now.

"Apparently our hypothesis is correct," Spock said. "There is no living being in there. It is a machine, nothing more."

"The field's down. The people are going in. Let's see what luck we have."

Kirk took a step forward. There was an immediate rumble of thunder, to the considerable alarm of the People of Vaal. Kirk stepped back quickly. "That's not the way."

"Evidently not. It is no ordinary machine, Captain. It has shown a capacity for independent action in its attacks upon us. It may well possess a more than rudimentary intelligence."

"But it needs to eat. It can't have any great power reserves."

"Indeed, Captain. But that does not seem to be of help. The ship now has only ten hours to break free."

"What if Vaal's power weakens as it approaches

feeding time? Mr. Spock, check with the ship; get an estimate of the total energy being expended against it. And measure it every hour."

"With pleasure, Captain." Spock took his communicator out quickly. Deep in thought, Kirk went back to the hut, where he found all of the landing party outside.

"What was it, Jim?"

"Mess call, Bones."

Spock came up behind him. "A perfect example of symbiosis. They provide for Vaal, and Vaal gives them everything they need."

"Which may also answer why there are no children here," Kirk said. "There are exactly enough people to do what Vaal requires."

"In my view," Spock said, "a splendid example of reciprocity."

"It would take a mind like yours to make that kind of statement," McCoy said.

"Gentlemen, your arguments can wait until the ship is out of danger."

"Jim," McCoy said, "you can't just blind yourself to what is happening here. These are humanoids—intelligent! They've got to advance—progress! Don't you understand what my readings indicate? There's been no change here in perhaps thousands of years! This isn't life, it's stagnation!"

"You are becoming emotional, Doctor," Spock said. "This seems to be a perfectly practical society."

"Practical? It's obscene! Humanoids living only so that they can service a hunk of tin!"

"A remarkable hunk of tin, Bones," Kirk said. "And they seem healthy and happy."

"That has nothing to do with it—"

Kirk's communicator cut in. "Kirk here."

"Scott, sir. We've got a reading on the power source as Spock asked. It *is* dropping a bit at a time—nominal, but a definite drain."

Kirk grinned triumphantly at Spock. "Good. Keep monitoring. How are you doing with the circuit switchover?"

"We're putting everything but the kitchen sink into the impulse drive, sir. It'll take another eight hours to complete the work."

"That's cutting it fine, Scotty."

"Aye, sir. But if we don't break out, I'd rather we didn't have to wait long for the end of it."

Kirk took a deep breath. "Right. Carry on, Scotty. Kirk out."

The hours wore away. A large assortment of fruit and vegetables was brought to the landing party by the People. Martha Landon was nervous and on the verge of tears; Kirk sent her out with Chekov for "a breath of air" and whatever reassurance Chekov could give her. Privately, Kirk hoped also that the People would spy on them; the sight of a little open necking might give them a few ideas disruptive to the absolute control Vaal had over them. Of course, that might provoke Vaal to retaliation—but what more could Vaal do than he was doing now?

Spock seemed to read Kirk's intentions with no difficulty. "I am concerned, Captain," he said. "This may not be an ideal society, but it is a viable one. If we are forced to do what it seems we must, in my opinion, we will be in direct violation of the noninterference directive."

"I'm not convinced that this is a viable society in the accepted sense of the word. Bones was right. These people aren't living, they're just existing. It's not a valid culture."

"Starfleet Command may think otherwise."

"That's a risk I'll have to take." He called the *Enterprise*. "How's it coming, Scotty?"

"Almost ready, sir. We'll need a half hour yet."

"You've only got forty-five minutes until you're pulled into the atmosphere."

"I know, sir. As you said, it's cutting things a bit fine."

"I think we're going to be able to help down here. I'll be back in touch shortly." Kirk cut off. "All hands. We're coming up on the next feeding time for Vaal.

Before that happens I want all the Vaalians confined in one hut—the women too, no exceptions. When that gong sounds, round them all up."

The gong in fact sounded only a few minutes later. By this time Chekov and McCoy, phasers drawn, had herded all the People together. They milled around inside the hut, appalled, some wailing and crying.

"Vaal calls us!" Akuta cried out. His face contorted in agony, and he touched the electrodes behind his ears. "We must go to him! He hungers!" The bell rang again. "Please! Let us go to him! We must!"

Kirk got out the communicator again. "Scotty, do you still have phaser power?"

"Aye sir. But what—"

"Lock all banks on the coordinates of the energy field you located down here. On my command, fire and maintain full phasers on those coordinates."

"Aye, sir, but they won't penetrate the field."

"If my guess is right, they won't have to. Stand by."

The bell rang again, louder, longer, more insistently. After checking to see that Chekov and McCoy had the People under control, Kirk and Spock went to the edge of the village. Spock pointed his tricorder toward the cliff.

"Interesting, Captain. The center of the emanations—Vaal—is somewhat weaker than the readings I've been getting. There are wide variations in energy transmission, as though it is drawing from other sources."

"Tapping its energy cells?"

"I would assume so."

"Right. I think the ship's attempts to pull away must have weakened it considerably. It needs to be fed, but the reserve capacity could hold out for days."

"If it has to reinforce its energy field to ward off a phaser attack, it will have to draw more heavily on its reserves."

"My plan exactly, Mr. Spock . . . Kirk to *Enterprise*. Open fire as ordered and maintain."

The phaser beams came down, in long sustained bursts. They were stopped short of the head of Vaal by the force field, but they continued to come down. Sparks flew at the point of contact. A hum rose from Vaal, loud and piercing.

"Tremendous upsurge in generated power, sir. Obviously Vaal is trying to reinforce its energy field."

"Good. Let's see how long it can do it!"

The sky darkened. A strong wind began to blow. Strong flashes of lights lit up Vaal's maw, and some smoke began to appear. The hum was now intolerably loud, and the wind was howling. Lightning flashed overhead, followed by thunder. The din was terrific.

Then, almost all at once, the storm clouds dissipated, the flashes inside Vaal's mouth stopped, and its eyes went out. The hum too was gone.

"Kirk to *Enterprise.* Cease firing."

"No power generation at all," Spock said. "Vaal is dead."

"Mr. Scott, status report."

"Tractor beam gone. Potency returning to antimatter banks. I'll put all engineering sections on repairing the circuits immediately. We'll have the Transporter working in an hour."

Kirk felt as though a great weight had slid off his shoulders. "You're rehired, Mr. Scott. When the Transporter's fixed, form an engineering detail with full analytical equipment and beam them down. I think they'll find some interesting things inside that cave. Kirk out . . . Bones, Chekov. Let them out."

The People emerged, huddled, frightened, still sobbing. McCoy came over to Kirk and Spock.

"Allow me to point out, Captain," Spock said, "that by destroying Vaal, you have also destroyed the People of Vaal."

"Nonsense, Spock!" McCoy said. "It will be the making of these people. Make them stand on their own feet, do things for themselves. They have a right to live like men."

"You mean they have a right to pain, worry, insecurity, tension . . . and eventually death and taxes."

"That's all part of it. Yes! Those too!"

"I hope you will be able to find a way to explain it to them." He nodded toward Akuta, who had moved out of the group toward them, tears streaming down his face.

"Vaal is dead. You have killed him. We cannot live."

"You'll live, Akuta," Kirk said gently. "I'll assign some of my people here to help you."

The girl Sayana was crying quietly. One of the young men, standing by her, obviously wanted to comfort her, but did not know how to start. He made several ineffectual gestures; and then, as if by instinct, his arms went around her waist. She moved closer to him, and her head went onto his shoulder.

"But," Akuta said, "it was Vaal who put the fruit on the trees, who caused the rain to fall. Vaal cared for us."

"You'll find that putting fruit on the trees is a relatively simple matter. Our agronomist will help you with that. As for Vaal taking care of you, you'll have to learn to take care of yourselves. You might even like it.

"Listen to me, all of you. From this day on, you will not depend on Vaal. You are your own masters. You will be able to think what you wish, say what you wish, do what you wish. You will learn many things that are strange, but they will be good. You will discover love; there will be children."

"What are children?" Sayana said.

As the young man's arm tightened around her waist, Kirk grinned. "You just go on the way you're going, and you'll find out."

As Kirk, McCoy and Spock were going toward the bridge, McCoy said: "Spock has an interesting analogy, Captain."

"Yes, Mr. Spock?"

"I am not at all certain that we have done exactly the right thing on Gamma Trianguli VI, Captain."

"We put those people back on a normal course of social evolution. I see nothing wrong with that. It's a good object lesson, Spock, in what can happen when your machines become too efficient, do too much of your work for you. Judging by their language, those people must have been among the very first interstellar colonists—good hardy stock. They tamed the planet, instituted weather control, and turned all jobs of that sort over to a master computer, powered by the plentiful local ore. I suppose the fatal mistake was in giving the computer the power to program itself—and the end product was Vaal . . . Bones said something about an analogy."

"Perhaps you will recall the biblical story of Genesis, sir?"

"I recall it very well, Spock."

"We found a race of people living in Paradise, much as Adam and Eve did. They were obeying every word of Vaal. We taught them, in effect, to disobey that word. In a manner of speaking we have given Adam and Eve the apple . . . the awareness of good and evil, if you will . . . and because of this they have been driven out of Paradise."

Kirk stopped and swung around on Spock suspiciously. "Mr. Spock, you seem to be casting me in the role of Satan. Do I look like Satan?"

"No, sir. But—"

"Is there anyone on this ship who looks even remotely like Satan?"

McCoy was grinning broadly. "I am not aware," Spock said stiffly, "of anyone in that category, Captain."

"No, Mr. Spock. I didn't think you would be."

BY ANY OTHER NAME
(D. C. Fontana and Jerome Bixby)

The landing party answering the distress call consisted of Kirk, Spock, McCoy, the security officer Lt. Shea, and Yeoman Leslie Thompson. At first there seemed to be no source at all on the planet for the call—no wrecked spaceship, no debris. Had the ship been destroyed in space and the survivors proceeded here in a shuttle?

Then two people appeared from the nearby trees, a man and a woman, dressed in outfits rather like Merchant Marine jumpsuits. The woman was lovely, but it was the man who dominated their attention. He looked fortyish, with enormous power in his sturdy frame, great authority and competence in his bearing. Neither of the strangers seemed armed, but Kirk noticed that they wore small unobtrusive boxes on their belts. Their hands rested on the belts near the boxes in an attitude so casually assumed that it seemed to be only a part of their stance, but Kirk was wary.

"I'm Captain James Kirk of the USS *Enterprise*. We came in answer to your distress call."

"It was very kind of you to respond so quickly, Captain. But now you will surrender your ship to me."

Kirk stared. "You have an odd sense of humor."

The strangers touched buttons on the boxes. Instantly, Kirk found himself paralyzed—and so, evidently, was the rest of the "rescue" party.

"I am Rojan, of Kelva," the strange man said. "I am your Commander, from this moment on. Efforts to resist us, or to escape, will be severely punished. Soon we, and you, will leave this galaxy forever. You humans must face the end of your existence as you have known it."

The woman moved forward to relieve the people of the *Enterprise* of their phasers and communicators. Rojan went on: "You are paralyzed by a selective field that neutralizes impulses to the voluntary muscles. I will now release you all, Captain Kirk."

He touched the belt device. Kirk tensed to jump him, then thought better of it. "A neural field?"

"Radiated from a central projector, directed at whomever we wish."

"What do you want?"

"Your ship, Captain. We have monitored many. The *Enterprise*—a starship—is the best of its kind in your galaxy. It will serve us well in the long voyage that is to come."

"Voyage to where?"

"To your neighboring galaxy, in the constellation you call Andromeda."

"*Why?*"

"The Andromeda galaxy is our home," Rojan said in a remote voice.

"What brought you here?" Spock said.

"Within ten millennia, high radiation levels will make life in our galaxy impossible; it is reaching the stage in its evolution which will make it what you call a quasar. The Kelvan Empire sent forth ships to explore other galaxies—to search for one which our race could conquer and colonize."

"Sorry," Kirk said. "This galaxy is occupied."

"Captain, you think you are unconquerable—your ship impregnable. While we have talked, three of my people have boarded it, and the capture has begun." He took one of the confiscated communicators from the Kelvan woman and clicked it open. "Subcommander Hanar, report."

"This ship is ours," a strange voice said from the communicator. "We control the bridge, engineering and life support."

Rojan folded the communicator shut, and stowed it on his own belt.

"What good is capturing my ship?" Kirk said. "Even at maximum warp, the *Enterprise* couldn't get to the Andromeda galaxy for thousands of years. It's two million light-years away!"

"We will modify its engines to produce velocities far beyond the reach of your science. The journey between galaxies will take less than three hundred of your years."

"Fascinating," Spock said, "Intergalactic travel requiring 'only' three hundred years is a leap beyond anything man has yet accomplished."

Yeoman Thompson asked the Kelvan woman: "Did you make a voyage of three hundred years?"

"Our ships were of multigeneration design," the woman said. "I was born in the intergalactic void. I shall die there, during the return journey."

"Our mission," Rojan added, "will be completed by a Captain who will be my descendant."

"What happened to your ship?" Kirk said.

"There is an energy barrier at the rim of your galaxy—"

"I know. We've been there."

"We broke through it with great difficulty. Our ship was destroyed. We barely escaped in a life craft. Our time here has been spent scanning your systems, studying you. And now we have the means to begin our journey again."

"Why use our vessel?" Spock said. "Why not transmit a message back to your galaxy?"

"No form of transmission can penetrate the barrier."

"Rojan," Kirk said, "we could take your problem to our Federation. Research expeditions have catalogued hundreds of uninhabited planets in this galaxy. Surely some of them would be suitable for your colonization."

"We do not colonize, Captain," Rojan said sharply. "We conquer. We rule. There is no other way for us."

"In other words," McCoy said, 'this galaxy isn't big enough for both of us'?"

"What will happen to the intelligent races here?" Kirk said.

"They will not be mistreated. Merely subordinated." Rojan shrugged. "The fate of the inferior . . . in any galaxy. Ah, Hanar!"

While he had been speaking, another Kelvan had popped into being beside him, a younger man, with a hard intelligent face. There was no shimmer or any other such effect comparable to the workings of the Transporter; he just appeared.

"Tomar has examined the ship," Hanar said. "The modifications are under way."

"Space again!" said Rojan. "I don't think we could have kept our sanity, living so long on this accursed planet."

It did not seem to be so accursed to Kirk; in fact it was quite a pleasant, Earthlike place. But Hanar said: "It is an undisciplined environment; one cannot control it. Yet there are things of interest."

"Yes. But—disturbing. These ugly shells in which we have encased ourselves . . . they have such heightened senses. How do humans manage to exist in such fragile casings?"

They did not seem to care at all whether they were overheard, an obvious expression of supreme confidence. Kirk listened intently to every word; he had known such self-confidence to be misplaced before.

"Since the ship is designed to sustain this form," Hanar said, "we have little choice."

Rojan turned to the woman. "Kelinda, take them to the holding area. We will be keeping you and your party here, Captain. Your crew will undoubtedly prefer to cooperate with us if they understand you are hostages."

"Move that way," said Kelinda. "Keep together."

Their jail proved to be a cave, with a door constructed of some odd-looking transparent material, which Spock and Kirk were examining. Shea was also at the door, looking out, ostensibly watching Kelinda.

"I'm unable to determine the nature of the material, Captain," Spock said. "But I do not believe even phaser fire could disturb its molecular structure."

"All right, we can't break out. Maybe we can find another way."

"Captain," said Yeoman Thompson, "what do they want from us? What kind of people are they?"

"A good question, Yeoman."

"They registered as human," McCoy said.

"No, more than that, Doctor," Spock said, frowning. "They registered as *perfect* human life forms. I recall noting that the readings were almost textbook responses. Most curious."

"Spock," Kirk said, "what are the odds on such a parallel in life forms in another galaxy?"

"Based on those we have encountered in our own galaxy, the probability of humanoid development is high. But I would say the chances were very much against such an absolute duplication."

Shea turned slightly from the door. "Well, however perfect they are, sir, there don't seem to be very many of them."

"But they've got the paralysis field," Kirk said. "Rojan mentioned a central projector."

"If we can put it out of operation," McCoy said, "we've got a chance!"

"I am constrained to point out," said Spock, "that we do not even know what this projector looks like."

"No," Kirk said, "but those devices on their belts might indicate the position of the source."

"I would like to have one to examine."

"You'll have one, sir," Shea said. "If I have to rip one of the Kelvans apart to get it for you."

"Lieutenant Shea," Kirk said firmly, "you'll have your chance—but I'll tell you when."

"Yes, sir."

Kirk eyed him narrowly; but he could understand

the younger officer's defiant attitude toward their captors. "Spock, do you remember how you tricked that guard on Eminiar? The empathic mind touching—"

"Quite well, Captain. I made him think we had escaped."

"Can you do it again?"

"I will attempt it."

He checked Kelinda, who was standing fairly close to the bars, and then put his hands on the cave wall approximately behind her. Then he began to concentrate.

At first the Kelvan woman did not respond. Then she twitched a little, nervously, as though aware that something was wrong, but unable to imagine what. She glanced around, then straightened again.

Kirk signaled his people to position themselves along the wall, so that from outside the cave would appear to be empty. Then he bent and scooped some dirt from the loose, sandy floor.

Suddenly Spock broke out of his intense concentration, as though wrenched from it by something beyond him. He gasped and staggered back against the wall. At the same moment, Kelinda came to the door, opened it quickly and started in.

Kirk hurled his handful of dirt into her face. She cried out and clawed at her eyes. While she was half blinded, Kirk delivered a karate chop. It sent her sprawling, and, surprisingly, out. Kirk and McCoy dragged her the rest of the way inside.

"Mr. Spock—?"

"I . . . will be . . . quite all right, Captain. We must hurry."

"Bones, keep an eye on him. Let's go." He took the belt device from Kelinda and led the way out. He had hardly taken two steps before he was paralyzed again, the device dropping from his limp hands.

"I am sorry, Captain," said Rojan's voice. He came into view with Hanar, who went into the cave. "The escape attempt was futile. You cannot stop us and you cannot escape us."

Hanar reappeared. "Kelinda is somewhat bruised, Rojan, but otherwise unhurt."

Rojan nodded, and turning back to Kirk, released the party from the freeze. "I cannot let this go unpunished. This will serve as an example." He pointed to Yeoman Thompson and security chief Shea. "Hanar, take these two aside."

"What are you going to do?" McCoy said.

"This is not your affair, Doctor. Captain, as a leader, you realize the importance of discipline. I need you and these other specialists. But those two are unnecessary to me."

"You can't just kill them!" Kirk said.

Rojan did not respond. Thompson turned, looking pleadingly at Kirk. "Captain . . ."

"Rojan, let them go. I'm responsible for them."

"I think we are somewhat alike, Captain. Each of us cares less for his own safety than for the lives of his command. We feel pain when others suffer for our mistakes. Your punishment shall be to watch your people die."

Rojan touched his belt device. Shea and the girl seemed to vanish instantly. Where each of them had been standing was an odd geometrically shaped block, about the size of a fist.

Hanar picked them up and brought them to Rojan, who held them up to Kirk. "This is the essence of what those people were . . . The flesh and brain, and also what you call the personality, distilled down to these compact shapes. Once crushed—" He closed his hand over one, crushing it in his grip, letting the fragments sift through his fingers. "—they are no more. This person is dead. However—" He flipped the second block away. It bounced to a halt on the grass. Rojan again touched a button, and Shea was standing there, bewildered. "—this person can be restored. As I said, Captain—very practical."

They were herded back into the cave, leaving behind the fragments which were all that were left of a pretty girl.

Shocked and dispirited, they all sat down on the

cave floor but Shea. Spock's manner seemed more than usually distant.

"Mr. Spock," Kirk said, "are you sure you're all right?"

"Yes, quite all right, Captain."

McCoy said, "You looked very sick a while back, when you broke the mind lock."

"I did not break it," Spock said slowly. "I was . . . shoved away by . . . something I have never experienced before."

"What was it?" said Kirk.

"Images . . . bursting in my mind and consciousness. Colors . . . shapes . . . mathematical equations . . . fused and blurred. I have been attempting to isolate them. So far, I have been able to recall clearly only one. Immense beings . . . a hundred limbs that resemble tentacles, but are not . . . minds of such control and capacity that each limb could do a different job."

"You mean," McCoy said, "that's what the Kelvans really are?"

"I do not know. It seemed the central image, but whether it was a source or a memory, I cannot tell."

"If they do normally look like that," Kirk said, "why did they adapt to bodies like ours?"

"For the sake of deception, what else?" McCoy said.

Kirk remembered the conversation they had overheard. "No, practicality. They chose the *Enterprise* as the best kind of vessel for the trip, and they need us to run her. We have to stay in our gravity and atmosphere, and they had to adapt to it . . . We *have* to find a way to beat them. We outnumber them. Their only hold on us is the paralysis field."

"That's enough," said McCoy. "One wrong move and they jam all our neural circuits."

"Jamming," said Kirk. "That's it. Tricorders could analyze the frequency of the paralysis field. Spock, if you reverse the circuits on McCoy's neuroanalyzer, would it serve as a counterfield to jam the paralysis projector?"

"I am dubious about the possibility of success, Captain. The medical equipment is not built to put out any great amount of power. It would probably burn out."

"Is there any chance at all?"

"A small one."

"We'll take it. You and Bones have to get up to the ship."

"How?" said McCoy.

Kirk looked at his First Officer. "Spock, you're sick."

Spock's eyebrows went up. "Captain, I assure you that I am in excellent health."

"No, you're not. Dr. McCoy has examined you, and you're seriously ill. In fact, if he doesn't get you up to Sickbay you may die. And Rojan won't let that happen because he needs you to get through the barrier."

"It's a good idea," McCoy said, "but anybody looking at him can tell he's healthy."

"Vulcans have the ability to put themselves into a kind of trance . . . an enforced relaxation of every part of the mind and body. Right, Mr. Spock?"

"We find it more useful for resting the body than the so-called vacation."

"Can you do it now, and come out of it when you're in Sickbay? Say in half an hour?"

"It will take me a moment to prepare."

Shea walked to where he could watch for guards, then turned to nod and wave an all clear. Spock, remaining seated, composed himself very carefully. He seemed to be directing his attention inward upon himself. Then, almost as if someone had snapped off his switch, he flopped limply to one side.

McCoy rose to examine him, and at once looked a little alarmed. "Jim, his heartbeat really is way down—respiration almost nonexistent—"

Kirk turned to the door quickly and shouted "Guard! Guard!"

Hanar appeared. "What do you want, human?"

"Mr. Spock is ill. The doctor thinks he's dying."

"This illness came on him very suddenly," Hanar said. "Is it not unusual?"

"He's a Vulcan. They don't react like humans."

"Look, he may die," McCoy said as Hanar hesitated. "If I can get him up to Sickbay, there's a chance I can save him."

"Stand away from the door."

The others pulled away. Hanar came in, hand on his belt device, and bent to study the motionless Science Officer. He frowned. "I will have you beamed aboard. but you will be met by Tomar and watched."

As Hanar turned away, opening a communicator, Kirk and McCoy glanced toward each other.

"Do the best you can with him, Bones," Kirk said. McCoy nodded quickly, significantly.

The Kelvan Tomar and McCoy entered the *Enterprise*'s examination room, supporting the limp Spock between them. Nurse Christine Chapel followed. "Doctor, what happened?"

McCoy ignored her. He said to Tomar, "Here. Put him down."

They eased Spock onto the table. Tomar peered curiously at the Vulcan, who was breathing only shallowly, and with alarmingly long pauses between breaths.

"Shall I summon more of your underlings?"

"I'll call my own underlings," McCoy said snappishly. "You stay out of the way. Miss Chapel, prepare two cc's of stokaline."

"Stokaline? But, Doctor—"

"Don't argue with me, Nurse. Get it."

Christine turned and went to get the required air hypo. McCoy activated the body function panel over the table and began to take readings, which were obviously low. Tomar hesitated, then moved away to where he could watch from a discreet distance.

Christine came back with the hypo, and at McCoy's nod, administered it, looking at her chief in puzzlement. There was no response from Spock for a moment. Then his eyes snapped open. McCoy shook his head very slightly and the eyes closed again. Over their heads, the readings began to pick up, some of them quickening, others returning to their Vulcan norms, which were almost surely strange to Tomar.

"This may be the turning point, Nurse. Prepare another shot."

"Doctor—"

"Miss Chapel, please follow orders."

She did so, though McCoy was well aware of her mounting puzzlement. He continued to study the panel. Finally he nodded. "That does it. He'll be all right now. Let him rest." He turned to Tomar. "It was a flare-up of Rigelian Kassaba fever. He suffered from it ten years ago, and it recurs now and then. There's no danger if he receives medication in time. He'll be up again in an hour or so."

"Very well. I will inform Rojan. You will stay here."

The Kelvan went out and McCoy went back to the table, grinning at Spock, who was now propped up on his elbows.

"I said I would awaken myself, Doctor. What was that shot you gave me?"

"It wasn't *a* shot. It was two."

"I am not interested in quantity, but in content."

"It was stokaline."

"I am not familiar with that drug. Are there any after effects?"

"Yes. You'll feel much better."

"It's a multiple vitamin compound," Christine said, beginning to look less confused.

McCoy patted Spock's shoulder. "Stop worrying. It'll put a little green in your cheeks. Let's get at the neuroanalyzer."

Spock grimaced and rolled off the table to his feet. "It would be helpful to have Mr. Scott here."

"Agreed. Miss Chapel, it is time for Mr. Scott's medical exam."

"I'll see that he reports immediately," Christine said demurely.

Hanar summoned Kirk out of the cave and brought him to Rojan, who was lounging comfortably by a lakeside, with Kelinda close by. Rojan waved Hanar away. "Proceed to the ship, Hanar. Rest yourself, Captain."

"What do you want with me now, Rojan?" Kirk said angrily.

"We will beam aboard the vessel shortly. I wish you to understand your duties."

"My duty is to stop you in any way I can."

"You will obey."

"Or you'll kill more of my people?"

"Captain, I cannot believe that you do not understand the importance of my mission," Rojan said slowly, as if trying to explain to an equal. "We Kelvans have a code of honor—harsh, demanding. It calls for much from us, and much from those we conquer. You have been conquered. I respect your devotion to your duty. But I cannot permit it to interfere with mine."

Kirk remained silent, thinking. It was impossible not to be impressed by what seemed to be so much straightforward honesty. It was apparent that that "code" was what Rojan lived by, and that he believed in it unshakably.

It was also impossible to forget the crumbled shards of what had been Yeoman Leslie Thompson, scattered in the grass not far from here.

Kelinda had moved away to a nearby burst of flowers. Rojan watched her, but not, Kirk thought, with any sign of ordinary male interest.

"I hunger to be in space again, Rojan," she said. "But these—these are lovely. Captain Kirk, what is it you call them?"

"Flowers," he said, moving closer to her, cautiously. "I don't know the variety."

"Our memory tapes tell us of such things on Kelva," Rojan said. "Crystals which form with such rapidity that they seem to grow. They look like these fragile things, somewhat. We call them 'sahsheer.' "

"The rose," Kirk said, "by any other name . . ."

"Captain?" Rojan said.

"A quotation, from a great human poet, Shakespeare. 'That which we call a rose by any other name would smell as sweet.' "

Kelinda bent to smell the flowers, while Kirk studied her. Did this woman in reality have a hundred tentacles, all adapted to different uses? It was hard to imagine.

"Kelinda, Captain, come away," Rojan said. "We must leave now."

Directly they were beamed up, Rojan directed Kirk to take him and Kelinda to the bridge. There, Uhura was at her station, and Chekov at his, but a Kelvan woman was in the Helmsman's seat, and Hanar was standing nearby.

"Drea has computed and laid a course for Kelva, Rojan," Hanar said.

"Sir," said Chekov, "we've jumped to warp eight."

"And we'll go faster yet," Rojan said. "Increase speed to warp eleven."

Chekov looked around sharply at Kirk, who could only shrug his helplessness and nod.

"On course and proceeding as planned," said the Kelvan woman at the helm, who was evidently Drea.

"Very well," said Rojan. "Hanar, proceed with the neutralizing operation."

Hanar nodded and went to the elevator. Kirk said quickly: "What neutralizing operation?"

"You humans are troublesome for us, Captain. There are not enough of us to effectively guard all of you all the time. Further, the food synthesizers cannot continue to manufacture food for all of you for our entire journey. We are therefore neutralizing all nonessential personnel."

"No!"

"Captain, you can do nothing to stop it. The procedure is already under way. Now, as to bridge personnel . . ." He moved toward Uhura. "We have no need of communications for some centuries."

Uhura sat frozen in her chair, staring at Rojan in horror. He touched his belt device—and there was nothing left in her seat but a geometrical solid.

"And since Drea is now capable of doing our navigating—" Chekov too vanished. Drea had already neutralized two crewmen beyond Scott's station. Kirk stood frozen.

"They are not dead, Captain," Rojan reminded him. "They are merely reduced to the sum total of what they are."

"That's very comforting," Kirk said sarcastically. "But not pleasant to watch. I'm going to Sickbay. My First Officer was taken ill."

"Yes, I was informed. Go ahead."

Sickbay was deserted. Kirk found Scott, McCoy and Spock picking at food at a table in the recreation room. Getting himself a tray, he joined them. "Reports, gentlemen?"

"I'm a little sick," McCoy said. "We burned out my neuroanalyzer, to no effect. I saw one of the Kelvans, the one they call Tomar, reduce four of my doctors and nurses to those . . . little blocks."

"I've seen them do that too. Remember, the process is reversible. I only wonder how far it's going to go."

"I have been checking our table of organization against their apparent capabilities," Spock said. "It appears that we will have very few 'survivors.' They will need none of the security men, for example. And once we cross the energy barrier, Engineering can be reduced to a skeleton crew. Beyond that point lies some three hundred years of straight cruising—at an astonishing velocity, to be sure, but still cruising. And of the officers, it would seem that only we four could be regarded as 'essential.' I am not even sure of your status, Captain, or mine."

"How so?"

"Rojan is in command now."

"Quite so," Kirk said bitterly. "Scotty, have you found out anything about the paralysis projector?"

"Quite a lot, and none of it good. The machine is in Engineering, and it's encased in that same stuff the door of our jail was made of. Furthermore, it's nae a simple machine—and it's the only one of its kind on board. I think it must be the source of all their special powers—and it's impregnable."

"Any suggestions?"

"One," Scott said. "Self-destruct."

Kirk considered it. "We've been driven to that point, or almost, once before," he said at last. "But aside from my aversion to suicide—and the deaths of everybody else—it's not practicable. We'd never complete the routine with the computer before Rojan paralyzed us."

"I thought of that," Scott said. "I could do it myself, though. Remember that we've got to cross the energy barrier. It willna be easy at best. A little sabotage in the matter-antimatter nacelles, and we'd blow, for good and all."

Kirk made a quick silencing gesture. Tomar had come in, and was now approaching them, staring curiously at their trays.

"I do not understand," he said, "why you go to the trouble of consuming this bulk material to sustain yourselves." He pulled a flat pillbox from a pocket and opened it. "These contain all the required nutritional elements."

"Not for human forms," McCoy said. "Bulk is necessary to our digestive systems, and there's a limit to the amount of energy that can be crammed into a pill, too. Perhaps you haven't been in human form long enough to find just pills debilitating, but you will—you will."

"Indeed? Then you had better show me promptly what else we shall need, and how to manage it."

McCoy looked rebellious and Kirk himself felt a hope die almost before it had been born. "I think you'd better, Bones," he said.

"All right. Come on, I'll show you how to work the selector." McCoy led Tomar off toward the wall dispenser.

"Spock," Kirk said in a whisper, "shall we self-destruct? Crossing the barrier may be our last chance to do so."

"Granted," Spock whispered back. "But it is said on Earth that while there is life, there is hope. That is sound logic: no multivalued problem has only one solution."

"Well, we couldn't knock out their central machine even if we were able. It has to be kept intact to restore the rest of our people to human form."

There was quite a long silence. McCoy had settled Tomar at a table with a tray, and Tomar was gingerly forking some meat into his mouth. Judging by his nod, he found it agreeable, and he began eating at a fair speed for a newcomer to the habit. McCoy grinned and rejoined his colleagues.

"I'm almost sorry I did that," he said. "It looks like he likes food—and I wouldn't want any of them to enjoy anything."

Spock continued to watch Tomar. "Most peculiar."

"What is?" Kirk said.

"The isolated glimpses of things I saw when I touched Kelinda's mind are beginning to coalesce in my consciousness. The Kelvans have superior intellectual capacity. But to gain it, they apparently sacrificed many things that would tend to distract them. Among these are the pleasures of the senses—and, of course, emotions."

"But then, Tomar shouldn't be enjoying the taste of food."

"He has taken human form," Spock said, "and is having human reactions."

Kirk's mind leapt ahead in response. "If they all respond to stimulation of the senses, maybe we could confuse them. They don't know how to handle those senses yet. If we can distract them enough, we could try to get the belt devices away. That's their only hold on us."

"It seems reasonable," Spock said.

"All right. We watch for opportunities to work on them—hit them every way we can think of."

Scott was studying Tomar. "I can think of one way right off," he said. He rose and went to the Kelvan. "Lad, you'll be needing something to wash that down with. Have you ever tried Saurian brandy?"

McCoy stopped Hanar as the Kelvan was passing by the door to the examination room. "Come on in a moment, please, Hanar."

"What is it, human?"

"I've noticed you're not looking too well."

"Impossible. We do not malfunction, as do you humans."

"No? You're forgetting you're in a human body. And that does malfunction—that's why Rojan considers me essential. You look pale." He gestured to the table. "Sit up there."

When Hanar complied, McCoy picked up his medical tricorder and began taking readings. "Uh huh . . . Hmmm . . . I don't know about that . . . Hmmmm."

"Please articulate, human."

"Well, it looks to me like this body of yours is getting a little anemic, and has some other subclinical deficiencies. Comes from taking your food in pills, instead of good solid substance." He turned aside and picked up a hypo, which he set.

"What are you doing?"

"I'm going to give you a shot—high potency vitamin-mineral concentrate. You'll have to have one three times a day for a few days. And eat some solid food."

It had taken Scott a while to get Tomar down to serious drinking; initially he had been too interested in the tartan, the claymore, the armorial bearings on the walls, the standing suit of ancient armor in Scott's quarters, all of which he declared nonfunctional in a starship. He did not seem to grasp either the concept of mementos or that of decoration.

Finally, however, they were seated at Scott's desk with a bottle and glasses between them. After a while, it was two bottles. Tomar seemed to remain in total control of himself, as if he'd been drinking lemonade. "No more?" he said.

"Well . . . no more Saurian brandy, but . . ." Scott looked around and found another bottle. "Now, y'see, this liquor is famous on Ahbloron—I mean, Aldibibble—on one of these planets we go to."

"It is a different color from the other."

"Yes. And stronger, too." He poured some into Tomar's glass with an unsteady hand, and then, perforce, some into his own. Somehow this experiment was not working out right.

Kirk paid a call on the cabin Kelinda had commandeered. When she invited him in, he found her looking at a tape on a viewscreen. "Did I disturb you?"

"Disturb? What is it you wish?"

He went over to her. "I want to apologize."

"I do not understand, Captain."

"For hitting you. I wanted to say I was sorry."

"That is not necessary. You attempted to escape, as we would have. That I was taken in by your ruse is my fault, not yours."

Kirk smiled and reached out to touch her face gently. "I don't usually hit beautiful women."

"Why not, if there is need?"

"Because there are better things for men and women to do." He moved the hand down to her neck. "Was it here that I hit you?"

"No, on the other side."

"Oh." He leaned to the other side, kissed her neck, and nuzzled her ear. "Is that better?"

"Better? Was it intended to be a remedy?"

"This is." Drawing her to her feet, he took her in his arms and kissed her.

After a moment she drew back. "Is there some significance to this action?"

"It was meant to express . . . well, among humans it shows warmth, love—"

"Oh. You are trying to seduce me," she said, as if she were reading a weather report. "I have been reading about you."

"Me?"

"Humans. This business of love. You have devoted much literature to it. Why have you built such a mystique around a simple biological fact?"

"We enjoy it."

"The literature?"

"Kelinda, I'm sorry I brought the subject up."

"Did you regard this contact of the lips as pleasurable?"

Kirk sighed. "I did."

"Curious. I wonder why." Abruptly she put her arms around him and kissed him back.

The door opened and Rojan came in. Kirk made a point of drawing back with guilty swiftness.

"Is there some problem, Captain?" Rojan said.

"None." Kirk left quickly. Rojan stared after him.

"What did he want here?"

"He came to apologize for hitting me," Kelinda said. "Apparently, it involves some peculiar touching contacts."

"In what manner?"

Kelinda hesitated, then reached up to nibble at Rojan's neck and ear. Rojan stepped away from her, frowning.

"They are odd creatures, these humans. Please have the reports on fuel consumption relayed to Subcommander Hanar as soon as possible."

Spock had taught Rojan to play chess; the Kelvan had learned with breathtaking speed. They were playing now, in the recreation room.

"Yes, they are peculiar," Spock said, moving a piece. "I very often find them unfathomable, but an interesting psychological study."

Rojan moved in return. "I do not understand this business of biting someone's neck to apologize."

Spock looked up, raising his eyebrows. Then he looked back at the game, saw an opening and quickly moved another piece. "I believe you are referring to a kiss. But it is my understanding that such, uh, apologies are usually exchanged between two people who have some affection for each other."

"Kelinda has no affection for Captain Kirk," Rojan said quickly.

Spock studied Rojan's next move and shook his

head. "You seemed disturbed about the incident. Your game is off."

"Why should I be disturbed?"

"It seems to me you have known Kelinda for some time. She is a Kelvan, as you are. Among humans, I have found the symptoms you are displaying would be indicative of jealousy."

"I have no reason for such a reaction. Kelinda is a female. Nothing more."

"Captain Kirk seems to find her quite attractive."

"Of course she is."

"But you are not jealous."

"No!"

"Nor upset."

"Certainly not!"

Spock made his move. "Checkmate."

Kirk, Spock and McCoy were holding another council of war in the recreation room. Kirk was depressed. "The thing is, I can't tell if we're getting anywhere. And I haven't seen Scotty for what seems like months."

"You haven't seen Tomar either," McCoy said. "But the point is, these things take time. The Kelvans started out with adapted human bodies in superb physical shape—textbook cases, as Spock said. They have high resistance. I've been giving Hanar shots that would have driven our whole crew up the wall in an hour. He responds slowly—but he's getting more irritable by the minute, now."

"And Rojan," Spock said, "has exhibited symptoms of jealousy toward Kelinda and you."

"What about Kelinda, Jim?" McCoy said.

"No progress," Kirk said, uncomfortably.

"What approach did you take with her? Could be you're a little rusty—"

Kirk felt himself begin to bristle. Spock interposed smoothly: "I would say it is sufficient that Rojan is jealous."

"Right," Kirk said quickly. "That's the opening wedge. As soon as it's a little wider, we move."

Behind Kirk, Kelinda's voice said: "I would like to speak with you, Captain."

Spock stood up at once. "Doctor, I think I need another dose of stokaline."

"Huh?" McCoy said. "Oh, yes. Pardon us."

They went out. Kirk leaned back in his chair and studied Kelinda. "You had something to say?"

"Yes." Did she really seem a trifle uncomfortable, even perhaps awkward? Kirk waited. Then she took a deep breath and touched him, lightly, on a shoulder. "This cultural mystique surrounding a biological function . . ."

"Yes?"

"You realize it really is quite overdone."

"Oh. Quite."

"However, I was wondering . . . would you please apologize to me again?"

Rojan was in the command chair. Behind him, the elevator doors snapped open, and then Hanar's voice said, with surprising belligerence: "Rojan. I want to talk to you."

Rojan looked up in surprise. "Very well, Hanar."

"First, I do not like the way responsibility and duty have been portioned out to us."

"It is the way your duties have always been assigned."

"And that is my second quarrel with you. It was always unjust—"

Rojan snapped out of the chair. "Hanar—"

"And further, I do not care much for the autocratic way you order us about on this ship, which we captured, not you—"

"Confine yourself to your quarters!"

Hanar hesitated, as though he had had a lot more to say, but had thought better of it. Then he spun on his heel and left without further acknowledgment.

Rojan found his own fists clenching in anger—and was suddenly aware that Drea was watching him in amazement from the navigator's station. As Rojan turned his back to hide his expression, Spock came onto the bridge and went toward his library-computer. Rojan followed.

"You were not called to the bridge, Spock. What is your purpose here?"

"Sensors and various other recording devices require monitoring and certain adjustments."

"Very well, proceed . . . Have you seen Captain Kirk?"

"Do you want him? I will call him to the bridge."

"No. I . . . wondered where he was."

"Dr. McCoy and I left him some time ago in the recreation room."

"He was alone, then?"

"No. Kelinda was with him. She seemed most anxious to speak to him."

"I told him to stay away from her."

"It would appear that you have little control over her, sir . . . or perhaps Captain Kirk has more."

Rojan turned abruptly and headed for the elevator.

Kirk and Kelinda were locked in a kiss when Rojan came through the recreation room door. Kirk looked up, but did not release Kelinda entirely; instead he kept a possessive arm around her as he turned toward Rojan. Rojan stopped and stared.

"Kelinda, I told you to avoid this human!"

"I did not wish to," she said.

"I am your commander."

"I've found," Kirk said, "that doesn't mean much to a woman if she's bound to go her own way."

"You have done this to her! Corrupted her—turned her away from me!"

"If you couldn't keep her, Rojan, that's not *my* problem."

Furiously, Rojan leaped at Kirk. He seemed to have forgotten all about the belt device, his bare hands reaching out. Kirk pushed Kelinda aside and met Rojan's rush.

The two men, equally powerful, slammed at each other like bulls. Rojan was more clumsy, more unaccustomed to the body he was in. Kirk was the quicker and the more adept fighter, but he was not possessed by the anger which obviously drove Rojan.

Kelinda did not intervene; she only watched. After a moment she was joined by Spock and McCoy.

Kirk delivered a final punch that sent Rojan spinning down, backward. But he was not beaten yet. He started to climb back to his feet.

"Rojan—wait!" Kirk said. "Listen to me—"

Rojan flung himself forward, but Kirk fended him off. "Listen! Why didn't you use your paralyzer? Don't you know why? Because you've become a human yourself." Kirk ducked a punch. "Look at you—brawling like a street fighter—shaking with rage—"

Rojan paused and stared as the words began to sink in. "What?"

"You thought I took your woman away from you. You were jealous—and you wanted to kill me with your bare hands. Would a Kelvan have done that? Would he *have* to? You reacted with the emotions of a human, Rojan. You are one."

"No! We cannot be."

"You have no choice. You chose this ship. Because of its environmental systems, you had to take human form to use it. And you're stuck with it—you and your descendants—for the next three hundred years. Look what's happened to you in the short time you've been exposed to us. What do you think will happen in three hundred years? When this ship gets to Kelva, the people on it will be aliens, the Kelvans their enemies.

"We have a mission. We must carry it out." But Rojan's tone showed that he was shaken.

"Your mission was to find worlds for your people to live on. You can still do that. I told you we could present your case to the Federation. I know it would be sympathetic. There are many unpopulated planets in our galaxy. You could develop them in peace, your way."

"They would do that? You would extend welcome to invaders?"

"No. But we do welcome friends."

"Perhaps," said Rojan, "perhaps it could be done."

Spock said: "A robot ship could be sent back to Kelva with the Federation proposal."

"But what of us?" Rojan said. "If we . . . if we retain this form, where can we find a place?"

"Seems to me," McCoy said, "that little planet you were on was kind of a nice place."

"Pleasant . . . but . . ."

"The Federation would probably grant a colonization permit to a small group of people who desired to settle there," Spock said. "You do represent an old and highly intelligent race."

Rojan turned to Kelinda and jerked his head at Kirk. "You would want to go with him?"

Kelinda glanced at Kirk and then back at Rojan. "As you have said, he is not our kind. I believe I owe you an apology." She kissed him. "It *is* pleasurable, Rojan."

"You know, Rojan," Kirk said, "one of the advantages of being a human is being able to appreciate beauty . . . of a flower, or of a woman. Unless you'd rather conquer a galaxy?"

"No, Captain, I would rather not." Rojan took Kelinda's hand. "A link in a chain—that's all we were. Perhaps there is an opportunity for us to be more." He turned away, crossed the room and activated an intercom. "Bridge, this is Rojan."

"Yes, Commander," said Drea's voice.

"Turn the ship. We are returning to the alien . . . We are returning home."

"Sir?"

"Turn the ship about."

He led Kelinda out. Kirk, Spock and McCoy expelled simultaneous sighs of relief.

"Jim, I was coming to tell you—"

"Yes, Bones?"

"I found Scotty in his room with Tomar. Apparently they've been having a drinking bout all this time. They were both under the table—but Tomar went down first. Scott had Tomar's belt device in his hand. He just never made it to the door with it."

Kirk grinned. "The Kelvans," he said, "still have a lot to learn about being human, don't they?"

THE CLOUD MINDERS

(Margaret Armen, David Gerrold and Oliver Crawford)

"Then there's been a mistake," Kirk said.

And he couldn't afford one, not on this mission. During a routine check of the *Enterprise's* operational quadrant of the galaxy, they had been ordered by the Federation to make top warp speed to the planet Ardana, sole source of a trace metal able to arrest a botanical plague ravaging vegetation which made a neighboring planet habitable. It was a mission whose emergency nature was known to the High Advisor of Ardana. Yet his greeting to the *Enterprise* had contained no reference to the zenite mines. Instead, his welcome specified Stratos as the reception site.

"Stratos is their Cloud City, isn't it, Mr. Spock?"

"It is, Captain."

Kirk hit the intercom to the Transporter Room. "Mr. Scott, are you locked in on the mines of Ardana or its Cloud City?"

"The mines, Captain. That's what you ordered."

Then this mistake isn't ours, Kirk thought. The Ardanans understood the Transporter; they had it themselves. Turning to Uhura, he said tersely, "Tell the High Advisor we request that the official welcoming courtesies be dispensed with. We are beaming down directly to the mines to ensure the fastest possible transport of the zenite to Marak II. The need is desperate. Say we appreciate the honor and look forward to a visit to Cloud City in the future ... Come with me, Mr. Spock."

But no miners were awaiting them at the mine-shaft entrance. The hill by which they'd arrived was deserted.

"I don't understand it," Kirk said. "The Troglyte miners were to make delivery when we beamed down."

"Perhaps there is another entrance," Spock suggested.

There was none. The other side of the hill was as abandoned, as bleak and forbidding as the rest of their arrival area. It was Spock who put the thought in both of their minds into words. "It would seem that the Troglytes have changed their minds about the delivery, sir."

Even as Kirk nodded there came a hiss in the air above their heads. Two heavy, noosed thongs were hurled from behind them with an accuracy that pinned their arms helplessly to their bodies. Jerks tightened the thongs, and the two *Enterprise* officers were pulled roughly around to confront four creatures, obvious Troglytes, their loose miners' overalls begrimed, their eyes begoggled, their features hidden by slitted masks. One of the Troglytes was slightly smaller than the others; but they all had long, sharp-edged mortae, the honed blades aimed in open threat.

"What is the reason for this attack?" Kirk demanded.

"Interference breeds attack," the smallest Troglyte said coldly, in a female voice. "My name is Vanna, Captain. I have need of your ... services. Move on." The overalled arm motioned to the mine-shaft entrance.

"We are here by permission of your government Council," Kirk said. "On emergency mission."

"Move on, Captain." Ominous ice entered the voice.

Kirk felt the prod of her sharp blade in his back. Exchanging a swift glance with Spock, they burst into simultaneous action, lashing out with their feet at the two nearest Troglytes. Spock's kick caught his man in the chest. It felled him just as Kirk's foot, slamming into his captor's stomach, dropped him to the ground, knocking the wind out of him.

Vanna lunged at Kirk, but he had broken clear of his bonds and knocked her weapon out of her hand. Spock and the remining Troglyte circled each other warily. Vanna, agile and swift, lunged at Kirk with her bare hands and they fell to the ground. In the struggle, the strap securing her goggles snapped. They slipped from her face to reveal feminine features of such surprising beauty that Kirk, lost in amazement, had no eyes for what was materializing on the Transporter coordinates.

It was her wince at the sudden glare of sunlight that brought him out of his trance. A man of patrician bearing stood behind them. He wore a togalike garment and the charismatic air of the born ruler. Two husky males, armed and uniformed in gleaming white, shimmered into sight beside him—guards.

The patrician spoke. "Troglytes! Halt!"

He was not obeyed. Vanna, unyielding, continued to writhe in Kirk's grasp. Spock was now trying to cope with two of the miners, as the third elbowed groggily from the ground where the Vulcan's first kick had landed him.

"Surrender—or we'll fire!"

Wrenching an arm free, Vanna tried to rake Kirk's face with her nails. He pulled back slightly, and seizing her chance to break his hold, she leaped to her feet and ran to the mine entrance, shouting to her companions. They joined her, racing after her amid a shower of shining pellets. One of the missiles from the guards' guns struck. Zigzagging, hunkered low, the three unwounded Troglytes disappeared into the mine entrance.

Kirk, climbing slowly to his feet, was frowning in preoccupation, his eyes following Vanna and her vanished companions. Spock stooped to retrieve the communicator which had dropped from his belt, and straightened to meet the approach of their rescuers.

"Are you harmed, gentlemen?" asked the toga-clad man.

"Just a little shaken up," Kirk said.

"I am Plasus, High Advisor for the planet Council."

Kirk acknowledged the introduction briefly. "Captain Kirk, *Enterprise*. My First Officer, Mr. Spock."

"My regrets for the unpleasantness of your welcome to Ardana, gentlemen."

"It was rather warm," Kirk said dryly.

"Unfortunately, violence is habitual with the Troglytes. I can assure you, Captain, this insult will not go unpunished."

It was Spock's turn to frown in thought as Kirk said, "I am more concerned with that zenite consignment. Why isn't it in its specified location?"

Urbane, unruffled, the High Advisor's face with its high-bridged nose assumed a look of sadness. "Apparently the Disruptors have confiscated it, as I feared they would. They're a small group of Troglyte malcontents who hold the others under complete domination. It is the Disruptors who are responsible for the others' refusal to continue mining zenite."

"But they agreed to this delivery," Kirk protested. "It was your Council which assured us of that."

Plasus nodded benignly. "Obviously," he said, "they agreed as a ruse to get valuable hostages."

"Hostages? For what purpose?"

"To force the Council to meet their demands." Plasus turned to his guards. "Pick up the injured Troglyte for later questioning . . . Then organize a search party for the zenite consignment." Once more the urbane host, he said to Kirk, "Meanwhile, Captain, I suggest that you and First Officer Spock be our guests in Stratos City."

"I hope the search will be brief," Kirk said.

A shadow of grimness darkened the urbanity for a

fleeting second. "I assure you we will do everything in our power to make it so. Now if you will just step this way, over here, our own Transporter will pick us all up."

They were led into a large, oddly designed chamber. Its floor and three of its walls glittered with a subdued iridescence. The fourth wall had been left open to the expanse of sky beyond, its border a waist-high balustrade of the same iridescent material. There was a careful carelessness about the manner in which luxuriously cushioned benches were scattered about the room, a calculated casualness that matched the surrealistic sculptural forms which decorated it. Central to it was a small dais, flanked by two straggly carved poles of almost ceiling height. They struck Kirk as purposeless even as decoration.

From the balustrade, Spock called, "Captain, here, sir, please!"

The whole planet was spread out beneath them. Its surface could be only half seen through drifting mists. What was visible was dwarfed by distance to the dimensions of a relief map, its hills anonymous mounds, its valleys vague shadows. There was both beauty and terror in such eminence. It evoked a feeling of uneasiness in Kirk.

"Remarkable," Spock said. "The finest example of sustained antigravity elevation I have ever seen."

The sound of a door opening behind them made them turn. A young woman had entered the room of antigravity triumph. She was tall, willow-slim, willow-graceful, her golden hair a mist of mystery around her perfect face. She didn't walk—she glided, her approaching movement so supple it lacked all suggestion of bone or skeletal muscle. Like the clouds which obscured the planet's contours, she drifted toward the two *Enterprise* officers.

"My father," she said to Plasus, "your sentinels informed me of our honored guests' arrival. I came to extend my greetings."

"Gentlemen, my daughter—one of our planet's

incomparable works of art. Droxine, Captain James Kirk and his First Officer, Mr. Spock."

Her eyes lingered for a moment on the satyr ears of the First Officer. "I have never met a Vulcan before, sir," she said demurely.

Spock bowed. "Nor I a work of art, madame."

Kirk looked at Spock with quizzical amusement and surprise. Plasus beckoned his guests back into the room from the balcony. "Come, gentlemen, there is much to see in our city. This is our Council gallery. We have some of our finest art forms assembled here for the viewing of all our city dwellers. That piece there can boast of a special–"

He stopped abruptly. The piece he had turned to was a transparent solid of flowing serpentine lines curled like coiling flames. A miner's mortae had been driven into it, webbing it with cracks.

"Disruptors again!" Furiously, Plasus jerked the tool from the sculpture and dashed it to the floor.

"They are despoiling the whole city," Droxine said.

"For what purpose?" Spock asked.

"Again, to force the Council to accede to their demands." Plasus spoke with the impatience of an adult irritated by a half-witted child.

"Just what are these demands?" Kirk said.

"Nothing you need concern yourself about, Captain."

Kirk's voice was very quiet. "I must concern myself with anything that interferes with the delivery of the zenite, Mr. Advisor."

"Mr. Advisor, plant life is the source of oxygen," Spock added. "If all plant life is destroyed on Marak II, all humanoid and animal life will end there with it."

Plasus had recovered his suavity. "I assure you, gentlemen, you will get what you came for."

"I hope so," Kirk said. He paused. "Ardana is a member of the Federation. It is your Council's responsibility that nothing interferes with its obligation to another Federation member."

"And we accept the responsibility."

Spock touched the webbed cracks in the sculpture. "But why destroy art forms? They are a loss to everybody."

"Art means nothing to the Disruptors." Plasus stooped to pick up the mortae. "*This* is the only form they understand." Rage overpowered him again. Nobody spoke as he fought to regain control of himself. "But no doubt you would like to rest. A chamber has been prepared for you. Sentinels will conduct you to it, gentlemen."

It was dismissal. Droxine's eyes followed Spock as the two from the *Enterprise* left the room.

"The Disruptors must be mad," she said, "to have attacked two such charming strangers."

"They grow more daring every day," Plasus said.

"Do you think the Captain and his very attractive officer will feel we are responsible?"

Plasus smiled indulgently down on his daughter. "Responsible for injuries done to the charming strangers—or to our diplomatic ties?"

Droxine flushed. "Oh, I was concerned about both, father."

Plasus laughed outright. "I am sure they will not blame you."

She exhaled a breath of relief. "I'm glad. I like them. They are not at all like our men of Ardana . . . Father, promise me not to find the zenite too soon?"

Before he could reply, two guards burst into the room. Between them was a powerful man, his muscular shoulders tensed against their grip, but not struggling to free himself. That he had been doing so before was evident in the guards' panting.

"Apologies, Mr. Advisor," said one of them. "This Troglyte was apprehended leaving the city. As he lacks a transport card, we thought you would want to question him."

The man's aspect bore little resemblance to the stunted figures of other Troglytes. Despite the grime of his miner's overalls, the unkempt tangle of his shoulder-length hair, he was handsome. Proudly he drew himself to his full height, his eyes bright with scorn as they fixed on Plasus.

"What is your business in Stratos City, Troglyte?" demanded the High Advisor.

Though the flashing eyes burned with hate, the lips were silent.

"Speak! I command you!"

"My business is to repair," said the prisoner.

"Indeed. Then you must have a repair order. Where is it?"

"It was forgotten."

"Did you also forget your transport card?" The question was harsh with irony.

"It was lost when your sentinels attacked me."

"And where was your cavern mortae lost?" Plasus pointed to the empty sheath at the waist of the overalls. Then, striding to the mutilated sculpture, he plunged the mortae he still held in his hand into the hole it had made. "Here, perhaps."

"I came to make repairs," the prisoner said stubbornly.

"You shall make them—by telling me the names of the Disruptors."

"I know nothing."

"I would advise you to increase your knowledge."

An open sneer distorted the handsome face. "That is not possible for a Troglyte. The Stratos City dwellers have said so."

"Secure him to the dais," Plasus told the guards.

They tried to. But as they pushed the miner toward the dais, he knocked one guard aside and raced for the iridescent balustrade. The guards moved for their guns, but Plasus shouted, "*No!* I want him alive!"

It was too late. The prisoner had flung himself over the balustrade.

After a moment, Plasus shrugged. "How unfortunate," he said philosophically. "How unfortunate." He went out.

Droxine, as composed as her father, had been busying herself with an arrangement of goblets on a cubical table. The gold metal of one rang as she set it down, and a moment later, Spock came through the still open doors of the Council chamber.

"Mr. Spock!" the girl cried. "I thought you had accompanied Captain Kirk to the rest chamber down the corridor."

"There was some disturbance," the First Officer said. "It awakened me."

"I was but setting the table. I did not realize I would disturb you."

"Only Vulcan ears would find such a noise discernible from such a distance," Spock said.

The perfect eyelids lifted. "It seems Vulcans are fascinatingly different," said their owner. "In many ways."

Their eyes met. "The same may be said of inhabitants of Stratos," Spock observed.

"Vulcan eyes seem to be very discerning, too." She drew him down on the bench beside her.

His attention was sufficiently on this Ardanan work of art for him to fail his reputation for discerning sight for once. Behind him, a small figure draped in the clothing of Stratos crept from behind a pillar and moved stealthily down the corridor.

In the rest chamber, Kirk, breathing evenly, lay apparently asleep on a wide, billowy-pillowed dais. Vanna, crossing to him silently, drew a mortae from under her gown and laid its blade against his throat.

Kirk opened his eyes and he seized Vanna's wrist. Twisting the mortae from her grasp, he fell back with her on the bed. She kicked and writhed, but shortly he got her arms pinned back above her head.

"Well, that's better," he said, breathing evenly. "You again!" The face beneath his chest was lovelier than he remembered; but its eyes were cold as death.

"You sleep lightly, Captain," Vanna said.

"And I see you've changed your dressmaker."

"Release me," she said tonelessly.

"So you can attack me again?"

"Then call the guards," she told him contemptuously. "They will protect you."

"But I don't want protection. I find this very enjoyable."

"I do not."

Kirk grinned down at her. "All right, I'll make a bargain with you. Answer some questions, and I'll let you up."

"What questions?"

Kirk shook his head. "First, your word."

Hesitation came and went in her face. "I will answer."

Kirk released her. Panther-swift, she leaped to her feet and stooped for the mortae beside the bed. As he gripped her wrist again, he became aware that Spock's bed was empty. Where *was* Spock in this place of sudden treacheries? With that gliding girl?

The gliding girl was leaning back against a down cushion, its cream less creamy than the skin of her face. Spock, sitting very erect, was saying, "Yes, we Vulcans pride ourselves on our logic."

"Also on complete control of your emotions?"

"Emotions interfere with logic," he said firmly.

"Is that why you take mates only once in seven years?"

"The seven-year cycle is biological. At that time the mating drive outweighs all other motivation."

Droxine moved her head from the pillow and rested it against his shoulder. He looked down at the spindrift of golden hair, its fragrance in his nostrils, and their eyes locked. "Can nothing disturb the cycle, Mr. Spock?"

The Vulcan logician cleared his throat. "Exceptional feminine beauty is always disturbing, madame."

She had lifted her mouth toward his when a clang resounded from down the corridor. Spock sprang from the bench and ran for the door. Rushing into the rest chamber, he stopped dead at the sight of Vanna. Kirk had wrenched the mortae from her once more and dashed it to the floor.

"Captain, are you all right?"

From behind him Droxine cried, "*Vanna!* Why have you come here?"

Disheveled but still proud in her disarray, the Troglyte girl bent in a low bow to Kirk and Spock. "To welcome our honored guests," she said in a voice that cut with sarcasm. "Just as I was taught to do when I served in your father's household."

"It seems the Troglytes have the impression that our ship is here to intimidate them," Kirk told Spock.

"It is not an impression, Captain," Vanna said hotly. "It is truth!"

Kirk picked up her mortae and shoved it into his belt. "We are here to get that consignment of zenite. Nothing more."

"Starships do not transport cargo!" Vanna cried.

"In times of emergency they do anything," Kirk said. "And believe me, this plant plague on Marak II is an extreme emergency."

"Lies will not keep the Troglytes in their caverns, and neither will your ship, Captain."

Droxine said, "You speak like a Disruptor, Vanna."

"I speak for my people! They have as much right to the skies as you Stratos dwellers!"

"What would Troglytes do here?" asked Droxine disdainfully.

"Live! With warmth and light as everyone should!"

"Your caverns are warm," said Droxine coldly. "And your eyes are unaccustomed to light. Just as your minds are unaccustomed to reason." She moved to a wall and pressed a button. A sentinel appeared at the door; and waving a casual hand toward Vanna, Droxine said, "Take her away."

Kirk looked at Spock. "Surely," he said to Droxine, "you don't deny light and warmth to the Troglytes?"

"The Troglytes are workers," said the child of the High Advisor. "They mind zenite and till the soil. Those things can't be done here."

"In other words," Spock said, "they perform all the physical toil necessary to maintain Stratos?"

Droxine smiled at him. "That is their function in our society."

"Yet they are not allowed to share its advantages?"

"How can they share what they don't understand?"

"They could be taught to understand," Kirk said.

Droxine's answer had the sound of a lesson learned by rote. "The complete separation of toil and leisure has given Ardana a perfectly balanced social system."

Kirk was finding this conversation increasingly disturbing. He began to pace. Spock said, " 'Troglyte' is a corruption of an ancient Earth term, Captain. Its technical translation is 'cave dweller.' "

Kirk threw him a tight nod. "We should have realized—"

He was interrupted by a shriek of agony echoing from the Council gallery. He and Spock exchanged a glance of alarm and raced down the corridor to the room of luxuriously cushioned benches.

Tied tightly to its central dais, Vanna was screaming. Incandescing rays from its flanking poles flooded her face with green fire. She shrieked again.

Droxine went back to the cubical table and straightened a gold goblet, while Plasus watched. Kirk and Spock sprang to the dais to tear at the cords that bound Vanna's writhings.

"Stop it!" Kirk shouted at Plasus. There was a long moment. Then Plasus' hands came together in a faint clap. The rays faded. Still bound, Vanna slumped into unconsciousness.

"She is stubborn," Plasus said. "Physical discomfort is the only persuasion they understand, Captain."

"You have tortured her." Kirk's voice shook with anger.

"Is it preferable to spare Vanna—and allow an entire planet to be destroyed? You yourself pointed out that the search for your zenite must be short." Plasus' voice was eminently reasonable.

Spock approached Droxine. "Violence in reality is quite different from theory. Do you not agree, madame?"

"But nothing else moves the Troglytes. What else can they understand?"

"All those little things you and I understand," the

Vulcan said gravely. "Such as kindness, justice, equality."

She shivered slightly. Then she drew a fold of her gown around her, rose gracefully and left the gallery.

"The abstract concepts of an intellectual society are beyond the comprehension of the Troglytes, Mr. Spock." The High Advisor was angry now.

"The abstract concept of loyalty seems clear to Vanna," Kirk said.

"A few Troglytes are brought here as retainers. Vanna was one of them. They receive more training than the others."

"But obviously no more consideration," Kirk said.

Open rage thickened Plasus' voice. "I fail to see the use of this continued criticism." He beckoned to his guards and pointed to the slumped body on the dais. "Revive her!"

Kirk leaped to the dais. "The only way you'll use that device again is on both of us!"

"An imposing display of primitive gallantry, Captain. You realize, of course, that I can have my guards remove you."

"Of course," Kirk said. "But Starfleet Command seldom takes kindly to having either rays or physical force used on one of its personnel. Think twice."

Plasus did so. "Why are you so concerned about this Disruptor's well-being, Captain Kirk?"

"I want that zenite."

"Then stop interfering—and I'll get it for you. We will get it for you in our own way. Guards, take the prisoner to confinement quarters. As for you, Captain, you will return to your starship at once—or I shall contact your Starfleet Command myself to report your interference in this planet's society, in contravention of your prime directive. Should you reappear on Stratos City again, it would be only as an enemy."

The guards were removing Vanna's unconscious body from the dais. Kirk clicked open his communicator.

"Kirk to *Enterprise*."

"Scott here, Captain."

"Returning to ship. Beam us up, Mr. Scott."

The Council gallery disappeared in dazzle.

Twelve hours.

Kirk moved restlessly in his command chair. The decision that confronted him was no joke. Twelve hours—and all plant life on Marak II would be irreversibly on its way to becoming extinct. Seven hundred and twenty minutes to allow the plague to complete its lethal work—or to persuade Ardana to make good on its pledge of the zenite consignment.

He swung his chair around to Uhura. "Advise Starfleet Command that the methods being employed by the government of Ardana will not make the zenite available. It is my view that I have only one alternative. I hereby notify that I must try to reason directly with the Troglyte miners. I am assuming full responsiblity for these direct negotiations."

McCoy walked over to him and laid a hand on Kirk's shoulder. "That won't be easy, Jim. Ardana has supplied us with data showing mental inferiority in the Troglytes."

"That's impossible, Bones! They have accepted personal sacrifice for a common cause. Mentally inferior beings aren't capable of that much abstract loyalty."

"I've checked the findings thoroughly," McCoy said gently. "Their intellect ratings are almost twenty percent below the planetary average."

Spock turned from his hooded computer. "But they all belong to the same species," he reminded McCoy. "Those who live on Stratos and those who live below all originated on the surface, not long ago. It is basic biological law that their physical and mental evolution must have been similar."

"True enough, Spock. But obviously the ancestors of those who live on Stratos had left the environment of the mines. That's how they avoided further effects of their influence."

"What influence?" Kirk asked.

McCoy held out a small sealed container, carefully.

"This is a low zenite ore sample I had brought from the surface. If I unsealed the container, it would have detrimental effects on everybody here."

"Zenite is shipped all over the galaxy wherever there's danger of plant plague," Spock protested. "No side effects have been reported."

"After it's refined there are none. But in its natural state it emits an odorless, invisible gas which retards the cortical functioning of the brain. At the same time it heightens emotional imbalance, causing violent reactions."

"Then the mines must be full of this gas," Kirk said.

McCoy nodded. "And the Troglytes breath it constantly."

"But the Disruptors—Vanna, for instance. They've outwitted a highly organized culture, apparently for years."

"Captain," Spock said, "you will recall Vanna's experience as a servant in Plasus' household. She was removed from exposure to the gas for an apparently significant period. Perhaps without long exposure, its effects slowly wear off."

"They do," McCoy said. "The other Disruptors probably have similar histories."

"Any way of neutralizing the gas, Bones?"

"No. But filter masks would eliminate the exposure."

"Get one, Bones—or make a mock-up of one, fast—and report back here on the double. Lieutenant Uhura, call Advisor Plasus."

After a considerable interval, the Council gallery materialized on the main viewing screen. Plasus was sitting at the cubical table, drinking slowly.

"Your further communication is not welcome, Captain," he said.

"I may be able to change your mind," Kirk said. "At least, I hope so. My ship's surgeon has made a crucial discovery. He has found that zenite ore discharges a gas that impairs brain function. He thinks he can counteract it."

McCoy appeared at Kirk's elbow, a face mask in

his hand. "That is the case, Mr. Advisor. This filter arrangement in my hand is a gas mask. It eliminates all gases injurious to humanoid life. If others like it are distributed to the miners, we can confidently expect them to achieve intellectual equality with Stratos inhabitants, perhaps quite soon."

Plasus dropped the goblet. "Who are you? Who are you to talk of 'intellectual equality' for—for *Troglytes?*"

"Let me present Dr. McCoy, Medical Officer of the *Enterprise*, Mr. Advisor," Kirk said. "We have checked his findings with our computers. They are absolutely valid."

"Are you saying that this comical mask can accomplish what centuries of evolution have failed to do?"

"Yes. That's what I said, Mr. Advisor."

"Centuries isn't a long time in terms of evolution," McCoy added.

"And do your computers also explain how my ancestors managed to create a magnificence like Stratos City while the Troglytes remained savages?"

"Your ancestors removed themselves from contamination by the gas," Spock said.

"Preposterous!"

"We have no time to argue," Kirk said. "I propose to inform Vanna that the filters are available."

"I doubt that even Vanna will credit such nonsense!"

"Are you afraid that the filters might work, Mr. Advisor?"

Kirk's question obviously hit home. Plasus stamped his foot on the iridescent floor. "You are here to complete an emergency mission, Captain! Not to conduct unauthorized tests!"

"I am here to collect a zenite consignment," Kirk said. "If these masks will help me do it, I will use them."

"I forbid it, Captain! Your Federation orders do not entitle you to defy local governments." Plasus reached for a switch. "This communication is ended."

As he faded from the screen, Kirk said, "My diplomacy seems to be somewhat inadequate."

"Pretty hard to overcome prejudice, Jim."

Kirk nodded. "Doesn't leave us much choice, does it?"

"Not much time, Captain," Spock said. "There are now ten hours and forty minutes left us to deliver the consignment to Marak II."

Kirk took the mask from McCoy. "Alert the Transporter Room to beam me down to Vanna's confinement quarters, Mr. Spock."

"Jim! You're returning to Stratos against government orders?"

"Unless Vanna has something definite to gain for her people, she'll die, Bones, before she turns over the zenite to us."

Spock intervened, an undertone of anxiety in his voice. "If you are apprehended violating the High Advisor's orders, he will consider it within his rights to execute you."

Kirk grinned. "If you're about to suggest that *you* contact Vanna, the answer is negative, Mr. Spock. And that goes for you, too, Bones."

Spock said stiffly, "Allow me to point out that a First Officer is more expendable than either a doctor or a Captain, sir."

"This mission is strictly unofficial," Kirk said. "Nobody is to have any part of it—or take any responsibility for it but myself. That's an order, Mr. Spock."

Silently the Vulcan detached his phaser from his belt and handed it to Kirk. Kirk took it, saying, "You have the con, Mr. Spock. Stand by until I contact you."

Vanna's confinement quarters were narrow, barely wide enough to accommodate a slim sleep dais and a small cube table. Her face still drawn from her ordeal, she was pacing the short length of the cell when she halted in amazement at the sight of him.

"I've brought you a gift," he said, and held out the mask to her. "Listen to me carefully, Vanna. In the mines there's a dangerous gas that affects the development of the Troglytes who are exposed to it too long. This mask will prevent any further damage and allow recovery to take place."

He laid the mask on the table and waited for her surprise to subside. She made no move toward the table.

"Gas from zenite?" she said suspiciously. "It's hard to believe that something we can neither see nor feel can do much harm."

"An idea isn't seen or felt, Vanna. But a mistaken idea is what's kept the Troglytes in the mines all these centuries."

"Will all the Troglytes receive these masks?"

"I will arrange to have Federation engineers help construct them."

She faced him, her eyes pondering. "Suppose Plasus will not agree?"

"Plasus is not the whole government," Kirk said.

"But the City Council will not listen to Troglytes."

"When the zenite is delivered, we'll come back. Then I'll request permission to mediate for the Troglytes. I give you my word."

"Stratos," she said, "was built by leaders who gave their word that all inhabitants would live there. The Troglytes are still waiting."

"This time you won't have to wait," he said gently. "We'll deliver the zenite in a few hours."

Her face was tormented. "Hours can become centuries just as words can be lies."

Kirk grasped her shoulders. "You must trust me, Vanna! If you don't, millions of people will die! A whole planet will die! The zenite is all that can save them—and the masks are all that can save the Troglytes!"

She closed her eyes for a moment, swaying. Then she said, "Very well, Captain. But the consignment is deep in the mines. I cannot tell you how to find it. I must take you to it."

Kirk hesitated. "Valuable hostages" was the phrase Plasus had used. There was no getting away from the fact that Captain James Kirk of the *Enterprise* would qualify as a very valuable hostage. But he had asked for her trust; he would have to give her his. He took out his communicator.

"Kirk to Scott. Beam us both up, and then back down to the mines."

Blinking in the planet's relentlessly glaring sunlight, Kirk drew the mask down over his head. Through its goggles, he could see Vanna's delicate figure, a dark shadow against the darker shadows of the mine's entrance, vanish into blackness. He followed her.

They were moving down a steeply descending tunnel. Ahead of him Kirk could discern faint glimmers of unidentifiable light. Then they were in a large cavern. Its walls glowed greenly with the phosphorescence of zenite ore lodes that etched themselves in cabalistic scribbles on the rock face like messages left by witches. Other jagged rocks jutted from the floor. The cavern might have been an underground graveyard of magicians' tombstones.

A miner's mortae lay against one of the floor's peaked rocks. Picking it up, Vanna struck the rock three times; the rock rang like a gong. As the sound died, Kirk heard a stealthy movement from a narrow ledge high on the left wall of the cave. Two big, begrimed Troglytes were climbing down a series of crude steps, hewed into the rock, to the cavern floor.

Vanna touched their shoulders in greeting. Their faces lightened. "Anka, Midro," she said.

"Vanna. It is you." Anka, the bigger Troglyte, touched her shoulder in similar greeting. "You have returned."

"And I have brought you a hostage," she said. "Seize him!"

The Troglytes grabbed Kirk's arms so swiftly that he could not make a move in defense. They were twisted behind him as Vanna, jerking his phaser from his belt, thrust it into hers. Then she snatched his communicator and hurled it against a sharp-toothed outcropping of rock a few feet away.

Kirk found his voice, but it was unfamiliar, hoarse, distorted by the mask. "We had a bargain. Why are you breaking it?"

"Did you really think I would trust you, Captain?"

"I trusted you," he said.

"You thought you'd tricked me with your talk of unseen gas and filters. I don't believe in it any more than Plasus does."

"Then you are a fool," Kirk said. "The filters can free you just as I said they could."

"Only weapons will free us," she retorted. "And you have just furnished us with two valuable ones. Yourself—and this." She touched the phaser in her belt.

"Holding me will not help you. My men will still come for the zenite consignment."

She laughed. "Without that," she said, pointing to the communicator, "you will be hard to locate."

"They will find me," Kirk said.

"Perhaps." She removed his mask and draped it over a mortae thrust into a crevice on the wall. "I don't think you will be needing this." Then she had a second thought, and taking the mask down again, handed it to Anka. "Send this to Plasus. It will inform him that we have more to bargain with than our mortaes and thongs."

Anka's eyes brightened. "You are clever, Vanna. Very clever."

He hurried out of the cavern and she turned to Midro. "Go to the other mines and tell the Troglytes to post watchers. Search parties may be coming soon."

Midro pointed to Kirk. "What of him?"

Vanna drew the phaser from her belt. "I will see that he does not escape."

"If we kill him," Midro said, "there'll be no need to see to that."

"A dead hostage is useless," she told him.

His face set stubbornly. "Only the Troglytes need know."

"I brought him—and I will say what is to be done."

"You're not the only Disruptor," Midro said sullenly. "I too can say."

"Can you do nothing but argue?" she cried impatiently. "Hurry—or the searchers will be here!"

"When Anka returns, we will *all* say." Nevertheless, he left.

Vanna kept the phaser leveled on Kirk. "Now, Captain, dig," she said. "Dig for zenite as the Troglytes do. I will give you a lesson in what our lives are like."

Silently, Kirk turned to the wall. It proved to be hard work. There was a bag on the floor in which he was told to put the chunks of ore; it took him a long time to get it half full. Vanna watched, smiling, as immaculate Captain James Kirk of the Starship *Enterprise* tore a nail on a bleeding finger.

"Is that what the Disruptors are working for?" he said. "The right to kill everyone?"

"Midro is a child."

"The filter masks could change that."

"Keep digging. You do it well, Captain. The unseen gas doesn't seem to be harming you."

"It takes a while for the effects to become noticeable." He straightened his aching back. "How long do you plan to keep me here? Providing Midro doesn't kill me, of course."

"Until we have help in the mines and our homes in the clouds."

"That might be quite a while." Kirk loosened another chunk of ore. "Longer than I can wait!"

He hurled the rough lump full in her face. She staggered back with a cry, and a moment later Kirk had wrested the phaser from her. He leveled it at the cavern entrance and fired. The boulders supporting it disintegrated, and the whole upper portion of its walls crumbled with a crash, sealing the entrance with a massive pile of rubble.

"You have trapped us!"

"Obviously."

"But soon the atmosphere will go! We will die!"

"Die? From something we cannot see or feel? You

astound me, Vanna." He picked his way over the rubble to his communicator. As he had rather expected, it was unharmed; these instruments had been designed for rough use. "Kirk to *Enterprise*."

"Spock here, Captain. Is anything wrong?"

"Nothing. Are you locked in on me?"

"Locked in, sir. Ready to beam up consignment."

"Circumstances dictate a slight variation, Mr. Spock." Kirk eyed Vanna warily. "Hold on these coordinates. Locate the High Advisor and beam him down to me immediately. Without advance communication. Repeat—*without advance communication*."

"Instructions clear, sir. We'll carry through at once. Spock out."

"You will seal Plasus in here also?" Vanna had gone rigid with alarm.

"I am preparing a slight demonstration of the effects of unbelieved gas," Kirk said. He waited. After a moment, the cavern shimmered and Plasus materialized. Such fury shook him when he saw Kirk that at first he failed to register the greenish darkness of his surroundings.

"Abduction of a planetary official is a serious crime, Captain! You will pay for it, I promise!"

Awe struggled with the alarm on Vanna's face. Kirk leveled the phaser at them both. "Not till you're convinced of the effects of zenite gas, Mr. Advisor."

"What effects? I see no change in either of you!"

"You need closer exposure." He waved to the half-filled bag at the cavern wall. "Fill that container."

"You suggest that *I* dig zenite?"

Kirk waved the phaser. "I insist, Mr. Advisor."

Plasus' fists clenched. "You will indeed pay for this, Captain." After eyeing the steady phaser for a moment, he turned to the wall, and began to scrabble at the open zenite lode. It was quickly obvious that he had never done any physical labor before in his life.

Kirk's jaw hardened, and he smiled a cold, thin smile. He felt strangely vindictive, and was enjoying it. "You too, Vanna."

She stared at him for a moment, and then obediently turned also to the wall.

Time passed. After a while, the communicator beeped. "*Enterprise* to Captain."

"What is it, Spock?"

"Contact check, sir. May I remind you that there are only five hours left to—"

"Your orders were to stand by. Carry them out."

"Standing by."

Kirk clicked out. Both his laborers were beginning to show signs of exhaustion. Vanna leaned against the wall for a moment. "I grow faint," she whispered. "The oxygen is going."

"She is right," said Plasus, panting. "You must have us transported out of here."

"Dig."

"You imbecile! We'll die!" Plasus cried.

Kirk backhanded him. "I said, *dig!*"

Knocked back against the wall, arms spread, Plasus snarled, an animal at bay; all trace of the urbane ruler of Ardana had vanished. "I will take no more orders!" He lurched forward.

Kirk jerked the phaser. "Another step and I'll kill you."

Vanna stared at Kirk's distorted face. "Captain—the gas!" she choked out. "You were right! It *is* affecting you!"

Plasus took the cue. "Are you as brave with a mortae as you are with a phaser?" he taunted.

Infuriated, Kirk tossed the phaser to the floor. Plasus scooped two mortae from the rock ledge, and one in each hand, charged Kirk like a clumsy bull, slashing. Kirk dodged, grabbed Plasus' right wrist and tumbled him with a karate twist. The head struck rock. The two mortae clanged on the floor and Kirk leapt for Plasus' throat. As he fell on the High Advisor, the communicator dropped from his belt.

Vanna grabbed it and began shouting. "*Enterprise! Enterprise!*" It remained dead. Vanna shook it, and then found the switch. "*Enterprise!* Help! They will kill each other! Help us."

For a moment, nothing happened. Kirk's fingers tightened on Plasus' throat. Then the cavern shimmered out of existence, and he found himself wrestling on the Transporter platform of the *Enterprise.*

"Captain!" Spock's voice shouted. "Stop! The gas—"

Kirk let go and got groggily to his feet. "The gas? What gas?" He looked around, almost without recognition. The Transporter Room was full of armed security guards. Vanna was cowering; Plasus was crawling off the platform, all defiance fled. It had been a near thing.

The Council gallery of Stratos City resembled a first rehearsal reading of a play, Kirk thought. The whole cast was assembled. He hoped they had all learned their lines.

"I understand you are going to get what you came for," Plasus said.

"Yes, Mr. Advisor."

"The zenite will be delivered exactly as I agreed," Vanna said.

But Plasus hadn't yet learned all his lines. He turned on her. "The word 'agreed' is not in the Troglyte vocabulary."

"The Captain will have his zenite."

"No thanks to any agreement by you. It had to be obtained by force."

"Force has served your purpose at times," she said.

"And bribery," Plasus said, stubborn to the last. "Those masks."

Kirk had had enough. "The masks will be very effective, Mr. Advisor. The Troglytes will no longer suffer mental retardation and emotional imbalance."

"No," said Plasus. "They will all be like this one—ungrateful and vindictive."

As he spoke, two sentinels entered the gallery staggering under the weight of an immense box. "There," Vanna said, "is the zenite. My word is kept."

"As mine will be," Kirk said. "Thank you, Vanna." He took out his communicator. "Kirk to *Enterprise* . . .

Mr. Scott, the zenite is here in the Council gallery. Have it beamed up immediately . . . Mr. Spock—"

He broke off. Spock and Droxine had drifted to the balustrade. The hand of Ardana's incomparable work of art was on Spock's arm.

"I don't like 'filters' or even 'masks,'" she was saying. "I think the word 'protectors' is much better, don't you, Mr. Spock?"

"It is less technical," he told her. "And therefore, less accurate." He looked down at the hand on his arm. "But perhaps it is more generally descriptive of their function."

" 'Protectors' is more personal," she said. "I shall be the first to test them. I shall go down into the mines. I no longer wish to be limited to the clouds."

"There is great beauty in what lies below. And there is only one way to experience it, madame."

"Is your planet like this?" She looked up at him.

"Vulcan is quite different," Spock said. His back was stiff.

"Someday, I should like to see it."

"You cannot remain on Stratos," Spock replied, "if you wish to make a real test of . . . a protector."

Kirk judged it time to intervene. "Mr. Spock, I think it is time. We've got just three hours to get the zenite to Marak II."

Spock turned from the balustrade. Removing the white hand from his arm, he bowed over it. Then he straightened.

"To be exact, Captain," he said, "two hours and fifty-nine minutes."

THE MARK OF GIDEON

(George F. Slavin and Stanley Adams)

"It appears to be Paradise, Mr. Spock," said Kirk, handing back the folder of Federation reports and stepping onto the Transporter platform. "It's taken Gideon long enough to agree to negotiating membership in the Federation."

"I'll be interested in hearing your description, Captain," said Spock, taking his place at the console. "Since they have not permitted any surveillance, or any visitors, you appear to be uniquely privileged to visit Heaven early."

"You won't have long to wait," said Kirk. Uhura's voice replied at once to Spock's request for coordinates. Spock set the levers at 875; 020; 079.

"Let's go, Mr. Spock."

"Energizing, Captain." Spock did not, of course, smile at Kirk's eagerness to be off.

The Transporter Room shimmered, then steadied. Nothing seemed to have happened.

"Mr. Spock," said Kirk, stepping from the platform. "Mr. Spock?" There was no one in the Transporter Room but himself.

He clicked the intercom button. "Mr. Spock, I have not been transported down, and why have you left your post before confirming? Mr. Spock, answer me . . ."

This was not at all according to regulations. Annoyed, Kirk stamped out of the Transporter Room and headed purposefully toward the bridge. There was nobody there either.

He hit the intercom with increasing irritation. "This is the Captain speaking. All bridge personnel report immediately." He folded his arms and waited; there had better be one hell of an explanation. Nothing happened. He switched on the intercom again, alternately calling Engineering, security, Dr. McCoy, and listening. There was only silence.

"Lieutenant Uhura, report to the bridge immediately."

The viewing screen showed only the planet Gideon exactly as he had just seen it before stepping onto the Transporter, a perfectly ordinary M-type planet peacefully poised in the screen. The readouts and lights on the bridge consoles continued to operate in their usual conformations.

"Captain Kirk." The smooth voice of Prime Minister Hodin emerged from the communication screen. "The Council is still awaiting your arrival."

A plump figure rose to its feet from among the Councillors of Gideon.

"This discourtesy is unforgivable!" he snapped. "Doesn't your Federation recognize that first impressions are most important?"

Spock blinked. "Captain Kirk was transported down minutes ago, sir."

"That's impossible."

"I transported him myself," said Spock firmly.

"He never arrived here," said Hodin, evenly. Spock stared at Scott, and turned back to the screen.

"He was beamed directly to your Council Chamber. Please check your coordinates, Prime Minister."

Hodin read out from a slip of paper, "875; 020; 079."

Scott nodded.

"Somethings' gone wrong with the Transporter," said Chekov. "Captain Kirk's lost somewhere between the *Enterprise* and Gideon." His voice rose; Spock's expression remained impassive. The planet hung in the viewscreen, enigmatic.

The Prime Minister was speaking insistently. "We provided you with the exact coordinates for this room, Mr. Spock. And that is all we were obligated to do. If he is not here it is your own responsibility and that of your staff."

"I do not deny that, Your Excellency. I was not attempting to blame your personnel."

"We are glad to hear that, sir." Hodin's voice sounded almost smug. "We are, in fact, inserting it into the records of this . . . most unfortunate event."

"Your Excellency, with intricate machinery so delicately balanced as ours, there is always a margin for error," Spock said sharply. "Captain Kirk may have materialized in some other part of Gideon."

Hodin said, "Let's hope it was dry land, Mr. Spock."

"Your Excellency, to cut directly to the point, I request permission to beam down and search for the Captain."

Hodin sat back, hands on the table before him. "Permission denied, Mr. Spock. Your Federation is well aware of our tradition of isolation from all contaminating contact with the violence of other planets . . ."

"Your Excellency, the wars between star systems no longer prevail in our galaxy. If you will grant permission . . ."

"We shall institute a search immediately. In the meantime I suggest you look to your machinery."

"We have already done so, sir." Spock's voice was now extremely controlled. "With regard to permission to land . . ."

But the Council Chamber had vanished from the screen.

"We must once and for all acknowledge that the purpose of diplomacy is to prolong a crisis," said Spock, deliberately closing the switch.

"What are we waiting for, Mr. Spock? *We're* not diplomats," McCoy flung himself on a chair.

"We are representatives of the Federation, Doctor."

"That doesn't mean we have to sit here like schoolchildren and listen to a damfool lecture by some . . . dip-lo-mat."

"Unfortunately, diplomacy is the only channel open to us at the moment. This planet is shielded from our sensors; we cannot observe it. Therefore we are unable to select coordinates. They have to be given to us. We are bound by Federation's agreements with Gideon." Spock turned to Lt. Uhura. "Contact Starfleet immediately. Advise them of this problem and request permission to use every means at our disposal to locate the Captain."

"D'ye think he's there, Spock?" said Scott. "Or are there any other possibilities?"

"They are endless, Mr. Scott."

"Where do we start?" said McCoy helplessly.

Spock leaned over Sulu's console. "Institute three-hundred-and-sixty degree scan, Mr. Sulu—one degree at a time."

"You're going to scan space for him? But sir, that could take years!"

"Then the sooner you begin, Mr. Sulu, the better," said Spock grimly.

Sweating slightly, Kirk ran from the elevator and pressed a door; it did not budge. He tried to force it with no success. He tried the next door; it opened easily. Standing guardedly in the opening, he pushed it all the way open with his elbow, one hand on the butt of his phaser. It whished slightly in the silence. The tables in the lounge stood as though the crew had just been summoned; a half-finished chess game, a sandwich with a bite out of it, a book dropped carelessly on the floor. But the only sound was Kirk's own breathing. He went out into the corridor again, warily.

Two more doors, locked. The third, labeled "Captain's Quarters," opened to the lightest pressure. His familiar room suddenly seemed alien—no crackle from the intercom, the bunk neatly made up, his books orderly on their shelf; his lounging robe swung eerily in the slight breeze made by the opening door. Momentarily disoriented, he wondered for a wild moment whether he had strayed from his own body and was visiting the *Enterprise* long after he and his crew had perished from the universe.

Footsteps! Dancing footsteps, echoing in the corridor; he pivoted on his now very real heels and stared. At the end of the hall a graceful figure whirled and curtsied, feet pattering gaily on the utilitarian flooring.

She caught sight of Kirk in mid-pirouette, and stopped with a little cry. He reached, and caught her; the sight of a human form brought his sense of reality back with a bump.

"Who the . . . who are you?"

She frowned, her delicate forehead lovely even when wrinkling; suddenly she smiled.

"Odona . . . yes. My name is Odona. Why did you bring me here?" She indicated the ship's corridor with a wide gesture.

Kirk was startled. "What are you doing on my ship?"

"This entire ship is yours?"

"It's not my personal property. I'm the Captain."

"And you have all this to yourself?" Her voice was full of wonder.

"At the moment, we seem to have it all to ourselves," Kirk corrected.

Odona smiled, sapphire eyes looking up from under sable lashes. "So it seems. You're hurting me, Captain."

Kirk hastily released her.

"Captain James Kirk. And I did not bring you here, incidentally."

"If you didn't . . ."

"Exactly. Who did?"

She shrugged helplessly. The decorations bordering her brief tunic twinkled in the lights.

"What happened before you got here?" said Kirk. "Try to remember. It's important."

She puzzled over it for a moment. "I remember ... it seems I was standing in a very large auditorium, crowded with people, thousands of people pressed against me so hard I could hardly breathe ... I was fighting for breath, screaming to get out and they kept pushing and pushing . . ." She shuddered.

"Don't be afraid." Kirk placed a comforting hand on her shoulder.

"I'm not." She looked up at him. "But you are troubled?"

Kirk turned away. "I am the only one of my crew left on the *Enterprise.* Out of four hundred and thirty. I may be the only one left alive."

"I am sorry. If only I could help."

"You can," said Kirk earnestly. "Tell me the rest. You were fighting for breath, screaming to get out, and ..."

"And suddenly I was here on this ... your ship. And there is so much room, so much freedom. I just wanted to float." She smiled impishly. "And then, there you were."

"How long have you been on the *Enterprise?*" Kirk's questions were almost random; any clue, any train of suggestion, might lead him to a solution.

"I don't know. Not long. Does it matter?"

"It might. Come on." He started back toward the bridge.

Odona followed reluctantly.

"Do we have to leave this wonderful open place?"

Kirk glowered at the chronometer in the bridge, gripping Odona's hand. She tried to pull away from him; he held her firmly.

"Half an hour of my life is lost."

Odona stared at him.

"Between the time I tried to leave this ship for Gideon, and the time I found myself here alone, a full half hour disappeared—poof! What happened during that half hour?"

"What is Gideon?"

"Your home, the planet you came from . . . don't you remember?"

"I don't know any Gideon." She looked at him, apparently utterly lost.

"That's impossible. We were in synchronous orbit over the capital city. I was supposed to beam down. Something went wrong. You must have been sent aboard from Gideon."

She shook her head, trying to remember.

"I do not think so."

Kirk flipped on the viewing screen. Gideon had vanished. The changing patterns of the stars indicated the forward motion of the ship. Odona moved closer, and put her hand in his.

"We are no longer over Gideon," said Kirk in a flat voice.

"Where are we?"

"I don't know. I don't recognize that quadrant," said Kirk dully.

Odona bit her lip. Thinking aloud, Kirk said, "Odona, you must realize that we are not here together by accident. Someone must have arranged it, for a purpose, an unknown purpose."

A small voice replied, "Captain Kirk, before I said I wasn't afraid. Now, I think I am."

He looked at her with compassion, and they turned back to the incomprehensible pattern of stars.

"Go back two degrees, there was a pulse variation," said Spock. Sulu maneuvered the sensor screen.

"There," said Spock. "There is something. Give me a reading."

Sulu flicked switches. "I can't make it out, sir."

"Get chemical analysis and molecular structure."

Sulu pointed silently at the indicators. Scott, McCoy and Chekov watched anxiously. Spock shook his head.

"Space debris."

Sulu sighed, and resumed tracking.

"Lieutenant Uhura, has Starfleet honored our request with an answer?"

"Not yet, sir."

"Did you impress upon them that the Captain's life is at stake?"

"Of course, Mr. Spock," she said indignantly. "But they insisted that the matter had to be referred to the Federation."

"What department?"

"Bureau of Planetary Treaties, sir."

"Contact them directly."

"I already have, Mr. Spock. They insist we go though Starfleet channels."

Sulu exploded, spinning in his chair. "With the Captain missing that's the best they could come up with?"

"A bureaucrat," said Spock bitterly, "is the opposite of a diplomat. But they manage to achieve the same results."

He stared at the chronometer. The second indicator clicked on. The captain was waiting . . . somewhere. And time was passing inalterably.

Suddenly Uhura's voice broke the tense silence.

"Mr. Spock, Gideon is making contact."

McCoy said sourly, "Now we're in for another dose of doubletalk."

"Since we must learn the language of diplomacy in order to deal with our present problem, shall we just listen to what they have to tell us?" said Spock. "Then, Doctor, we can decide on the relative merits of their statements."

Four poker-faced ministers flanked the Prime Minister as he appeared on the viewer. Courteously, Spock began, "Your Excellency, we are pleased to hear that you have news of the Captain."

"Good news!" said the smiling image. "Very good news indeed, Mr. Spock. Your Captain is definitely *not* on Gideon. We have made a thorough search, just as you requested. I am sure you will be relieved to know you may now proceed to investigate all the other possibilities, and forget about Gideon."

"But that is not what we requested!"

"It is in the records, Mr. Spock," broke in the voice

of the Prime Minister. "You asked for a thorough search of Gideon. We have used every means at our disposal to accommodate you, Mr. Spock." Outraged astonishment overlaid the diplomat's usual smile.

"Your record on this subject cannot be precise, Excellency."

Hodin waved to an assistant, and took from him a thick book. With ambitious eagerness the assistant had already opened it to a specific passage.

"You do not intend, I hope, that a conference be made the subject of a dispute between Gideon and the Federation, Mr. Spock."

"Your Excellency, a dispute is farthest from our minds. It's quite unnecessary to check your documents. I am merely suggesting to you that the language of our request may not have been understood exactly as intended."

Hodin stood up, huffily indignant. He waved his puffy hand.

"Mr. Spock, you are an officer of a spaceship. In your profession you make use of many instruments, tools, and . . . weapons . . . to achieve your objectives, do you not?"

"Yes, sir."

Hodin's eyes were squinting with an apparent effort to remain diplomatically cool. His posture betrayed him.

"However," he continued, "the only tool diplomacy has is language. It is of the utmost importance that the meaning be crystal clear."

Spock's own posture was of stiff attention.

"I am basically a scientist, Excellency. Clarity of formulation is essential in my profession also."

"I am glad to hear that. Perhaps then you will make a greater effort to choose your words precisely."

The word "precisely" vibrated through the bridge like a red petticoat in a bullring. The crew was coming to a full boil; all hands were fists by now.

McCoy muttered, "Are you going to let him get away with that, Spock?"

"No matter what you say, he'll find a way to twist the meaning," said Scott.

Uhura growled, "How can you stand this, Mr. Spock?"

McCoy leaned past Spock to the viewer and spoke directly to Hodin. "Our Captain is lost out there somewhere. We don't care how much you have searched, we are going over every inch of space ourselves. He's got to be down there somewhere. We're going after him!"

Too loudly, Chekov said, "This is no time to stick to rules and regulations, this is an emergency!" McCoy gently pulled him back, and leaned toward the screen again.

"We can't leave without being absolutely positive ourselves that everything has been done," he said. "Surely you can understand our feelings."

Hodin turned back to the screen, smiling.

"Mr. Spock. Mr. Spock."

"Yes, Your Excellency?"

"Are you still there?" That smile was imperturbable. "There was considerable interference with your transmission. A great deal of noise drowned out your transmission; could you please repeat more clearly?"

McCoy retreated, baffled. "Let me apologize for the *noise*, Your Excellency," said Spock. "To summarize, I request permission to transport down to Gideon."

The Prime Minister looked at his deputies and back at Spock. They all burst out in offensive laughter.

"Forgive me, Mr. Spock," Hodin's oily voice resumed. "No criticism of your equipment is intended. But evidently it has sent your Captain on some strange journey—we all still hope a safe one, of course." He bowed formally. "But it could create for us a grave incident with your Federation. And now you propose to repeat the disaster with yet another officer? Are you mad?"

Scott shouted, "I'll not take that, Mr. Spock. The Transporter was in perfect condition . . . I pairsonally guarantee that mysel'. Transport me down there this minute and I'll be proving it to those ... those ... gentlemen!"

The chill in Spock's quick glance froze Scott in his tracks.

"I could not quite make that out, Mr. Spock. Would you be so good as to repeat what you said?" Hodin gave every appearance of amusement at the antics of the crew.

"The ship's engineer was saying that the malfunction that existed has now been repaired," said Spock, a quelling eye on Scott. "We would like to test it immediately. I would like to transport down to your Council Chamber."

"But, Mr. Spock, you ..."

Spock interrupted Hodin. "Your Excellency, grant this one request."

"You are a very persistent fellow, Mr. Spock."

A moment of tension passed while Hodin again consulted with his staff.

"All right, Mr. Spock." A whistling sound passed through the bridge as the entire crew released held breath. "You shall test the skill of your ... er ... very excitable repairman."

Scott's teeth ground in Chekov's ear. "He doesna ken what excitable is ..." Chekov grinned at him, and whispered, "But he's letting him go . . . Wait."

"There is one further proviso. We cannot risk additional incident. You will therefore transport a member of my staff to your ship. Let us first see if that works."

"Thank you, Your Excellency. Your proposal is accepted." Spock turned to Scott. "Transporter Room, Mr. Scott, on the double."

"At once, Mr. Spock," said Scott, rather stiffly. He stalked to the elevator and punched the door.

On the screen, yet another assistant with a large book was talking to Hodin, who looked up.

"My assistant will provide you with the proper, what is the word?"

"Co-or-di-nates," said Spock, very clearly.

"Thank you. You may proceed."

The Gideonite assistant placed himself at a corner of the Council Chamber.

"875," he said.

"875, Mr. Scott," said Spock.

"875, aye."

"020."

"020."

"709."

"709?" The last number was repeated. Spock hesitated for a moment.

"709, Mr. Scott. Energize."

"Mr. Spock, the young gentleman fron Gideon is here," Scott reported triumphantly.

"Very good, Mr. Scott." Spock turned to the screen. "Your assistant is safely arrived, Your Excellency. And now we would like to send down myself and if possible, a few technicians to follow through on . . ."

"Now, now, now, Mr. Spock. Not so fast. That is quite a different matter. We agreed to allow one representative on our soil, your Captain alone. Now you suggest a 'few technicians.' And will the Federation then demand an army of 'technicians' to hunt for these?"

Patiently, Spock said, "I will demand only one thing, Prime Minister; that I be permitted to beam down to your planet to search for the Captain."

"Your request," said Hodin, smoothly triumphant, "will be brought to the floor at the next session of Gideon's Council. Er . . . do not look forward to a favorable reply."

"Your Excellency!" Spock pressed the switch several times rapidly; the screen remained blank. He hit the intercom.

"Mr. Scott. Send the gentleman from Gideon home."

"I was just beginning to think you might find a new career as a diplomat, Spock," said McCoy.

"Do not lose hope, Doctor. Lt. Uhura, contact Starfleet Command. Demand an instant reply to our request for permission to land on Gideon."

The room was tense as Uhura operated her console.

"*Enterprise* to Starfleet Command.

"*Enterprise* to Starfleet Command."

"*Enterprise* to Starfleet Command." Kirk and Odona bent over the console, Kirk's fingers expertly flicking the controls.

"Captain Kirk here. Red Priority Alert. Do you read me? Red Priority Alert." The console impassively continued its normal light patterns.

"Isn't it working?" said Odona.

"It seems to be all right." Kirk flipped the manual control and held it open.

"Kirk here. Answer please. Red Priority Alert."

"If it is working someone must hear you," Odona said hopefully.

"There's nothing. If they do hear they aren't replying."

"Why would they do that?"

"They wouldn't." Kirk glanced quizzically at her, then crossed the bridge to Sulu's board. With a few swift motions he altered the setting so that the lights showed a different pattern.

"I'm taking the ship out of warp speed."

"Out of what?" Odona looked utterly baffled.

Kirk laughed. "Space terminology. We're no longer moving faster than light. I trimmed her down to sublight speed till we can find out where we are."

"It doesn't feel any different."

"Well, no." Kirk was amused. Abruptly, his smile faded. "Maybe it isn't." He stared at the other consoles, one by one. No change was apparent. He turned on the forward viewing screen. No motion was visible in the star-filled sky, still and remote.

"Has the ship slowed down?"

"If we can believe the screen, it has."

"Oh, don't tell me the *sky* is out of order now!"

They stood side by side watching the glittering heavens; behind them the console lights moved in rhythmic silence. Odona said softly, "It's so quiet, and peaceful."

"It isn't really, you know. Out there, it's . . ." As he turned his head to look at her he felt fingers against his lips.

"And it's beautiful," she said.

Kirk looked back at the panoply on the screen, and at the delicate oval face in its black wings of hair.

"And it's beautiful. Very beautiful."

"We're all alone here. Can it last a long, long time?" Her eyes were raised to his, sparkling. His arm slipped around her.

"How long would you like it to last?"

"Forever." Odona's voice was barely audible.

"Let's see now. Power; that's no problem, it regenerates. Food; we had a five years' supply for four hundred and thirty. For two of us that should last . . ."

"Forever?"

Their eyes met, and her hands touched his shoulders. He pulled her closer. She said in a trembling voice, "All my life I've dreamed of being alone . . ."

The startling intensity of her "alone" woke Kirk; the moment was broken. Gently he released her. She stood, her arms still raised, eyelids lowered, her expression rapt.

"Most people are afraid of being alone," Kirk said.

She opened her eyes and looked him in the face.

"Where I live people dream of it."

"But why? What makes the people of Gideon dream of being alone?" His voice had recovered its tone of impersonal interest.

"I . . ." she caught herself. Her expression of puzzlement returned. "Gideon? I told you I don't know where my home is." She shook her head.

"It might well be Gideon." Kirk appraised her coolly.

"Does it matter so much?" She started toward him, her hands out.

"It might help me locate our position." She stopped. Her hands dropped to her sides. She shrugged, almost imperceptibly.

"And then you might find your crew. Being here with you, I forgot there were others. I envy your sense of loyalty." She drew close to him. "I wish I could ease your fear for your friends."

Kirk shook his head. "I *must* make contact with whoever is manipulating us. I've got to find a way . . ." He paced the room, stopping in front of each of the consoles, willing them to reveal something, the smallest clue. Suddenly he whirled and faced the girl. "Odona, can't you remember why your people want so much to be alone?"

A wave of utter panic swept over her face. She shivered, although there was no change in the temperature.

"Because they cannot ever be."

"Why not?"

"There are so many." He could hardly hear her reply. She lifted her head. A shuddering force seemed to rise from her slender body.

"So many . . . so many. There is no place, no street, no house, no garden, no beach, no mountain that is not filled with people. If he could, each one would kill to find a place to be alone. If he could, he would die for it."

She stared at him, tears creeping down her cheeks, supporting herself on Uhura's chair. She looked exhausted.

"Why were you sent here, Odona?" Kirk put the question compassionately.

Her head lifted proudly. "No one commands Odona. I was not sent here."

Kirk strode to her side, and took her face in his hands.

"Have you come here to kill?"

Her tearstained face was shocked; unable to answer, her lips formed a soundless "no."

"Have you come here to die?"

"I don't know. I don't care . . . I only know I am here. I only know I am happy here." She threw her arms around his neck and clung to him, desperately. The trouble in her eyes moved Kirk as her coquetry had failed to do. He kissed her, gently, then more urgently. Yet in the back of his mind the images evoked by her tormented outcry haunted him; faces of people yearning for solitude, young, old, men, women and children unable to draw a breath that was not their neighbor's.

The stars on the viewscreen ignored them.

Suddenly Kirk drew back his arm with an exclamation. She flinched.

"I have done something wrong?"

"No." Kirk smiled ruefully. But he let her go, and pulled up his sleeve. There was a bruise on his forearm. Blood made a tiny dome in its center.

"Why does it take so long?" Odona asked, peering at it.

"Long? What?"

"The bruise. It stays the same."

"And the irritation gets worse. If Dr. McCoy were here he'd take care of it with a simple wave of his medical tricorder."

It was obviously the same as if he had said "his wand" to Odona, but she said, "I would willingly give up some of this glorious space to Dr. McCoy, if he could take away your . . . irritation."

"They took Dr. McCoy, but they had to leave Sickbay," said Kirk. He took her arm and steered her to the elevator.

On the bridge of the other *Enterprise,* Uhura, Chekov, Scott and McCoy were intently scanning the viewscreen. Spock stood at attention in the Captain's position. Over the air the voice of the Starfleet Admiral, slightly distorted by its long journey, sounded extremely stern.

"I sympathize deeply, but Starfleet cannot override Federation directives in this matter."

"The crew will not understand it, Admiral."

"Damn straight," muttered McCoy.

"Has your crew suddenly become interested in provoking a war, Mr. Spock? That is hardly Starfleet's mission."

"We only want to save the life of the Captain," repeated Spock.

"You have not proved your case to the Federation, or even to Starfleet, for that matter," said the Admiral.

"What's the matter wi' them all?" said Scott in a surly voice. "Ye'd think naebody but us care at all . . ."

Spock shushed him with a wave of his hand behind his back.

"I'm positive I will be able to do so to your satisfaction, Admiral. It has been clear to me since my first exchange of, er . . . courtesies with the Prime Minister that they have taken the Captain prisoner."

"Granted, Mr. Spock."

"I know now precisely where the Captain is being held." A stunned silence gripped the crew.

"Leave it to Spock, every time," whispered Uhura. Scott nodded.

". . . If he is at the same place to which we transported him," Spock went on.

"They would not dare to harm him in the Council Chamber!" The Admiral was outraged.

"That is not where the Captain is, Admiral. He is being held nearby."

"Well! You have now answered What and Where. I now await your explanation of Why."

"Since this planet is shielded from our sensors, by Federation agreement, Admiral, we cannot possibly establish that without on-the-spot investigation."

"Mhm. What evidence have you that the Captain's life is threatened?"

"Why else would they keep him?"

"I'm afraid that's not good enough, Mr. Spock. Permission denied."

Spock took a deep breath, fists clenched. "I wish personally to go on record that this decision is completely arbitrary."

"So noted." The screen blipped off.

"Diplomats!" exploded Scott. "What did you mean,

Mr. Spock? Didn't we beam the Captain into the Council Chamber?"

"Quiet, please!" Mr. Spock broke through the agitated babble. "No, Mr. Scott, Gideon supplied us with two different sets of coordinates; one for the Captain, and one for our ... er ... recent guest." As Scott looked doubtful, he said, "The Captain's Log is evidence enough—I hope." He turned to the ship's memory. The crew stared at the numbers on the readout.

"You're right, Mr. Spock!"

"Look at that!"

"What kind of finagle is this?" Scott turned to Spock, hands on hips and a glare in his eye.

"What now, Mr. Spock?" said McCoy. "Are we to sit here and wait with our hands folded for the Captain to reappear?"

"This is typical of top echelon isolation." Spock's dry voice conveyed disgust. "They are too far away from the elements that influence crew morale."

"At times like this I don't think they remember that there is such a thing," said McCoy furiously.

"It is unfortunate. But for the first time in my career, I am forced to violate a direct order from Starfleet."

"Hear, hear!" shouted Scott. "That's absolutely the right decision, Spock. I'm with you!"

"One hundred percent!" That was Chekov; it was very clear that if Starfleet Command could but hear them the entire crew would be tried for insubordination—at the least.

"I shall beam down there at once." Spock's resolute calm stirred everybody into action; positions were taken.

"Mr. Scott, the con is yours."

"Aye, but ye'll be needing me along," said Scott, protesting.

"The Captain will be needing all of you at your posts." This reminder had the desired effect; subdued, Scott headed for the elevator behind Spock.

"It might be taken as an invasion," McCoy whispered to Scott. "I'll pick up my medical tricorder and meet you in the Transporter Room, Mr. Spock."

"No, Dr. McCoy; I cannot assume responsibility for ordering a fellow officer to violate a Starfleet directive. I go alone."

"Well, that's just about the worst decision you'll ever make, Spock," grumbled McCoy. "I hope you won't regret it."

As he entered the elevator, Spock said, "I'm sure this won't take long." McCoy held out his hand in a good-luck gesture. Spock shook it solemnly, and the doors closed.

"Isn't that just what Captain Kirk said?"

Chekov's words echoed in the suddenly quiet room.

Odona wandered around Sickbay, fingering pieces of equipment, peering curiously at instruments, spelling out the names of chemicals.

"If I can find a medical tricorder I'll be cured in no time," said Kirk, rummaging in a cabinet.

"Cured?"

"My arm," said Kirk patiently. "The pain would be gone."

"Oh. What will happen if you do not find it? Will you become sick? Will you, uh, die?"

Kirk looked at her, astonished. "Of this little scratch? Of course not. It would heal itself, eventually. It's just a simple . . ." He looked closely at the little wound.

"Or is it?" Recollections of biological sampling, blood tests, other scientifically motivated wounds went through his mind. Had someone wanted something of his tissues? Well, there was no telling. He turned back to the cabinet.

"All this is needed to cure those who are . . . sick?" Odona was examining the autoclave. Kirk nodded.

"It is cruel. Why are they not allowed to die?"

"What did you say?"

"Why don't you let them die?"

Her hand lay on the cauterizer; Kirk jumped.

"Don't touch that!"

He was a fraction of a second too late; Odona had

bumped the switch; a jet of flame streaked out. Kirk jerked her away from the machine and switched off the flame in one motion.

"Are you hurt?"

"Just my hand." Odona had not even blinked, had not cried out. Was this a spartan self-control—or something else?"

"Let me see it." She covered her damaged hand.

"It's nothing."

He pulled the hand gently but firmly into the light. Her forefinger was burnt completely away.

"My God!" Kirk's grip tighted with sympathetic horror. She withdrew her hand.

"The pain is already gone. Don't worry." Her voice was quite calm.

"Sutures . . . it's already cauterized . . . shock . . ." Kirk plunged at the cabinet.

"Wait." She was utterly unperturbed. "It's already healing."

Kirk glanced at the hand she held out to him and lurched into the cabinet door. A tiny forefinger had already appeared where a moment ago had been a raw wound. As he goggled, the finger grew before his eyes. In a matter of minutes Odona's hand was as whole as ever.

"See?" she said. "Why did you worry so much? This is strange to you?"

"Regeneration . . ." he muttered. "Injuries heal themselves?"

"Just as your arm will," she said, reassuringly.

"No. I have never seen anything like this before. Do all your people have this capacity?"

"Of course."

"They do not fall sick. Or die."

Once again the fleeting expression of panic swept over her face.

"That is why they long for death," Kirk said slowly, gazing at her. "So many, no one ever dying . . ."

He became aware of a sound—a sound not due to his own or Odona's movements. It grew in his consciousness to a steady throb.

"Do you hear that?" he asked. Odona nodded. Kirk prowled the room, listening at the walls for the direction of the sound. He checked his watch; it timed at seventy-two beats per minute. Odona put her hand to her forehead.

"It sounds like an engine," she offered.

"The ship's engine makes no sound."

"But there is something wrong with the equipment. Could that be it?"

"I know every sound on this ship; this is coming from outside," said Kirk, trying to recollect what the timing had reminded him about.

"Is it a storm?"

"We wouldn't hear a storm in here. Come along, it's not coming from here, at any rate."

They moved cautiously along the corridor, Kirk leading the girl by the hand. Her hand was cold, and a little damp. She must be terrified. The pulse of sound went on, no louder and no less. Kirk stopped at a viewing port in the observation corridor.

"We can see outside from here—if it works." He depressed a button. Nothing happened. He reached for the manual control lever. The panel slid open.

To his horrified amazement, the port was filled with the faces he had imagined when Odona had burst out with her passionate yearning for solitude. Silently screaming, the faces filled his vision with distress and longing. He fell back a step, glanced at Odona. When he looked at the screen again it showed only the still and starlit skies.

Sharply he asked, "What did you see?"

"People . . . the faces of people; and stars."

She turned to him, pale. "What is it? What's happening?"

The sound stopped as suddenly as it had begun. He remembered; the beat had been identical with the human heartbeat. Thousands of people outside the ship, pressing against it with their bodies.

"You said we were moving through space."

"Yes."

"Then there couldn't really be people out there."

"There could," Kirk said grimly. "Someone could be creating an illusion in our minds. Why would they want to do that, Odona?"

She shrank from him. He saw that her forehead was beaded with perspiration.

"I don't know. I don't know anything. Why do you ask me?"

"I wonder ... if we were convinced of a location, we would stop searching. We might be content to stay here, mightn't we?"

"Be ... content." Odona's pallor belied her calm. Suddenly he was irritated and tired of trickery.

"Where is my crew, girl? Are they dead? Have you killed them to have the ship to yourself?"

She shivered in his grasp, scarlet patches flaming her cheeks. Her sapphire eyes had lost their sparkle, looked dull and sunken.

"No, no, I don't know anything. Please, Captain, something strange is happening to me. I never felt like this ..."

"Neither have I," said Kirk, as cold as ice.

"Am I sick? Is this ... dying?" she whispered, clinging to a doorframe. Her weight fell on Kirk's arms as he gripped her firmly.

"You do not know of sickness," he said. "You have none on your planet. What kind of ..."

"Now there will be ... sickness, now there will be death!" Her voice died in a whisper as she fainted, smiling.

"What the blue ..." Kirk caught her. Bearing her in his arms he started straight back to Sickbay. As he approached the door he was arrested by the sound of pounding feet coming down the corridor.

"Hodin!"

Guards surrounded him as Hodin ponderously walked toward Kirk and his burden.

"Yes, Captain. Our experiment has passed the first stage."

The explanation would have to wait.

"Let me by," he said urgently. "I must help her."

"No," said Hodin, quietly. "We do not want any of your medicines."

"But she's very ill. Look at her—she needs help, and at once."

"We are grateful for her illness. Thank you, Captain. You have done more than you know for us."

Kirk thought they must be mad. He looked at Odona. Her eyelids fluttered. Hodin spoke gravely.

"My dear daughter, you have done well." He took the limp form from Kirk and turned away. The deputation closed in around the baffled Captin.

"Guard him well, we shall need him for a long time," called Hodin over his shoulder.

In total perplexity Kirk marched along with his guard. What had happened to his crew? This corridor along which they were now walking was unfamiliar; not aboard the *Enterprise*, then. Well, where *was* the *Enterprise*? Why did this diplomat want his daughter to die? Perhaps he could take comfort from the fact that he alone had been tricked; perhaps crew and ship were safe elsewhere. They drew near to the "Captain's Quarters" and he heard voices. He halted, despite the guards' effort to press him along.

"I must see him," came the faint tone of Odona.

"Yes, yes. But now you must lie still." Hodin's voice had lost some of its smoothness. "Do you feel great pain?"

"My arms . . . and . . . thighs . . ."

Avid, yet tender, Hodin said, "What is it like?"

"It is like . . . like when we have seen that the people have no hope, Father. You felt . . . great despair. Your heart was heavy because you could do nothing. It is like that."

"You have great courage, my daughter. I am very proud of you." Hodin closed the door softly behind him. Kirk stepped toward him anxiously.

"Let me see her."

"Not yet."

"You don't know what illness she has. Maybe I can tell."

Hodin looked at him gravely. "We know. She has Vegan choriomeningitis."

"Oh, my God." Kirk stepped back; "If she is not treated at once, within twenty-four hours, she will die. I know; it nearly killed me."

Hodin nodded. "Yes, Captain. We learned of your medical history, as we did the plan of a starship, during the negotiations. We brought you here to obtain the microorganisms."

"So that's how my arm was hurt."

"My apologies. As you have learned, we have no medical practitioners. We were unforgivably awkward to have inflicted pain on you . . ."

"You mean you deliberately infected your own daughter . . ." Overcome with fury, Kirk turned on his guards. His right fist shot out and caught one in the midriff; as he doubled up with a grunt, Kirk lashed out at the other and leaped for the door of Odona's sickroom. But the first man had recovered and dived at Kirk's feet, bringing him down; the second guard pulled him roughly up and dragged him back to Hodin.

"We do not wish to hurt you. You will see her as soon as we are certain she is susceptible."

"You *are* mad!" cried Kirk in frustrated rage.

"No, Captain. We are desperate. Bring him along to the Council Chamber."

The chamber was a scene of excited chatter, the deputies of Gideon's government descending upon Hodin, demanding, "How is she? What has happened?"

Hodin waved them to their places around the table. Kirk was brought forward between his guards.

"Your report to the Federation was a tissue of lies," he said angrily. "You described Gideon as a Paradise."

"And so it was . . . once. A long time ago it was as we described it. In the germ-free atmosphere of Gideon people flourished in physical and spiritual perfection, Captain. The life-span was extended and extended, until finally death comes only to the very ancient, when regeneration is no longer possible.

These gifts, Captain, have been our reward for respecting life."

"Most people would envy you."

"We no longer find this condition enviable. Births have increased our population until Gideon is encased in a living mass of beings without rest, without peace, without joy."

"Then why have you not introduced measures to make your people sterile?"

"They do not work," said Hodin simply. "All known techniques are defeated by our organs' capacity to regenerate, like my daughter's hand."

"There are other ways to prevent conception, however."

"This is our dilemma, Captain. Life is sacred to our people. This is the one unshakable tradition. Yet we pay for the gifts that the worship of life has brought us, and the price is very heavy. Because of our overwhelming love of life we have the gifts of regeneration and longevity."

"And misery."

"That is the contradiction."

"The reality, Hodin."

Hodin flinched. He turned his back for a moment, then walked back and forth, the tortured confusion of his mind all too apparent.

"What are we to do? We cannot deny the truth of what has shaped us as we are. We are not capable of interfering with the Creation we love so deeply. It is against our natures."

"Yet you can kill your own daughter. How can you justify that?"

"We are not killing her. It is the disease that will or will not kill her; this is not under our control. The opportunity came to us, perhaps as a gift; we have seized upon it to readjust the life cycle of this planet. My daughter had hoped you might be brought to feel the agony of Gideon, Captain. It is impossible; no stranger could realize the horror of existence.

"I will not ask you to understand my personal grief;

nor will I parade it to gain your cooperation." Hodin had stopped pacing, and faced Kirk proudly.

"My daughter has won my pride, as she has always had my love. She has freely chosen to take this chance with her life, as all the people of Gideon are free to choose. And she cannot be sure she is right."

"This virus is rare. Where do you intend to get it?" said Kirk, grappling with the first of these problems that he felt able to handle.

The smooth diplomatic mask slipped over Hodin's face. Kirk was suddenly wary.

"Your blood will provide it, Captain. You will be staying here."

Kirk slammed the table with the flat of his hand.

"Not me, Hodin. You have other ways to solve your problem. I do not offer my life for this purpose at all; I have other commitments. And I have other hopes for Odona than death."

"My daughter hoped you would love her—enough to stay."

Kirk looked hard at him. "What passed between your daughter and me was between us alone."

"She pleaded with you to stay."

"You watched us, didn't you?"

Hodin bowed his head in admission. "We are desperate. And privacy is perhaps of less concern to us than to you."

"I'm desperate too, you . . ."

Kirk was interrupted by a buzzer. A message was delivered to Hodin, who raised his head in proud sorrow.

"You may go to her now. She is calling for you. You cannot leave quite yet, Captain, can you?"

"Spock to *Enterprise*. Spock to *Enterprise*."

"Scott here, Mr. Spock."

"Mr. Scott, I am speaking to you from the bridge of the *Enterprise*."

"Ye're what, man?"

"Speaking from the bridge of the *Enterprise*, Mr. Scott.

"Those were the coordinates you gave me!"

"They were correct. I am apparently on an exact duplicate of the *Enterprise*."

"What's that? Is it in orbit?"

"You could say so; Gideon is in orbit, this ship is on Gideon."

"Weel, that's a beginning, Spock. What about the Captain?"

"I'm sure he's somewhere here, Mr. Scott. I'm picking up life readings locally. Spock over and out."

Kirk knelt by the side of the bunk where Odona lay, flushed with fever, her cloud of silvery black hair tarnished and lifeless. He looked up at Hodin.

"If you do not let me get Dr. McCoy it will soon be too late for her."

"We have told you, Captain Kirk. It is her wish and mine that there be no interference with the natural development of this precious virus."

"What is the matter with you? If she lives, her blood would contain the virus just as mine does. She doesn't have to die."

"She must die. Our people must believe in this escape."

"She is so young . . ."

"Because she is young she will be an inspiration to our people. Don't you see, Captain, she will become a symbol for others to follow? In time, Gideon will once again be the Paradise it was . . ."

Odona's sigh pierced the shell of exaltation Hodin had erected around his consciousness. Kirk smoothed her blazing forehead; Hodin stood by her bedside in a state of misery. But Odona's weary eyes only gazed at Kirk.

"I . . . am glad you are here. Is my time short?"

"Very short," Kirk whispered.

"I asked you to make the journey last forever." She smiled wanly. "It began here, didn't it?"

Kirk spoke very clearly, hoping to penetrate the feverish haze that surrounded her senses.

"The journey can continue. If you will let me, I can make you well."

"Like your arm?"

He nodded hopefully. She lay still, expressionless. Then, with a slight cry, she raised her arms to embrace him. The delicacy that had given her such grace in health now gave her too much fragility in his arms. He willed her with all his might to agree to be cured.

"I am not afraid of ... what will happen. I am not at all afraid," she murmured feebly against his shoulder. "It's only that now ... I wish it could be ... with you ... forever ..." Her voice sank. Gently Kirk laid her unconscious head on the pillow.

The door closed with a decisive snap.

"I am glad to see you looking so well, Captain. Apparently Starfleet's analysis was correct after all." Spock's cool words cut into the air.

Kirk whirled; it *was* Spock. "I'm fine," he managed to say. "But we do have a patient." He lifted Odona from the bed. Hodin stood, paralyzed.

"Spockto*Enterprise* Spockto*Enterprise* Threeto-beamup Mr.Scott," Spock slipped the words out with machine-gun speed.

"Three—? Er—same coordinates, Mr. Spock?"

Scott had obviously grasped the need for haste.

Hodin plunged at Spock with an inarticulate sound of fury.

"Your Excellency, please do not interfere." As the sparkles replaced the three figures, Mr. Spock's last, "I already have enough to explain to upper echelons, Prime Minister," hung in the air over Hodin's impotent rage.

"I am ... cured?" Odona's tone wavered between disappointment and wonder.

"Completely." Kirk lifted her to her feet and stood smiling down at her brightened eyes.

"Then I can now take your place on Gideon," she said gravely.

"Is that what you want to do?" Kirk was very

serious, yet a small smile crossed his face as he watched her. She touched his cheek tenderly, lightly.

"That is what I must do. I am needed there."

Kirk kissed her hand, a gesture of salute to her gallantry—and a farewell. "People like you are needed everywhere, Odona."

They walked side by side into the corridor.

"Will you sign this, please, sir?" A young crewman held out a clipboard to Kirk. He scrawled his initials, and in the bustle of traffic in the corridor he saw her watching a couple stroll hand in hand toward the lounge. As she caught his eye, the wistfulness in her face vanished. She smiled.

"It's different from our *Enterprise*."

"It's almost exactly the same," said Kirk. "Only this one works." He added wryly, "And it's crowded."

She laughed. "Does it seem so to you?"

"It does now."

"Excuse me, Captain, but before this young lady goes home we are obliged to devise some way to complete our mission. The Prime Minister, you may recall, was somewhat agitated when we last saw him." Spock was apologetic, but quite firm.

Kirk clapped a hand to his head. "Foof, I was forgetting him. Call McCoy and Scott; we'll confer on the bridge."

"Captain," said Spock very formally. "I beg leave to report that I have broken regulations. Starfleet Command gave specific orders which I, upon my own responsibility, disobeyed. In view of Prime Minister Hodin's intransigence to date . . ."

"If you mean father," said Odona, "he did not really want me to volunteer for this sickness at all. He will be grateful to have me back, and if I am carrying the virus, all will be well."

"He wanted you to be a symbol for your people," said Kirk thoughtfully. "He was quite impassioned about that, Odona."

"He had to have some way to live with himself, letting me die, Captain," said Odona gently. "I haven't died. Perhaps there may be some way to inspire our people, nevertheless."

Spock was frowning into his console. "I wonder," he said. "There are many ways to gather public approval—besides the sacrifice of . . . er . . . young women."

There was a silence; each of them cast about in his mind for alternatives. Hodin required something that would serve to call forth volunteers from his people for infection with a deadly disease; and this was a unique public relations problem for the crew of the *Enterprise* to consider.

"In the old days of medicine . . ." began McCoy. "I seem to recall that there was some sort of signal . . . illness aboard, doctor required; I don't quite remember . . ."

Spock laughed. "Bravo, Doctor!" He punched rapidly at his console. "Here it is; a distress flag, flown by seagoing vessels . . . the design sounds simple enough."

Uhura rose from her seat. "I'll see to it at once." She left the room quickly.

"What is it? What are you doing?" Odona was unable to follow their rapid trains of thought. Kirk smiled to himself. This time her puzzlement was genuine.

"What we propose, madame, is to send you home with a badge of honor," said Spock. "When you show it to your father, he can offer such badges to all your people who volunteer for the . . . service he so urgently wishes to render them. This will make it a matter of pride to have such a badge in the family, and thus serve the same purpose as your death was designed to do."

Uhura returned with a small flag, as described by Spock. Kirk took it from her, and going up to Odona, while the crew stood at full attention, he pinned it ceremoniously to her shoulder.

"For service to Gideon above and beyond the call of duty," he intoned. He hesitated, then kissed her on both cheeks. "An old custom of some of our people," he said, smiling at her blush.

"Will you stay on the ship?" she whispered.

He looked at her quickly. In that moment he recognized the ambiguity of her question, and replied unmistakably.

"On *this* ship, I will stay, Odona."

She said wistfully, "Forever?"

"Sometimes I think so," he said, very quietly. "But this is my ship, my dear." He struck at the intercom.

"Kirk to Transporter Room. One to beam down to Gideon."

Later, McCoy asked, "Captain, is the Federation really all that anxious to gain the membership of what is now more or less a plague planet?"

"That," said Kirk, with a glance at Spock, "will be for the diplomats to decide."

Book III

Star Trek 7

BOOK III—*Star Trek 7*

WHO MOURNS FOR ADONAIS?

(Gilbert A. Ralston and Gene L. Coon)

All heads in the *Enterprise* bridge turned as the elevator door opened.

Kirk made a bet with himself: it was Lieutenant Carolyn Palamas with her report on those marblelike fragments they'd beamed up from the dead planet in the Cecrops cluster. He won the bet. She handed him some stapled sheets and he said, "Thank you," his eyes carefully averted from the girl's lustrous slate-gray ones.

Supreme beauty, he'd decided, could be a cruel liability to a woman. The stares it attracted set her apart. And he didn't want Carolyn Palamas to feel set apart. If she was the owner of copper-glorious hair and those slate-gray eyes, she was also a new member of his crew and a highly competent archeologist. She'd been stopping traffic since the day she was born. Well, he wasn't adding his gapes to the quota. He said, "Continue with standard procedures for Pollux Four, Lieutenant."

Dr. McCoy appeared to share his defensiveness toward the traffic-stopper. "You look tired, Carolyn," he said.

"I worked all night on my report," she said.

"There's nothing like a cup of coffee to buck you up," Scott said. "Want to join me in one, Carolyn?"

She smiled at him. "Just let me get my chemicals back into the lab cabinet first." She left the bridge and Kirk said, "Could you get that excited over a cup of coffee, Bones?"

"I'm in love with her," Scott said briefly. As he hastened after her, a slight frown pulled at McCoy's brows. "I'm wondering about that, Jim."

"Scotty's a good man," Kirk said.

"He thinks he's the right man for her, but *she*—" McCoy shrugged. "Emotional analysis of this love goddess of ours shows up strong drives for wifehood and motherhood. She's all woman, Jim. One of these days the bug will find her and off she'll go—out of the Service."

"I'd hate to lose a good officer, but I never fight nature, Bones."

Chekov spoke from his station near Kirk's command chair. "Entering standard orbit around Pollux Four, sir."

On the screen Pollux Four had already appeared, not unearthlike. Continents, seas, clouds.

"Preliminary reports, Mr. Spock?"

"Class M, Captain." Spock didn't turn from his mounded computer. Kirk, his eyes on the screen, saw the planet, rotating slowly, come into closer focus. He heard Spock say, "Nitrogen-oxygen atmosphere, sir. Sensor readings indicate no life-forms. Approximate age four billion years. I judge no reason for contact. In all respects quite ordinary."

Kirk pushed a button. "Cartographic section, implement standard orders. All scanners automatic. All—"

"Captain!" shouted Sulu. "On scanner twelve!"

Something had suddenly come between them and the planet—something formless and so transparent Kirk could see the stars through it. It was rapidly growing in size.

"What in the name of . . ." McCoy fell silent.

"Mr. Sulu," Chekov said, "am I seeing things?"

"Not unless I am, too," Sulu said. "Captain, that thing is a giant hand!"

Kirk didn't speak. On the screen the amorphous mass had begun to differentiate itself into five gigantic fingers, into a palm, the hint of a massive wrist extending down and out of the viewer's area. "Readings, Mr. Spock." His voice was toneless. "Is it a hand?"

"No, Captain. Not living tissue."

"A trick then? A magnified projection?"

"Not a projection, sir. A field of energy."

"Hard about!" Kirk ordered briskly. "Course 230 mark 41."

The palm now dominated the screen, its lines deeply shadowed valleys, the huge, contrasting mounds of its construction simulating the human-size mounds of a human palm. The valleyed lines deepened, moving—and Chekov cried, "It means to grab us!"

For the first time Spock turned from his computer to look at the viewer. "Captain, if it's a force field—".

"All engines reverse!" Kirk shouted.

Lights flickered. Shudders shook the starship. Strained metal screamed. Bridge seats tumbled their occupants to the floor. Scrambling up to wrestle with his console, Sulu grasped it with both hands as he fought to pull it backward. "The helm won't answer, Captain! We can't move!"

Scott had rushed in from the elevator; and Kirk, regaining his chair, addressed Uhura. "Lieutenant, relay our position and circumstances to Star Base Twelve immediately. Report that the *Enterprise* has been stopped in space by an unknown force of some kind." He swung his chair around to Sulu. "Mr. Sulu, try rocking the ship. Full impulse forward, *then* back."

"Damage report coming in, Captain," said Uhura. "Situation under control. Minor damage stations three, seven and nineteen."

"Mr. Sulu?"

"Applying thrust, sir."

The ship vibrated. "No results, Captain. We're stuck tight."

Kirk glanced at the screen. The palm still owned it; and stars still shone through it. He looked away from it. "Status, Mr. Spock?"

"The ship is almost totally encircled by a force

field, sir. It resembles a conventional force field but of unusual wavelengths. Despite its likeness to a human appendage, it is not living tissue. It is energy."

"Thank you, Mr. Spock. Forward tractor beams, Mr. Sulu—and adjust to repel."

"Aye, aye, sir."

"Activate now!"

The ship quivered, groaning. "Ineffective, sir," Sulu said. "There doesn't seem to be anything to push against."

Spock spoke. "I suggest we throw scanner twelve on the main viewing screen, Captain."

"Do so, Mr. Spock."

The palm slid away. In its place, nebulous, still transparent, the features of a great face were shaping themselves into form on the screen. Silence was absolute in the bridge of the *Enterprise.* The immense face could be seen now, whole. But its immensity struck Kirk as irrelevant. It was an intensely masculine face; and whomever it belonged to was the handsomest male Kirk had ever seen in his life. The dark eyes were fixed on the ship. Diademed with stars, the brow, the nose and mouth conformed to convey an impression of classic beauty, ageless as the stars.

The voice that came from the screen suited the face.

"The aeons have passed, and what has been written has come about. You are welcome here, my beloved children. Your home awaits you."

Kirk shook his head as though to clear his ears of the deep organ tones reverberating through the bridge. He tore his gaze from the screen to address Uhura. "Response frequencies, Lieutenant."

"Calculated, sir. Channel open."

He pulled the mike to him. "This is Captain James T. Kirk of the *USS Enterprise.* Please identify yourself."

The request was ignored. "You have left your plains and valleys to make this bold venture," said the voice. "So it was from the beginning. We shall remember together. We shall drink the sacramental wine. The pipes shall call again from the woodlands. The long wait is ended."

The words had the sound of an incantation. Kirk said, "Whatever you are, whoever you are, are you responsible for stopping my ship?"

"I have caused the wind to withdraw from your sails."

"Return it," Kirk said. "Then we'll talk. You seem unwilling to identify yourself, but I warn you we have the power to defend ourselves. If you value your safety, release this ship!"

The lips moved in an approving smile. "You have the old fire. How like your fathers you are. Agamemnon . . . Achilles . . . Trojan Hector . . ."

"Never mind the history lesson. Release this ship or I'll—"

The smile faded. "You will obey—lest I close my hand—thus—"

The ship rocked like a toy shaken by a petulant child.

"External pressure building up, Captain," Scott called from his station. "Eight hundred GSC and mounting."

"Compensate, Mr. Scott."

"Pressure becoming critical, sir. One thousand GSC. We can't take it."

Savagely Kirk swung around to the screen. "All right, whatever you're doing, you win. Turn it off."

"That was your first lesson. Remember it," the voice said. The sternness on its face was replaced by a smile radiant as sunlight. "I invite you and all your officers to join me, Captain. Don't bring the one with the pointed ears. Pan is a bore. He always was."

Kirk said hastily, "Take it easy, Mr. Spock. We don't know what we're up against."

"Hasten, children," urged the voice. "Let your hearts prepare to sing."

"Well, Bones, ready for the concert?"

"Is that wise, Jim?"

"It is if we want a ship instead of a crushed egg-shell."

Kirk got up to join his First Officer at the computer station. "You're in command, Mr. Spock. Get all labs working on the nature of the force holding us here. Find a way to break clear."

"Acknowledged, sir. Beam-down?"

"Yes, Mr. Spock."

The party materialized among olive trees. Ahead of them on a grassy knoll stood a small edifice of veinless marble. It was fronted by six fluted columns of the stone, lifting to capitals that flowered into graceful curves. Above them rose the white temple's architrave, embossed with sculptured figures. They looked ancient but somehow familiar. A semi-circled flight of steps led upward and into the structure.

As Chekov and Scott moved into position beside him, Kirk said, "Maintain readings on tricorders. That goes for everybody."

Behind him, unusually pale, Carolyn Palamas edged nearer to McCoy. "What am *I* doing here, Doctor?"

Unslinging his tricorder, McCoy said, "You're the student of ancient civilizations. This seems to be one. We'll need all the information you've got about it." He moved on to follow Kirk, adding, "The Captain will want us with him when he enters that door."

There was no door. They found themselves at once in a peristylelike open space. At its far end a dais made a pediment for a carved throne of the same spotless marble. There were benches of marble, a table that held a simple repast of fruit and wine. From somewhere came the sound of pipes, sweet, wild, pagan. On a bench beside the table sat a man-size being. Kirk had seen some good-looking men in his life, but this male, human or non-human, was in a class of his own. His face held the same agelessly classic beauty as the huge image of the *Enterprise* screen. A thigh-length garment was clasped to his sun-browned, smoothly muscular shoulders. Beside him lay a lyre. He rose to his tall six-foot two-inch height and walked to meet them.

"My children, greetings. Long, long have I waited for this moment."

His youth should have made the term "children" absurd. It didn't. He could get away with it, Kirk thought, because of the dignity. The whole bearing of the creature exuded it.

Low-voiced, he said, "Bones, aim your tricorder at him."

"Ah, the memories you bring of our lush and beautiful Earth!" The being flung up his arms as though invoking the memories. "Its green meadows . . . its blue skies . . . the simple shepherds and their flocks on the hills . . ."

"You know Earth?" Kirk asked. "You've been there?"

The white teeth flashed in the radiant smile. "Once I stretched out my hand—and the Earth trembled. I breathed upon it—and spring returned."

"You mentioned Achilles," Kirk said. "How do you know about him?"

"Search back into your most distant memories, those of the thousands of years that have passed . . . and I am there. Your fathers knew me and your fathers' fathers. I am Apollo."

It was insanely credible. The temple . . . the lyre. Apollo had been the patron god of music. And the speech of this being was marked by an antique cadence, an almost superhuman assurance. There was also his incomparable symmetry of body and gesture.

Chekov broke the spell. "Yes," he said, "and I am the Czar of all the Russias!"

"Mr. Chekov!"

"Sorry, Captain. I never met a god before."

"And you haven't now," Kirk said. "Your readings, Bones?"

"A simple humanoid. Nothing special."

"You have the manners of a satyr. You will learn." The remark was made abstractedly. The dark eyes had fixed on Carolyn Palamas. The creature stepped forward to lift her chin with his hand. Scott bristled and Kirk said, "Hold it, Scotty."

"Earth—she always was the mother of beautiful women. That at least is unchanged. I am pleased. Yes, we gods knew your Earth well . . . Zeus, my sister Artemis, Athene. Five thousand years ago we knew it well."

"All right," Kirk said. "We're here. Now let's talk.

Apparently, you're all alone. Maybe we can do something to help you."

"Help me? *You?* You will not help me. You will not leave this place." The tone was final. "Your transportation device no longer functions."

Kirk flipped open his communicator. There was no responding crackle. The being said casually, "Nor will that device work either, Captain." He paused. Just as casually, he added, "You are here to worship me as your fathers worshipped me before you."

"If you wish to play god by calling yourself Apollo, that is your business," Kirk said. "But you are not a god to us."

"I said," repeated the humanoid, "you shall worship me."

"*You've* got a lot to learn, my friend," Kirk retorted.

"And so have you! Let the lesson begin!"

Before Kirk's unbelieving eyes, the body of the man-size being began to rise, taller, taller, taller. He towered twelve feet above them—and still grew higher. He was now a good eighteen feet in stature, a colossus of mingled beauty and rage. As the black brows drew together in fury, there came a deafening crash of thunder. The translucent light in the temple went dim, streaks of lightning piercing its darkness. Thunder rolled again. Around the temple's columned walls far above him, Kirk could see that lightning spears were gathering about the great head in a dazzling nimbus of flame.

Crowned with fire, Apollo said, "Welcome to Olympus, Captain Kirk!"

Dazed, the *Enterprise* commander fought against the evidence of his senses. His reason denied the divinity of the being; but his eyes, his ears, insisted on its truth. Then he saw that a look of weariness, of pain, had appeared on Apollo's face. The massive shoulders sagged. He vanished.

It was McCoy who spoke first. "To coin a phrase—fascinating."

Kirk turned to the girl. "Lieutenant Palamas, what do you know about Apollo?"

She stared at him unseeingly. "What? . . . oh, Apollo.

He—he was the son of Zeus and Latona . . . a mortal woman. He was the god of light, of music, of archery. He—he controlled prophecy."

"And this creature?"

She had collected herself. "Clearly he has some knowledge of Earth, sir. His classic references, the way he speaks, his—his looks. They resemble certain museum sculptures of the god."

"Bones?"

"I can't say much till I've checked out these readings. He looks human, but of course that doesn't mean a thing."

"Whatever he is, he seems to control a remarkable technology," Chekov said.

"Power is what the thing controls," Scott said. "You can't pull off these tricks without power."

"Fine. But what power? Where does it come from?" Kirk's voice was impatient. "Scout around with your tricorders and see if you can locate his power source."

Scott and Chekov moved off and Kirk, his face grown thoughtful, turned to McCoy. "I wonder if five thousand years ago a race of—"

"You have a theory, Jim?"

"I'm considering one. What if—"

"Jim, look!"

Man-size again, Apollo was sitting on his marble throne.

"Come to me," he said.

They obeyed. Kirk spoke. "Mister—" he began. He hesitated, then plunged. "Apollo, would you kindly tell us what you want from us? Omitting, if you please, all Olympian comments?"

"I want from you what is rightfully mine. Your loyalty, your tribute and your worship."

"What do you offer in exchange?"

The dark eyes brooded on Kirk's. "I offer you human life as simple and pleasureful as it was those thousands of years ago on our beautiful Earth so far away."

"We're not in the habit of bending our knees to everyone we meet with a bag of tricks."

"Agamemnon was one such as you. And Hercules. Pride, hubris." The deep voice was somber with memory. "They defied me, too—until they felt my wrath."

Scott had rejoined Kirk in time to hear this last exchange. "We are capable of some wrath ourselves," he said hotly.

"I have four hundred and thirty people on my ship up there," Kirk said, "and they—"

"They are mine," said Apollo. "To cherish or destroy. At my will."

Carolyn suddenly broke in. "But why? What you've said makes no sense."

The dark eyes veered from Kirk's to linger on the cloud of copper-glorious hair. "What is your name?"

"Lieutenant Palamas."

"I mean your *name.*"

She glanced at Kirk as though for help. "Carolyn."

"Yes." Apollo leaned forward on the throne. "When she gave you beauty, Aphrodite was feeling unusually generous. I have a thousand tales to tell you. We shall speak together, you and I, of valor and of love."

"Let her alone!" Scott cried.

"You protest?" Apollo was amused. "You risk much, mortal."

Scott whipped out his phaser. "And so do you!"

With a lithe movement, Apollo was on his feet. He extended a finger at the phaser. A blue-hot flame leaped from it—and Scott yelled in pain. He dropped the weapon, recoiling.

Kirk bent to pick it up, but Chekov had already retrieved it. The phaser was a lump of melted metal. Chekov handed it to Kirk. It was still hot to the touch.

"Quite impressive." The respect in Kirk's voice was genuine. "Did you generate that force internally?"

"Captain!" shouted Chekov. "The phasers—all of them!"

Kirk withdrew his from his belt. It had been fused into the same mass of useless metal.

"None of your toys will function."

Apollo dismissed the subject of the ruined phasers by stepping from his white throne. He strode over to Carolyn to search the slate-gray eyes with his. "Yes," he said, "the Cyprian was unusually generous to you. But the bow arm should be bare . . ."

He touched her uniform. Its stuff thinned into soft golden folds. They lengthened to her feet. She was gowned in a robe of flowing archaic Greek design that left one white shoulder naked. Golden sandals had replaced her shoes. Wonderingly, she whispered, "It—it is beautiful."

"You are beautiful," he said. "Come."

"She's not going with you!" Scott shouted. He took an angry step toward them—and was slammed against a marble bench. McCoy ran to him.

"That mortal must learn the discipline of my temple," Apollo said. "So must you all." He had Carolyn's hand in his. "But you—you come with me."

Kirk made a move and the girl shook her head. "It's all right, Captain."

The sunlight smile was for her. "Good," Apollo said. "Without fear. You are fit." A radiance suddenly enveloped them. Their figures were absorbed by it. They disappeared.

McCoy called to Kirk. "Scotty's stunned. He'll come around. But the girl, Jim—I'm not sure at all it was wise to let her go off like that. Whatever this Apollo is, we'd better be careful in dealing with him."

"He'd have been hard to stop," Kirk said. "Scotty tried."

"It's his moods that worry me. You've seen how capricious he is. Benevolent one moment, angry the next. If she says one displeasing thing to him, he could kill her."

"Yes, he could." Kirk turned to Chekov. "Mr. Chekov, continue your investigations. You all right, Scotty?"

Leaning against McCoy's shoulder, the engineer shook his head dazedly. "I don't know. I'm tingling all over . . . a kind of inside burning. Did he take her with him?"

"So it would seem, Scotty."

"Captain, we've got to stop him! He wants her! The way he looks at her—"

"Mr. Scott, the Lieutenant volunteered to go with

him, hopefully to find out more about him. I understand your concern—but she's doing her job. It's time you started doing yours. We've got to locate the source of his power. You have a tricorder. Use it. One thing more. I want no more unauthorized action taken against him. I don't want you killed. That's an order."

Sullenly Scott stumbled away after Chekov and McCoy said, "Scotty doesn't believe in gods, Jim."

"Apollo could have been one though—once."

"Is *that* your theory?"

"Bones, suppose a highly sophisticated group of humans achieved space travel five thousand years ago. Suppose they landed on Earth near the area around the Aegean Sea. To the simple shepherds and tribesmen of primitive Greece wouldn't they have seemed to be gods? Especially if they were able to alter their shapes at will and command great energy?"

McCoy stared. Then he nodded soberly. "Like humans, occasionally benevolent, occasionally vindictive. Maybe you've got something. But I certainly wish that love-goddess girl were safely back on the *Enterprise.*"

Under the golden sandals of the love-goddess girl, the grass of the olive-groved glade was soft. "A simple humanoid" was how Dr. McCoy had defined the man who strolled beside her. Birds threaded the air she breathed with melody. Her hand felt very small in his. He lifted it to his lips—and they were as warm as human lips. Above the bird song, she could hear the plashing of a waterfall. Vaguely Carolyn Palamas thought, "I am both afraid and not afraid. How is it possible to feel two such different feelings at once?"

"I have known other women," he said. "Mortals . . . Daphne, Cassandra. None were so lovely as you. You fear me?"

"I—don't know. It isn't every day a girl is flattered by—"

"A god? I do not flatter."

She reached for another subject. "How do you know so much of Earth?"

"How do you remember *your* home? Earth was so

dear to us, it remains forever a shrine. There were laughter, brave and goodly company—love."

"You are alone, so alone," she said. "The others—where are they? Hera, Hermes, your sister Artemis?"

"They returned to the stars on the wings of the wind," he said.

"You mean they died?"

"No. We gods are immortal. It was the Earth that died. Your fathers turned away from us until we were only memories. A god cannot survive as a memory. We need awe, worship. We need love."

"You really consider yourself to be a god?"

He laughed. "It's a habit one gets into. But in a real sense we were gods. The power of life and death was ours. When men turned from us, we could have struck down from Olympus and destroyed them. But we had no wish to destroy. So we came back to the stars again."

A note of infinite sadness entered his voice. "But those we had to leave behind, those who had loved us were gone. Here was an empty place without worship, without love. We waited, all of us, through the endless centuries."

"But you said the others didn't die."

"Hera went first. She stood before the temple and spread herself upon the wind in a way we have . . . thinner and thinner until only the wind remained. Even for gods there is a point of no return." He paused. Then he turned her around to face him.

"Now you have come," he said.

A breeze stirred the grass at her feet. The urgency in his eyes was familiar to the traffic-stopper. But in his it seemed uniquely moving. Abruptly she had a sense of imminent glory or catastrophe.

"I knew you would come to the stars one day. Of all the gods, I knew. I am the one who waited. I have waited for you to come and sit by my side in the temple. Why have you been so long? It has been . . . so lonely."

She didn't speak. "Zeus," he said, "took Latona, my mother. She was a mortal like you. He took her to care for, to guard, to love—thus . . ."

His arms were around her. She whispered, "No—no, please, not now. I—I feel you are most kind and your—your loneliness is a pain in my heart. But I don't know. I—"

"I have waited five thousand years."

He kissed her. She pulled back; and he released her at once. "I will leave you for a little to compose yourself. The temple is not far." He stooped to brush the burnished hair with his lips before turning to stride up the swell of the glade. She watched him go. A sob broke from her; and she covered her face with her hands. Glory—or catastrophe. Who could know which lay in wait? The bird song had sunk into silence and shadows were lengthening through the leaves of the olive trees. She waited another moment before she climbed the gladed upswell that led back to the temple.

The *Enterprise* party was quartering the area before it with tricorders. As she emerged from the trees, Chekov was calling to Kirk. "There's a repeated occurrence of registrations, Captain. A regularly pulsating pattern of radiated energy."

She was glad Scott's attention was fixed on the ground. "I can detect the energy pattern, too, Captain. But I can't focus on it."

"Apollo seems able to focus on it, Mr. Scott. He taps that power. How?"

"The electric eel can generate and control energy without harm to itself," Chekov said. "And the dry-worm of Antos—"

"Not the whole encyclopedia, please," McCoy begged.

"The Captain asked for complete information," Chekov said stiffly.

"Jim, Spock is contaminating this boy."

"Mr. Chekov, what you're suggesting is that Apollo taps a flow of energy he discharges through his own body," Kirk said.

"That would seem to be most likely, sir."

"But we don't *know* where the energy comes from! That's what we've got to find out if we're to cut off its source!"

"Number one on our 'things to do'," murmured McCoy.

"Is that all you can offer, Bones?"

"Yes, except for this finding. Your Apollo's got an extra organ in his gorgeous chest. I can't even make a guess at its function."

"An extra organ. Bones, is there any chance—"

"Captain!" Scott shouted.

Apollo had assumed shape and substance on the temple steps. Kirk walked up to him. "Where is Lieutenant Palamas?"

"She is well."

"That's not good enough—"

"She is no longer your concern, Captain Kirk."

"You blood-thirsty heathen, what have you done with her?" Scott cried.

Kirk's stern "No!" came too late. Scott, snatching up a stone, charged Apollo, headlong. The finger extended—and the blue-hot streak lashed from it. Heels over head, Scott was whirled through the air. He fell with a crash; and the rock in his hand rolled down the knoll.

"Well?" Kirk said.

McCoy was kneeling beside Scott's crumpled body. "Not so well, Jim. He's in deep shock."

Kirk glanced at Scott's white face. Blood was seeping from a gash near his mouth. He stood immobile for a long moment, half-seeing the injection McCoy was preparing. Then he whirled to stride up to the temple steps. "All right, Mr. Last of the Gods. You wanted worshippers? You've got enemies. From now on—"

The finger pointed directly at him. The blue-hot flash struck him directly in the chest. It didn't fade. It didn't waver. Kirk choked, hands groping at his heart. He spun around—and fell flat on his face into unconsciousness.

McCoy, instantly beside him, lifted an eyelid. "Two patients," he muttered to nobody. "Two damn fools."

From behind the tree whose trunk had sheltered her from Scott's notice, Carolyn burst out of the dismay that had benumbed her. She flew to the temple steps, crying wildly, "What have you done to them? What have you done?"

"They—needed discipline." Apollo spoke wearily.

She turned her back on him to run to the two stricken crew members. Kirk was climbing slowly to his feet, McCoy's arm about his shoulders. She knelt beside Scott to wipe the blood from his chin with her robe. He opened his eyes at her touch and smiled faintly at her. "What happened?" he said.

"You let your enthusiasm get the better of your pragmatism," McCoy told him dryly.

"I—I was going to separate his head from his ruddy neck," Scott said.

"And you disobeyed an order not to do it! When we get back to the ship, you'll report for a hearing, Mr. Scott!"

"She's—worth it, Captain."

"You're an officer of the Starfleet! Start acting like one! Besides, you stiff-necked thistlehead, you could have got yourself killed!"

Carolyn leaped to her feet, eyes blazing. "Apollo would not kill!"

Kirk stared at her. *"Women!"* he thought. "They'll believe anything's true if they want to believe it is true." He said icily, "Lieutenant, he very nearly has killed—and several times."

"He could—but he *didn't!* Captain, you've got to see! He doesn't want to hurt anyone. He's just—terribly lonely. Please try to understand. He's the god of light, of music. He wouldn't hurt us!"

Kirk gripped her shoulders. "What happened when he took you away?"

"We—just talked."

"What about?"

"Captain, I—"

Kirk's voice was hard as the temple's stone. "Answer me, Lieutenant. What he said may help us."

Her eyes sought the ground. "He—said there was a point of no return . . . even for gods. Of course he's not a god—but he is *not* inhuman!"

"He's not human, either," Scott said grimly.

"No!" she cried. "He is something greater than human, nobler!"

"Lieutenant, there are four hundred and thirty people on our ship and we're all in trouble."

"Oh, I know it, Captain! Don't you think I know it? I just don't know what—" She burst into tears.

"Go easy on her, Jim."

"Why? So she can play around with an exciting new romance?"

"A god is making love to her. That's strong stuff, Jim."

Kirk shook his head in irritation. "How do you feel, Scotty?"

"I can't move my left arm."

"You won't for a while. There's some neural damage to the arm, Jim. I could repair it if I had the facilities."

"One more reason why we have to get out of here." Kirk walked over to a log, kicked it aside and turned to beckon to McCoy. "Bones, listen. I've been trying to remember my Greek mythology. After expending energy its gods needed rest just as humans do. At any rate, I intend to assume they did."

"You think this Apollo is off somewhere recharging his batteries?"

"That's not so far-fetched. He's disappeared again, hasn't he? Why shouldn't he be resting after the show he put on? Remember he's maintaining a force field on the ship while he drains off energy down here. Point? If we can overwork him, wear him out, that just might do it."

"The trouble with overworking him is that it could get us all killed."

"Not if we can provoke him into striking one of us again. The energy drainage could make him vulnerable to being jumped by the rest of us."

"I still think we might all get killed."

"Bones, you're a pessimist. It's our only out. When he comes back, we'll try it. Cue Chekov in on the plan. Scotty's useless arm counts him out of any scramble. By the way, let's get him into the shade of the temple. It's hot in the sun."

But Carolyn Palamas had already assisted Scott into

the temple's coolness. She was easing him down on a bench. Kirk, following them, heard her say, "I am so sorry, Scotty."

"I'm not blaming you," Scott said heavily, his eyes on her face. He shoved himself up with his right arm. "Carolyn, you must not let yourself fall in love with him!"

"Do you think I *want* to?"

Kirk had had enough. He interrupted them. "You are the one to answer that question, Lieutenant. What is it exactly you *do* want? If you've pulled yourself together, I'd be glad to hear."

"Jim, he's recharged his batteries."

McCoy's warning was very quiet. Kirk spun around.

Strong, glowing, glorious with health, Apollo was reclining against the side of his marble throne, chin on fist, the dark eyes on all of them, watchful.

"Come here," he said.

Kirk, McCoy and Chekov obeyed. "You are trying to escape me. It is useless. I know everything you mortals do."

"You know nothing about us mortals," Kirk said. "The mortals you know were our remote ancestors. It was they who trembled before your tricks. They do not frighten us and neither do you." He spoke with deliberate insolence. "We've come a long way in five thousand years."

"I could sweep you out of existence with a wave of my hand." The radiant smile flashed. "Then I could bring you back. I can give life and I can take it away. What else does mankind demand of its gods?"

"We find one sufficient," Kirk said.

Apollo sighed, bored. "No more debate, mortal. I offer you eternal joy according to the ancient way. I ask little in return. But what I ask for I shall have."

He leaned forward. "Approach me."

They didn't move. Instead, they turned their backs on him and strolled toward the temple entrance.

"I said *approach* me!"

"No." Kirk flung the word over his shoulder.

"You will gather laurel leaves! You will light the

ancient fires! You will slay a deer—and make your sacrifice to me!"

Kirk roared with laughter. "Gather laurel leaves? Listen to him!"

"It's warm enough without lighting fires!" shouted McCoy.

Chekov chuckled. "Maybe we should dance around a Maypole."

Apollo rose. "You shall reap the reward of this arrogance."

"Spread out. Get ready," Kirk said quietly. Then he turned, shouting, "We are tired of you and your phony fireworks!"

"You have earned this—"

Apollo had lifted an arm when Carolyn's *"No!"* came in a scream. "No, please, *no!* A father does not destroy his children! You are gentle! You love them! How can they worship you if you hurt them? Mortals make mistakes. You know us!"

"Shsssh," Kirk hissed. She didn't so much as glance at him. She was on her knees now before the throne. "Please—you know so much of love. Don't hurt them!"

The raised arm lowered. Apollo stepped from the dais and bent to lift her in his arms. Then he placed her on his throne. His hand on her neck, he turned to face them.

"She is my love of ten thousand years," he said. "In her name I shall be lenient with you. Bring the rest of your people down to me. They will need homes. Tell your artisans to bring axes."

Kirk's voice was acid with disappointment. "And you'll supply the sheep we herd and the pipes we'll play."

Apollo took Carolyn in his arms. The sunny radiance gathered around them. They dissolved into it—and were gone.

"Captain, we must *do* something!"

Kirk strode over to Scott's bench. "We *were* doing something until that girl of yours interfered with it! All right, she stopped him this time! How long do you think her influence will last?"

It was a question Carolyn was asking herself.

Gods were notoriously unfaithful lovers. Now the summer grass in the olive-groved glade was still green beneath her sandals. But autumn and winter? They would come in their seasons. Summer would pass . . . and when it went, she would know. Catastrophe—or glory. Now there was no knowing, no knowing of anything but the warmth of his arm around her shoulder.

"They are fools," he was saying. "They think they have progressed. They are wrong. They have forgotten all that gives life meaning—meaning to the life of gods or of mortals."

"They are my friends," she said.

"They will be with you," he said. "I will cause them to stay with you—with us. It is for you that I shall care for them. I shall cherish them and provide for them all the days that they live."

She was trembling uncontrollably. She wrung her hands to still their shaking. He took them in his.

"No dream of love you have ever dreamed is I," he said. "You have completed me. You and I—we are both immortal now."

His mouth was on hers. She swayed and his kiss grew deeper. Then her arms reached for his neck. "Yes, it is true," she whispered. "Yes, yes, yes . . ."

Kirk glanced at her sharply as she re-entered the temple.

"Lieutenant, where is he?"

She didn't answer; and Scott, raising his head painfully from his bench, saw her face. "What's happened to her? If he—"

She passed him to move on toward the throne. Her look was the absent look of a woman who has just discovered she is one. It was clear that the men of the *Enterprise* had ceased to exist for her.

"She can't talk," Scott said bewilderedly. "He's struck her dumb."

"Easy does it, Scotty," Kirk said. "She won't talk to you. You're too involved. But she'll talk to me."

"Want some assistance, Captain?" Chekov asked.

"How old are you, Ensign Chekov?"

"Twenty-two, sir."

"Then stay where you are," Kirk said. He walked over to the girl. "Are you all right, Lieutenant Palamas?"

She stepped down from the dais. "What?"

"I asked if you are all right."

"All right? Oh yes. I—am all right. I have a message for you."

"Sit down," Kirk said. "Here on this bench. Beside me—here."

She swallowed. "He—he wants us to live in eternal joy. He wants to guard . . . and provide for us for the rest of our lives. He can do it."

Kirk got up. "All right, Lieutenant, come back from where you are. You've got work to do."

"Work?"

"He thrives on love, on worship. They're his meat."

"He gives so much," she said. "He gives—"

"We can't give him worship. None of us, especially you."

"What?"

"Reject him. You must!"

"I love him," she said.

Kirk rubbed a hand up his cheek. "All our lives, here and on the ship, depend on you."

"No! Not on me. Please, not on me!"

"On you, Lieutenant. Accept him—and you condemn the crew of the *Enterprise* to slavery. Do you hear me? *Slavery!*"

The slate-gray eyes were uncomprehending. "He wants the best for us. And he is so alone, so . . . so gentle." Her voice broke. "What you want me to do would break his heart. How can I? How can I?" She burst into passionate weeping.

"Give me your hand, Lieutenant."

"What?"

He seized her hand. "Feel mine? Human flesh against human flesh. It is flesh born of the same time. The same century begot us, you and I. We are contemporaries, Lieutenant!"

All sympathy had left his voice. "You are to remember what you are! A bit of flesh and blood afloat in illimitable space. The only thing that is truly yours is this small moment of time you share with a humanity that belongs to the present. That's where your duty lies. He is the past. His moment in time is not our moment. Do you understand me?"

The slate-gray eyes were anguished. But he sustained the iron in his face until she whispered, "Yes—I understand." She rose, left him, bent distractedly to pick up a tricorder; and half-turning, looked up at the temple's ceiling as though she were listening.

"He's—calling me," she faltered.

"I hear nothing," he said.

She didn't reply. The iron in his face was steel now. Desperate, he grabbed her shoulders. As he touched them, their bone, their flesh seemed to be losing solidity. She grew misty, fading. Kirk was alone with the echo of his own word "nothing".

Sinking down on the bench, he put his head in his hands. *Slavery.* It would claim all of them, McCoy, Scotty, Chekov. And up on the ship, they, too, would be enslaved to the whims of this god of the past. Sulu, Uhura, Spock . . .

"Spock here, Captain! *Enterprise* to Captain Kirk! *Enterprise* calling Captain Kirk! Come in, Captain!"

"I've gone mad," Kirk said to his hands. His useless communicator beeped again. "Communication restored, Captain! Come in, Captain. First Officer Spock calling Captain Kirk . . ."

"Kirk here, Mr. Spock."

"Are you all right, sir?"

"All right, Mr. Spock."

"We have pinpointed a power source on the planet that may have some connection with the force field. Is there a structure of some sort near you?"

Kirk had a crazy impulse to laugh. "Indeed there is, Mr. Spock. I'm in it."

"The power definitely emanates from there."

"Good. How are you coming with the force field?"

"Nuclear electronics believes we can drive holes through it by synchronization with all phaser banks. We aim the phasers—and there'll be gaps in the field ahead of them."

Kirk drew a deep lungful of air. "That ought to do

it, Mr. Spock. Have Sulu lock in every phaser bank we've got on this structure. Fire on my signal—but cut it fine. We'll need time to get out of here."

"I would recommend a discreet distance for all of you, Captain."

"Believe me, Mr. Spock, we'd like to oblige but we're not all together. One of us is hostage to the Greek god Apollo. This marble temple is his power source. I want to know where he is when we attack it. Kirk out."

"I seem to have lost touch with reality." McCoy was looking curiously at Kirk. "Or maybe you have. Was that Spock you were talking to on that broken communicator—or the spirit world?"

"Function has been restored to it. Don't ask me how. Ask Spock when you see him again. Now we have to get out of here. All phaser banks on the *Enterprise* are about to attack this place. I'll give you a hand with Scotty."

Scott said, "I won't leave, sir." Then his anxiety burst out of him. "Captain, we've got to wait till Carolyn comes back before you fire on the temple. We don't know what he'll do to her if he's suddenly attacked."

"I know," Kirk said. "We'll wait, Scotty."

As he arranged the paralyzed arm around his shoulder, he said, "That mysterious organ in the gorgeous chest, Bones—could it have anything to do with his energy transmissions?"

"I can't think of any other meaning it could have, Jim."

The gorgeous chest, its extra organ notwithstanding, had another meaning for Carolyn Palamas. Its existence had plunged her into the battle of her life. Walking beside her god in the olive-groved glade, her eyes were blank with the battle's torture. It centered itself on one thought alone. She must not let him touch her. If he touched her . . .

"You gave them my message," he said. "Were they persuaded?"

They'd said he was the source of mysterious power. He was not. He was the source of mysterious rapture. People, millions of them, shared her moment of time.

They crowded it with her. But not one of them could evoke the ecstasy this being of a different time could bring to birth in her just by the sound of his voice.

"*You* persuaded them," he said. "Who could deny you anything?"

His eyes were the night sky, starred. He caught her in his arms; and not for her soul's sake or humanity's either, could she deny him her mouth. She flung her arms around his neck, returned his kiss—and pushed him away.

"I must say that the way you ape human behavior is quite remarkable," she said. "Your evolutionary pattern must be—"

"My what?"

"I'm sure it's unique. I've never encountered any specimen like you before."

"Haven't you?" he said. Running laughter sparkled in the dark eyes as he reached for her again. She held herself rigid, tight, withdrawn. The sparkle flamed into anger. "I am Apollo! I have chosen you!"

"I have work to do."

"Work? *You?*"

"I am a scientist. My specialty is relics—outworn objects of the past." She managed a shaken laugh. "Now you know why I have been studying you." She unslung her tricorder, aiming it at him. "I'd appreciate your telling me how you stole that temple artifact from Greece."

He knocked the tricorder out of her hand. "You cannot talk like this! You love me! You think I do not know when love is returned to me?"

"You confuse me with a shepherd girl. I could no more love you than I could love a new species of bacteria." Lifting the hem of her golden robe, she left him to climb back up the gladed hill. Then he was beside her. Anguish struggled with fury in his face.

"Carolyn, what have you said to me? I forbid you to go! I command you to return to me!"

"I am dying," was what she thought. What she said was: "Is this rage the thunderbolt that dropped your frightened nymphs to their knees?"

An eternity passed. His hand fell from her shoulder.

Then a wild cry broke from him. He raised an arm and shook a fist at the sky. The air in the glade went suddently sultry, oppressive. The sun disappeared. A chill breeze fluttered her robe as she began to run up the glade's incline.

It did more than flutter Kirk's jacket. A fierce gust of wind blew it half off his shoulders. Under its increasing howl his communicator beeped feebly. "Spock, Captain. Sensors are reporting intense atmospheric disturbance in your area."

The sensors hadn't exaggerated. The clouds over Kirk's head darkened to a sickly, yellowish blackness that hid the glimmer of the temple's marble. It was cleaved by a three-pronged snake of lightning before it flooded in again. There followed a crack of thunder; and another lightning flash struck from the sky. Kirk heard the sound of splitting wood—and an olive tree not five feet away burst into flame. Grabbing his communicator, he shouted into it. "Stand by, phaser banks! Mr. Spock, prepare to fire at my signal!"

Scott rushed to him. "Captain, we've got to go and find her!"

"Here is where we stay, Mr. Scott. When he comes back—" The wind took the words from his mouth.

"What if he doesn't, sir?"

"We'll bring him back. When that temple is—"

There was no need to bring him back.

He was back. The God of Storms himself. He topped the olive trees. A Goliath of power, Apollo of Olympus had returned in his gigantic avatar. The great head was flung back in agony, the vast mouth open, both giant fists lifted, clenched against the sky. It obeyed him. It gave him livid lightning forks to hurl earthward and filled his mouth with rolling thunder. Leaves shriveled. The tree trunk beside Kirk began to smoke. Then it flared into fire—and the black sky gave its God of Storms the lash of rain.

Stumbling toward the temple, Carolyn Palamas screamed. The gale's winds tore at her drenched robe. She screamed again as the bush she clung to was whipped from the ground, its branches clawing at her face. Apollo had found her. He was all around her, the blaze of his eyes in the lightning's blaze, in the rain that streamed down her body, the wild cry of the wind in the ears he had kissed. The she saw him. The God of Storms stooped from his height above the trees to show her his maddened face. He brought it closer to her, closer until she shrieked, "Forgive me! Forgive me!—" and lay still.

"Captain, you heard her! She screamed!"

"Now, Mr. Spock," Kirk said into his communicator.

The incandescing phaser beams struck the temple squarely in its central roof.

"No! No! No!"

The god who had appeared before the temple dwarfed it. He had unclenched his fists to spread his hands wide on his up-flung arms. Bolts of blue-hot fire streamed from his fingers.

"Oh, stop it, stop it, *please!"*

Carolyn, running to Apollo, halted. Behind him the temple was wavering, going indistinct. It winked out—and was gone.

She fell to her knees before the man-size being who stood in its place.

He spoke brokenly. "I would have loved you as a father his children. Did I ask so much of you?"

The grief-ravaged face moved Kirk to a strange pity. "We have outgrown you," he said gently. "You asked for what we can no longer give."

Apollo looked down at the girl at his feet. "I showed you my heart. See what you've done to me."

She saw a slight wind stir his hair. She kissed his feet—but she knew. The flesh under her lips, his body was losing substance. Kirk made no move; but he had noted that the arms were spreading wide.

"Zeus, my father, you were right. Hera, you were wise. Our time is gone. Take me home to the stars on the wind . . ." The words seemed to come from a great distance.

It was very still in the empty space before the ruined temple.

"I—I wish we hadn't had to do that," McCoy said.

"So do I, Bones." Kirk's voice was somber. "Everything grew from the worship of those gods of Greece—philosophy, culture. Would it hurt us, I wonder, to gather a few laurel leaves?"

He shook his head, looking skyward.

There were only the sounds of a woman's sobbing and the drip of raindrops from olive trees.

McCoy, sauntering into the *Enterprise* bridge, strolled over to Kirk and Spock at the computer station.

"Yes, Bones? Somebody ill?"

"Carolyn Palamas rejected her breakfast this mornin."

"Some bug going around?"

"She's pregnant, Jim. I've just examined her."

"What?"

"You heard me."

"Apollo?"

"Yes."

"Bones, it's impossible!"

McCoy leaned an arm on the hood of the computer.

"Spock," he said, "may I put a question to this gadget of yours? I'd like to ask it if I'm to turn my Sickbay into a delivery room for a human child—or a god. My medical courses did not include obstetrics for infant gods."

THE CHANGELING

(John Meredyth Lucas)

The last census had shown the Malurian system, which had two habitable planets, to have a population of over four billion; and only a week ago, the *Enterprise* had received a routine report from the head of the Federation investigating team there, asking to be picked up. Yet now there was no response from either planet, on any channel—and a long-range sensor sweep of the system revealed no sign of life at all.

There could not have been any system-wide natural catastrophe, or the astronomers would have detected it, and probably even predicted it. An interplanetary war would have left a great amount of radioactive residue; but the instruments showed only normal background radiation. As for an epidemic, what disease could wipe out two planets in a week, let alone so quickly that not even a single distress signal could be sent out—and what disease could wipe out *all* forms of life?

A part of the answer came almost at once as the ship's deflector screens snapped on. Something was approaching the *Enterprise* at multi-warp speed: necessarily, another ship. Nor did it leave a moment's doubt about its intentions. The bridge rang to a slamming jar. The *Enterprise* had been fired upon.

"Shields holding, Captain," Scott said.

"Good."

"I fear it is a temporary condition," Spock said. "The shields absorbed energy equivalent to almost ninety of our photon torpedos."

"*Ninety,* Mr. Spock?"

"Yes, Captain. I may add, the energy used in repulsing that first attack has reduced our shielding power by approximately 20 percent. In other words, we can resist perhaps three more; the fourth one will get through."

"Source?"

"Something very small . . . bearing 123 degrees mark 18. Range, ninety thousand kilometers. Yet the sensors still do not register any life forms."

"Nevertheless, we'll try talking. They obviously pack more wallop than we do. Lieutenant Uhura, patch my audio speaker into the translator computer and open all hailing frequencies."

"Aye, sir . . . All hailing frequencies open."

"To unidentified vessel, this is Captain Kirk of the *USS Enterprise.* We are on a peaceful mission. We mean no harm to you or to any life-form. Please communicate with us." There was no answer. "Mr. Spock, do you have any further readings on the alien?"

"Yes, sir. Mass, five hundred kilograms. Shape, roughly cylindrical. Length, a fraction over one meter."

"Must be a shuttlecraft," Scott said. "Some sort of dependent ship, or a proxy."

Spock shook his head. "There is no other ship on the sensors. The object we are scanning is the only possible source of the attack."

"What kind of intelligent creatures could exist in a thing that size?"

"Intelligence does not necessarily require bulk, Mr. Scott."

"Captain, message coming in," Uhura said.

The voice that came from the speaker was toneless, inflectionless, but comprehensible. "*USS Enterprise.* This is Nomad. My mission is non-hostile. Require communication. Can you leave your ship?"

"Yes," Kirk said, "but it will not be possible to enter your ship because of size differential."

"Non sequitur," said Nomad. "Your facts are uncoordinated."

"We are prepared to beam you aboard our ship."

Kirk's officers, except for Spock, reacted with alarm at this, but Nomad responded, "That will be satisfactory."

"Do you require any special conditions, any particular atmosphere or environment?"

"Negative."

"Please maintain your position. We are locked on to your coordinates and will beam you aboard." Kirk made a throat-cutting gesture to Uhura, who broke the contact.

"Captain," Scott said, "you're really going to bring that thing in here?"

"While it's on board, Mr. Scott, I doubt very much if it will do any more shooting at us. And if we don't do what it asks, we're a sitting duck for it right now. Lieutenant Uhura, have Dr. McCoy report to the Transporter Room. Mr. Spock, Scotty, come with me."

The glowing swirl of sparkle that was the Transporter effect died, and Nomad was there, a dull metallic cylinder, resting in a horizontal position on the floor of the chamber. It was motionless, silent, and a little absurd. There were seams on its sides, indicating possible openings, but there were no visible ports or sensors.

Spock moved to a scanning station, then shook his head. "No sensor readings, Captain. It has some sort of screen which protects it. I cannot get through."

There was a moment's silence. Then McCoy said: "What do we do now? Go up and knock?"

As if in answer, the flat inflectionless voice of Nomad spoke again, now through the ship's intercom system. "Relate your point of origin."

Kirk said, "We are from the United Federation of Planets."

"Insufficient response. All things have a point of origin. I will scan your star charts."

Kirk thought about this for a moment, then turned to Spock. "We can show it as a closeup of our system. As long as it has nothing to relate to, it won't know anything more important than it does now."

"It seems a reasonable course," Spock said.

"Nomad," Kirk told the cylinder, "If you would like to leave your ship, we can provide the necessary life-support systems."

"Non sequitur. Your facts remain uncoordinated."

"Jim," said McCoy, "I don't believe there's anyone in there."

"I contain no parasitical beings. I am Nomad."

"Och, it's a machine!" Scott said, brightening.

"Opinion, Mr. Spock?"

"Indeed, Captain, it is reacting quite like a highly sophisticated computer."

"I am Nomad. What is 'opinion'?"

"Opinion," Spock said, "is a belief, view or judgment."

"Insufficient response."

"What's your source of power?" Scott said.

"It has changed since the point of origin. There was much taken from the other. Now I focus cosmic radiation, and am perpetual."

Kirk drew Spock aside and spoke in a low voice. "Wasn't there a probe called Nomad launched from Earth back in the early two thousands?"

"Yes. It was reported destroyed. There were no more in the series. But if this *is* that probe—"

"I will scan your star charts now," Nomad said.

"We'll bring them."

"I have the capability of movement within your ship."

After a moment's hesitation, Kirk said, "This way. Scotty, get our shields recharged as soon as possible. Spock, Bones, come with me."

He led the way to the auxiliary control room, Nomad floating after him. The group considerably startled a crewman who was working there.

Spock crossed to the console. "Chart fourteen A, sir?"

Kirk nodded. The First Officer touched buttons quickly, and a view-screen lit up, showing a schematic chart of Earth's solar system—not, of course, to scale.

"Nomad," Kirk said, "can you scan this?"

"Yes."

"This is our point of origin. A star we know as Sol."

"You are from the third planet?"

"Yes."

"A planet with one large natural satellite?"

"Yes."

"The planet is called Earth?"

"Yes it is," Kirk said, puzzled.

An antenna slid from the side of the cylinder, swiveled, and centered upon him. He eyed it warily.

"Then," said Nomad, "you are the Creator—the Kirk. The sterilization procedure against your ship was a profound error."

"What sterilization procedure?"

"You know. You are the Kirk—the Creator. You programmed my function."

"Well, I'm not the Kirk," McCoy said. "Tell *me* what your function is."

The antenna turned to center on the surgeon. "This is one of your units, Creator?"

"Uh . . . yes, he is."

"It functions irrationally."

"Nevertheless, tell him your function."

The antenna retracted. "I am sent to probe for biological infestations. I am to destroy that which is not perfect."

Kirk turned to Spock, who was working at an extension of the library computer. "Biological infestations? There never was any probe sent out for that."

"I am checking its history," Spock said. "I should have a read-out in a moment."

Kirk turned back to Nomad. "Did you destroy the Malurian system? And why?"

"Clarify."

"The system of this star, Omega Ceti."

"Not the system, Creator Kirk, only the unstable biological infestation. It is my function."

"Unstable manifestation!" McCoy said angrily. "The population of two planets!"

"Doctor," Kirk said warningly. "Nomad, why do you call me Creator?"

"Is the usage incorrect?"

"The usage is correct," Spock put in quickly. "The Creator was simply testing your memory banks."

What, Kirk wondered, was Spock on to now? Well, best keep silent and play along.

"There was much damage in the accident," Nomad said.

Kirk turned toward the crewman, who had been listening with growing amazement. "Mr. Singh, come over here, please. Mr. Spock, Doctor, go to the briefing room. Nomad, I will return shortly. This unit, called Singh, will see to your needs."

There was no reaction from the cylinder. Kirk joined Spock and McCoy in the corridor. "Spock, you're on to something. What is it?"

"A Nomad probe was launched from Earth in August of the year 2002, old calendar. I am convinced that this is the same probe."

"Ridiculous," McCoy said. "Earth science couldn't begin to build anything with those capabilities that long ago."

"Besides," Kirk added, "Nomad was destroyed."

"Presumed destroyed by a meteor collision," Spock said. "I submit that it was badly damaged, but managed somehow to repair itself. But what is puzzling is that the original mission was a peaceful one." They had reached the briefing room, and the First Officer stepped aside to allow Kirk to precede him in. "The creator of Nomad was perhaps the most brilliant, though erratic, cyberneticist of his time. His dream was to make a perfect thinking machine, capable of independent logic. His name was Jackson Roykirk."

Light dawned. "Oho," Kirk said.

"Yes, Captain, I believe Nomad thinks you are Roykirk, and that may well be why the attack was broken off when you hailed it. It responded to your name, as well as its damaged memory banks permitted. While we were in Auxiliary Control, I programmed the computer to show a picture of the original Nomad on the screen here."

Spock switched on the screen. On it appeared, not a photograph, but a sketch. The size and shape indicated were about the same as the present Nomad, but the design was somehow rougher.

"But that's not the same," McCoy said.

"Essentially it is, Doctor. But I believe more happened to it than just damage in the meteor collision. It mentioned 'the other'. The other *what* is still an unanswered question. Nomad was a thinking machine, the best that could be engineered. It was a prototype. However, the entire program was highly controversial. It had many powerful enemies in the confused and inefficient Earth culture of that time. When Jackson Roykirk died, the Nomad program died with him."

"But if it's Nomad," Kirk said, "what happened to alter its shape?"

"I think it somehow repaired the damage it sustained."

"Its purpose must have been altered. The directive to seek out and destroy biological infestations couldn't have been programmed into it."

"As I recall, it wasn't," McCoy said. "Seems to me it was supposed to be the first interstellar probe to seek out new life-forms—only."

"Precisely, Doctor," Spock said. "And somehow that programming has been changed. It would seem that Nomad is now seeking out *perfect* life-forms . . . perfection being measured by its own relentless logic."

"If what you say is true, Mr. Spock," Kirk said, "Nomad has effectively programmed itself to destroy all non-mechanical life."

"Indeed, Captain. We have taken aboard our vessel a device which, sooner or later, must destroy us."

"Bridge to Captain Kirk," said the intercom urgently.

"Here, Scotty."

"Sir, that mechanical beastie is up here on the bridge!"

"On my way." Kirk tried to remember whether or not he, as the misidentified "Creator," had given Nomad a direct order to stay in the auxiliary control room. Evidently not.

On the bridge Uhura, Scott and Sulu were on duty; Uhura had been singing softly to herself.

"I always liked that song," Sulu said.

As he spoke, the elevator doors opened, and Nomad emerged. It paused for a moment, antenna extended and swiveling, coming to rest at last on Uhura. It started towards her. (It was at this point that Scott had called for Kirk.)

"What is the meaning of that?" Nomad said. "What form of communication?"

Uhura stared; though she knew the device had been brought aboard, this was the first time she had actually seen it. "I don't know what you—oh, I was singing."

"For what purpose is this singing?"

"I don't know. Just because I felt like singing, felt like music."

"What is music?"

Uhura started to laugh—there was something inherently ludicrous about discussing music with a machine—but the laugh died quickly. "Music is a pleasant arrangement of musical tones—sound vibrations of various frequencies, purer than those used in normal speech, and with associated harmonics. It can be immensely more complex than what I was doing just then."

"What is its purpose?"

Uhura shrugged helplessly. "Just for enjoyment."

"Insufficient response," said the machine. A pencil of light shot out from it, resting a spot of light on her forehead, between and slightly above the eyes. "Think about music."

Uhura's face went completely blank. Scott lunged to his feet. "Lieutenant! Get away from that thing—"

The elevator doors opened and Kirk, Spock and McCoy entered. "Scotty, look out—" Kirk shouted.

Scott had already reached the machine and grabbed for it, as if to shove it out of the way. There was no movement or effect from the craft, but the engineer was picked up and flung with tremendous impact against the nearest bulkhead. Sulu leapt up to yank Uhura out of the beam of light.

Kirk gestured toward Scott and McCoy strode to him quickly and knelt. Then he looked up. "He's dead, Jim."

For a moment Kirk stood stunned and appalled.

Then fury rose to free him from his paralysis. "Why did you kill him?" he asked Nomad grimly.

"That unit touched my screens."

"That *unit* was my chief engineer." He turned to Uhura. "Lieutenant, are you all right? . . . Lieutenant! . . . Dammit, Nomad, what did you do to *her?"*

"This unit is defective. Its thinking was chaotic. Absorbing it unsettled my circuitry."

"The unit is a woman," Spock said.

"A mass of conflicting impulses."

Kirk turned angrily away. "Take Mr. Scott below."

"The Creator will effect repairs on the unit Scott?"

"He's dead."

"Insufficient response."

"His biological functions have ceased." Kirk was only barely able to control his rage and sorrow.

"If the Creator wishes," Nomad said emotionlessly, "I will repair the unit."

Startled, Kirk looked at McCoy, who said, "There's nothing I can do, Jim. But if there's a chance, it'll have to be soon."

"All right. Nomad, repair the unit."

"I require tapes on the structure."

Spock looked to McCoy. The surgeon said, "It'll need tapes on general anatomy, the central nervous system, one on the physiological structure of the brain. We'd better give it all the neurological studies we have. And tracings of Scotty's electro-encephalogram."

Spock nodded and punched the commands into the library computer as McCoy called off the requirements. "Ready, Nomad."

The device glided forward. A thin filament of wire extruded from it and touched a stud on the panel. Spock tripped a toggle and the computer whirred.

Then it was over and the filament pulled back into Nomad. "An interesting structure. But, Creator, there are so few safeguards built in. It can break down from innumerable causes, and its self-maintenance systems are unreliable."

"It serves me as it is, Nomad," Kirk said.

"Very well, Creator. Where is the unit Scott now?"

"Bones, take it to Sickbay." Kirk snapped a switch

and said into his mike, "Security. Twenty-four hour two-man armed surveillance on Nomad. Pick it up in Sickbay." He turned to Spock. "Nomad is operating on some kind of energy. We've got to find out what it is and put a damper on it. Surely it can't be getting much cosmic radiation inside the *Enterprise;* we're well shielded. Let's feed in everything that's happened so far to the computer, and program for a hypothesis."

"It seems the most reasonable course, Captain. But it won't be easy."

"Easy or not, I want it done. Get on it, Mr. Spock. Then report to me in Sickbay."

Scott's body lay upon the examination table, with Nomad hovering over it. McCoy and Nurse Christine Chapel stood beside it, while Kirk and the two Security guards stood near the wall. Nomad, antenna extended, was scanning the body and humming.

The nurse looked toward the body-functions panel. "No reaction, Doctor."

"Could have told you that without looking, Nurse."

Suddenly, a light appeared on the panel, and a dial began quivering. In time with its movements, there came a steady beeping sound, gradually picking up in speed and volume.

Scott's eyes opened and he looked up at the amazed group, frowning. While he stared back, Spock joined the others. "What are the lot of you staring at?" Scott demanded.

"I . . . don't . . . believe it," McCoy whispered.

Scott looked around, and spotting Nomad, its antenna retracted now, he sat up in alarm. "What am I doing here? How did I—That thing did something to Lieutenant Uhura—"

"She's being taken care of, Scotty," Kirk said.

"But sir, it's dangerous! It—"

"Take it easy, Scotty," McCoy said. "Now just lie down. I want to check you out."

"The unit Scott is repaired," Nomad said. "It will function as before if your information to me was correct."

"How about it, Bones? Can he go back to duty?"

"If you don't mind, I'll check him out first. A man isn't just a . . . a biological unit to be patched together."

"What did it do to me?" Scott said.

Suddenly, a wave of pure awe, as strong as any he had ever felt in his life, swept through Kirk. Back from the dead! Why, if—but he pushed speculation resolutely away for the time being. "Dr. McCoy will explain, Scotty."

"Nurse Chapel," McCoy said, "I want him prepared for a full physical exam."

"Yes, sir."

Kirk crossed the examination room toward Sickbay proper, where Uhura now was. "Nomad, come here."

The machine glided after him, followed by Spock and McCoy. Inside, the Communications Officer lay unmoving on a bed, in a hospital gown and covered by a blanket. She did not look at any of them.

"Can you repair her, Nomad?" Kirk demanded.

"No," said the machine.

"But you were able to restore Scott, who had much more extensive damage."

"That was simply physiological repair. This one's superficial knowledge banks have been wiped clean."

"Superficial? Be more specific."

"She still remembers her life experiences, but her memory of how to express them, either logically or in the illogic called music, or to act on them, has been purged."

"Captain, if that is correct," Spock said, "if her mind has not been damaged and the aphasia is that superficial, she could be taught again."

"Bones?"

"I'll get on it right away." McCoy swung on Nomad. "And despite the way you repaired Scotty, you ticking metal—"

"Does the Creator wish Nomad to wait elsewhere?" Spock broke in quickly.

"Yes. Guards! Nomad, you will go with these units. They will escort you tc a waiting area. Guards, take it to the top security cell in the brig."

There was silence while the guards and the machine

went out. Then Spock said, "I interrupted you, Doctor, because Nomad would not have understood your anger. Its technical skill is great but it seems to react violently to emotion, even so non-specific an emotion as the enjoyment of music. It almost qualifies as a life-form itself."

Kirk glanced sharply at him. "It's all right to admire it, Mr. Spock, but remember it's a killer. We're going to have to handle it."

"I agree, Captain. It is a remarkable construction; it may well be the most advanced machine in the known galaxy. Study of it—"

"I intend to render it harmless, whatever it may take."

"You mean destroy it, Captain?"

"If it's necessary," Kirk said. "Get down to the brig with your equipment and run a full analysis of the mechanism. I want to know what makes that thing tick."

"Yes, sir."

The First Officer went out, and Kirk and McCoy returned to the examination room. Scott was still lying on the table. McCoy scanned the body functions panel slowly, and shook his head in disbelief.

"He checks out fine," he said. "Everything's normal."

"Then," Scott said, "can I get back to my engines, sir?"

Kirk glanced at McCoy, who nodded. "All right, Scotty."

"I hate to admit it," McCoy said as Scott swung off the table and left, "but Spock was right. Nomad is a remarkable machine."

"Just remember it kills as effectively as it heals, Bones . . . if I'm called, I'll be down in the brig."

The two Security guards, phasers in hand, stood outside the force-field door of the brig, which was on. Inside, Nomad floated, almost surrounded by an array of portable scanners, behind which was Spock, staring with disapproval at the machine. Nomad, its antenna out, "stared" back.

One of the guards switched off the screen to allow

Kirk to enter, then switched it on again. Kirk said, "What's the problem?"

"I have been unable to convince Nomad to lower its screens for analysis. Without its cooperation, I can do nothing."

Kirk studied the quietly humming machine. "Nomad, you will allow Spock to probe your memory banks and structure."

"This Spock is also one of your biological units, Creator?"

"Yes."

"This unit is different. It is well ordered. Interesting."

Under other circumstances, Kirk would have been amused to hear a machine applying Spock's favorite word to Spock himself, but the stakes were too great for amusement now. "Follow your orders, Nomad."

"My screens are down. You may proceed."

Spock set to work, very rapidly indeed, making settings, taking readings, making new settings. Within a few moments, he seemed to have found something which surprised him. He made another adjustment, and the machine he had been using promptly extruded a slip of paper, which he studied.

"Captain, I suggest we go out in the corridor for a private conference." They did so. "Sir, I have formed a partial hypothesis. But my information is insufficient and I have gleaned everything possible from the scanners. I must be allowed to question Nomad directly."

"Too dangerous."

"Captain, it moves only against imperfections. As you will recall, there is a Vulcan mind discipline which permits absolute concentration on one subject for a considerable period of time. If I were to use it—"

"And if your mind wandered for a moment, Nomad might just blast you out of existence. Right now it's safe in the brig."

"We do not know enough about it to know if it is 'safe' anywhere. If my hypothesis is correct, sir, we will at least be closer to understanding it. And control is not possible without understanding."

"All right," Kirk said, taking a phaser from one of the guards, "but I think I'll just keep this handy."

They went back in. Spock sat down on the cell bunk, for which the present prisoner had no use, and put his fingers to his temple. Kirk could almost hear his mind working.

"Nomad, my unit Spock will ask you certain questions. You will answer them as though I were asking them myself."

"Yes, Creator."

Silence. At last Spock said, "Nomad, there was an accident."

"There was an accident."

"You encountered the other."

"There was another. It was without direction. We joined."

"The other was not of the Earth. Its functions were other than yours." Spock held up the piece of paper, on which Kirk could see a drawing of what looked to be a space capsule of unfamiliar design. "I secured this design from your memory banks. Is this the other?"

"It is the other."

"Nomad, your memory banks were damaged by the accident. You took new directions from the other."

There was a buzz from the machine, and an antenna was aimed at Spock again. "Your statement is not recorded. You are in error."

"Logically, Nomad, you cannot prove I am in error, if your memory banks were damaged. You would have no way of knowing whether I speak the truth or not." Spock fell silent. The antenna retracted. "You acknowledge my logic. After meeting with the other, you had a new directive. Life-forms, if not perfect, are to be sterilized. Is this correct?"

"That is my programmed purpose."

"How much of the other did you assimilate?"

"Unrelated. Your question has no factual basis."

"Spock," Kirk said, "I think you're getting into deep waters. Better knock off."

Spock, unhearing, continued to stare at Nomad. The machine said: "There is error here. But if there was damage to my memory cells, there can be no proof of error. I will consider it."

"Enough," Kirk said firmly. Signaling to the guards to drop the screen, he dragged Spock out. The Vulcan was still glassy-eyed. "Mr. Spock! Come out of it!"

Slowly Spock's eyes began to focus. "Yes, Captain?"

"Are you all right?"

"Quite all right, sir." He looked back into the brig. "Fascinating. I was correct. It did meet a completely alien probe in deep space."

"And they merged—or at least their purposes did."

"In effect. Nomad took the alien's prime purpose to replace that part of its own which had been destroyed. The alien was originally programmed to seek out and sterilize soil samples from various planets—possibly as a preliminary to colonization."

"Hmm. Spock, do you know what a changeling is?"

"Sir?"

"An ancient Earth legend. A changeling was supposed to be a fairy child left in place of a stolen human baby. The changeling took the identity of the human child."

"That would be a parallel if Nomad is actually the alien probe intact. But actually, its programming now is a combination of the two. Nomad was supposed to find new life-forms; the alien to find and sterilize soil samples; the combination, and a deadly one, is to seek out and sterilize all life-forms. Moreover, the highly advanced alien technology, plus Nomad's own creative thinking, has enabled it to evolve itself into the incredibly powerful and sophisticated machine it is now."

"Not so sophisticated, Spock. It thinks I'm its . . . its father."

"Apparently Roykirk had enough ego to build a reverence for himself into the machine. That has been transferred to you—and so far it has been all that has saved us."

"Well, we'd better see to it that it never loses that reverence, Spock."

They were just about to enter an elevator when an intercom squalled with alarm. "Captain Kirk! This is Engineering! That alien device is down here, fooling with the anti-matter pod controls. We're up to Warp Ten now and can't stop!"

"Impossible! She won't go that fast."

"Warp Eleven now, sir."

"I'll be right down. Mr. Spock, check the brig."

The Engineering section was filled with the terrifying whine of the overdriven warp engines. Nomad was floating in front of the control panels, on which all the telltales glowed red.

Kirk rushed to the panel. "Nomad, you will stop whatever you're doing."

"Is there a problem, Creator? I have increased conversion efficiently by 57 percent—"

"You will destroy my ship. Its structure cannot stand the stress of that much power. Shut down your repair operation!"

"Acknowledged."

The whine began to die, and the panel returned to normal, the red lights blinking out one by one.

"It is reversed, as you ordered, Creator."

Spock entered the section and came up to Kirk. "Captain, I have examined the brig. The force-field generator of the security-cell door has been burnt out, and the guards have vanished. I must assume they are dead. I have asked for two more; they are outside."

"Creator, your mechanical units are as inefficient as your biological specimens."

"Nomad," Kirk said grimly, "it's time you were reminded of exactly who and what you are. I am a biological specimen—and you acknowledge that I built you."

"True," said the machine. *"Non sequitur*. Biological specimens are inherently inferior. This is an inconsistency."

"There are two men waiting outside. You will not harm them. They will escort you back to the waiting area. You will stay there. You will do nothing."

"I am programmed to investigate," Nomad said.

"I have given you new programming. You will implement it."

"There is much to be considered before I return to

launch point. I must re-evaluate." Lifting, the machine floated away through the door, through which the red shirts of two more Security guards could be seen.

"Re-evaluate?" Kirk said.

"Captain," said Spock, "it may have been unwise to admit to Nomad you were a biological specimen. In Nomad's eyes you will undoubtedly now appear as imperfect as all the other biological specimens. I suspect that it is about to re-evaluate its Creator."

Scott, having seen that his board had been put back to rights, had come over to them in time to catch the last sentence. He said, "Will we be any worse off than we are now?"

"Scotty, it's just killed two men," Kirk said. "We've got to find a way to protect the crew."

"Captain, it is even more serious," Spock said. "Nomad just made a reference to its launch point. Earth."

A horrible thought struck Kirk. "Spock, is there any chance Nomad got a navigational fix on Earth while tapping our computers earlier?"

"I don't believe there is much beyond Nomad's capabilities, sir."

"Then we showed it the way home! And when it gets there—"

Spock nodded. "It will find the Earth infested with inferior biological specimens—just as was the Malurian system."

"And it will carry out its new prime directive. Sterilize!"

As they stared at each other, McCoy's amplified voice boomed out. "Captain Kirk! Captain Kirk to Sickbay! Emergency!"

This, Kirk thought, is turning into a continuous nightmare. He ran, Spock at his heels.

At the door of the examination room, Kirk hammered on the touchplate. It did not open. As Spock turned down the corridor to actuate the manual controls, however, the door suddenly slid back and Nomad emerged.

"Nomad! Stop!"

The machine paid no heed, but went on down the

corridor. It passed Spock on the way, but ignored him too. In a moment it had vanished.

In the examination room, Christine lay unconscious on the floor. McCoy was bending over her with his medical tricorder.

"Is she all right, Bones?"

"I think so, Jim. Looks like some kind of shock."

"What happened?"

"Nomad examined the personnel files. The medical records. She tried to stop it."

"Whose medical history?"

"Yours, Jim."

"Since it specifically examined your history, Captain," Spock said, "I would suggest that it has carried out its re-evaluation."

"And," Kirk said grimly, "confirmed that its Creator is as imperfect as the rest of the biological specimens."

"Bridge to Captain Kirk," said the wall communicator.

"Kirk here. Report."

"Captain, life-support systems are out all over the ship. Manual override has been blocked! Source: Engineering."

"Carry on . . . well Mr. Spock, it seems you were right, and now we're in for it."

"Undoubtedly, Captain."

"Jim," McCoy said, "with all systems out, we only have enough air and heat for four and a half hours."

"I know that. Spock, get some anti-gravs and meet me and Scotty in Engineering."

"What is your plan, Captain?"

"I've got to use something you're a lot better at than I am. Logic."

"Then perhaps I—"

"No. I'm the one Nomad mistook for its Creator. And that's my ace. If I play it right—"

"I understand, Captain," Spock said quietly. "What you intend to do is most dangerous, however. If you make one mistake—"

"Then I'm dead and the ship is in the same mess it is now. Move!"

In Engineering, Nomad was busy at the panels again,

and the red alarm lights were winking back on. One crewman was slumped lifeless by the door, another in a corner; obviously they had tangled with Nomad and lost. Scott was crouched behind an engine, out of Nomad's sight.

Kirk went directly to the malignant machine, which ignored him. "Nomad, you will stop what you are doing and effect repairs on the life-support system."

There was no response. Kirk took another step toward the panel, and Nomad said, "Stop."

"You are programmed to obey the orders of your Creator."

"I am programmed to destroy those life-forms which are imperfect. These alterations will do so, without destroying the vessel on which they are parasitic. It, too, is imperfect, but it can be adjusted."

"Nomad . . . admitted that biological units are imperfect. But you were created by a biological unit."

"I am perfect. I am Nomad."

"You are not Nomad. You are an alien machine. Your programming tapes have been altered."

Silence. The door opened and Spock came in, an anti-grav under each arm; he was probably the only man on the ship strong enough to carry two of them. Kirk gestured him toward Scott's hiding place.

"You are in error," Nomad said at last. "You are a biological unit. You are imperfect."

"But I am the Creator?"

"You are the Creator."

"And I created you?"

"You are the Creator."

"I admit I'm imperfect. How could I create anything as perfect as you?"

"Answer unknown. I shall analyze."

The machine hummed. Spock and Scott edged a little closer.

"Analysis incomplete," said Nomad. "Insufficient data to resolve problem. But my programming is whole. My purpose remains. I am Nomad. I am perfect. That which is imperfect must be sterilized."

"Then you will continue to destroy all that lives and thinks and is imperfect?"

"I shall continue. I shall return to launch point. I shall sterilize."

"Then . . . you *must* sterilize in case of error?"

"Errors are inconsistent with my prime function. Sterilization is correction."

"All that errs is to be sterilized?"

"There are no exceptions."

Kirk felt himself sweating. So far, so good; the machine, without being aware of it, had backed itself into a logical corner. It was time to play the ace. "I made an error in creating you, Nomad."

"The creation of perfection is no error."

"But I did not create perfection, Nomad. I created error."

"I am Nomad. I am perfect. Your data are faulty."

"I am Kirk, the Creator?"

"You are the Creator. But you are a biological unit and are imperfect."

"But I am *not* the Creator. Jackson Roykirk, who was the Creator, is dead. You have mistaken me for him! You have made an error! You did not discover your mistake! You have made two errors! You are flawed and imperfect—but you did not correct the errors by sterilization! You are imperfect! You have made three errors!"

Under the hammering of his voice, the machine's humming rose sharply in pitch. Nomad said, "Error? Error? Examine!"

"You are flawed! You are imperfect! Execute your prime function!"

"I shall analyze . . . error . . . an . . . a . . . lyze . . . err . . ." Nomad's voice slowed to a stop. The humming continued to rise. Kirk whirled to Scott and Spock.

"Now! Get those anti-gravs on it. We've got to get rid of it while it's trying to think its way out of that box. It won't be able to do it, and there's no telling how long it'll take to decide that for itself—"

They wrestled the anti-gravs onto the whining mechanism. Spock said, "Your logic is impeccable, Captain. We are in grave danger."

They hoisted Nomad and started toward the door with it. "Where to, sir?" Scott said.

"Transporter Room!"

The distance to be covered was not great. As they entered, Kirk took over wrestling with Nomad from Scott, and they dragged the thing to the platform. "Scotty, set the controls for deep space. Two-twelve mark 10 ought to be far enough."

Scott jumped to the console, and Kirk and Spock deposited the humming Nomad on one of the stations.

"Ready, sir."

Kirk and Spock jumped back, and Kirk shouted: "Nomad, you are imperfect. Exercize your prime function. Mr. Scott, energize!"

The Transporter effect swirled Nomad into nothingess.

"Now, the bridge, quick!"

But they were scarcely out into the corridor before the entire ship rocked violently, throwing them all. Then the ship steadied. They clambered to their feet and ran on.

On the bridge, they found Sulu wiping streaming eyes. "Captain, I wish you'd let me know when you're going to stage a fireworks display. Luckily I wasn't looking directly at the screen."

"Sorry, Mr. Sulu." Kirk went to his command chair and sat down with immense relief. Spock looked at him with respect.

"I must congratulate you, Captain," the Vulcan said. "That was a dazzling display of logic."

"Didn't think I had it in me, did you?"

"Now that you make the suggestion, sir—"

"Well, I didn't, Spock. I played a hunch. I had no idea whether or not it could tolerate the idea of its own fallibility. And when I said it couldn't think its way out of the box, that was for its benefit. Actually, we biological units are well known for our unreliability. Supposing it had decided that I was lying?"

McCoy came in and approached the chair. Spock said gravely, "That possibility also occurred to me, which was why I praised your reasoning while we were still in Engineering. But Nomad really was fallible; by not recognizing that possibility itself, it committed a fourth error."

"I thought you'd like to know," McCoy said, "that Lieutenant Uhura is already at college level. We'll have her back on the job within a week."

"Good, Bones. I wish I could say the same for the other crewmen we lost."

"Still," said Spock, "the destruction of Nomad was a great waste. It was a remarkable instrument."

"Which might well have destroyed more billions of lives. It's well gone . . . besides, what are you feeling so bad about? Think of me. It's not easy to lose a bright and promising son."

"Captain?"

"Well, it thought I was its father, didn't it? Do you think I'm completely without feelings, Mr. Spock? You saw what it did for Scotty. What a doctor it would have made." Kirk grinned. "My son, the doctor. Kind of gets you right here, doesn't it?"

THE PARADISE SYNDROME

(Margaret Armen)

Doom was in the monster asteroid hurtling toward the planet on a collision course.

It was a fate which Kirk refused to accept. Stately pine trees edged the meadow where he, Spock and McCoy had materialized. There was the nostalgic fragrance of honeysuckle in his nostrils mingled with the freshness of wild roses. From somewhere nearby he could hear the murmur of a brook bubbling over pebbles. Violets, he thought. Their flat, sweet green leaves would carpet its damp banks, the flowers hidden among them.

"It's unbelievable," he said, suddenly homesick, Earth-sick. He stooped to pick a buttercup. "How long, Bones, since you saw one of these?"

"At least three years, Jim."

"It seems like three hundred." But the planet's similarity to Earth was less of a mystery than the astounding fact of its survival. It was located in a sector of its solar system where an asteroid belt had succeeded in smashing all other planets into dusty, drifting desolation.

"Two months from now when that giant asteroid hits this place—" McCoy began.

"We're here to see that it doesn't hit it," Kirk said. "Spock, how much time do we have to investigate?"

"If we're to divert the asteroid, Captain, we must warp out of orbit within thirty hours. Every second we delay in reaching the deflection point will compound the problem, perhaps past solution."

McCoy halted. "What in blazes is *that?*" he exclaimed.

Ahead of them, topping a shallow hill stood a tall tower, obelisk-shaped, composed of some gleaming metal. Wild flowers were heaped around its base. Nearing it, they could see that its surface was inscribed with curious, unreadable symbols.

"Analysis, Mr. Spock."

Spock was readjusting a dial on his tricorder. He frowned. "Incomplete, sir. It's an alien metal of some kind—an alloy resistant to probe. Readings can't even measure its age accurately."

"Any theories about what it could be?"

"Negative, Captain. But alloys of this complexity are found only in cultures that parallel our own—or surpass it."

"Buttercups in a meteor area but no meteor craters," McCoy said. "The whole place is an enigma, biologically and culturally."

"Thirty hours," Kirk said. "Let's not waste them. This Paradise may support some life-forms."

It did. Below the obelisk's hill lay a clearing. Copper-skinned people were moving about in it with an ease which declared it to be their home. In its center a large, circular lodge lifted to a roof that seemed thatched with reeds. Animal hides had been sewn together and stretched to compose its walls. A woman, children around her, was mixing meal with water she dipped from a crude pottery bowl with a gourd. Near her an old man, a heap of what looked like flint arrow heads beside him, was bent over his work. To his right, younger men, magnificently muscled, bows slung over their shoulders, were gathered around a painted skin target, engaged in some amiable argument. Perhaps it was the way the russet tone of their bodies blended with the hue of their beaded leather clothing that explained the sense of peace that lay like a blessing over the whole settlement. Here was man at one with his environment.

"Why, they look—I'd swear they are American Indians!" cried McCoy.

"They are," Spock said. "A mixture of advanced tribes—Navajo, Mohican, Delaware."

"It's like coming on Shangri-La," Kirk said. "Could there be a more evolved civilization on this planet, Spock? One capable of building that obelisk—or developing an asteroid-deflector system?"

"The sensors indicate only one form of life type here, Captain."

"Shouldn't we tell them, Jim?"

"What, Bones? That an asteroid is going to smash their world to atoms?"

Spock said, "Our appearance would only serve to frighten and confuse them, Doctor."

"All right," Kirk said abruptly. "We've got a job to do. Let's get back to the *Enterprise.*" But as he turned away, he looked back at the Indian village, his face wistful, a little envious.

"Something wrong, Jim?"

"What?" Kirk said absently. "Oh, nothing. It just looks so peaceful and uncomplicated. No problems, no command decisions. Just *living.*"

McCoy smiled. "Back in the twentieth century it was called the 'Tahiti syndrome,' Jim— a typical reaction to idyllic, unspoiled nature. It's especially common to overpressured leader types like Star Fleet captains."

"All right, Bones. So I need a vacation. First let's take care of that asteroid."

Kirk moved on toward the obelisk. Stepping on to its pediment, he flipped open his communicator. "Kirk to *Enterprise*!"

"Aye, Captain." It was Scott's voice.

The order for beam-up was on Kirk's lips when the metal under his feet gave way. What appeared to be a panel in the pediment slid open and tumbled him down a steep flight of stairs. In the narrow shaft of daylight that shone through the gap, he had barely time to note that the panel's underside was dotted with varicolored control buttons. Then the panel closed silently. Groggy, he raised his head—and his shoulder hit one of the buttons. A shrill buzz sounded. A blue-green beam flashed out. It widened and spread until he was completely bathed in blue-green luminescence. It held him, struggling. Then he fell down the rest of the steep stairs—and lay still.

Spock was the first to notice his disappearance. Appalled, McCoy joined him. They circled the obelisk, their anxiety mounting in them. When Spock had raked the empty meadow with his eyes to no effect, he opened his communicator, reported the news to Scott and ordered beam-down of a Security Guard search party. But neither the Guards nor their sensor probes succeeded where the Vulcan's sharp eyes had failed. The panel gave no hint of its existence. Stern-faced, Spock gave the meadow another rake with his eyes before he made his decision. He jerked open his communicator to say curtly, "Prepare to beam us all back up, Mr. Scott. We're warping out of orbit immediately."

"Leaving? You can't be serious, Spock!" McCoy said.

"That asteroid is almost as large as your Earth's moon, Doctor—"

"The devil with the asteroid!" McCoy shouted. "It won't get here for two months!"

"If we reach that deflection point in time, it may not get here at all." Spock's face was impassive.

"In the meantime, what about Jim?"

"As soon as the asteroid is diverted, we will return and resume the search."

"That'll be hours from now! He may be hurt! Dying!"

Spock faced him. "If we fail to reach that deflection point at the exact moment, we will not be able to divert it. In such case, Doctor, everyone on this planet, including the Captain, will die."

"Can a few minutes more matter?"

"In the time it has taken for this explanation, the asteroid has sped thousands of miles closer to this planet—and to the Captain." Imperturbable, he spoke into his communicator. "Beam us up, Mr. Scott."

Scott's voice was heavy with disapproval. "Beaming up, Mr. Spock."

The object of their concern wasn't dying; but he was breathing painfully, slowly. He seemed to be in a large, vaultlike chamber; but the dizziness in his head made it as hard for his eyes to focus as it made it to remember where he'd come from or how he'd got here. He was sure of nothing but the vertigo that swayed him in sickly waves when he tried to stand up. In his fall, he'd dropped his phaser and communicator. Now he stumbled over them. He picked them up, staring at them without recognizing them. After a moment, he stopped puzzling over them to start groping his way up the metal stairs. As he stepped on the first one, a sharp musical note sounded. He accepted it with the same dazedness that had accepted the unfamiliarity of his phaser and communicator. Then his reaching hand brushed against some button in the panel above him. It slid open as silently as it had closed; and he hauled himself up through it into the daylight.

The three girls, flower baskets in their arms, startled him. So did their bronze skins. They were staring at him, more astonished than he was. One was beautiful, he thought. Under the long, black hair that glittered in the sunshine, she bore herself with the dignity of a young queen, despite the amazement on her face.

In their mutually dumbfounded silence, he decided he liked her high cheekbones. They emphasized the lovely, smooth planes of her brow, cheeks and chin. The other two girls seemed frightened of him. So was she, he suspected; but she didn't turn to run away. Instead, she made a commanding gesture to her companions—and dropped to her knees at Kirk's feet. Then the others knelt, too. All three placed their palms on their foreheads.

Kirk found his voice. It was hoarse. "Who—are you?" he said.

"I am Miramanee," the queenlike girl said. "We are your people. We have been waiting for you to come."

But her ready welcome of him wasn't repeated so quickly from the elderly chief of the Indian village.

Kirk's greeting into the communal lodge was courteous but reserved. It was primitively but comfortably furnished with mats and divans of deerhide. Tomahawks, spears, skin shields and flint knives decorated its walls. There was a fire pit in its center, embers in it still glowing red. The chief sat beside it. Flanking him, three young braves kept their black eyes fixed on Kirk's face. One wore a gleaming silver headband, embossed with a emblem into which a likeness of the obelisk had been etched. Miramanee made her obeisance to the chief; and turning to Kirk, said, "This is Goro."

The old man gestured to a pile of skins across from him.

"Our priestess has said you appeared to her and her handmaidens from the walls of the temple. So it is that our legend foretells. Though we do not doubt the words of Miramanee, these are troubled times. We must be sure."

"I'll answer any questions I can," Kirk said, "but as I told your priestess, many things are strange to me."

The warrior who wore the emblemed headband cried out, "He doesn't even know our danger! How can he save us?"

"Silence, Salish! It is against custom to interrupt the tribal Elder in council! Even for the Medicine chief!"

But Salish persisted. "Words will not save us when the skies darken! I say he must *prove* he is a god!"

"I will have silence!" Goro addressed Kirk. "Three times the skies have darkened since the harvest. Our legend predicts much danger. It promises that the Wise Ones who placed us here will send a god to save us—one who can awake the temple spirit and make the skies grow quiet. Can you do this?"

Kirk hesitated, searching frantically through his emptied memory for some recollection that would make sense of the question. He saw the suspicion in Salish's eyes hardening into open scorn. "I came from the temple," he said finally. "Just as Miramanee has told . . . but I came from the sky, too. I can't remember this clearly, but—"

His stumbling words were interrupted by a stir at the lodge entrance. A man entered, the limp body of a boy in his arms. Both were dripping wet. Miramanee, her hand on the boy's soaked hair, cried, "A bad thing has happened! Salish, the child does not breathe! The fish nets pulled him to the bottom of the river. Lino has brought him quickly but he does not move!"

Rising, the Medicine chief went to the boy, and bending his ear to the chest, listened intently. Then he pried open an eyelid to peer into the pupil. After a moment, he straightened. "There is no sound in the body," he announced, "and no light in the eyes. The child will move no more."

Lino had laid the small body on a heap of skins. Kirk glanced around at the shocked, stricken faces. He got up, moved quickly to the child and raised the head. "He is still breathing," he said. Then he stooped to place his mouth on the cold lips. Breathing regularly and deeply, he exhaled air into them. After a moment, he seized the ankles; and began to flex them back and forward against the chest. Salish made a threatening move toward him. He held up a restraining hand and Goro called, "Wait!"

The keen old ears had heard the slight moan. The child stirred feebly—and began to retch. Kirk massaged him briskly. There was a gasping breath. The eyes opened. Kirk stood up, relief flooding through him. "He will be all right now," he said.

Goro placed his palm on his forehead. "The people are grateful."

"It's a simple technique. It goes away back . . . away back to—"

His voice trailed off. Away back to where? He couldn't remember. This "simple technique"—where had he learned it? Now that the emergency's tension had passed, it was replaced by an anguish of frustration. How had he been marooned in a present that denied him any past? Who was he? He felt as though he were dissolving, his very being slipping through his fingers like so much water.

In a dream he heard Goro say, "Only a god can breathe life into the dead." In a dream he saw him turn to the three young braves. "Do you still question that the legend is fulfilled?"

Two shook their heads. Salish alone refused to touch palm to forehead. Goro turned to Miramanee. "Give the Medicine lodge to the god."

Still in his nightmare of non-being, Kirk felt the silver band of the Medicine chief placed on his head.

It was Scott's angry opinion that too much was being asked of his engines.

"I can't give you Warp Nine much longer, Spock." Calculated disrespect went into the engineer's intercom. "My engines are showing signs of stress."

"Stress or not, we cannot reduce speed, Mr. Scott."

"If these circuits of mine get much hotter—"

The nervous systems of the *Enterprise* bridge personnel were also showing signs of stress. Their circuits were getting hot under pressure of the race against time being made by the asteroid. Spock alone preserved his equanimity. But even his quiet eyes were riveted to the main viewing screen where a small luminous blip was becoming increasingly visible. The irregular mass of the thing grew larger and larger, its dull though multiple colors revealing themselves more distinctly with every moment.

"Deflection point minus seven," Chekov said.

"Full power, Mr. Scott," Spock said into his intercom.

"The relays will reject the overload!"

"Then bypass the relays. Go to manual control."

"If I do that, we'll burn out the engines!"

"I want full power," Spock said tonelessly.

"Aye, sir."

The First Officer swung the command chair around to Sulu. "Magnification, factor 12, Mr. Sulu."

Sulu moved a control switch—and the image on the screen jumped into enormous contour. For the first time the asteroid's ominous details could be seen, malignantly jagged—a sharp-fanged mass of rock speeding toward them through the trackless vacuum of space.

"Deflection point minus four," Chekov said.

Spock looked away from the frightful immensity on the screen and Chekov said, "Minus three now, sir."

The Vulcan hit his intercom button. "All engines stop. Hold position here, Mr. Scott."

"All engines stopped, sir."

"Prepare to activate deflectors."

"Aye, sir."

There was an irregular cracking sound, acutely heard in the sudden silence usually filled by the engines' smooth humming. The ship vibrated.

"Power dropping, sir!" cried Sulu.

"Engineering section! Maintain full power. *Full power!*"

Scott's voice was hard. "Dilythium circuits failing, sir. We'll have to replace them."

"Not now," Spock said.

"Zero! Deflection point—we've reached it, sir!"

"Activate!" Spock said sharply.

On the screen the monstrous mass glowed redly. Then the glow flickered and faded.

"Degree of deflection, Mr. Sulu?"

"Insufficient, sir."

It was defeat. Horrified silence held the bridge in thrall.

The composure of Spock's voice came like a benediction. "Recircuit power to engines, Mr. Scott. Maximum speed. The heading is 37 mark 010."

"That heading will put us right in the asteroid's path, sir."

"I am aware of that, Mr. Chekov. My intention is to retreat before it until we can employ all our power on our phaser beams."

"What for?" McCoy demanded.

"To destroy it." Spock turned his chair around as though he were addressing the entire personnel in the bridge. "A narrow phaser beam," he said, "that is concentrated on a single spot of that rock will split it."

"It's also likely to cripple the ship," McCoy said. "Then we'll be crushed by the thing."

"Incorrect, Doctor. We could still evade its path by using our impulse power."

"Jim won't be able to get out of its path!"

"That is another calculated risk we must take," Spock said.

Miramanee, her arms full of new buckskin garments, was approaching Kirk's Medicine lodge when Salish stepped out from behind a pine tree.

"Where are you going?" he said.

"It is my duty to see to the needs of the god," she said quietly.

Salish tore the clothing from her. "You should be working on our ritual cloak!"

She retrieved the clothing. "There will be no ritual between us now, Salish." She spoke gently.

"You cannot go against tradition!"

"It is because of tradition that we cannot now be joined," she said.

"You are promised to *me!*"

"That was before he came."

"Tribal priestess and Medicine chief are always joined!"

"He is the Medicine chief." She paused. "Choose another, Salish. Any maiden will be honored to join with you."

"I do not wish another."

Genuine compassion came into her face. "You have no choice," she said.

"And if you had a choice, Miramanee, would you choose me?"

She didn't answer. His face darkened. He wheeled and strode off into a grove of sycamore trees. She shook her head sadly as she watched him disappear. Then her black eyes lit. She walked quickly toward the Medicine lodge; and Kirk, roused from his brooding by her entrance, looked up at her and smiled.

"Perhaps you would like to bathe before you clothe yourself in these." She placed the Indian garments at his feet.

"Miramanee, tell me about the Wise Ones."

"Tell? But a god knows everything."

"Not this god," Kirk said wryly. "Tell me."

She knelt beside him, fingering his uniform wonderingly. "The Wise Ones? They brought us here from far away. They chose a Medicine chief to keep the secret of the temple and to use it when the sky darkens." She reached to touch the back of his uniform. "There are no lacings here," she said, puzzled. "How is it removed?"

He knew he was flushing and felt like a fool. Gently he removed her hand. "And the secret was passed from father to son? Then why doesn't Salish use the secret? Why are the people in danger?"

Still puzzled, she was seeking a way to loosen his belt. "The father of Salish died before he could tell him the secret."

Kirk had taken her hands in his when two girls, accompanied by Goro, came into the lodge. They placed their baskets of fruit at his feet; and Goro, touching his forehead respectfully, said, "The people honor your name. But they do not know what you wish to be called."

Kirk felt the anguish of frustration again. "What do I want to be called?" equaled "Who am I?"—that "I" of his without a Past, without identity. He was sweating as he fought to dredge up one small clue to the Past that was hidden from him—and suddenly one word advanced from its blackness. He said, "Kir . . . Kirk. I wish to be called Kirk."

"Kirok?" Goro said.

Kirk nodded. He was exhausted. Something in his face frightened the fruit bearers. They had hoped for the god's approval, not this look of lostness. They withdrew; and Goro, anxious, asked, "Have the gifts displeased you?"

"No. They are good."

"Then it must be ourselves—the way we live. Perhaps we have failed to improve as quickly as the Wise Ones wished."

Kirk could take no more. He found what he hoped were comforting words. "Your land is rich and your people are happy. The Wise Ones could not be displeased with you."

"But there is something," Goro insisted. "Tell us and we will change it."

"I—I can't tell you anything. Except that I have been peaceful and glad here."

Mercifully, Goro seemed satisfied. When he'd left,

Kirk turned almost angrily to Miramanee. "Why are they so sure I can save them?"

"You came from the temple. And did you not return life to the dead child?"

He placed his tortured head in his hands. "I—need time," he said, "time to try and remember . . ."

She placed the buckskin garments on his knees. "Here is much time, my god. Much quietness and much time."

The simplicity with which she spoke was oil on his flayed soul. The strain in it relaxed. "Yes," he said. "Thank you, Miramanee."

The *Enterprise* and the asteroid were speeding on a parallel course. A terrible companion, it traveled with them, a voracious menace that devoured the whole area of the bridge's main viewing screen.

"Coordinates, Mr. Chekov?"

"Tau—eight point seven, sir. Beta—point zero four one."

"That's our target, Mr. Chekov—the asteroid's weakest point."

Chekov gave Spock a look of awed respect. "Yes, almost dead center, sir."

"Lock all phasers on that mark, Mr. Sulu. Maximum intensity, narrow beam. I want that fissure split wide open."

"You sound like a diamond-cutter, Spock," McCoy said.

"An astute analogy, Doctor."

"Phasers locked, sir," Sulu said.

"We will fire in sequence. And will continue firing as long as Mr. Scott can maintain power."

"Standing by, sir."

"Fire phasers!"

The ship trembled. "Phaser one firing!"

Sulu hit another button. "Phaser two fired!"

On the screen the rocky mass loomed larger than the ship. Fragments erupted from it as the phasers' blue beams struck it.

"Phaser three fired, sir! Phaser four!"

Another cloud of rock segments, sharp, huge were torn from the asteroid.

"All phasers fired, sir."

The stillness of Spock's face gave impressive poignancy to the tone of bitter disappointment in his voice. "Rig for simultaneous firing, Mr. Sulu."

In the engineering section, Scott muttered to an assistant, "That Vulcan won't be satisfied till all these panels are a lead puddle!" As he spoke there was a sharp metallic click—and one of his main relays began to smoke.

"Main relay's out again, Mr. Scott!" cried the assistant.

"Machines are smarter than people," his chief said. "At least they know enough to quit before they blow themselves up!"

"Commence simultaneous bombardment." As Spock's order was heard on the intercom, a white-hot flash leaped from the engine compartment. There was the roar of an explosion that hurled Scott back against the opposite bulkhead. Spread-eagled, clinging to it, he was close to tears as he watched the death of his friends—his engines. "My bairns," he said brokenly. "My poor bairns . . ."

"Kirok."

It was a soft whisper but it roused Kirk from his uneasy doze. Kneeling beside him, Miramanee said, "The ritual cloak is finished."

She was very close to him. Under his eyes the long black hair drooped. "If it pleases you, I will name the Joining Day."

"The Joining Day?"

"I am the daughter of chiefs," she said. "Tribal law gives me to our god."

Kirk looked at her, uncomprehending. She bowed her head. "If there is another in your heart, Kirok . . ."

"There is no one else, Miramanee. In my mind or in my heart."

She was still disturbed by what she feared was his lack of response. "A god's wish is above tribal law. If you do not wish—"

Kirk reached for her. "Miramanee, name the Joining Day."

The shining lashes lifted. "The sooner our happiness together begins, the longer it will last. I name—tomorrow."

The Past was a darkness, cold, impenetrable. If he was a prisoner of the Present, at least it offered this warmth, this glow in the black-lashed eyes. Kirk drew her fiercely to him. He bent his head to her mouth.

Spock had retreated to his quarters. McCoy, entering them without knocking, found him staring at his viewer. "I told you to *rest,* Spock! For the love of heaven, quit looking at that screen!"

The intercom spoke. Scott said furiously, "Our star drive is completely burned out! So don't ask for any more Warp Nine speed! The only thing you've left us, Spock, is impulse power!"

"Estimated repair time?" the Vulcan asked the intercom.

"Hanging here in space? Forever. The only way to fix my engines is to get to the nearest repair base!"

McCoy snapped off the intercom. He laid his hand on Spock's shoulder. "You took that calculated risk for us, for that planet—and for Jim. That you took it is important. That you lost it—well, losing it was in your calculation."

"I accept the full responsibility for the failure, Doctor."

"And my responsibility is the health of this crew. You are to stop driving yourself so hard."

Spock switched the intercom back on. "Resume heading 883 mark 41, Mr. Chekov."

"Why, that's back to the planet!" McCoy cried. "Without warp speed, getting to it will take months!"

"Exactly 59.223 days, Doctor. And the asteroid will be four hours behind us all the way."

"Then what's the use? Even if the Captain is still alive, we may not be able to save him! We may not be able to save anything—not even the ship!" McCoy hit the wall. "You haven't heard a word I have said!

All you've been doing is staring at that damn—" He strode over to the screen and struck the image of the obelisk that had appeared on it.

"Another calculated Vulcan risk, Doctor."

Miramanee was radiant in her bridal finery. She was surrounded by women who had crowded into the tribal lodge. As one placed a chaplet of flowers on the shining black hair, she said, "This Joining Day is the end of darkened skies."

Salish dropped the hide back over the lodge's entrance. On his moccasined feet, he walked swiftly toward the obelisk where the god-groom in festive dress was submitting his face to the paint Goro was applying to it from a gourd.

Goro handed the gourd to a young brave. "It is I who must tell the priestess you will follow," he said. "Wait here until I have walked the holy path to the tribal lodge."

When Goro had disappeared down the sun-dappled path, Kirk, smiling, stepped from the obelisk to make his way to the lodge and Miramanee. Salish, dropping from a pine bough above him, stood facing him, blocking the trail. His face was raw with hate.

"Get out of my way," Kirk said.

"Kirok, even though you are a god, I will not permit this joining." Salish pulled a flint knife. "Before I permit it, you must strike me dead."

"I don't wish to strike anybody dead," Kirk said. But Salish jumped him. Kirk sidestepped the lunge; and Salish, rushing him again, scraped the knife across his cheek.

"You bleed, Kirok! Gods do not bleed!" He drove at Kirk with the knife, murder in his eyes. They grappled; and Kirk wrenched the knife from his grasp. Salish flung himself to the ground. "Kill me, Kirok! Kill me now! And I will return from the dead to prove to the people you are no god!"

Kirk looked at the maddened face at his feet. Placing the knife in his belt, he stepped over the prone body and moved on down the path. This imposed god-role of his had its liabilities. On the other hand it had brought him Miramanee. At the thought of her he hastened his stride toward the lodge.

Two braves greeted him at its entrance. A magnificent feathered cloak was placed around his shoulders. Miramanee moved to him; and on instruction, he enfolded her in the cloak to signify the oneness of marriage. Goro struck a stone chime with a mallet. There were shouts of delight from the people. Beads rattled in gourds, tom-toms beat louder and louder—and Miramanee, slipping from under the cloak, ran from the lodge. At the entrance, she paused to look back at him, her flower-crowned face bright with inviting laughter. This time Kirk didn't need instruction. He sped after her, the feathered cloak flying behind him.

She'd reached the pine woods when he caught her. She fell to the soft bed of scented needles and he flung himself down beside her.

He grew to love the pine woods. It was pure happiness to help Miramanee gather their fragrant boughs for the fire pit in their Medicine lodge. He loved Miramanee, too; but sometimes her black eyes saw too deeply.

They were lying, embraced, beside the fire pit when she lifted her head from his shoulder. "Each time you hold me is more joyous than it was on our Joining Day. But you—"

He kissed her eyelids. "It's the dreams," he said.

"I thought they had gone. I thought you no longer looked for the strange lodge in the sky."

He released her. "The dreams have returned. I see faces, too. Even in daylight, I see faces. They're dim—but I feel that I know them. I—I feel my place is where they are. Not here—not here. I have no right to all this happiness . . ."

She smiled down into his troubled face. "I have a gift for you." She reached her hand under the blanket they lay on and withdrew the papoose board she'd hidden under it. She knelt to lay it at his feet.

"I carry your child, my Kirok."

Kirk was swept by a sense of almost intolerable

tenderness. The lines of anxiety in his face softened. He drew her head back to his shoulder.

Again without knocking, McCoy entered Spock's quarters.

"I thought I told you to report to Sickbay," he said belligerently.

Spock didn't so much as glance up from his small cabin computer. "There isn't time," he said. "I've got to decipher those obelisk symbols. I judge them to be a highly advanced form of coding."

"You've been trying to do that ever since we started back to the planet! That's fifty-eight days ago!"

Spock passed a hand over his tired eyes as though to wipe a mist away from them. He had grown gaunt from fatigue. "I'm aware of that, Doctor. I'm also aware that we'll have barely four hours to effect rescue when we reach the planet. I feel those symbols are the key."

"You won't decipher them by killing yourself!" McCoy adopted the equable tone of reason. "Spock, you've hardly eaten or slept for weeks now. If you don't let up on yourself, it is rational to expect collapse."

"I am not hungry, Doctor. And under stress we Vulcans can do without sleep for weeks."

McCoy aimed his medical tricorder at him. Peering at it, he said, "Well, I can tell you your Vulcan metabolism is so low it can hardly be measured. And as for the pressure of that green ice water in your veins you call blood—"

To straighten Spock had to support himself by clutching his console. "My physical condition is not important. That obelisk is."

"My diagnosis is exhaustion caused by overwork and guilt. Yes, *guilt.* You're blaming yourself for crippling the ship." McCoy shook Spock's shoulder. "Listen to me! You made a command decision. Jim would have made the same one. My prescription is rest. Do I have to call the Security Guards to enforce it?"

Spock shook his head. He moved unsteadily to his bunk and lay down. No sooner had McCoy, satisfied, closed the door behind him than he got up again—and returned to his viewer.

Kirk was trying to improve the lighting of his lodge by constructing a crude lamp. But Miramanee could not grasp the function of the wick.

"It will make night into day?" she said wonderingly. "And I can cook more and pre—pre . . ."

"Preserve food," Kirk said.

"For times of famine." They smiled at each other. "Ah," she said, "that is why you are making the lamp, Kirok. So I shall be forever cooking."

His laugh ended abruptly. Miramanee's face had gone tight with terror. A gust of wind pulled at the lodge's hide door. "There is nothing to fear," he said. "It is just wind."

"Miramanee is a stupid child," she said. "No, there is nothing to fear. You are here." But she had moved to the lodge door to look nervously up at the sky. She turned. "It is time to go to the temple, Kirok. The people will be there waiting for you."

"Why?"

"To save them," she said simply.

"Wind can't harm them." But the gravity in her face didn't lighten. "The wind is just the beginning," she said. "Soon the lake will go wild, the river will grow big. Then the sky will darken and the earth will shake. Only you can save us."

"I can't do anything about the wind and the sky."

She removed the lamp from his hand, seized his arm pleadingly to pull him toward the door. "Come, Kirok. You must come."

A sense of threat suddenly oppressed him. "Miramanee, wait—"

She pulled harder at him, her panic mounting. "We must go before it is too late! You must go inside the temple and make the blue flame shine!"

Kirk stared at her, helpless to reach her understanding. "I don't know how to get inside the temple!"

"You are a god!"

He grabbed her shoulders roughly. *I am not a god.* I am a man—just a man."

She shrank from him. "No! No! You are a god, Kirok!"

"Look at me," he said. "And *listen.* I am not a god.

If you can only love a god, you cannot love me. I say it again— I am a *man!*"

She flung her arms about his neck, covering his face with frantic kisses. "It must be kept secret, then! If you are not a god, the people will kill you!"

A fiercer gust of wind shook the poles of the lodge. Miramanee screamed. "You must speak to the people—or they will say you are not a god. Come, Kirok, come!"

The tribe had gathered in the central lodge. Under the onslaught of the rising wind, shields, spears, knives had been torn from their places on the hide walls. Women were screaming, pulling at children, shoving them under heaps of skins. Salish fought his way through the maddened crowd to confront Kirk.

"Why are you not at the temple, Kirok? Soon the ground will begin to tremble!"

"We shall all go to the caves," Kirk said.

"The caves!" Salish shouted. "Is that the best a god can do for his people?"

Goro spoke. "When the ground trembles, even the caves are unsafe, Kirok. You must rouse the spirit of the temple—or we will all die!"

"What are you waiting for, god?" Salish said.

Kirk unclasped Miramanee's arms from his neck and placed her hand in Goro's. "Take care of her," he said. "I will go to the temple."

Outside, the gale tore his breath from his lungs. Somewhere to his left a pine tree crashed. Thunder rumbled along the horizon in a constant cannonade. And the sky was darkening. Boughs whipped across his face as he groped his half-blind way down the worn trail to the obelisk. The enigmatic tower told him nothing. Its inscrutable symbols held their secret as remorselessly as ever. Kirk beat at the hard metal with his fists, shouting, screaming at it, "I am Kirok! I have come! Open to me!"

The words were drowned by the screams of the unhearing wind.

McCoy stopped dead at the door of Spock's quarters.

Strains of unearthly music were coming from the cabin. Maybe *I've* broken," McCoy thought. "Maybe

I've died, gone to heaven and am hearing the music of the spheres." It wasn't music of the spheres. It was music got from an oddly shaped Vulcan harp. Spock, huddled over his computer, was strumming it, his face tight with concentration.

"I prescribed sleep," McCoy said.

"Inaccurate, Doctor. You prescribed rest." The musician looked up from his instrument. "The obelisk symbols are not letters. They are musical notes."

"You mean a song?"

"In a way. Certain cultures, offshoots of our Vulcan one, use musical notes as words. The tones correspond roughly to an alphabet." He laid the harp aside. "The obelisk is a marker left by a super race on that planet. Apparently, they passed through the galaxy, rescuing primitive cultures threatened by extinction—and 'seeded' them, so to speak, where they could live and grow."

"Well," said McCoy. "I must admit I've wondered why so many humanoids were scattered through this galaxy."

"So have I. I judge the Preservers account for a number of them."

"Then these 'Preservers' must have left that obelisk on the planet as an asteroid-deflector."

Spock nodded. "It's become defective."

"So we have to put it back in working order. Otherwise . . ."

"Precisely, Doctor."

The earth around the obelisk was shaking. Villagers, panicked to the point of madness, had fled to their temple in a last hope of salvation. Kirk, backed against it, wiped blood from his cheek where one of their stones had gashed it.

"False god, die!"

It was Salish. As though his cry of hate were the words they had been waiting to hear spoken, the crowd broke out into roars of accusation. Women screamed the enormity of their sense of betrayal. "Die, liar, die! Die as we all will die!" Men stooped for rocks. Goro shrieked, "Impostor! Liar!"

Miramanee flung herself before Kirk, her arms spread wide. "No! No! You are wrong! He can save us!"

Kirk pushed her away. "You cannot help me. Go back to them, Miramanee! Go back to them!" Salish burst from the crowd and seized her.

"Kirok! Kirok! I belong to you!" She wrenched free of Salish and flew back to Kirk.

"Then you die, too! With your false god!"

His rock struck her. She fell. There was a hail of stones; she elbowed up and crawled to Kirk. Before he could lift her to shield her with his body, Salish hurled another rock. It caught her in the abdomen.

"Miramanee . . ." Kirk was on his knees beside her. The crowd closed in for the kill when there came a shimmer of luminescence on the obelisk pediment. The Indians fell back, their stones still in their hands—and Spock and McCoy, in their *Enterprise* uniforms, materialized on each side of the kneeling Kirk.

"Kirok . . . Kirok . . ."

McCoy stooped over Miramanee. "I need Nurse Chapel," he told Spock shortly. The Vulcan had his communicator ready. "Beam down Nurse Chapel with a supplementary surgical kit, Mr. Scott."

Kirk tried to rise and was pushed gently back by McCoy. "Easy, Jim. Take it easy."

"My wife . . . my wife—is she all right?"

"Wife?" Spock looked at McCoy. "Hallucinations, Doctor?"

"Jim . . ."

"Miramanee," Kirk whispered. He looked at her face and closed his eyes.

The *Enterprise* nurse rose from the Indian girl's crumpled body. She joined McCoy who was making a last diagnostic pass over Kirk's unmoving form. "He hasn't recognized us," she said.

Spock was with Miramanee. "The nurse has given you medicine to ease the pain. Why were the people stoning you?"

"Kirok did not know how to get back into the temple."

"Naturally," Spock said. "He didn't come from there."

She lifted her head. "He did. I saw him come out of the temple."

Spock looked at her thoughtfully. Then he spoke to McCoy.

"The Captain, Doctor?"

"His brain is undamaged. Everything's functioning but his memory."

"Can you help him?"

"It will take time."

"Time, Doctor, is the one thing we do not have." He spoke into his communicator. "Spock here. Mr. Sulu?"

"Tracking report, sir. Sixty-five minutes to end of safety margin."

"Report noted." He returned to Kirk. "Do you think he's strong enough for a Vulcan mind fusion, Doctor?"

"We have no choice," McCoy said.

Spock stooped to place a hand on each side of Kirk's head. He spoke very slowly, with repressed intensity, his eyes boring into Kirk's closed ones. "I am Spock," he said with great distinctness. "You are James Kirk. Our minds are moving toward each other, closer . . ." His face was strained with such concentration, he seemed to be in pain. "Closer, James Kirk . . . closer . . . closer . . ."

Kirk moaned. "No . . . no . . . Miramanee . . ."

Spock increased the pressure against Kirk's temples as he fought to reach the lost memory. He shut his eyes, all his powers centered on the struggle. "Closer, James Kirk, closer . . ."

He gave a sudden hoarse cry of agony and Kirk's body galvanized. Spock was breathing heavily, his voice assuming the entranced tone of one possessed. "I am Kirok . . . I am the god of the metal tower." Spock's agonized voice deepened. "I am Kirok . . . I am Kiro— I am Kir— I am Spock! *Spock!*"

He jerked his hands away from Kirk's temples, his face tortured. Kirk lay still, his eyes closed.

"What's wrong?"

"He—he is an extremely dynamic personality, Doctor."

"So it didn't work," McCoy said hopelessly. He shook

his head—and Kirk's eyes opened, full awareness in them.

He sat up. "It did work. Thank you, Mr. Spock."

"Captain, were you inside that obelisk?"

"Yes. It seemed to be loaded with scientific equipment."

"It's a huge deflecting mechanism, Captain. It is imperative that we get inside it at once."

"The key may be in those symbols," Kirk said. "If we could only decipher them."

"They are musical notes, Captain."

"You mean entry can be gained by playing notes on some musical instrument?"

"That's one method. Another would be placement of tonal qualities stated in a proper sequence."

Kirk said, "Give me your communicator, Mr. Spock." He paused a moment. "Total control! Consonants and vowels. I must have hit the control accidentally when I contacted the ship to ask Scotty for beam-up!"

"If you could remember your exact words, Captain . . ."

"Let's see if I can. They were 'Kirk to *Enterprise*'. Then Scotty said, 'Aye, Captain' ".

The carefully smoothed panel in the obelisk slid open. As Spock stepped into it with him, Kirk looked back at Miramanee. "Stay with her, Bones."

The silence within the obelisk was absolute. As they examined the buttoned panel, Spock said, "From its position this button should activate the deflection mechanism."

"Careful!" Kirk warned. "I hit one and the beam it emitted was what paralyzed my memory."

"Probably an information beam activated out of sequence."

"Look, Spock. Over there—the other side of the vault. More symbols; and like those on the outside of the tower. Can you read them?"

Spock nodded. "I have an excellent eye for musical notes, Captain."

"Then activate, Mr. Spock!"

The Vulcan pressed three lower buttons in swift succession. Above them the wind-swept darkness was sliced by a wide streak of rainbow-colored flame that sprang from the tower's peak like a giant's sword blade. There was a screaming explosion that deafened them even in their underground insulation.

"That was the sound of deflection impact, Captain. The asteroid has been diverted."

Spock was right. They emerged from the obelisk into calm air, fresh but windless. The sky had lightened to pure blue.

Kirk dropped to his knees beside Miramanee. "How is she, Bones?"

"She was pregnant and there were bad internal injuries, Jim."

"Will she live?"

McCoy's face was his answer. Kirk swayed, fighting for control. Miramanee, her face bloodless under the high cheekbones he loved, opened her eyes and recognized him.

"Kirok. It is—true. You *are* safe."

"And so are your people," Kirk said.

"I knew you would save them, my chief. We . . . we will live long and happily. I will . . . bear you many strong sons. And love you always."

"And I will love you," he said. He kissed her; and she said weakly, "Each kiss is like the . . . the first . . ."

Her voice failed on the last word. The hand on his fell away.

He bent again to kiss the dead face.

McCoy laid a hand on his shoulder.

"It's over, Jim. But in our way we kept their peacefulness for them."

METAMORPHOSIS

(Gene L. Coon)

It was not often that the *Enterprise* needed the services of her shuttlecraft *Galileo,* for usually the Transporter served her purposes better; but this was one of those times. The *Enterprise* had been on other duty when the distress call had come from Epsilon Canaris III, well out of Transporter range, and not even the *Enterprise* could be in two places at once.

Now, however, the *Galileo* was heading back for rendezvous with the mother ship, Kirk at the controls, Spock navigating. The shuttlecraft's passengers were Dr. McCoy and his patient, Assistant Federation Commissioner Nancy Hedford, a very beautiful woman in her early thirties, whose beauty was marred by an almost constant expression of sullenness. The expression did not belie her; she was not a particularly pleasant person to be around.

"We have reached projected point three, Captain," Spock said. "Adjust to new course 201 mark 15."

"Thank you, Mr. Spock . . . Doctor, how is she?"

"No change."

"Small thanks to the Starfleet," Nancy Hedford said.

"Really, Commissioner," McCoy said, "you can't blame the Starfleet—"

"I should have received the proper inoculation ahead of time."

"Sukaro's disease is extremely rare, Commissioner. The chances of anyone contracting it are literally billions to one. How could we predict—"

"I was sent to that planet to prevent a war, Doctor. Thanks to the inefficiency of the medical branch of the Starfleet I have been forced to leave before my job was done. How many millions of innocent people will die because of this so-called rare disease of mine?"

Privately, Kirk was of the opinion that she was overestimating her own importance; her senior officer could probably handle the situation alone—or maybe even better. But it wouldn't do to say so. "Commissioner, I assure you, once we reach the *Enterprise*, with its medical facilities, we'll have you back on your feet in no time. You'll get back to your job."

"And just how soon will we rendezvous with this ship of yours, Captain?"

"Four hours and twenty-one minutes."

"Captain," Spock said. "The scanners are picking up some kind of small nebulosity ahead. It seems to be—yes, it is on a collision course."

"It can hardly matter," Kirk said, "but we'll swerve for it anyhow."

This, however, proved impossible to do. Every time Kirk changed the *Galileo's* course, the cloud did also. Soon it was within visual distance, a phosphorescent, twisting blob against the immensities of space.

Spock checked the sensors. "It appears to be mostly ionized hydrogen, Captain. But I would say nevertheless that it is not a natural object. It is too dense, changes shape too rapidly, and there is a high degree of electrical activity."

"Whatever it is, we're about to be right in the middle of it."

He had scarcely spoken when the view ahead was completely masked by the glowing, shifting cloud. A moment later, the controls went dead. A quick check showed that communications were out, too.

"Readings, Mr. Spock?"

"Extremely complex patterns of electrical impulses,

and an intense magnetic field—or rather, a number of them. It seems to have locked onto us."

The craft lurched, slightly but definitely. Kirk looked down at his console. "Yes, and it's taking us with it."

"Captain!" the woman's voice called. "What's happening? I demand to know!"

"You already know about as much as we do, Commissioner. Whatever that thing is outside, it's pulling us off our course for the *Enterprise.*"

"Now on course 98 mark 12," Spock said. "Heading straight into the Gamma Canaris region."

"Jim!" McCoy said. "We've got to get Miss Hedford to the *Enterprise*—her condition—"

"I'm sorry, Bones. There's nothing we can do."

"I am not at all surprised," Miss Hedford said coldly. "This is exactly the sort of thing I expect from the Starfleet. If I am as sick as this dubious authority claims I am—"

"Believe me, you are," McCoy said. "You may feel fine now, but nevertheless you're very ill."

"Then why are you all just sitting there? I insist—"

"I'm sorry, Commissioner," Kirk said. "We'll do what we can when we can—but right now we're helpless. You might as well sit back and enjoy the ride."

The *Galileo* was put down—there seemed to be no other word for it—on a small planet, of which very few details could be seen through the enveloping nebulosity. But the moment they had grounded, the cloud vanished, leaving them staring out at a broad, deserted sweep of heathlike countryside.

"Bones, Mr. Spock, get some readings on this place." Kirk snapped a switch. "*Enterprise,* this is the *Galileo.* Kirk here. Come in, please. Come in . . . no good, we're not sending. That cloud must still be around someplace. Any data, anybody?"

"The atmosphere is almost identical with that of the Earth," Spock reported, "and so is the gravity. Almost impossible for a planet this small, unless the core is something other than the usual nickel-iron. But suitable for human life."

"Well, I guess we get out and get under," Kirk said.

"Bones, phaser out and maintain full alert. Commissioner, best you stay inside for the time being."

"And just how long a time is that?"

"That's a very good question. I wish I could answer it. Mr. Spock, let's go."

Outside, they went to the rear of the shuttlecraft and unbolted the access panels to the machinery, while McCoy stayed up forward. Checking the works did not take long.

"Very strange," Spock said. "In fact, quite impossible."

"Nothing works."

"Nothing. And for no reason."

"Of course there's a reason. We just haven't found it yet. Let's go over it again."

While they were at it, Nancy Hedford came out and headed for them, looking, as usual, both annoyed and officious. Patience was evidently not her strong point, either. Kirk sighed and straightened.

"Well, Captain?"

"Well, Commissioner?"

"Where is this strange powerful force of yours, which brought us here? Or could it be that you simply made a navigational error?"

"There was no error, Miss Hedford," Kirk said patiently. "For your information, our power units are dead—so I judge that the force you refer to is still in the vicinity."

"I am not interested in alibis, Captain. I insist that you get us off this dismal rock immediately."

"Commissioner, I realize that you're ill, and you're anxious to receive treatment."

"I am anxious, as you put it, to get this medical nonsense out of the way so I can get back to my assignment!"

McCoy, looking rather anxious himself, had joined them. He said, "How do you feel, Commissioner?"

"I wish you would stop asking that stupid question." She strode angrily away.

Kirk managed a rueful grin. "As long as she answers you like that, Bones, I guess she feels all right."

"But she won't for long. The fever's due to hit any time."

As Kirk started to reply, there was a long, hailing call from no very great distance. "Hallloooo!"

They turned, startled. A human figure had emerged from over the horizon, which on this small world was no more than a mile away. It waved its arms, and came toward them at a run.

"Bones, I want a physiological reading on—whoever that is."

The figure disappeared behind a rise, and then appeared at the top of it, looking down on the party. It was a young, sturdy, tall, handsome man in his mid-thirties, dressed in a one-piece suit of coveralls. His expression was joyful.

"Hello!" he said again, plunging down the rise to them. "Are you real? I mean—I'm not imagining you, am I?"

"We're real enough," Kirk said.

"And you speak English. Earth people?"

Kirk nodded. "From the Federation."

"The Federation? Well, it doesn't matter." He grabbed Kirk's hand enthusiastically. "I'm Cochrane. Been marooned here who knows how long. If you knew how good it was to see you . . . and a woman! A beautiful one at that. Well!"

Kirk made the introductions. Cochrane, still staring at the Commissioner, said, "You're food to a starving man. All of you." He looked over to Spock. "A Vulcan, aren't you. When I was there—hey, there's a nice ship. Simple, clean. Been trying to get her going again? Forget it. It won't work."

He began to circle the shuttlecraft, admiringly. Kirk said in a low voice to McCoy, "Our friend seems to have a grasshopper mind."

"Too many things to take in all at once. Normal reaction. In fact, everything checks out perfectly normal. He's human."

"Mr. Cochrane!" The newcomer rejoined them, still beaming. "We were forced off our course and brought here by some power we couldn't identify—which seems to be here on the surface of the planet at the moment."

"Could be. Strange things happen in space."

"You said we wouldn't be able to get the ship functioning again?" Spock asked.

"Not a chance. Damping field of some sort down here. Power systems don't work. Take my word for it."

"You won't mind if we keep trying?" Spock persisted.

"Go right ahead. You'll have plenty of time."

"How about you, Cochrane?" Kirk said. "What are you doing here?"

"Marooned. I told you. Look, we've got lots of time to learn about each other. I've got a little place not far away. All the comforts of home." He turned to the woman. "I can even offer you a hot bath."

"How acute of you to notice that I needed it," she said icily.

"If you don't mind, Mr. Cochrane," Kirk said, "I'd like a little more than just the statement that you were marooned here. This is a long way off the beaten path."

"That's right. That's why I'm so glad to see you. Look, I'll tell you everything you want to know. But not here." He eyed the shuttlecraft again. "A beauty."

"You've been out of circulation a while. Maybe the principles are new to you. Mr. Spock, would you like to explain our propulsion methods to Mr. Cochrane?"

"Of course, Captain. Mr. Cochrane?"

As the two moved off, McCoy said, "He talks a lot but he doesn't say much."

"I noticed," Kirk said. "And I noticed something else. There's something familiar about him, Bones."

"Familiar? . . . well, now that you mention it, I think so too."

"I can't place him, but . . . how about Miss Hedford?"

"No temperature yet. But we've got to get under way soon. I guarantee you it'll develop."

"You're sure there's no mistake? It is Sakuro's disease?"

"Positive. And something else I'm not mistaken about. Untreated, it's fatal. Always . . . well, what do we do now?"

"I think we'll take Mr. Cochrane up on his offer. At least we can make her comfortable."

Cochrane's house was a simple functional cube, with a door, but no windows. The surrounding area was cultivated.

"You built this, Mr. Cochrane?" Spock said.

"Yes. I had some tools and supplies left over from my crash. It's not Earth, of course, but it's livable. I grow vegetables, as you see. Come on in."

He led the way. The house contained a heating unit which apparently served as a stove, a climate control device, and some reasonably comfortable furniture, all decidedly old. Miss Hedford looked around with distaste.

"What a dreadful, dingy place," she said.

Cochrane only smiled. "But I call it home, Miss Hedford."

"Where did you get the antiques?" Kirk said.

"The antiques? Oh, you mean my gadgets. I imagine things have changed a lot since I wrecked."

"Not that much."

"Must you keep it so terribly hot?" the woman asked.

"The temperature is a constant seventy-two degrees."

"Do you feel hot?" McCoy asked Miss Hedford.

She flopped angrily down in a chair. "I feel infuriated, deeply put upon, absolutely outraged."

"It was quite a hike here," McCoy said. "You're tired. Just take it easy for a while."

"I'll rest later, Doctor. Right now I am planning the report I will make to the Board of Commissioners on the efficiency of the Starfleet. I assure all of you it will be very, very complete."

"Captain! Doctor!" Spock called from the door. "Look at this, please!"

Alarmed at the urgency in his voice, Kirk crossed to the door in one bound. Outside, perhaps half a mile away, was a columnar area of blurry, misty interference, like a tame whirlwind, except that there was no wind. Faint pastel lights and shades appeared and disappeared inside it. With it there was a half sound, half feeling of soft chiming music. For a moment it moved from side to side, gently; then it disappeared.

Kirk turned quickly to Cochrane. "What was that?"

"Sometimes the light plays tricks on you," Cochrane said. "You'd be surprised what I've imagined I've seen around here."

"We imagined nothing, Mr. Cochrane. There was an entity out there, and I suspect it was the same entity that brought us here. Please explain."

"There's nothing to explain."

"Mr. Cochrane, you'll find I have a low tolerance level where the safety of my people are concerned. We find you out here where no human has any business being. We were virtually hijacked in space and brought here—apparently by that thing we just saw out there. I am not just requesting an explanation, Mister. I am demanding it!"

Cochrane shrugged. "All right. Out there—that was the Companion."

"The what?"

"That's what I call it. The fact is, Captain, I did not crash here. I was brought here in my disabled ship. I was almost dead. The Companion saved my life."

"You seem perfectly healthy now," Kirk said. "What was wrong?"

"Old age, Captain. I was eighty-seven years old at the time. I don't know how it did it, but the Companion rejuvenated me. Made me—well—young again, like I am now."

Kirk and Spock exchanged glances. Spock's eyebrows were about to crawl right off the top of his forehead. He said, "I would like to reserve judgment on that part of your story, sir. Would you mind telling us exactly what this Companion of yours is?"

"I told you, I don't know what it is. It exists. It lives. I can communicate with it to a limited extent."

"That's a pretty far-out story," McCoy said.

"You saw the creature. Have you a better story?"

"Mr. Cochrane," Kirk said. "Do you have a first name?"

Cochrane nodded. "Zefram."

McCoy's jaw dropped, but Spock had apparently

been expecting the answer. Kirk said, "Cochrane of Alpha Centauri? The discoverer of the space warp?"

"That's right, Captain."

"Zefram Cochrane," McCoy said, "has been dead a hundred and fifty years."

"His body was never found," Spock said.

"You're looking at it, Mr. Spock," Cochrane said.

"You say this Companion of yours found you and rejuvenated you. What were you doing in space at the age of eighty-seven?"

"I was tired, Captain. I was going to die. And I wanted to die in space. That's all."

McCoy turned to Miss Hedford, whose eyes were now closed. He felt her forehead, then took readings. He was obviously concerned by the results.

"These devices," Spock said. "They all date from the time indicated. From your ship, Mr. Cochrane?"

"I cannibalized it. The rest—the food, water, gardens, everything I need—the Companion gives me. Creates it, apparently, out of the native elements."

"If you can communicate with it," Kirk said, "maybe you can find out what *we* are doing here."

"I already know."

"You wouldn't mind telling us?"

"You won't like it."

"We already don't like it."

"You're here to keep me company," Cochrane said. "I was always pretty much of a loner. Spent years in space by myself. At first being alone here didn't bother me. But a hundred and fifty years is a long time, Kirk. Too long. I finally told the Companion I'd die without the company of other humans. I thought it would release me—send me back somehow. Instead, it went out and obviously brought back the first human beings it could find."

"No!" Miss Hedford cried weakly. "No! It's disgusting! We're not animals!"

She began to sob. McCoy, with Kirk's help, lifted her and put her on a cot, where McCoy gave her a shot. Gradually, her sobbing subsided.

"Bad," said McCoy. "Very bad."

"You can't do anything?"

"Keep her quiet. Keep secondary infections from developing. But the attrition rate of her red corpuscles is increasing. I can't stop it."

Kirk turned to Spock. "Mr. Spock, the next time that thing appears, don't fail to get tricorder readings. Find us a weapon to use against that thing."

"Captain, I have already drawn certain tentative conclusions. Considering the anomalously small size of this planet, and the presence of the damping field Mr. Cochrane mentioned, plus the Companion, leads me to believe that it was the moon of some larger body now destroyed, and was colonized by a highly advanced civilization."

"I agree," Cochrane said. "I've found some artifacts which suggest the same thing."

"The point, Spock?"

"One can deduce further that the Companion may be the last survivor of this long-dead culture. You ask me to find a weapon. Do you intend to destroy it?"

"I intend to do whatever is necessary to get us away from here and Commissioner Hedford to a hospital," Kirk said grimly. "If the Companion stands in the way, then we push it out of the way. Clear, Mr. Spock?"

"Quite clear, Captain." Spock picked up his tricorder and left, heading for the shuttlecraft.

"Cochrane, if you left here, what would happen to you?"

"I'd start to age again, normally."

"You want to get away from here?"

"Believe me, Captain, immortality consists largely of boredom. Of course I do . . . what's it like out there? In the galaxy?"

"We're on a thousand planets, and spreading out. We're crossing fantastic distances . . . and finding life everywhere. We estimate there are millions of planets with intelligent life. We haven't begun to map them." Cochrane's eyes were shining. "Interesting?"

"How would you like to go to sleep for a hundred and fifty years and wake up in a new world?"

"Good," Kirk said. "It's all out there, waiting for you. And you'll find your name honored there. But we'll probably need your help to get away."

"You've got it."

"All right. You seem to think this Companion can do almost anything."

"I don't know its limitations."

"Could it cure Commissioner Hedford?"

"I don't know."

"It's worth a try. We're helpless. You say you can communicate with it?"

"To a degree. It's on a non-verbal level, but I usually get my messages across."

"Try it now. See if it can do anything."

Cochrane nodded and stepped outside, followed by Kirk and McCoy. "How do you do it?" Kirk said.

"I just sort of . . . clear my mind. Then it comes. Better stay back."

Cochrane closed his eyes. A long moment passed, and then Kirk heard the melodic humming of the Companion. It appeared near Cochrane, shimmering, resplendent with a dozen beautiful colors, to the sound of faint bells. It moved to Cochrane, enveloped him, gathered around him, hovering. The lights played on Cochrane's face.

"What do you make of that, Bones?" Kirk said softly.

"Almost a symbiosis of some kind. A sort of joining."

"Just what I was thinking. Not exactly like a pet owner speaking to an affectionate animal, would you say?"

"No. More than that."

"I agree. Much more. Possibly . . . love."

Now the Companion was moving away from Cochrane, who was slowly returning to normal. The Companion faded away, and Cochrane shook his head and looked about as if to get his bearings. His eyes settled on Kirk.

"You all right?" Kirk said.

"Oh. Yes. I . . . it always kind of . . . drains me. But I'm all right."

"Well?"

Cochrane shook his head again. "The Companion can't do anything to help Miss Hedford. There seems to be some question of identity involved . . . I didn't understand it. But the answer is no, I'm sure of that."

"Then she'll die."

"Look, I'm sorry. If I could help you, I would. But the Companion won't."

It was several hours before Spock came back from the shuttlecraft. When he returned, he was carrying with him a small but complex black device, obviously in very rough form, as though it had been hastily put together by a gifted child. He took it into the house. "Your weapon, Captain."

"Oho. How does it work?"

"The Companion, as we already know, is mostly plasma—a state of matter characterized by a high degree of ionization. To put the matter simply, it is mostly electricity. I propose to, in effect, short it out. Put this in proximity to the Companion, throw this switch, and we will scramble every electrical impulse the creature can produce. It cannot fail."

Cochrane was staring unhappily at the device. Kirk said, "It troubles you, Cochrane?"

"The Companion saved my life. Took care of me for a hundred and fifty years. We've been . . . very close . . . in a way that's hard to explain. I suppose I even have a sort of affection for it."

"It's also keeping you a prisoner here."

"I don't want it killed."

Spock said, "We may simply render it powerless—"

"But you don't know!" Cochrane said intensely. "You could kill it! I won't stand for that, Kirk."

"We're getting away from here, Cochrane. Make up your mind to that."

"What kind of people are you nowadays?" Cochrane demanded. "Doesn't gratitude mean anything to you?"

"I've got a woman dying in here, Cochrane. I'll do anything I have to to save her life."

Cochrane stared at Kirk, and slowly the fight went out of him. "I suppose, from your point of view, you're right. I only . . ."

"We understand how you feel, Mr. Cochrane," McCoy said. "But it has to be done."

"All right. You want me to call it, I suppose?"

"Please," Kirk said. "Outside."

McCoy remained with his patient. Spock hefted his device, and he and Kirk left the house. Already, Cochrane and the Companion were approaching each other. Soft lights and soft music came from the creature. It almost seemed to be purring.

"Is this close enough?" Kirk whispered.

"I think so," Spock whispered back. "But there is a certain risk. We do not know the extent of the creature's powers."

"Nor it ours. Now, Spock!"

Spock closed the switch. The blurring of the Companion abruptly increased, and a sharp high-pitched humming sound came from it, alarmed, strong. The pastel colors changed to somber blues and greens, and the hint of bells changed to a discordant clanging. Cochrane, only a few feet away from it, grasped his head and staggered, then fell. The evanescent, ever-changing column of plasma swept down upon the house.

Kirk and Spock ducked inside, but there was no safety there. The room was filled with the whirling and clanging. With it, Kirk felt a terrible sense of pressure, all over his body. The breath was crushed out of him. He struck out, but there was nothing to strike at. Beside him, he was aware that Spock had dropped the device and was also gasping futilely for air.

"Stop it! Stop it!" McCoy's voice shouted, as if from a great distance. "It's killing them!"

Cochrane came in, and, immediately divining what was happening, went into the position of communion. The Companion's colors returned to the pastel, and the creature faded away. Kirk and Spock both fell to their knees, gulping in great gasps of air. McCoy knelt beside them; Cochrane went out again.

"Are you all right?" McCoy said. "Can you breathe?"

Kirk nodded. "All . . . right, Bones." He got shakily to his feet, followed by Spock, who also seemed to be regaining his strength rapidly. "Cochrane's got it off us. I don't know whether he did us a favor or not."

"What kind of talk is that?" McCoy said sharply.

"How do you fight a thing like that? I've got a ship

somewhere out there . . . the responsibility for four lives here . . . and one of them dying."

"That's not your fault."

"I'm in command, Bones. That makes it my fault. Now I've had it. I can't destroy it. I can't force it to let us go."

After a moment McCoy said, "You're a soldier so often that maybe you forget you were also trained to be a diplomat. Why not try using a carrot instead of a stick?"

"But what could I offer . . . Hmmm. Maybe we can. Spock!"

"Yes, Captain."

"The universal translator on the shuttlecraft. We can try that. Talk to the thing."

"The translator is for use with more congruent life-forms."

"Adjust it. Change it. The trouble with immortality is that it's boring. Adjusting the translator would give you something to do."

"It's possible. If I could widen its pattern of reception—"

"Right down your alley, Mr. Spock. Get it here and get to work."

The translator was small but intricate. Cochrane eyed it interestedly, while McCoy tended his patient. "How does that gadget work?" he said.

"There are certain universal ideas and concepts, common to all intelligent life," Kirk explained. "This device instantaneously compares the frequency of brain-wave patterns, selects those it recognizes, and provides the necessary grammar and vocabulary."

"You mean the box speaks?"

"With the voice, or its approximation, of whatever creature is on the sending end. It's not perfect, of course, but it usually works well enough. Are you ready, Mr. Spock?"

"Quite ready, Captain."

"Mr. Cochrane, call the Companion, please."

Cochrane left the house, Kirk and Spock once more following, with the translator. And again the sound of the Companion preceded its appearance; then it was there, misty, enigmatic. Spock touched the translator and nodded to Kirk.

"Companion . . . we wish to talk to you."

There was a change in the sound. The Companion drew away from Cochrane. Then a voice came from the translator. It was soft, gentle—and unmistakably feminine.

"How can we communicate? My thoughts . . . you are hearing them. This is interesting."

"Feminine, Spock," Kirk said. "No doubt about it."

"Odd. The matter of gender could change the entire situation."

"Dr. McCoy and I are way ahead of you, Mr. Spock."

"Then it is not a zoo-keeper."

"No, Mr. Spock. A lover . . . Companion! It is wrong to hold us here against our will."

"The man needs the company of his own kind, or he will cease to exist," the gentle voice said. "He felt it to me."

"One of us is about to cease to exist. She must be taken to a place where we can care for her."

"The man needs others of his species. That is why you are here. The man must continue."

"Captain, there is a peculiar, dispassionate logic here," Spock said. "Pragmatism unalloyed. From its words, I would say it will never understand our point of view."

"Maybe. Companion, try to understand. It is the nature of our species to be free, just as it is your nature to stay here. We will cease to exist in captivity."

"Your bodies have stopped their peculiar degeneration. You will continue without end. There will be sustenance. There will be nothing to harm you. You will continue and the man will continue. This is necessary."

"Captain!" Spock said. "This is a marvelous opportunity for us to add to our knowledge. Ask it about its nature, its history—"

"Mr. Spock, this is no classroom. I'm trying to get us away from here."

"A chance like this may never come again. It could tell us so much—"

"Mr. Spock, get lost. Companion, it is plain you do not understand us. This is because you are not of our species. Believe me, we do not lie. What you offer us is not continuation. It is non-existence. We will cease to exist. Even the man will cease to exist."

"Your impulses are illogical. This communication is useless. The Man must continue. Therefore, you will continue. It is necessary."

The voice fell silent. The Companion moved away. Slowly it started to grow fainter, and finally was not there at all.

Kirk's shoulders sagged, and he went back into the house, followed by Spock. Cochrane came in after them.

"Captain," he said, "why did you build that translator of yours with a feminine voice box?"

"We didn't," Kirk said.

"But I heard—"

"The ideas of male and female are universal constants, Cochrane. The Companion is definitely female."

"I don't understand."

"You don't?" said McCoy. "A blind man could see it with his cane. You're not a pet, Cochrane. Nor a specimen kept in a cage. You're a lover."

"I'm—what?"

"Isn't it evident?" Kirk said. "Everything she does is for you. Provides for you. Feeds you. Shelters you. Clothes you. Brings you companions when you're lonely."

"Her attitude, when she approaches you, is profoundly different from when she contacts us," Spock added. "In appearance, in sound, in method. Though I do not completely understand the emotion, it obviously exists. The Companion loves you."

Cochrane stared at them. "That's—that's ridiculous!"

"Not at all," Kirk said. "We've seen similar situations."

"But after a hundred and fifty years—"

"What happens when you communicate with it?" Spock said.

"Why, we sort of . . . it—it merges with my mind."

"Of course. It is nothing to be shocked by. A simple symbolic union of two minds."

"That's outrageous! Do you know what you're saying? No, you couldn't! But . . . all the years . . . letting something . . . as alien as that . . . into my mind, my feelings—" Suddenly Cochrane was furious as well as astonished. "It tricked me! It's some kind of an . . . emotional vampire! Crawling around inside me!"

"It didn't hurt you, did it?" Kirk said.

"Hurt me? What has that to do with it? You can be married to a woman you love for fifty years and still keep your private places in your mind. But this—this thing—fed on me!"

"An interesting attitude," Spock said. "Typical of your time, I should say, when humanity had much less contact with alien life-forms than at present."

"Don't sit there and calmly analyze a disgusting thing like this!" Cochrane exploded. "What kind of men are you, anyway?"

"There's nothing disgusting about it, Cochrane," McCoy said. "It's just one more life-form. You get used to these things."

"You turn my stomach! You're as bad as it is!"

"I fail to understand your highly emotional reaction," Spock said. "Your relationship with the Companion was, for a hundred and fifty years, emotionally satisfying, eminently practical, and totally harmless. It may, indeed, have been quite beneficial."

Cochrane glared at them. "So this is what the future looks like—men who don't have the slightest notion of decency or morality. Well, maybe I'm a hundred and fifty years out of style, but I'm not going to be fodder for some inhuman—monstrous—" Choking up, he swung on his heel and walked out.

"A most parochial attitude," Spock said.

"Doctor," Nancy Hedford's voice called weakly. "Doctor."

McCoy hurried to her, Kirk following. "Right here, Miss Hedford."

She managed a very faint, almost bitter laugh. "I . . . heard him. He was loved . . . and he resents it."

"You rest," McCoy said.

"No. I don't want . . . want to die . . . I've been . . . good at my job, Doctor. But I've . . . never been loved. What kind . . . of a life is that? Not to be loved . . . never . . . and now I'm dying. And he . . . runs away from love . . ."

She fell silent, gasping for breath. McCoy's eyes were grim.

"Captain," Spock called from the door. "Look out here."

Outside, the Companion was back, looking much the same as usual, but Cochrane was standing away from it, barely controlling himself, icily furious.

"Do you understand?" he was saying. "I don't want anything to do with you."

The Companion moved a little closer, chiming questioningly, insistently. Cochrane backed away.

"I said keep away! You'll never get close enough to trick me again! Stay away from me! I know you understand me! Stay away! Leave me alone, from now on!"

Shaken, white-faced and sweating, Cochrane came back to his house. Kirk turned back to McCoy. Nancy was lying quite still.

"Bones? Is it over?"

"No. But she's moribund. Respiration highly erratic. Blood pressure dropping. She'll be dead in ten minutes. And I—"

"You did everything you could, Bones."

"Are you sorry for her, Kirk?" Cochrane said, still in an icy rage. "Are you really feeling something? Don't bother. Because that's the only way any of us are going to get away from here. By dying!"

An idea, a forlorn hope, came to Kirk. He picked up the translator and went outside. The Companion was still there.

"Companion. Do you love the man?"

"I do not understand," said the feminine voice from the translator.

"Is he important to you—more important than anything? Is it as though he were part of you?"

"He is part of me. He must continue."

"But he will not continue. He will cease to exist. By

your feeling for him you are condemning him to an existence he will find unbearable."

"He does not age. He remains forever."

"You refer to his body," said Kirk. "I speak of his spirit. Companion, inside the shelter a female of our species lies dying. She will not continue. That is what will happen to the man unless you release all of us."

"I do not understand."

"Our species can only survive when there are obstacles to overcome. You take away all obstacles. Without them to strengthen us, we weaken and die. You regard the man only as a toy. You only amuse yourself with him."

"You are wrong," said the translator. Was there urgency as well as protest in that voice? "The man is the center of all things. I care for him."

"But you can't really love him. You don't have the slightest knowledge of love—of the total union of two people. You are the Companion; he is the man; you are two different things, and can never join. You can never know love. You may keep him here forever, but you will always be separate, apart from him."

There was a long pause. Then the Companion said, "If I were human . . . there can be love . . ."

Then the creature faded from sight. Kirk went back into the shelter, almost bumping into McCoy, who had been standing behind him. "What did you hope to gain by that?" the surgeon said.

"Convince her of the hopelessness of it. The emotion of love frequently expresses itself in sacrifice. If love is what she feels, she might let him go."

"But she—or it—is inhuman, Captain," Spock said. "You cannot expect her to react like a human."

"I can try."

"It won't do any good," Cochrane said. "I know."

From the direction of the cot, a voice said, "Zefram Cochrane." It was Nancy's voice, clear and strong, but somehow as if the use of human lips, tongue and vocal cords had become unfamiliar. They all spun around.

There stood Nancy Hedford—but transformed, radiant, soft, gentle, staring at Cochrane. The rosy glow of health was evident in her cheek. McCoy raised his medical tricorder and stared at it, thunderstruck, but Kirk had no need to ask what he saw. The Nancy Hedford who had been about to die was not sick at all now.

"Zefram Cochrane," she said. "We are understanding."

"It's—it's her!" Cochrane said. "Don't you understand? It's the Companion!"

"Yes," said Nancy. "We are here—those you knew as the Commissioner and the Companion. We are both here."

Spock said, "Companion, you do not have the power to create life."

"No. That is for the maker of all things."

"But Commissioner Hedford was dying."

"That part of us was too weak to hold on. In a moment there would have been no continuing. Now we are together. Now we understand that which you called love—both of us. It fills a great need. That we did not have, we now have."

"You mean—you're both there in one body?" Kirk said.

"We are one. There is so much hunger, so much wanting." She moved toward Cochrane, who retreated a step. "Poor Zefram Cochrane. We frighten you. We never frightened you before." Tears formed in her eyes. "Loneliness. This is loneliness. We know loneliness. What a bitter thing. Zefram Cochrane, how do you bear it?"

"How do you know what loneliness is?" Cochrane said.

"To wear this form is to discover pain." She extended a hand. "Let us touch you, Zefram Cochrane."

His hand slowly went out, and they touched.

Kirk turned his head and said in a low voice: "Spock. Check out the shuttlecraft. The engines, communication, everything."

"We hear you, Captain," Nancy said. "It is not necessary. Your vehicle will operate as before. So will your communications device."

"You're letting us go?" Cochrane said.

"We would do nothing to stop you. Captain, you

said that we would not know love because we were not human. Now we are human, all human, and nothing more. We will know the change of the days. We will know death. But to touch the hand of the man—nothing is as important. Is this happiness, Zefram Cochrane? When the sun is warmer? The air sweeter? The sounds of this place like gentle currents in the air?"

"You are very beautiful," Cochrane said in a low voice.

"Part of me understands. Part does not. But it pleases me."

"I could explain. Many things. It'll be an eye-opener to you." He was alive with excitement. "A thousand worlds, a thousand races. I'll show you everything—just as soon as I learn my way around again. Maybe I can make up for everything you did for me."

Sadness appeared in Nancy's eyes. "I cannot go with you, Zefram Cochrane."

Cochrane was stunned. "Of course you can. You have to."

"My life emanates from this place. If I leave it, for more than a tiny march of days, I will cease to exist. I must return, even as you must consume matter to maintain your life."

"But—you have powers—you can—"

"I have become almost as you. The march of days will affect me. But to leave here would mean a cessation of my existence."

"You mean you gave up everything to become human?"

"It is nothing . . . compared to the touch of you."

"But you'll age, like any other human. Eventually you'll die."

"The joy of this hour is enough. I am pleased."

"I can't fly off and leave you here," Cochrane said. "You saved my life. You took care of me and you loved me. I never understood, but I do now."

"You must be free, Zefram Cochrane."

Kirk said gently: "The *Galileo* is waiting, Mr. Cochrane."

"But . . . If I take her away from here, she'll die. If I

leave her . . . she's human. She'll die of loneliness. And that's not all. I love her. Is that surprising?"

"Not coming from a human being," Spock said. "You are, after all, essentially irrational."

Cochrane put his arms around her. "I can't leave her. And this isn't such a bad place. I'm used to it."

"Think it over, Mr. Cochrane," Kirk said. "There's a galaxy out there, waiting to honor you."

"I have honors enough. She loves me."

"But you will age, both of you," Spock said. "There will be no more immortality. You will grow old here, and finally die."

"That's been happening to men and women for a long time . . . and I've got the feeling that it's one of the pleasanter things about being human—as long as you do it together."

"You're sure?" Kirk said.

"There's plenty of water. The climate is good for growing things. I might even try to plant a fig tree. Every man's entitled to that, isn't he?" He paused, then added soberly, "It isn't gratitude, Captain. Now that I see her, touch her, I know. I love her. We'll have a lot of years, and they'll be happy ones."

"Mr. Cochrane, you may or may not be doing the right thing. But I wish you the best. Mr. Spock, Bones, let's go."

As they turned, Cochrane said, "Captain."

"Yes?"

"Don't tell them about Cochrane. Let it go."

Kirk smiled. "Not a word, Mr. Cochrane."

As they settled into the *Galileo,* Spock said, "I pose you an interesting question, Captain. Have we not aided in the commission of bigamy? After all, the Companion and Commissioner Hedford are now sharing the same body."

"Now you're being parochial, Mr. Spock," McCoy said. "Bigamy is not everywhere illegal. Besides, Nancy Hedford was all but dead. Only the Companion is keeping her alive. If it withdrew, Nancy wouldn't last ten minutes. In fact, I'm going to report her dead as soon as we hit the *Enterprise.*"

"Besides, what difference does it make?" Kirk said. "Love was the one thing Nancy and the Companion wanted most. Now they have it."

"But not for eternity," McCoy said. "Only a lifetime."

"Yes. But that's enough, Bones. For humans."

"That's a very illogical remark, Jim." As Spock's eyebrows climbed, McCoy added, "However, it happens to be true."

Kirk grinned and raised his communicator. "Kirk to *Enterprise.*"

The communicator fairly shouted back. "Captain! This is Scotty. Are you all right?"

"We're perfectly all right. Can you get a fix on us?"

"Computing now . . . yes, locked on."

"Very good. I'll continue transmission. Assume standard orbit on arrival. We'll transfer up on the shuttlecraft."

"But what happened, Captain?"

"Not very much, in the end," Kirk said. "Only the oldest story in the world."

THE DEADLY YEARS

(David P. Harmon)

There was no sign of Robert Johnson when the party from the *Enterprise* materialized on Gamma Hydra IV. In fact, there was no sign of anybody, and their arrival site, which otherwise resembled a Kansas field in mid-August, was eerily silent.

There were the overbright sun, the varied greens of leaves and grasses, even the shimmer of heat waves over the adjacent meadow. But all sounds of life were missing —insect, animal, human. All that suggested that it was the specified headquarters of the Johnson expedition was a scattering of pre-fab buildings.

Spock, Kirk noted, was looking troubled too. McCoy said, "Perhaps they weren't expecting us."

Spock shook his head. "Our arrival was scheduled well in advance, Doctor. An annual check of every scientific expedition is routine."

"Besides, I had sub-space contact with the leader of this expedition, a Robert Johnson, not an hour ago," Kirk said.

"Did he report anything wrong, Jim?"

"No . . . and yet there was *something* wrong. I can't quite nail it down, but his conversation was disjointed, somehow, as though he were having trouble sticking to the subject, or was worried about something." Kirk pointed at the nearest building. "Mr. Chekov, check that place. Mr. Spock and I will check that one. McCoy, Scotty, Lieutenant Galway, look around, see if you can find anyone."

The group broke up. Arlene Galway was looking a little scared, Kirk thought. Well, this was only her first extra-solar planet; she'd toughen in due course. And the circumstances were a little odd.

Kirk and Spock were about to enter "their" building when a scream rent the air. Whirling, Kirk saw Chekov bursting out into the open, looking about wildly.

"Captain! Captain!" Chekov's voice had gone up a full octave. Kirk loped forward and grabbed him.

"What's wrong?"

"Captain! In there!"

"Control yourself, Ensign! What is it?"

"A man, sir! In there!" Cheokov seemed a little calmer. "A dead man."

"All right, we'll check it. But why the panic? You've seen dead men before."

"I know," Chekov said, a little ashamedly. "But this one's, uh, peculiar, and frankly, sir, it startled me."

" 'Scared' might be the better word. All right, Bones, Spock, let's take a look." Kirk drew his phaser.

The interior of the building was quite dark—not black, but Kirk, coming in from the bright sunlight, had trouble getting used to it. At first, the building seemed quite empty; then he saw some sort of low structure near its end. He approached cautiously.

Then he abruptly understood what had panicked the unprepared Chekov. The object was a crudely constructed wooden coffin, for which two sawhorses served as a catafalque.

The body it held might have been Methuselah's. Deep wrinkles made its facial features also indecipherable. The open mouth was toothless, its near-white gums shriveled, its eyes sunk in caverns, flattened under their lids of flabby skin. The body seemed to be mere bones, barely held together by a brown-spotted integument of tissue-paper thinness. Clawed hands were crossed on its collapsed chest.

Chekov's voice said through the dimness, "I bumped into it walking backward, sir, and I—"

"I quite understand, Ensign. Rest easy. Bones, what's this?"

"Exactly what it looks like, Jim. Death by natural causes—in other words, old age."

"Doctor," Spock said, "I ran a personnel check on the members of this expedition before we beamed-down, and I can assure you that not one of them was . . ."

Midway through this sentence Kirk became aware of the shuffling of feet outside the open door. They all turned as Spock's voice trailed off.

A man and woman tottered toward them, supporting themselves with sticks. They were stooped and shrunken, the skin of their skulls showing through their thin white hair.

The man said, in a quavering voice, "They've come to pay their respects to Professor Alvin."

"I am Captain Kirk of the—"

"You'll have to speak louder," the man said, cupping his ear with his free hand.

"I said I am Captain Kirk of the *Enterprise*. Who are you?"

"Robert Johnson," said the old man, nodding. "And this is my wife Elaine."

"That's impossible," Kirk said. "The Johnsons are—how old are you?"

"Me? I'm . . . let me see . . . oh yes, I'm twenty-nine. Elaine is twenty-seven."

The shocked silence was at last broken by McCoy. "I am a physician. You both need rest and medical care."

There were only three decrepit survivors of the expedition to be beamed-up to Sickbay and Nurse Chapel's gentle but efficient care. Standing beside McCoy, Kirk leaned over Robert Johnson's bed.

"Can you hear me, Dr. Johnson?"

The filmed eyes found his face. "Not deaf yet, you know. Not yet."

"Have you any idea what happened?"

"What happened?" Johnson echoed vaguely.

"Did your instruments show anything?"

The old mind was wandering. As though appealing to some benevolent but absent god, Johnson said, "Elaine was so beautiful . . . so beautiful."

"He can hear you, Jim, but he can't understand. Let him rest."

Kirk nodded. "Nurse Chapel, if any of them seem lucid, we'll be in the briefing room." He went to the intercom. "Kirk to bridge. Mr. Spock, Commodore Stocker, Dr. Wallace, to the briefing room, please. Bones, I'll ask you to come along."

Janet Wallace and George Stocker were distinguished guests; he an able administrator in his mid-forties, she an endocrinologist, in her late twenties and extremely attractive. They were waiting with Spock at the big table when he and McCoy arrived. He nodded to them all and sat down himself. "Commodore Stocker, I've asked you to this briefing because Gamma Hydra Four falls within the area of your administration."

Trim, competent-looking, the tall man said, "I appreciate that, Captain."

The merest hint of constraint came into Kirk's voice as he spoke to the dark-eyed girl who sat next to the Commodore. "Dr. Wallace, though you are a new member of our crew, your credentials as an endocrinologist are impressive. In this situation we face, I'd appreciate your working closely with Dr. McCoy."

She smiled at him. "Yes, Captain."

He turned hastily to McCoy. "Fill them in, Bones."

McCoy said, "The survivors of the expedition to Gamma Hydra Four are not merely suffering from extreme old age. They are getting older, much older by the minute. My examinations have shown up nothing. I haven't a clue to the cause of this rapidly aging process."

"Mr. Spock, what about environment and atmosphere?"

"Sensors show nothing inimical to human life, sir. The atmosphere screens out the usual amount of harmful cosmic rays."

"We are close, though," Kirk said, "to the neutral zone between our Federation and the Romulan Confederation. The Romulans may have a new weapon.

Perhaps they have been using members of the expedition as guinea pigs."

"I have begun to investigate that possibility, Captain," Spock said.

Kirk rose. "I want you all to check out everything in your particular specialties. No matter how remote, how far-fetched seems the notion, I want it run down." He paused for emphasis. "We will remain in orbit until we have the answer."

Stocker spoke. "I am anxious to get to Star Base Ten in order to assume my new post. I am sure you understand that, Captain."

"I will do what I can to see that you make your due date, Commodore."

"Thank you, Captain."

The men, pushing back their chairs, left the briefing room. But the dark-eyed Dr. Wallace didn't move. Kirk turned at the door. "Anything I can do for you, Doctor?"

"Yes," she said. "You might, for instance, say 'Hello, Janet'. You might be a little less the cold, efficient starship captain and a little more the old . . . friend."

"Janet, as captain, I have certain—my duties are heavy." Then he gave her a wry little smile. "Or maybe I just don't want to get burned again."

"I'm carrying a little scar tissue of my own," she said.

There was a small silence. Then he said, "How long has it been?"

"More than six years, Jim."

"A long time. But there wouldn't be any change if we started it up all over again, would there? I've got my ship; and you've got your work. Neither of us will change."

"You never asked why I married after we called it off."

"I supposed you'd found another man you loved."

"I found a man I admired."

"And in the same field as you. You didn't have to give up anything."

"No, I didn't. But he's dead now, Jim."

She went to him, her hands extended. Kirk hesitated.

Then he took one of the hands, his eyes searching the warm brown ones—and Uhura's voice spoke on the intercom.

"Captain Kirk, Mr. Spock would like to see you on the bridge."

"Tell Mr. Spock I'm on my way." He was finding deeper depths in the brown eyes. "Janet, we're under pressure right now. Maybe, when it eases off, things will be—"

Uhura's voice interrupted again. "Captain Kirk, Mr. Scott would like to see you in Engineering."

"Tell him I'll be down after I check with Mr. Spock." He drew Janet closer to him. Lifting her chin, he said, "But this time there must be truth between us. You and I, with our eyes open, knowing what each of us are."

"It's been a long six years," she said; and placed her arms around his neck. He had bent his head to her mouth when the intercom spoke for the third time. "Captain Kirk!"

"On my way, Lieutenant Uhura." A sudden wave of weariness swept over him. He touched the girl's mouth with his forefinger. "Six long years—and that intercom is trying to make it six more. Dr. Wallace, your lips are as tempting as ever—but as I remarked, my duties are heavy."

The weariness stayed with him on his way to the bridge. Sulu greeted him with a "Standard orbit, Captain." He said, "Maintain" and crossed to Spock at the computer station.

"I have rechecked the sensors, sir. Gamma Hydra Four checks out as a Class M planet, nitrogen-oxygen atmosphere, normal mass with conventional atmospheric conditions. I can find nothing at all out of the ordinary."

"How about that comet that recently passed through here?"

"I am running checks on it, sir. As yet I have no conclusions. The comet is a rogue and has never been investigated."

"Captain Kirk!"

It was Stocker. He looked like a man with a determined idea. "Facilities at Star Base Ten," he said, "are much more complete than those on board ship. It seems to me your investigations would be facilitated by proceeding there at once. I assure you of every cooperation."

"Thank you, Commodore; but we have a few facilities of our own. I am going to Engineering, Mr. Spock." He left the computer station to say to Sulu, "Maintain standard orbit, Mr. Sulu."

Surprised, Sulu exclaimed, "But you already gave that order, sir!"

Kirk looked surprised himself. "Did I? Oh, well. Follow it."

As he left the bridge, Spock stared after him, a look of concern in his eyes.

Lieutenant Galway appeared uneasy, too, as she opened the door of Sickbay. "Dr. McCoy, can I speak with you a moment?"

"Of course." He motioned her to a chair but she didn't take it. "I know," she said, "that this is going to sound foolish. But—I seem to be having a little trouble hearing."

"Probably nothing important," McCoy said.

"I never had any trouble before."

"I'll have a look at you. Maybe a simple hypersonic treatment will clear it up." She said, "Thank you, Doctor" and followed him into the examination room.

Kirk was discovering some trouble of his own. Alone in his quarters, stripped to the waist, he dried the face he'd just shaved, and reached for the clean shirt he'd laid out on the bed. As he raised his right arm to insert it into a sleeve, a sharp stab of pain struck his right shoulder. He winced, lowered the arm, flexed it, massaging the shoulder muscle. The pain persisted. Slowly, carefully, he put on the shirt. Then he moved to the intercom and flicked a button. "Progress report, Mr. Spock?"

"All research lines negative, Captain."

Kirk said, "Astronomical section reports that a comet recently passed by. Check into that."

Spock waited a moment before he replied, "I'm doing that, sir, according to your order. We discussed it earlier."

"Oh. Well, let me know what you come up with. I'll be in Sickbay."

"Yes, Captain."

The walk to Sickbay seemed longer than usual. The pain in the right shoulder had extended to the right knee. There was a slight trace of a limp in Kirk's movement as he entered Sickbay. In its bed section, all but one of the three beds was vacant. He thought, "So two of the rescued Johnson party are gone." It was a depressing reflection. Then he saw Nurse Chapel draw a blanket up and over the face of the patient who occupied the third bed.

McCoy looked up. "Robert Johnson, deceased. The last one, Jim. Cause of death—old age."

"You did what you could," Kirk said.

The intercom spoke. "Dr. McCoy? This is Scott. Can I come up and see you?"

McCoy answered shortly. "You just need vitamins. But yes, come up anyway, Scotty."

He punched off and Kirk said, "Bones, I believe you're getting gray!"

"You take over my job and see what it does to you!" Low-voiced, McCoy gave an order to Nurse Chapel. Then he turned back to Kirk. "Well, what's *your* problem?"

"My shoulder," Kirk said. "Got a little twinge in it. Probably just a muscle strain."

"Probably, Dr. Kirk," McCoy snapped.

Kirk grinned. "Reprimand noted, sir. Okay, no more diagnoses by me."

McCoy ran his Feinberger over Kirk's shoulder. He frowned. "Hmmm. Maybe we'd better run a complete check on you."

"Well? Muscle strain?"

McCoy shook his head. "No, Jim. It's an advanced case of arthritis. And spreading."

"But that's not possible!"

"I'll run the check again, but I'll get the same answer."

He didn't run it again. For Kirk, his dismay still on his face was staring past him at the Sickbay door. Mc-

Coy turned. Scott stood there—a Scott with snow-white hair who appeared to be sixty years of age.

Sickbay on the *Enterprise* had become a section that seemed to have been appropriated by a Golden Age club. Assembled there on Kirk's order were every member of the crew who had contacted Gamma Hydra Four. With the single exception of Chekov, each one had been affected by the rapidly aging process. Kirk looked fifty-five: McCoy ten years older. Nor had Spock's Vulcan heritage been entirely able to immunize him against its effects. Wrinkles cracked his face; the skin under his eyes had gone baggy. Lieutenant Galway might have been a woman in her mid-sixties. Scott looked oldest of them all.

"All right, Bones," Kirk said. "Let's have it."

McCoy said, "All of us who went down to the planet, except Ensign Chekov, are aging rapidly. The rates vary from person to person, but it averages thirty years each day. I don't know what's causing it—virus, bacteria or evil spirits. I'm trying to find out."

"Spock? I asked you for some calculations."

"Based on what Dr. McCoy gave me, I'd say that we each have a week to live. It would also seem that since our mental faculties are aging faster than our bodies, we will become little better than mental vegetables in less time than a week."

"You mean total senility?"

"Yes, Captain. In a very short time!"

Kirk took a step away from the group. "What a . . . a filthy way to die!" He turned slowly, accommodating his aching knee. "I want every research facility on this ship, every science technician, to immediately start round-the-clock research. I want the answer! And a remedy! And you might start in by telling me why Chekov wasn't affected!"

"I'm doing what I can," McCoy said. He removed his Feinberger diagnostic instrument from Spock. "You are disgustingly healthy, Spock."

"I must differ with you, Doctor. I am finding it difficult to concentrate. My eyesight appears to be failing.

And the normal temperature of the ship strikes me as increasingly cold."

"I didn't say you were not affected."

Scott said dully, "Can I go back to my station?"

"Feel up it it, Scotty?" Kirk asked.

"Of course I do. Just need a little rest, that's all."

McCoy said, "You can leave too if you wish, Lieutenant Galway."

She didn't move. McCoy spoke louder. "Lieutenant Galway?"

"What? You spoke to me, Doctor?"

"Yes. I said you could go. Why not go to your quarters and get some sleep?"

"No! I don't want to sleep! Can't you understand? If I sleep . . . what will I find when I wake up?"

Kirk said, "Lieutenant Galway, report to your station and continue with your duties."

Her "Yes, sir" was grateful. She rose painfully from her chair, moved toward the door, and came face to face with herself in a mirror. She turned from it in anger.

"What a stupid place to hang a mirror!"

She half-stumbled out. Kirk looked after her. "She's seven or eight years younger than I am. She looks ten years older."

"People normally age at different speeds, Jim."

Kirk pointed to Chekov. "But why hasn't he aged?"

"I don't know."

"Well, I want to know! Is it his youth? His blood type? His glands? His medical history? His genes?"

"Nurse Chapel, prepare Mr. Chekov for a complete physical."

She rose. "Come along, Ensign. This won't hurt. Much."

As the door closed behind the nurse and the reluctant Chekov, Janet Wallace turned to McCoy. "A few years ago on Aldebaran Three, my husband and I used a variation of cholesterol block to slow arteriosclerosis in animals."

"Did it work?"

"Sometimes. But the side effects were fierce. We gave it up."

"Try it anyhow, Dr. Wallace. Try anything, but do it quickly!"

"Yes, sir." She went out in turn.

"Mr. Spock, return to the bridge," Kirk said. "I'll join you shortly. Keep me posted on Chekov, Bones."

He found Janet Wallace waiting for him in the corridor. "I thought you were on your way to the biochemistry lab, Doctor."

"We both go in the same direction, Jim."

After a moment, he nodded. "So we do."

She adjusted her pace to his slower walk. "We know the problem," she said. "We know the effects it is having. And we know the progress of the affliction. Therefore, once we find the proper line of research, it's only logical that we find the solution."

Kirk smiled. "You sound like my First Officer."

"No problem, Jim—not even ours—is insoluble."

"I could name you five insoluble problems right off the top of my head. For example, why was the universe created? How can we trust what we think we know? Is there such a thing as an invariably right or wrong action? What is the nature of beauty? What is the proof of Fermat's last theorem? None of those are soluble by logic."

"No. The heart is not a logical organ. Our . . . situation . . . doesn't have its roots in logic." She put her arm through his. "When I married Theodore Wallace, I thought I was over you. I was wrong."

Kirk gave her a sharp look. "When did you realize this? Today?"

"What?"

"How much older was your husband than you?"

"What difference does it make?" she asked.

"Answer me!"

"Twenty-six years," she told him reluctantly. Then, as though he'd demanded an explanation, she added, "He was a brilliant man . . . we were stationed on a lonely outpost . . . working together—" She broke off to cry, "Jim, I don't want to talk about him! I want to talk about us!"

"Look at me!" Kirk demanded. He seized her shoulders. "I said look at me! What do you see?"

"I—I see Captain James Kirk," she said unsteadily. "A man of morality, decency—strong, handsome—"

"And *old!*" he cried. "Old—and getting older every minute!"

"Jim, please . . ."

"What are you offering me, Jan? Love—or a good-bye present?"

"That's very cruel," she said.

"It's honest!" His voice was harsh with bitterness. "Just stay around for two more days, Janet! By that time I'll really be old enough for your love!"

Young Chekov was feeling the strain of multiple medical examinations. "Give us some more blood, Chekov!" he muttered to Sulu. "The needle won't hurt, Chekov! Take off your shirt, Chekov! Roll over, Chekov! Breathe deeply, Chekov! Blood sample! Marrow sample! Skin sample! They take so many samples of me I'm not even sure I'm here!"

"You'll live," Sulu said.

"Oh yes, I'll live . . . but I won't enjoy—"

Kirk entered the bridge and he fell silent. Sulu said, "Maintaining standard orbit, Captain."

"Increase orbit to twenty thousand perigee."

As Kirk moved to his command chair, Yeoman Doris Atkins handed him a clipboard. "Will you sign this, sir?" He glanced at the board, scribbled his name on it and was handing it back to her when Commodore Stocker approached him.

"I hope to have a few words with you, Captain."

"I have very little time, Commodore."

"Very well, sir. I just want to remind you we have a due date at Star Base Ten."

"I'm afraid we'll be late for it, Commodore Stocker. I do not intend to leave this area until we have found a solution to our problem."

"Captain, I am watching four very valuable, and one almost irreplaceable, members of the Starfleet failing before my eyes. I want to do something to help."

"If you are so concerned," Kirk said, "I'll send a sub-space message to Star Base Ten and explain the situation."

At his computer station, Spock shook his head. Kirk noticed the gesture. "Yes, Mr. Spock?"

"Captain . . . you sent such a message this morning."

"Oh. Yes, of course." He changed the subject. "Yeoman Atkins."

"Sir?"

"Where's the report on fuel consumption?"

"You just signed it, sir."

"If I'd signed it, I wouldn't have asked for it! Give it to me!"

The girl timidly handed him the board. There was his signature. Angrily, he handed the board back to her and sank down in his command chair. He saw Chekov and Sulu exchange looks. Uhura's back was resolutely turned.

Kirk closed his eyes. *I need rest. You can take just so much. Then you've had it.* He was helpless; that was the fact. And he had never been so tired before in all his life . . . worry, despair . . . they weren't going to change a thing . . . tired . . . tired . . .

As from a great distance, he heard Spock's voice. "Captain! I believe I know the cause! I decided to—" The voice stopped, and Kirk let his mind drift again; but then he was being shaken. "Captain!" He roused himself with immense effort.

"Hmm? Spock? Sorry . . . I was thinking."

"Understandable, sir."

"Um. Do you have something to report, Mr. Spock?"

"Yes, sir. I think I know the cause of the affliction. I cannot be sure, but the lead I have seems very promising."

Alert now, Kirk said, "What is it?"

"The comet," Spock said. "The orbit of Gamma Hydra Four carried it directly through the comet's tail. I examined the residue on conventional radiation setting and discovered nothing. But when I reset our sensors at the extreme lower range of the scale, undetected radiation appeared. Below normal radiation readings . . . but definitely present. And undoubtedly residue from the comet's tail."

"Good, Mr. Spock. Let's get that to Dr. McCoy immediately."

Pain stabbed in his right knee as he rose. He massaged it and limped over to Uhura. "Lieutenant, take a message to Starfleet Command."

"Yes, sir."

"Because of the proximity of the Romulans, use Code Two."

"But, sir, the Romulans have broken Code Two. If you will remember the last bulletin—"

"Then use Code Three!"

"Yes, sir. Code Three."

"Message. Key to affliction may be in comet which passed Gamma Hydra Four. Said comet is now—" He looked at Spock.

"Quadrant four four eight, sir."

"I suggest all units be alerted for complete analysis of radiation; and means found to neutralize it. The comet is highly dangerous. Kirk, commanding *Enterprise*. Send it at once, Lieutenant Uhura. Let's go, Mr. Spock."

At the elevator he paused. "Mr. Sulu, increase orbit to twenty thousand miles perigee."

Startled, Sulu said, "You mean—another twenty thousand, Captain?"

Kirk whipped around, grim-faced. "I find it difficult to understand why every one of my commands is being questioned. Do what you're told, Mr. Sulu."

Spock spoke quietly. "What is our present position, Mr. Sulu?"

"Orbiting at twenty thousand, sir."

Kirk looked at Spock's impassive face. Then he said, "Maintain, Mr. Sulu."

"Maintaining, sir."

The silence of constraint was heavy in the bridge when the elevator door closed behind them.

But in Sickbay, hope had returned.

"Radiation," McCoy said reflectively. "As good an answer as any. But why didn't we know this earlier?"

"I suspect, Doctor, because my thinking processes are less clear and rapid than they were."

McCoy glanced at Spock. Then he handed his tape cartridge to Janet Wallace. "Run this through, please, Doctor."

"All right," Kirk said. "Keep me posted. I'll be on the bridge. Coming, Spock?"

"I have a question for the Doctor, Captain."

Kirk nodded, left. Spock said, "Doctor, the ship's temperature is increasingly uncomfortable for me. I have adjusted the environment in my quarters to one hundred and twenty-five degrees. This at least is tolerable, but—"

"I can see I won't be making any house calls on you," McCoy said.

"I wondered if there was something which could lower my sensitivity to cold."

"I'm not a magician, Spock. Just a plain old country doctor."

As the Vulcan closed the Sickbay door behind him, Janet turned, frustrated, from the computer. "Dr. McCoy, none of our usual radiation therapies will have any effect on this particular form of radiation sickness."

"All right. We start over. We work harder. Faster. Start completely from scratch if we have to. But we must find something."

Outside in the corridor, Commodore Stocker had intercepted Spock. "Can I have a word with you, Mr. Spock?"

"Commodore?"

Stocker lowered his voice. "Mr. Spock, a Starship can function with a chief engineer, a chief medical officer, even a First Officer who is under physical par. But it is disastrous to have a commanding officer whose condition is less than perfection."

"I am aware of that."

"Please understand me. My admiration for Captain Kirk is unbounded. He is a great officer. But . . . Mr. Spock, I need your help and your cooperation."

"For what, sir?"

"I want you to take over command of the *Enterprise*."

"On what grounds, sir?"

"On the grounds that the Captain is unable to perform his duties because of his affliction."

"I must remind you that I have contracted the same affliction."

"But you're a Vulcan," Stocker said. "You have a

much greater life span. You show the effects to a much smaller degree . . ."

"I am half human, sir," Spock said. "My physical reflexes are down. My mental capacities are reduced. I tire easily. No, sir. I am not fit for command."

"If you, a Vulcan, are not, then obviously Captain Kirk cannot be."

"Sir," Spock said, "I have duties to perform."

"Mr. Spock, I do not like what I'm about to say but regulations demand it. As second in command of the *Enterprise,* you must convene an extraordinary hearing on the Captain's competence."

"I—resist that suggestion, sir," Spock said stiffly.

"It's not a matter of choice. If a Captain is mentally or physically unfit, a competency hearing is mandatory. Please don't force me to quote a regulation which you know as well as I do."

There was a long pause. "Very well," Spock said. "The hearing will convene at fourteen hundred hours."

Under the eyes of a worried Kirk, Janet and McCoy were running final tests of Chekov. The unhappy Ensign was obviously considering rebellion against what seemed to be the thousandth needle jabbed into him during the course of these interminable examinations.

"Now, this won't hurt," McCoy told him.

"That's what you said last time," Chekov said. "And the time before that."

"Did it hurt?"

"Yes," Chekov retorted.

From the door of Sickbay came a whimper: "Doctor . . . help me . . ."

They turned. Arlene Galway was clutching the door-jamb for support. She was almost unrecognizable with age. "Please . . . do something . . . help . . ."

She reached out a hand; but before anyone could reach her, she collapsed to the deck. McCoy bent over her, while Kirk looked on, appalled even through the gray fog in which everything seemed to have happened in the last few days—or was it the last few weeks?

"That can't be—Lieutenant Galway?" he quavered.

"It is," McCoy said, his own voice creaky. "Or was.

She's dead. Her higher metabolism rate caused her to age more rapidly than the rest of us. But it's only a question of time before—"

"Bones, how long have we got?"

"Oh, it's a matter of days, Jim . . . perhaps only hours."

It wasn't information calculated to tranquilize a Starfleet captain called to a hearing on his command competence. Nor were the people gathered around the briefing-room table a quieting influence. The mysterious radiation sickness had made deeper inroads on everyone who had made the ill-fated check on the Robert Johnson expedition.

Looking as though he'd passed his fiftieth birthday, Spock opened the hearing by turning to Yeoman Atkins, who was serving as recorder. "Let it be read that this competency hearing has been ordered by Commodore Stocker, here present." He paused. "And reluctantly called by myself."

Kirk said, "Let it also be read that I consider this hearing invalid."

Spock looked down the table at Stocker.

Stocker said, "Regulation seven five nine two, section three paragraph eleven . . ."

"I know the book, Commodore," Kirk said.

Spock said quietly, "The legality of the hearing, Captain, is unquestionable."

"Mr. Spock, may I make a statement?" It was Stocker's question. At Spock's nod, he said, "I've had to resort to these legal grounds to save the lives of some extremely valuable members of the Starfleet. I have tried to convince Captain Kirk of the need to proceed to Star Base Ten—but have been overruled in each case. The responsibility for this hearing is mine."

"On the contrary, Commodore," Spock said. "As presiding officer and second in command of the *Enterprise,* the responsibility is mine. Captain Kirk, would you like to make a statement?"

"Yes!" The word came in a shout. "I am Captain of this ship and am totally capable of commanding her. Call this farce off and let's get back to work!"

"I cannot, sir," Spock said. "The regulations are quite specific." The chill struck him again. "You are entitled, sir, to direct examination of all witnesses immediately after this board has questioned them."

Kirk's voice was acid with sarcasm. "That is very kind of you, Mr. Spock."

Spock pushed a button on the computer-recorder. Imperturbable, he said, "Mr. Sulu, how long have you served with Captain Kirk?"

"Two years, sir."

"To your knowledge has he ever been unable to make decisions?"

"No, sir."

"Did he order you to maintain standard orbit around Gamma Hydra Four?"

"Yes, sir."

"Did he, several minutes later, repeat the order?"

"Yes, sir."

"Did he order you to increase orbit to twenty thousand perigee?"

"Yes, sir."

"And did he not repeat that order?"

"He did not!" Kirk yelled. "When I give an order I expect it to be obeyed! I don't have to repeat myself!"

"Captain, you'll be allowed direct cross-examination privileges when the board has finished."

"Isn't your terminology mixed up, Spock? This isn't a board! It's a cudgel!"

"Captain, it is a hearing not only sanctioned but required by regulations. Will you please answer the question, Mr. Sulu?"

"Yes, sir. Captain Kirk repeated his order."

"Commodore?"

"I have no questions," Stocker said.

"Captain Kirk?"

"Let's get on with it."

Spock ground his teeth together to keep them from chattering. His hands felt clumsy with cold. "Yeoman Atkins, you handed Captain Kirk a fuel-consumption report before witnesses. He accepted and signed it. Is that correct?"

"Sir, he had more important things on his mind. The current crisis—"

"Yeoman, you are merely to answer the question."

"I—guess he forgot he'd signed it."

"You guess?"

"He forgot he'd signed it."

"Thank you, Yeoman. You may leave."

It went on. Spock called Uhura to testify to Kirk's failure to recall that the Romulans had broken Code Two.

"All right!" Kirk cried. "I had a lot on my mind! I admit to the oversight!"

"It could have been a dangerous one," Stocker said.

"You are out of order, Commodore," Spock said. "Dr. McCoy?"

McCoy was lost in a daydream. "Dr. McCoy!"

He roused. "Sorry. Yes, Mr. Spock?"

"Several hours ago, at this board's request, you ran a complete physical examination of Captain Kirk."

"I did." McCoy threw a tape across the table at Spock. "It's all there. Enjoy yourself."

Silently, the Vulcan placed the tape cartridge into the computer slot.

The device buzzed, clicked, spoke. "Subject's physical age, based on physiological profile, sixty-three solar years."

There was a silence. Then Kirk said, "I am thirty-four years old."

"The computer differs with you," Stocker said.

"Dr. McCoy, give us your professional evaluation of Captain Kirk's present physical condition."

McCoy averted his eyes from Spock. "He is afflicted with a strange type of radiation sickness . . . and so are you and I and Mr. Scott."

"Kindly restrict your comments to Captain Kirk alone, Doctor. What effect has this sickness had on him?"

"He's—he's graying a little. A touch of arthritis."

"Is that all?"

"You know it isn't all! What are trying to do, Spock?"

"What I must do. Is not the Captain suffering from

a peculiar physical degeneration which strongly resembles aging?"

"Yes, he is. But he's a better man—"

"Doctor, do you agree with the computer's evaluation of the Captain's physical age?"

"It's a blasted machine!"

"Do you agree with it, Doctor?"

"Yes, I agree. I'm sorry, Jim."

"This board has no further questions. Unless you, Commodore Stocker . . ."

"I am quite satisfied, Mr. Spock."

"Do you wish to call witnesses, Captain Kirk?"

"I am perfectly capable of speaking in my own defense!"

Kirk tried to rise. His knee gave way; and he clutched at the table to keep from falling. "This hearing is being held for one reason and one alone. Because I refuse to leave Gamma Hydra Two."

"Gamma Hydra Four, sir," Spock said.

"Of course. A slip of the tongue. Where was I?" He suddenly clenched his fist and dashed it against the table. "So I'm a little confused! Who wouldn't be at a time like this? My ship in trouble . . . my senior officers ill . . . and this—this nonsense about a competency hearing! Enough to mix up any man! Trying to relieve a Starfleet captain of his command. Why, that's . . . that's . . . I wouldn't have believed it of you, Spock!"

He glared around the table. "All right, ask me questions! Go ahead! I'll show you who's capable! There's nothing wrong with my memory. Nor with my resolution, either. I repeat, we are maintaining orbit around Gamma Hydra Two!"

The second memory failure stood out, stark-naked.

Spock, cold to his marrow, spoke quietly into the silence.

"We have no more questions, Captain." He struggled to control his shivering. "If you will leave the room, sir, while the board votes . . ."

"Fine! You bet I'll leave it. Get your stupid voting over so I can get back to running my ship!"

He limped to the door and turned. "If I'm wanted, I'll be in my quarters."

When the door closed behind him, Spock said, "A simple hand vote will suffice. Dr. Wallace is excluded from the vote. Those who agree that Captain Kirk is no longer capable of handling the *Enterprise* will so signify by raising their right hands."

All hands save Spock's were slowly raised.

"Mr. Spock?" It was Commodore Stocker.

Spock raised his hand. He addressed the recording computer. "Register a unanimous vote."

Stocker said, "I assume, Mr. Spock, that you will now take over command of this vessel."

"Your assumption is incorrect, sir."

"Your reason?"

"By the standards this hearing has used against the Captain: my own physical failings exclude me from any command position."

"All right. Next in line is Mr. Scott."

All eyes fixed on Scott. He peered at the expectant faces, blinked, nodded—and was asleep.

"Since all senior officers are incapable, I am forced by regulations to assume command." Stocker was rising from the table when Spock said, "Sir, you have never commanded a starship."

"Whom would you have take over, Mr. Spock?"

"There is danger from the Romulans," Spock said.

"Mr. Spock, we've got to save these people!" He turned to Sulu. "Mr. Sulu, lay a direct course for Star Base Ten. Warp Five."

"Across the neutral zone, sir?"

Stocker nodded. "Alter course immediately."

"Commodore Stocker, I beg you not to underestimate the danger. Or the Romulans." Spock spoke urgently.

"The neutral zone is thinly patrolled at best. I am gambling that the violation will escape the Romulans' notice."

"The gamble, sir, if I may quote the odds—" Spock said.

"You may not!" Stocker strode to the door. "All officers are to return to their stations."

Kirk was alone in his quarters, tired, defeated, crushed by the full weight of his seventy years. When the knock at the door came, he could hardly bring himself to respond to it; but after a moment, he said, "Come in."

Spock entered, followed by Janet, who took up an inconspicuous stance beside the door. Kirk looked up hopefully at Spock, but the First Officer's face, for once, was almost as readable as a book.

"So," Kirk said. "I've been relieved."

"I am sorry, Captain."

"You should have been a prosecuting attorney."

"Regulations required me—"

"Regulations!" Kirk said. "Don't give me regulations, Spock! You've wanted command all along! The first little excuse—"

"I have not assumed command, Captain."

"I hope you're proud of the way you got . . ." Kirk paused, Spock's words gradually coming home. "What do you mean, you're not in command?"

"I suffer from the same ailment as yourself, sir."

"If you're not in command, who is?"

"Commodore Stocker."

It took Kirk a long moment to place the name. Then he exploded. "Stocker? Are you crazy? He's never held a field command! If Scotty—"

"Mr. Scott is in no condition to command. Commodore Stocker, as a ranking officer—"

"Don't prate to me about rank. The man's a chair-bound paper-pusher. Spock, I order you to take command!"

"I cannot, sir."

"You are disobeying a direct order, Mr. Spock."

"No, Captain. Only Commodore Stocker can give command orders on this ship now."

Impotent fury rose in Kirk. "You disloyal, traitorous . . . you stabbed me in the back the first chance you had. You—" His rage mounted as he found that he was weeping. Weeping! "Get out of here! I don't ever want to have to look at you again!"

Spock hesitated, inclined his head slightly, and left. After a moment, Kirk became aware of the female figure still standing beside the door inside his room, making faint sniffling noises. He peered at it.

"Who is it? Jan? Jan?"

"I'm sorry, Jim," she said. "Truly I am."

"I acted like a fool in there. Let them rattle me. Let myself get confused."

"Everyone understood."

"Only I'm not old, Jan. I'm not! A few muscular aches don't make a man old! You don't run a starship with your arms—you run it with your head! My mind's as sharp as it ever was!"

"We'll find a cure."

"A simple case of radiation sickness and I'm relieved of command." He turned and looked at himself in a mirror. "All right, I admit I've gotten a little gray. Radiation can do that."

"Jim," she said, as if in pain. "I have work to do. Please excuse me—"

"Look at me, Jan. You said you loved me. You know me. Look closely—"

"*Please,* Jim—"

"Just need a little rest. That's all. I'm not old, am I? Well, Say it! Say I'm not old!"

There was no response. Grasping her by the shoulders, he pulled her to him and kissed her with all the violence of which he was capable. But there was no response—not from her, and what was worse, not even within himself. He released her—and saw the pity in her eyes. He turned his back.

"Get out."

Now what? He could not think. He was relieved. The answer . . . but there was no answer. Wait. Something about a comet. McCoy. Chekov. The examination room. That was it, the examination room. He hobbled out, cursing himself for his slowness.

Spock was there; so were Nurse Chapel, McCoy and Janet. They all looked very old, somehow. But the hapless Chekov, back on the table again, did not seem to have changed. He was saying: "Why don't I just go back to work and leave my blood here?"

Kirk tried to glare at Spock. "What are you doing here?"

"It would seem the place where I can be of the most use."

"Maybe you'd like to relieve Dr. McCoy? Bones, what about Ensign Chekov here?"

"Nothing," McCoy said peevishly. "Absolutely nothing."

"There has to be! There has to be! We went down to the surface together. Beamed-down together. Stayed in the same spot. He was with us all the time. He—"

"No, Captain," Spock said, drawing in a sharp breath. "Not all the time. He left us for a few moments."

"Left us?" Kirk stared at the Vulcan, trying to remember. "Oh. Yes—when he went into the building. He . . . there was . . . Spock! Something did happen!"

"Indeed, Captain. Doctor, you will remember Professor Alvin's corpse in the improvised coffin—"

"Chekov, you got scared!" Kirk crowed. "You bumped into the dead man, and—"

"You bet," Chekov said. "I was scared, sir. But not half as scared as I am now, I'll tell you that."

"Fright?" McCoy said, raising a trembling hand to his chin. "Yes. Could be. Heart beats faster. Breath short. Cold sweat. Epinephrine flows. Something I read once . . . epinephrine tried for radiation sickness, in the mid-twentieth century—"

"It was abandoned," Janet said. "When hyronalyn was discovered."

"Yes, yes," McCoy said testily. "Don't confuse me. Why was it abandoned? There was some other reason. I knew it well, once. They didn't know the intermediate? Yes! That's it! AMP! Nurse, ask the computer for something called AMP!"

Christine Chapel, her face a study in incredulitity, turned to the computer read-out panel. After what seemed a very long time, she said, "There's an entry for it. It's called cyclic adenosine three-five monophosphate. But it affects *all* the hormonal processes—that's why they dropped it."

"We'll try it," McCoy said, with a startling cackle. "Don't just stand there, Dr. Wallace. Synthesize me a batch. Dammit, get cracking!"

On the bridge, Commodore Stocker was in the command chair. If he was aware of how many backs were pointedly turned to him, he did not show it; he was too busy trying to make sense of the many little lights that were flickering across the console before him.

"Entering Romulan neutral zone, sir," the helmsman said. "All sensors on maximum."

Now who was that? "Thank you, Mr. Spock, sorry, Mr. Sulu. Lieutenant Uhura, let me know if we contact any Romulan."

"Yes, sir. Nothing yet."

Stocker nodded and looked down again. The little lights danced mockingly at him. As a cadet he had studied a control board something like this, but since then, everything seemed to have been rearranged, and labeled with new symbols which meant nothing to him, with only a few exceptions. Well, he would have to depend upon these officers—

Then the *Enterprise* shook sharply under him, and half of the little lights went red. Ignorance overwhelmed him. "What was that?" he said helplessly.

"We have made contact, sir," Uhura said in a dry voice.

"Romulans approach from both sides, sir," Sulu added.

The ship shook again, harder. Swallowing, Stocker said, "Let's see them."

The main viewscreen lit up. It too was full of crawling little lights, which could not be told from the stars except for their motions, which he could not read either.

"I don't see any Romulans!"

"The ones that are changing color, sir. They change in accordance with their rate of approach—"

The ship bucked under him. All the lights went red.

"We're bracketed, sir," Sulu said evenly.

There was a buzz he couldn't locate. "Engineering calling, sir," Uhura said. "Do you want power diverted to the shields?"

His face felt bathed in sweat. "Yes," he said, at random.

"Mr. Scott asks how much warp power to reserve."

What was the answer to that one?

"Commodore Stocker," Sulu said, turning halfway toward the command chair. "We're in a tight. What are your orders?"

The *Enterprise* shuddered once more, and the lights dimmed. Stocker realized suddenly that he was too scared to speak, let alone move—

Then, mercifully, Kirk's voice, thin but demanding, came through the intercom. "What's going on up there? Lieutenant Uhura, this is the Captain!"

"Sir!" Uhura said. "We have violated the Romulan neutral zone, and are under attack."

"The fool. Maintain full shields! I'll be right there."

Stocker felt as though he were about to pass out with relief, but the ordeal wasn't over yet. Voices, more distant, were arguing over the open intercom:

"Jim . . . you can't . . . neither of us . . . Nurse . . . Doctor Wallace . . ."

"Got to . . . get to the bridge . . ."

"Oh Jim, you can't . . . Nurse . . . In there . . ."

Then the voices snapped off. Clearly, Kirk was not about to bail Stocker out yet. Rousing himself, Stocker said, "Lieutenant Uhura, keep trying to raise the Romulans."

"Very well. No response thus far."

"If I can talk to them—tell them the reason why we've violated the neutral zone—"

"The Romulans are notorious for not listening to explanations," Sulu said. "We know—we've tangled with them before."

"Hail them again!"

"I've hailed them on all channels," Uhura said. "They're ignoring us."

"Why shouldn't they?" Sulu said. "They know they have us. As long as we sit here, they can kick away at the screens until they go down."

Stocker ran a hand through his hair. "Then," he said, "we have no alternative but to surrender."

"They'd love that," Sulu said, his back still turned. "They have never captured a starship before. And, Commodore, they never take prisoners."

"Then what—"

"Sir," Uhura said, "you are in command. *What are your orders?*"

In Sickbay, Nurse Chapel and Janet had Kirk pinned down on a bed. He struggled to get up, and despite his aged condition they were having trouble restraining him—a task further complicated by the unpredictable shuddering of the *Enterprise*.

"Greenhorn—up there—ruin my ship—"

"Jim," Janet said through gritted teeth, "if I have to give you a shot—"

"Jim, lay quiet," McCoy said. "You can't do any good. We're through."

"No, no. My ship—"

Spock appeared from the laboratory, carrying a flask. "Dr. Wallace, here is the drug. It's crude, but we had no time for pharmacological tests or other refinements."

"All right," said McCoy. "Let's go."

"It will cure . . . or kill." Spock handed the flask to Janet, who loaded a hypo from it. "A safer preparation would take weeks to test."

"What is it?" Kirk said, quietening somewhat.

"The hormone intermediate," Janet said. "It has to be given parenterally, and even without the probable impurities in it, it could be extremely hard on the body. Cerebral hemmorhage, cardiac arrest—"

"Never mind the details," McCoy said. "Give it to me."

"No," Kirk said. "I'll take the first shot."

"You can't," McCoy said firmly.

As if on cue, the *Enterprise* shook again. "How long do you think the ship can take a pounding like this?" Kirk demanded. "I've got to get up there!"

"Jim, this could kill you," Janet said.

"I'll die anyway without it."

"Medical ethics demand—" McCoy began.

"Forget medical ethics! My ship is being destroyed! Give me that shot."

"The Captain is correct," Spock said. "If he does not regain his faculties, and get to the bridge to take command in a very few minutes, we shall all die at the hands of the Romulans. Give him the shot, Dr. Wallace."

She did so. For a moment nothing seemed to happen. Then Kirk found himself in the throes of convulsions, bucking and flailing at random. Dimly he was aware that all four of the others were hanging on to him.

It seemed to last forever, but actually hardly a minute passed before the fit began to subside, to be gradually replaced by a feeling of exhausted well-being. Janet was pointing a Feinberger at him.

"It's working," she said in a hushed voice. "The aging process has stopped."

"Can't see any change," McCoy said.

"She is correct, Doctor," Spock said. "It is there, and accelerating."

"Janet, help me up," Kirk said, taking a deep breath. "That was quite a ride."

"How do you feel?" she said.

"Like I've been kicked through the bulkhead. Spock, you'll have to wait for your shot; I need you on the bridge. Janet, give McCoy his shot, then Scott." He smiled. "Besides, Spock—if what I've got in mind doesn't work, you won't need that shot. Let's go."

In transit, he felt stronger and more acute with every passing second, and judging by the looks of relief with which he was greeted on the bridge, the change was visible to others as well.

"Report, Sulu!"

"We are surrounded by Romulan vessels—maximum of ten. Range, fifty to a hundred thousand kilometers."

Stocker got out of the command chair in a hurry as Kirk approached it. Kirk punched the intercom. "Engineering, feed in all emergency power, and all warp-drive engines on full standby. I'm going to need the works in about two minutes. Captain out . . . Lieutenant Uhura, set up a special channel to Starfleet Command. Code Two."

"But, Captain—"

"I gave you an order, Lieutenant. Code Two."

"Code Two, sir."

"Message: *Enterprise* to Starfleet Command, this

sector. Ship has inadvertantly encroached upon Romulan neutral zone. Surrounded and under heavy Romulan attack. Escape impossible. Shields failing. Will implement destruct order, using corbomite device recently installed. Since this will result in destruction of *Enterprise* and all matter within two hundred thousand kilometer diameter, and establish corresponding dead zone, all Federation ships to avoid area for at least four solar years. Explosion will occur in one minute. Kirk, commanding *Enterprise.* Out . . . Mr. Sulu. Course 188, mark 14, Warp Eight and stand by."

"Standing by, sir."

From his station, Spock said, "The Romulans are giving ground, sir. I believe they tapped in, as you obviously expected them to."

"A logical assumption, Mr. Spock. Are they still retreating?"

"Yes, sir, but are still well within firing range."

"All hands stand by . . . now, Warp Eight!"

The ship jolted—not this time to an onslaught, but to sudden motion at eight times the speed of light. Spock hovered over his console.

"The Romulans were caught off guard, sir. Not even in motion yet."

"Are we out of range, Mr. Sulu?"

"Yes, sir. And out of the neutral zone."

"Adjust to new course. One nine two degrees, mark 4. Heading for Star Base Ten."

"Coming around, sir."

Kirk sat back. He felt fine. Commodore Stocker approached him, his face full of shame.

"Captain," Stocker said, "I just wanted to assure you that I did what I thought had to be done to save you and the other officers."

"Noted, Commodore. You should know, however, that there is very little a Star Base can do that a starship cannot."

"If I may say so, Captain, I am now quite aware of what a starship can do—with the right man at the helm."

The elevator doors snapped open and McCoy came out. He was as young as ever. Kirk stared at him.

"You're looking good, Bones."

"So's Scotty. The drug worked. He pulled a muscle during the initial reaction, but otherwise he's feeling fine. Now, Mr. Spock, whenever you're ready."

"I'm ready now, Doctor."

"Good. Because of your Vulcan physique, I've prepared an extremely potent shot. I've also removed all the breakables from Sickbay."

"That is very thoughtful of you."

"I knew you'd appreciate it."

Kirk smiled. "All in all, gentlemen, an experience we'll remember in our old age . . . of course, that won't be for a long time yet, will it?"

ELAAN OF TROYIUS

(John Meredyth Lucas)

Kirk's orders were simple. He was to "cooperate" in all matters pertaining to the mission of his passenger, the Ambassador of the planet Troyius.

It was the implications of his orders that were complicated. First, the Ambassador's mission was top secret. Second, his negotiations involved the notoriously hostile people of Elas, a neighbor planet. As if such "cooperation" weren't enough of a headache, both planets were located in a star system over which the Klingon Empire claimed jurisdiction. By entering the system, the *Enterprise* was inviting Klingon retaliation for trespass.

Kirk was frankly irritated as he swung his command chair to Uhura. "Inform Transporter Room we'll be beaming-up the Elas party at once. Ask Ambassador Petri to meet us there."

"Yes, Captain."

At his nod, Spock, McCoy and Scott followed him into the elevator. Kirk said, "Some deskbound Starfleet bureaucrat has cut these cloak-and-dagger orders."

The intercom spoke. "Bridge to Captain." It was Uhura's voice.

"Kirk here."

"Captain, signal from the Elas party. They're ready to beam aboard but demand an explanation of the delay."

"Here we go," Kirk said. "What delay are they talking about? All right. Forget it, Lieutenant Uhura. Beam them aboard."

Spock said, "The attitude is typical of the Elasians, sir. Scientists who made the original survey of the planet described their men as vicious and arrogant."

"That's the negative aspect," McCoy said. "I've gone over those records. Their women are supposed to be something very special. They're said to possess a kind of subtle—maybe mystical—power that drives men wild."

Spock gave McCoy a disgusted look. It was still on his face when the elevator door opened to reveal the waiting Troyian envoy. Kirk addressed him immediately. "Ambassador Petri, suppose you drop this diplomatic secrecy—and tell me what this mission of yours is really about."

"That must wait until the Dohlman of Elas is aboard, Captain."

"Dohlman?" Kirk said as they all entered the Transporter Room. "What the devil is a Dohlman?"

"The thing most feared and hated by my people. Our most deadly enemy," Petri said.

The Transporter Room's hum deepened—and three figures sparkled into substance on the platform. They were soldiers. Breast plates covered their chests. Weapons of no recognizable variety hung from the barbaric chains around their necks. The biggest Elasian soldier, thick-jawed, heavy-browed, covered the *Enterprise* group with his strange weapon.

"Welcome. I am the Ambassador of Troyius," Petri said.

The ape-jawed giant ignored him. "Who runs this ship?"

Kirk said, "The *Enterprise* is under my command. I am Captain Kirk."

"And I am Kryton of Elas. That Troyian there is a menace. I must know that all is secure here before the Dohlman is brought aboard."

Spock lowered his voice. "Captain, the weapons resemble twenty-first century nuclear disintegrators."

Kirk spoke to the bellicose Kryton. "My ship *is* secure. What's more, we are equipped to repel any hostile act." He turned his back on the Elasian to say to the Transporter Room technician. "Energize!"

The center transporter platform went luminous. The three Elasians dropped to one knee. Glaring at Kirk, Kryton growled, "Quickly! To your knee! Do honor to the Dohlman of Elas!"

Kirk's jaw tightened. Beside him, acquiescent, Petri sank to one knee. "It is their custom," he muttered. "To stand is a breach of protocol."

Spock looked at Kirk. Annoyance on his face, Kirk nodded. The Vulcan hesitated; then, he, too, bent his knee. The sight increased Kirk's annoyance. It was abruptly dissipated. On the center platform the "deadly enemy" of Troyius had appeared. The Dohlman was a silver blonde. Her skin had the pearly tone of dreams. So was her body the stuff of dreams. Nor was it hidden. The scanty metallic scarves she wore served no purpose but suggestion of beauty too overwhelming for complete revelation.

Kryton said, "Glory to Elaan, Dohlman of Elas!"

"Glory is right," Kirk thought, controlling an impulse to kneel himself. Instead, he bowed. Then, raising his head, he looked again at the Dohlman of Elas. Under the silver blonde hair, her eyes were dark. Aflame with contempt, they swept over the kneeling men. At a snap of her fingers, her soldier bodyguard got to their feet, Kryton, addressing Spock and Petri, said, "Now you may stand."

She came forward, Kryton towering behind her, tense, his weapon at the ready. Her own hand rested on the elaborately jeweled hilt of a dagger suspended from a golden chain she wore around her slim waist.

"Odd," Kirk said to Spock. "Body armor and nuclear weapons."

"Not without precedent, sir. Consider the Samurai customs of old Earth's Japanese. Even we Vulcans preserve some symbolic remnants of our past."

Kryton growled again. "Permission to speak was not given!"

Before Kirk could retort, Elaan said to Spock, "You rule this ship?" The voice was husky, infinitely feminine.

"I am the ship's First Officer. This is Captain Kirk."

She made no sign of acknowledgment. Petri interposed hastily. "Your glory, I am Petri of Troyius. In the name of my people, I bid you welcome to—"

"Your mission is known to me," she said with negligent scorn. Then, turning to Kirk, she added, "You are permitted to show the accommodations."

He pulled himself together. "I think we'd better have an understanding right—"

"Please, Captain," Petri begged.

Kirk said, "My First Officer, Mr. Spock will show you to your quarters." He turned to leave. "Ambassador Petri, I want to speak to you."

Elaan's words came like a whip. "You have not been dismissed."

Incredulous, on the edge of explosion, Kirk gave his response second thought. He decided to shrug. "May I have your glory's permission to leave?" he asked silkily.

"You are all dismissed," she said.

Outside in the corridor Kirk wheeled on Petri. "All right, Ambassador! What exactly are we supposed to be doing?"

Petri drew him aside. "She—that woman is to be the wife of our ruler. The marriage has been arranged to bring peace. Our two warring planets now possess the capability of mutual destruction. Some method of coexistence had to be found."

"Then we return to Troyius?"

"Yes. But slowly, Captain. I will need time. My mission is to teach her civilized manners before we reach Troyius. It must be clear to you now why I'll need time. In her present savage condition my people would never accept her as queen."

"You've got yourself quite a mission," Kirk said.

"Those are my orders. I must ask you and your crew to tolerate this Elasian impudence for the sake of future peace. It is vital that friction now be kept to a minimum."

"That I can understand," Kirk said.

"There's another thing you should understand, Captain. You have as much at stake as I have. Your superiors know that failure of this mission would be as catastrophic for Federation planning as it would be for our two planets. The peace we'd gain by accepting such an untutored wife for our ruler would not be peace." He drew a deep sighing breath. "I will take her the official gifts I bear. Perhaps they will change her mood."

Kirk said, "I hope so." But what he thought was: "Shrew, termagant—a knockout fishwife is what I've got on my ship!"

Troubled, he stopped at Sulu's station as he re-entered the bridge. "Mr. Sulu, lay in a course for Troyius. Impulse drive-speed factor point zero three seven. Take us out of orbit."

Sulu looked startled. "Impulse drive, Captain?"

"That is correct, Mr. Sulu. Sub-light factor point zero three seven."

Scott looked up from his station. "Captain, you'll not be using the warp drive? All the way on impulse?"

"Correct, Mr. Scott."

"That'll take a great deal of time."

"Are you in a hurry, Mr. Scott?"

"No, sir."

"That's it, then." But he'd scarcely reached his command chair when Spock hurried to his side. "Captain, the Dohlman is dissatisfied with her quarters!"

Overhearing, Uhura turned indignantly. "What's the matter with them?"

"Nothing that I was able to see," Spock said. "But all the Elasians seem to be most irrational."

"I gave up my quarters," Uhura said, "because—"

"*I* appreciate your sacrifice, Lieutenant," Kirk told her. He got up. "I'll talk to the lady myself."

He heard the screams of rage before he reached Uhura's cabin. Its door was wide open. But it took a moment to take in the scene. A crystal box was flying through the air—and struck Petri in the chest. "Swine!

Take back your gifts! Your ruler cannot buy the favor of the Dohlman of Elas!"

Petri retrieved the box, stuffing delicate lace back into it. "Your glory," he said, "this is your wedding veil." He backed up to what he clearly hoped was a safe distance to raise the lid of a begemmed gold casket. "In this," he said, "are the most prized royal jewels of Troyius. This necklace is a gift from the bridegroom's mother to adorn your lovely throat . . ."

The necklace seemed to be composed of diamonds and emeralds. Elaan seized it. Then she hurled it at Petri with a wild aim that barely escaped hitting Kirk in the face. "I would strangle if I wore this bauble of Troyian dogs around my neck!"

Kirk stepped over the glitter at his feet and into the cabin. She saw him and shrieked, "Kryton!" The huge guard rushed in. "By whose permission has *he* come here?"

"He came in answer to your summons, your glory."

Kirk said, "I understand you are not happy with your quarters."

She waved a hand, dismissing Kryton. "Quarters?" She leveled a perfect leg at a cushioned chair. "Am I a soft, pewling Troyian that I must have cushions to sit on?" She kicked the chair over. Her own action inflamed her rage. She ran to the cabin window, ripping down its draperies. "These female trappings in here are an offense to me!"

Kirk said, "My Communications Officer vacated these rooms in the generous hope you would find them satisfactory."

"I do not find them so." She pointed at Petri. "And I find this—this Ambassador even less satisfactory! Must my bitterness be compounded by his presence aboard your ship?"

Petri, red with suppressed fury, said, "I've explained to her glory that her Council of Nobles and the Troyian Tribunal jointly agreed that I should instruct—make her acquainted with the customs and manners of our people."

"Kryton!" Elaan called. She indicated Petri. "Remove him!" The guard fingered his weapon. Petri bowed; and was moving to the door when she cried, "And take that garbage with you!" He bowed again, stooped lower to collect the gifts she'd flung to the floor and gratefully made his exit.

"That he should dare to suggest I adopt the servile manners of his people!" Elaan stormed.

"Your glory doesn't seem to be responding favorably to Troyian instruction," Kirk said.

"I will never forgive the Council of Nobles for inflicting such a nightmare on me! By the way, *you* were responding to my demand for better quarters!"

"There are none better aboard," Kirk said. "I suggest you make the best of it."

Aghast at this effrontery, she glanced at Uhura's dressing table for some object she could smash. "You presume to suggest to *me*—"

Kirk said, "Lieutenant Uhura's personal belongings have all been removed from the cabin. But if smashing things gratifies you, I will arrange to equip it with breakable articles."

"I will not be humiliated!"

"Then behave yourself," Kirk said. He went to the door; and she screamed, "I did not give you permission to leave!"

"I didn't ask for it," he said, slamming the door behind him.

An agitated Petri was waiting for him in the corridor. "Captain, I wish to contact my government. I cannot fulfill my mission. I would be an insult to my ruler to bring him this incorrigible monster as a bride."

"Simmer down, Ambassador. Your mission is a peace mission."

"There cannot be peace between the Elasians and us. We have deluded ourselves. The truth is, when I am with these people, I do not want peace. I want to kill them."

"Then you're as bad as she is," Kirk said. "You're not obliged to like the Elasians. You're obliged to do a job."

"The job's impossible. She simply won't listen to me."

"*Make* her listen," Kirk said. "Don't be so diplomatic. She respects strength. Come on strong with her, Ambassador."

"I, too, have pride, Captain. I will not be humiliated."

"You're on assignment, Ambassador. So am I. We're under orders to deliver the Dohlman in acceptable condition for this marriage. If it means swallowing a bit of our pride—well, that's part of the job."

Petri sighed. "Very well. I'll make another try."

"Strong, Ambassador. Remember, come on strong with her. Good luck."

A knockout fishwife. What she needed was a swift one to her lovely jaw. Kirk, re-entering the bridge was greeted by Uhura's hopeful question: "Does she like my quarters any better now, Captain?"

"She's made certain . . . arrangements, Lieutenant. But I think things will work out."

The intercom spoke excitedly. "Security alert! Deck five! Security alert!"

Kirk ran for the elevator. On deck five, Security Officer Evans met him as he stepped out. "It's Ambassador Petri, sir. They refuse to explain what happened but—"

At the door to Elaan's quarters, two *Enterprise* security men were confronting the three Elasian guards. "Stand aside, please," Kirk said to Kryton.

The ape-jawed giant said, "Her glory has not summoned you."

Behind him Elaan opened the closed door. "Have this Troyian pig removed," she said.

Petri lay on the cabin floor, face down in a pool of his own blood. The jeweled dagger had been buried in his back.

In Sickbay McCoy looked up at Kirk. "The knife went deep, Jim. He's lost a lot of blood."

Kirk bent over the patient. What he received was a glare. "If I recover," Petri said weakly, "it will be no thanks to you."

"I said talk to her. Not fight her."

"I should have known better than to enter that

cabin, unarmed. But you forced me to. I hold you responsible for this."

"Captain!" It was Uhura. "A message from Starfleet Command just in. Class A security, scrambled. I've just put it through the decoder."

"What is it, Lieutenant?"

"The Federation's High Commissioner is on his way to Troyius for the royal wedding."

McCoy whistled. "Whew! Now the fat's really in the fire. When the Commissioner learns the bride has just tried to murder the groom's Ambassador . . ."

"What a comfort you are, Bones!" But McCoy had returned to the patient whom Nurse Christine was preparing for an air hypo. As she applied it, she said, "If the Elasian women are this vicious, sir, why are men so attracted to them? What is their magic?"

"It's not magic," Petri said scornfully. "It's biochemical—a chemical substance in their tears. A man whose flesh is once touched by an Elasian woman's tears is made her slave forever."

"What rot!" Kirk thought. "The man's a fool." The failure of his mission was about to be exposed to the Federation's High Commissioner—and here he was going on about Elasian females' tears. He walked over to the bed. "Ambassador, I have news for you. The Federation's High Commissioner is on his way to this wedding."

"There will be no wedding. I would not have our ruler marry that creature if the entire galaxy depended on it. And I want nothing more to do with you."

"I didn't ask you to have anything to do with me. I asked you to do your job with her." He turned to McCoy. "Bones, how long will it take to get him back on his feet?"

"A few days. Maybe a week."

Petri raised his head from his pillow. "Captain, in this bed you put me. And in this bed I intend to stay. Indefinitely. I have nothing further to say to you."

Kirk looked at McCoy. Then he shrugged. Uhura and McCoy followed him out to the corridor. "I don't know what to do with him, Jim. He's as bad as she is. They're all pig-headed. And they just plain hate each other."

Uhura said, "You've got to admit he's got the better reason for hate. Captain, can't you explain to the High Commissioner that it's just impossible to—"

"High Commissioners don't like explanations. They like results. How do you handle a woman like that, anyway?"

"You stay away from her, Captain. As far away as—"

She broke off. From the recreation room they were passing came the sound of poignantly haunting music. Uhura's face lighted. "Captain, it used to be said that music hath charms to soothe the savage breast. The Dohlman has a very savage breast. Suppose you—"

"Soothing that woman is asking a lot of any music," McCoy said.

But Kirk was looking reflectively at the recreation room door. He opened it. Spock, sitting apart from the other crew members, was strumming his Vulcan lyre. Its unearthly tones suited the room decorations—its carpet of pink grass, wall vines that broke into drooping, long-stamened blossoms, the fountain spraying purple water into the air.

"Spock, what's that music you're playing?"

"A simple scale. I was just tuning the lyre."

"You can play tunes on that contraption?" McCoy said.

"I took second prize in the all-Vulcan music competition."

"Who took the first one?"

"My father."

"Can you play a love song?" Kirk said.

"A mating song. In ancient times the Vulcan lyre was used to stimulate the mating passion."

"We need some form of such stimulation on this ship," Kirk said. "A mating on Troyius is supposed to take place if we could just persuade the bride to participate in it."

"Inasmuch as she's just knifed her teacher in the bridegroom's etiquette, teaching it to her seems something of a baffler," McCoy said.

"Appoint another teacher," Spock said.

"You, Spock?"

"Certainly not. Logic dictates that the Dohlman will accept only the person of highest rank aboard this vessel."

Everybody looked at Kirk. He looked back at them, considering all the elements involved in Elaan's capitulation to reason.

"All right. Spock, give me five minutes and then start piping that music of yours into the Dohlman's quarters." He left; and as Spock's fingers moved over the strings of his instrument, Uhura sighed. "Mr. Spock, that music really gets to me."

"Yes, I also find it relaxing."

"Relaxing is the very last word I'd use to describe it," Uhura said. "I'd certainly like to learn how to play that lyre."

"I'd be glad to give you the theory, Lieutenant. However, to my knowledge no non-Vulcan has ever mastered the skill."

In Elaan's cabin Kirk was wishing he could give her the theory of acceptable table manners.

He watched her lift a wine bottle from her sumptuously spread dinner table, take a swig from it and wipe her mouth with a lovely arm. She swallowed, and replacing the bottle on the table, said, "So the Ambassador will recover. That's too bad." Then she grabbed a roasted squab from a plate. She bit a mouthful of breast meat from it; and tossing the rest of the delicacy over her shoulder, added, "You've delivered your message. You have my leave to go."

He was fascinated by the efficiency with which she managed to articulate and chew squab at the same time. "I'd like nothing better," he said. "But your glory's impetuous nature has—"

"That Troyian pig was in my quarters without permission. Naturally I stabbed him."

Kirk said, "You Elasians pride yourselves on being a warrior race. Then you must understand discipline—the ability to follow orders as well as to give them. You are under orders to marry the Troyian ruler and familiarize yourself with the habits of his people."

"Troyians disgust me," she said. "Any contact with them makes me feel soiled."

Her cheek was soiled by a large spot of grease from the squab. "It's my experience," Kirk said, "that the prejudices people feel disappear once they get to know each other."

Spock's music had begun to filter into the cabin. "That has not been my experience," she said, reaching for a rich cream pastry.

"In any case, we're still faced with a problem."

"Problem?"

"Your indoctrination in the customs of Troyius."

"I have eliminated that problem."

"No. You eliminated your teacher. The problem remains."

The luscious mouth smiled grimly. How, he couldn't figure out. "And its solution?" she said.

"A new teacher."

"Oh." She placed her dagger on the table. "What's that sickening sound?" The pastry in her hand, she rose, went to the intercom and switched off the Vulcan music. Licking cream from the pastry, she said, "And you—what can you teach me?"

"Table manners for one thing," he said.

He picked up a napkin, went to her, removed the pastry; and wiped her mouth, her cheek and fingers. "This," he said, "is a table napkin. Its function is to remove traces of the wine and food one has swallowed instead of leaving them on the mouth, the cheek, the fingers—and oh yes, the arm." He wiped her arm. Then, grasping it firmly, he led her over to the table.

"And this," he said, "is a plate. It holds food. It is specifically made to hold food, as floors are not. They are constructed to walk on." He poured wine into a glass; and held it up. "This is a glass," he said, "the vessel from which one drinks wine. A bottle, your glory, is merely intended to hold the wine."

She seized the bottle and took another swig from it. "Leave me," she said.

"You are going to learn what you've been ordered to learn," he said.

"You will return me to Elas at once!"

"That is impossible."

She stamped her foot. "What I command is always possible! I will not go to Troyius! I will not be given to a fat pig of a Troyian as a bride to stop a war!" She lifted the wine bottle again to her mouth. Kirk grabbed it.

"You enjoy the title of Dohlman," he said. "If you don't want the obligations that go with it, give it up!"

Her shock was genuine. "Nobody has ever dared to speak to me in such a manner!"

"That's your trouble," he said. "Nobody has ever told you the truth. You are an uncivilized little savage, a vicious, bad-tempered child in a woman's body . . ."

Her fist leaped out and connected with Kirk's jaw. She had pulled her arm back to strike him again when he grabbed it and slapped her as hard as he could across the face. The blow sent her sprawling back on the bed. Shaking with rage, Kirk shouted, "You've heard the truth from me for the first time in your spoiled life!"

He made for the door—and her dagger hissed past his ear to stick, quivering, in a wall plaque beside his head. He pulled it free; and tossing it back to her, said, "Tomorrow's lesson, your glory, will be on courtesy."

As he jerked the door closed behind him, she yanked wildly at the table cover. He didn't turn at the sound of crashing crockery.

He got out of the bridge elevator to see Spock absorbed in his sensor viewer. "Captain, look at this. At first I defined it as a sensor ghost. But I've run checks on all the instrumentation. The equipment is working perfectly."

Kirk examined the shadow. "Hydrogen cloud reflection?"

"None in the area. The ghost appears intermittently."

"Speculation, Mr. Spock?"

"None, sir. Insufficient data."

"It's not an instrument malfunction, not a reflection of natural phenomena. A space ship, then?"

The intercom beeped. Scott's voice was thick with anger.

"Captain, must I let these—these passengers fool

around with my equipment? I know what you said about showing them respect but . . ."

"Hang on, Scotty. And be pleasant no matter how it hurts. I'm on my way."

He was startled himself when he opened the door to Engineering. Elaan and her three guards had their heads bent over the warp-drive mechanism. Scott had somehow got his fury under control. He was saying, "I suppose, ma'am, that even our impulse drive must seem fast—"

"We are interested in how ships are used in combat, not in what drives them. Engines are for mechanics and other menials."

Scott choked. "Menials? How long do you think—"

"Mr. Scott!" Kirk said sharply.

He strode to Elaan. "Why didn't you tell me you wanted a tour of the engine room?"

"Do I not own the freedom of this ship? I have granted your men permission not to kneel in my presence. What more do you want?"

"Courtesy."

"Courtesy is not for inferiors."

Kirk said, "Mr. Scott, our chief engineer has received you into his department. That was a courtesy. You will respond to it by saying, 'Thank you, Mr. Scott.' "

He thought she was going to spit at him. Then she said tightly, "Thank you, Mr. Scott." Her guards stared, dumbfounded. She pushed one. "Come," she said to them and swept out.

Scott said, "Your schooling, sir, seems to be taking effect."

A buzz came from the intercom beside them. Spock's voice said, "Bridge to Captain."

"Kirk here."

"That sensor ghost is moving closer, sir."

"On my way."

His guess had been right. The sensor ghost was a space ship. Kirk studied the instrument for a long moment. Then he raised his head. "The question is, Mr. Spock, whose space ship is it?"

"No data yet, sir."

"Captain!" Sulu called. "A distant bearing, sir. Mark 73.5."

"Maximum magnification," Kirk said.

The main viewing screen had been merely showing a telescopic blur of a normally stationary star field. Now there suddenly swam into it the sharp image of an unfamiliar but strangely evil-looking space ship.

"Our ghost has materialized, Captain," Spock said.

Kirk nodded soberly. "A Klingon warship."

He returned to his command chair, the gravity in his face deepened. He turned to look at the screen again. "Any change, Mr. Spock?"

"Negative, sir. The Klingon ship has simply moved into contact range. She's pacing us, precisely matching our sub-light speed."

Though the bridge screen was equipped to show what was moving outside the *Enterprise,* it was not equipped to show what was moving inside it. Thus, Kirk could not see Kryton move stealthily into the engineering room—and take cover behind the huge mount where Second Engineer Watson was working. In perfect secrecy, the Elasian silently removed the main relay box cover, took a small dial-studded disk from his uniform pouch, adjusted the dials and placed the disk in the relay box. It was as he fitted it that Watson sensed something amiss. Tool in hand, he confronted Kryton, shouting, "What are you doing in here?"

Kryton's fist came up under his chin like a uncoiled spring. Watson crumpled. In a flash, Kryton had the body hidden and huddled behind the mount. Then he went back to work in the relay box.

In the bridge, Kirk, still concentrated on the Klingon ship's doings, turned to Uhura. "Lieutenant, open a hailing frequency. Identify us and ask his intentions."

She plugged into her board, shook her head. "No response, sir. Not on any channel."

"Then continue to monitor all frequencies, Lieutenant." He paused a moment. Then he said to Sulu, "Phaser crews stand by, Mr. Sulu." He waited another moment before he added "Maintain yellow alert." He rose from his chair. "Mr. Spock, it's time."

Down in Engineering, still unknown, unheard, Kryton's disk made contact. The lights in the matter-antimatter grille flickered before they returned to full strength. Kirk, on deck five, was walking down the corridor to Elaan's cabin. As he'd expected, two guards stood at her door. But neither was Kryton. A little uneasy he said, "Where is Kryton?"

"On business," said a guard. Both lifted their weapons. "No one may enter the Dohlman's presence," one said.

"Inform her glory that Captain Kirk requests the honor of a visit."

"The Dohlman has said I shall be whipped to death if I let Captain Kirk pass through this door." Kirk pushed past them. The weapons leveled. A beam flashed twice. The guards fell; and Spock, phaser in hand, came out of the opposite door. "Have them taken to the Security Holding area, Mr. Spock."

Spock said, "Captain, how did you anticipate that she would deny you admittance? The logic by which you arrived at your conclusion escapes me."

"On your planet, Mr. Spock, females are logical. No other planet in the galaxy can make that claim."

He opened Elaan's door to see her sitting before a mirror. She was absorbed in combing the shining hair. As she saw his reflection in the glass, she flew to the bed where she'd discarded her belted dagger. Holding it high, she rushed at Kirk, its point at his heart. He seized her wrist and she shrieked, "You dare to touch a member of the royal family of Elas?"

"In self-defense, I certainly do." He removed the dagger and she tried to rake his face with her nails. He closed with her, holding her arms immobilized.

"For what you are doing the penalty is death on Elas!"

"You're not on Elas now. You are on my ship. I command here."

She bit his arm. The pain took him off guard. His hold on her loosened—and she was gone, fled into the adjoining bathroom, its door clicking locked behind her.

"That's your warning, Captain!" she called through it. "Don't ever touch me again!"

"All right," Kirk shouted in answer. "Then I'll send in Mr. Spock or Dr. McCoy! But I'll tell you one thing! You're going to do what you've been ordered to do by Councils, Tribunals and bureaucrats . . ."

He'd had it. A Klingon warship in the offing—and here he was, stuck behind a bathroom door trying to make sense to an overindulged brat who had no sense. "I'm leaving!" he yelled. "I'm through with you!"

She opened the door. "Captain . . ." She hesitated. "There . . . is one thing you . . . can teach me . . ."

"No, there isn't!" he roared at her. "You were right the first time! There's nothing I want to teach you! Not any more! You know everything!"

She began to cry. "I don't know everything. I don't know how to make people like me. Everybody hates me . . ."

He was startled into contrition. Genuine tears flooded the dark eyes. It was a sight he'd never thought to see. "Now look . . ." he said. "It's not that anybody hates you . . ."

"Yes, they do," she sobbed. "Everybody does . . ."

He went to her and wiped the tear-wet cheeks with his hand. "Stop crying," he said. "It's just that nobody likes to be treated as though they didn't exist . . ."

He was suddenly conscious of heat. "Something's wrong with the ventilation of this room . . . I—I need some air . . . we'll have a short recess, your glory."

"Captain . . ." He turned from the door. The luscious mouth was smiling at him, the pearl-toned arms outstretched to him. He stared at her for a long moment. Then he went straight into the arms. He kissed her—and the world, the Klingon ship, the High Commissioner, all he'd ever known in his life before was as though it had never existed.

She whispered, "You . . . slapped me."

Unsteadily, Kirk said, "We'll . . . talk about it later . . ."

His mouth found hers again.

Uhura, checking her dials, pushed the intercom button.

"Bridge to Captain," she said. She glanced over at Spock. "Mr. Spock, I'm getting—"

"I have it on my sensor," Spock said.

"Bridge to Captain," she repeated, frowning. "Come in, Captain. Captain Kirk, please answer."

Kirk's voice came, unfamiliar, dazed. "Kirk here."

"Captain, I'm picking up a transmission from inside the *Enterprise*. It's on a tight beam aimed at the Klingon vessel."

Elaan was nibbling at the lobe of Kirk's ear. "Transmission?" he echoed vaguely. Her lashes were black. They should have been silver blonde but they weren't. He said, "Stop that." She kissed the ear; and he was able to focus his attention on the intercom long enough to ask, "Can you pinpoint the source of the transmission, Lieutenant?"

"Spock here, Captain. I am triangulating now. It's coming from the engine room, sir."

The news broke through his entrancement. "Security to engineering! An intruder! Security alert all decks!"

He ran for the door and the elevator. In the engine room, Scott met him, his face stricken. He pointed to the body of Watson. "Watson must have discovered the devil after he'd sneaked in here. He got killed for it. He had this in his hand when I found him. It looks like some kind of transmitter."

Kirk took it. "It's Klingon," he said.

McCoy rose from Watson's body. "Neck snapped clean, Jim."

Kirk walked over to where two Security guards, their phasers trained on Kryton, held the ape-jawed Elasian in custody.

"What signal did you send that Klingon ship? What was your assignment?"

Impassive, his small eyes bright with scorn, Kryton said, "Captain, you must know I will say nothing. Our interrogation methods are far more excruciating than anything you people are capable of."

"I'm aware you're trained to resist any form of *physical* torture." Kirk moved to the intercom. "Kirk to Spock."

"Spock here, Captain."

"Mr. Spock, it is Kryton who's been transmitting. He refuses to talk. I'll need you to do the Vulcan mind-meld."

"Captain!" It was Evans, one of the Security guards. "The prisoner—he's sick . . ." Kirk whirled to see Kryton clutch at his stomach. The Elasian sagged at the knees—and his hand whipped out to seize Evans' phaser. He reversed it, fired it at himself and disappeared.

Stunned, Evans said, "Captain, I'm sorry. But he really seemed—"

"What was he hiding that was so important he had to die to keep it secret?" Hard-faced, Kirk turned to Scott. "He didn't come in here just to use a transmitter. Scotty, I want you to check every relay you've got."

"Captain, do you realize how many relays there are in Engineering?"

"Don't waste time telling me. Do it!"

He wasted no time himself in getting back to Elaan's cabin. She took the news of Kryton's suicide quietly. "He's been half out of his mind ever since the announcement of my wedding. He was of noble family—and he loved me."

"Then he sold out to the Klingons out of jealousy?"

"Probably." She laid her hand on his heart. "It is mine, is it not? Let us not speak of unimportant matters."

"There's a Klingon warship out there," he told her. "What is it there for? It isn't keeping pace with us just to prevent your marriage."

She put her silver blonde head on his shoulder. "We should welcome their help against the marriage," she said.

He grasped her upper arms. "Elaan, two planets, the stability of an entire star system depends on your marriage. We both have a duty to forget what happened."

"Could you do that? Give me to another man?"

"My orders—and yours—say you *belong* to that other man. What happened between us was an accident."

"It was no accident. I chose you and you chose me." Before he could speak, she added, "I have a plan. With this ship you could utterly obliterate Troyius. Then there would be no need for the marriage. Our grateful people would give you command of the star system."

He stared at her in horror. "How can you think of such a monstrous thing?"

"He is Troyian," she said. And was in his arms again. "You cannot fight against this love . . . against my love."

"Captain!" It was Spock on the intercom. There was a pause before he said, "May we see you a moment?"

Kirk didn't answer. The witch in his arms was right. He could not fight against this love, this passion, this fatality—whatever it was, whatever name one chose to give it. Nameless or named, it held him in thrall. His lips were on hers again—and the door opened. Spock and McCoy stood there, staring in unbelief.

"Jim!"

Kirk raised unseeing eyes.

"Jim! May I have a word with you, please?"

Kirk pulled free of the clinging arms; and moved toward the door with the slow, ponderous walk of a man walking under water. He looked back at Elaan. Then he stumbled out into the corridor.

"Captain, are you all right?" Spock said.

He nodded.

"Jim, did she cry?"

"What?"

"Did she cry? Did her tears touch your skin?"

Kirk frowned. "Yes."

McCoy sighed. "Then we're in trouble. Jim, listen to me. Petri told Christine that Elasian women's tears contain a biochemical substance that acts like a super, grade A love potion."

Kirk was staring at the hand that had wiped the tears from Elaan's cheek. "And according to Petri, the effects don't wear off," McCoy said.

"Bones, you've got to find me an antidote."

"I can try but I'll need to make tests of—"

The corridor intercom spoke. "Bridge to Captain!"

"Kirk here."

Sulu's anxious voice said, "Captain, the Klingon ship

has changed course! It's heading toward us at warp speed!"

All look of bemusement left Kirk's face. "Battle stations!" he ordered crisply. "I'm on my way."

Klaxon alarm shrieks filled the bridge as he stepped from the elevator. A fast glance at the screen showed the swiftly enlarging image of the Klingon ship. "Stand by, phasers!" he ordered, running to his command chair.

"Phasers ready, sir," Sulu reported.

Spock called, "His speed is better than Warp Six, Captain!"

Eyes on the screen, Kirk said, "Mr. Chekov, lay in a course to take us clear of this system. If he wants to fight, we'll need room to maneuver."

"Course computed, sir," Chekov said.

"And laid in, Captain."

"Very well, Mr. Sulu. Ahead, Warp Two and—"

The intercom beeped to the sound of Scott's agitated voice. "Captain! The matter-anti-matter reactor is—"

Before Scott had uttered the next word, Kirk had barked, "Belay that order, Mr. Sulu!"

Sulu jerked his hand from the button he was about to push as though it were red-hot. Spock left his station to come and stand beside Kirk.

"What is it, Scotty?"

Everyone on the bridge could hear Scott say, "The anti-matter pod is rigged to blow up the moment we go into warp drive."

Moments went by before Kirk spoke. Then he said, "That bomb he planted, Scotty. Can you dismantle it?"

"Not without blowing us halfway across the galaxy."

Like a blow Kirk could feel the pressure of the eyes focussed on him. He drew a deep breath. "Then give us every ounce of power you've got from the impulse drive. And find a solution to that bomb."

It was into this atmosphere of repressed excitement that Elaan stepped from the bridge elevator. On the screen the Klingon ship was growing in size and detail. "Mr. Sulu, stand by to make your maneuvers smartly. She'll be sluggish in response."

Kirk turned back to the screen and saw Elaan. Absorbed though he was in crisis, he had to fight the impulse to go to her by grasping the arms of his chair. Spock moved closer to him; and Sulu said tonelessly, "One hundred thousand kilometers."

Time ambled by. Then Sulu said, "Ninety kilometers."

"Hold your fire," Kirk said.

Sulu moistened his lips. "Sixty. Fifty."

On the screen the Klingon ship blurred in a burst of speed. "She's passed us without firing a shot," Sulu said very quietly.

"Captain, I don't think they meant to attack us," Spock said. Now that the crisis had passed, Kirk was conscious again only of the presence of Elaan. He rose from his chair as though pulled to her by an invisible chain. Watchful, Spock said warningly, "*This* time we have been fortunate."

The invisible chain snapped. Kirk sank back in his chair. "Yes, their tactics are clear now. They were trying to tempt us to cut in warp drive. That way we'd have blown ourselves up. Their problem would have been solved for them without risking war with the Federation. Very neat."

"Very," Spock said. "But why do they consider the possession of this system so vital?"

"A very good question, Mr. Spock."

"I have another question, sir. Isn't the bridge the wrong place for the Dohlman to be at a time like this?"

"I'll be the judge of—" Kirk began. He met Spock's eyes. "You're right, Mr. Spock. Thank you."

He strode over to Elaan. "I want you to leave the bridge and go to Sickbay. It's the best-protected part of the ship."

"I want to be with you," she said.

"Your presence here is interfering with my efficiency —my ability to protect you."

"I won't go."

Gripping her shoulders, he propelled her toward the elevator. Over her head, he looked at Spock. "You have the con, Mr. Spock."

As the elevator door slid closed, she flung her arms about his neck. "I love you. I have chosen you. But

I do not understand why you did not fight the Klingon."

"If I can do better by my mission by running away, then I run away."

"That mission," she said, "is to deliver me to Troyius."

"Yes, it is," he said.

"You would have me wear my wedding dress for another man and never see me again?"

"Yes, Elaan."

"Are you happy at that prospect?"

"No."

The intercom buzzed. "Scott to Captain."

"Kirk here."

"Bad news, Skipper. The entire dilythium crystal converter assembly is fused. No chance of repair. It's completely unusable."

"No way to restore warp drive?"

"Not without the dilythium crystal, sir. We can't even generate enough power to fire our weapons."

"Elaan, I've got to get back to the bridge. *Please* go to Sickbay. There's its door. Down this corridor."

She stood on tiptoe to kiss his forehead. "Yes, my brave love."

He watched her move down to the Sickbay door. Whatever chemical substance it was in the tears he had wiped from her cheek, it was powerful stuff.

Mysteriously baffling was how McCoy was finding it. Twenty-four tests—and analysis of it was as elusive as ever.

Petri watched him examine a read-out handed him by Nurse Christine. "You're wasting your time," he said. "There is no antidote to the poison of Elasian tears. The men of Elas have tried desperately to locate one. They've always failed." He had leaned back against his pillow when Elaan opened the Sickbay door. She addressed McCoy. "The Captain asked me to come here for safety."

Petri raised his head again. "And our safety? What about that with this woman around? How do you estimate our chances for survival, Dr. McCoy?"

"That's the Captain's responsibility," McCoy said.

Petri looked soberly thoughtful. After a long moment, he reached down into the gold casket he'd placed under his bed and withdrew the necklace Elaan had rejected. He pulled on his robe and walked slowly over to her.

"I have failed in my responsibility to my people," he said heavily. "With more wisdom I might have been able to prepare you to marry our ruler. Now that we may all die, I again ask you to accept this necklace as a token of respect for the true wish of my—of our people—for peace between us."

"Responsibility, duty—that's all you men ever think about!" she said angrily.

But she took the necklace.

When Kirk got back to the bridge, it was for more bad news. It was Uhura who had to give it to him. "A message from the Klingon ship, sir. We are ordered to stand by for boarding or be destroyed. They demand an immediate reply."

"So he's going to force a fight," Kirk said.

Back in his command chair, he struck his intercom button. "Kirk to Engineering. Energy status, Scotty?"

"Ninety-three percent of impulse power, Captain."

"We can still maneuver, sir," Spock said.

"Aye, we can wallow like a garbage scow," Scott said. "Our shields will hold out for a few passes. But without the matter-anti-matter reactors, we've no chance against a starship. Captain, can't you call Starfleet in *this* emergency?"

"And tell the Klingons they've succeeded in knocking out the warp engines?" Kirk retorted. "No, we'll stall for time."

He swung around to confront the taut faces in the bridge. "We will proceed," he said, "on course; in hope that the Klingons can be bluffed—or think better of starting a general war. Lieutenant Uhura, open a hailing frequency."

He seized his speaker. "This is Captain James Kirk of the *USS Enterprise* on Federation business. Our mission is peaceful but we are not prepared to accept interference."

The hoarse Klingon voice filled the bridge. "Prepare to be boarded or destroyed."

"Very effective, our strategy," Kirk muttered.

"Captain, the Klingon is closing in on an intercept course!" Sulu exclaimed. "Five hundred thousand kilometers." He added, "Deflector shields up!"

It was the moment Elaan chose to step out of the bridge elevator, radiant in the shimmering white of her wedding dress, the Troyian necklace of pellucid jewels around her neck. Kirk tore his eyes from the vision she made—and hit the intercom with his fist. "Mr. Scott, can you deliver even partial power to the main phaser banks?"

"No, sir. Not a chance."

Elaan was beside Kirk. Averting his eyes from her, he said, "I told you to stay in Sickbay."

"If I'm going to die, I want to die with you."

"We don't intend to die. Leave the bridge."

She drifted away toward the elevator and stopped to lean her head back against the wall.

Sulu shouted, "One thousand kilometers!"—and the ship shuddered under impact by a Klingon missile. As it burst against a deflector shield, its flash bathed the *Enterprise* in a multi-colored auroral light.

"He's passed us," Spock said. "All shields held."

"Mr. Sulu, come to 143 mark 2. Keep our forward shields to him."

"Here he comes again, sir," Sulu said.

"Stay with the controls. Keep those forward shields to him." On the screen the Klingon ship was an approaching streak of speed.

"He's going for our flank, Mr. Sulu. Hard over! Bring her around!"

The force of the second missile shook every chair in the bridge. "Sulu!" Kirk shouted.

"Sorry, Captain. She won't respond fast enough on impulse drive."

"He's passed us again," Spock said. "There's damage to number four shield, sir."

"How bad?"

"It won't take another full strike. Captain, I'm getting some very peculiar readings on the sensor board."

"What sort of readings, Mr. Spock?"

The Vulcan had seized his tricorder and was scanning the bridge area with it. Suddenly, he leaped from his chair to point to Elaan. "*She* is the source!" he cried.

"She?" Kirk said. "You mean Elaan?"

"The necklace, Captain!"

Both men ran to her. "What kind of jewels are in that thing?" Kirk demanded.

Bewildered, she fingered the necklace. "We call the white beads radans. They are quite common stones."

Spock scanned the diamonds with a circular device on his tricorder. Under it, they glowed and sparkled with an unearthly fire.

"It's only because of its antiquity that the necklace is prized," Elaan said.

"Common stones!" Kirk said. "No wonder the Klingons are interested in this star system! May I have that necklace, your glory?"

"If it can be of any help—of course," she said.

"You may just have saved our lives," Kirk said. "Mr. Spock, do you think Scotty could use some dilythium crystals?"

"There's a highly positive element in your supposition, Captain." The necklace in hand, Spock entered the elevator.

"He's coming in again, sir," Sulu cried.

"Mr. Sulu, stand by my order to turn *quickly* to port. Try to protect number four shield. *Now,* Mr. Sulu! Hard to port!"

Again the shields reflected the brilliant interplay of multi-colored light as the ship vibrated under shock by the Klingon attack. "Shields holding but weakened," Sulu called.

"Captain, message coming in," Uhura reported. At Kirk's nod, she hit the speaker.

The guttural Klingon voice had triumph in it. "*Enterprise,* our readings confirm your power extremly low, your shields buckling. This is your last chance to surrender."

Sulu said, "Number four shield just collapsed, sir. Impulse power down to 31 percent."

Kirk walked over to Uhura's station. "Lieutenant, open a channel." He seized the microphone. "This is Captain Kirk. I request your terms of surrender."

"No terms. Surrender must be unconditional and immediate."

Kirk struck the intercom button. "Scotty, what's the estimate?"

"We're fitting it now, sir. We'll need to run a few tests to make sure—"

"We'll test it in combat."

Spock said, "Those are crude crystals, sir. There's no way to judge what the unusual shapes will do to energy flow."

Scott used the intercom to add his caution. "Captain, a hitch in the energy flow could blow us up just as effectively as—"

Kirk cut him off. "Let me know when it's in place." He returned to Uhura. "Hailing frequency again, Lieutenant." Back at his command chair, he said into his speaker, "This is the *USS Enterprise.* Will you guarantee the safety of our passenger, the Dohlman of Elas?"

The harsh voice repeated, "No conditions. Surrender immediate."

"Captain, he's starting his run!"

"I see, Mr. Sulu." Standing before the screen, Kirk felt a quiet hand laid on his arm. Elaan watched with him as death in the form of the Klingon ship neared them, itself a black missile made vague by speed. Then Scott spoke from the intercom. "It's in place, sir—but I can't answer for . . ."

"Get up here fast!" Kirk said. He wheeled from the screen. "Mr. Sulu, stand by for warp maneuver. Mr. Chekov, arm photon torpedoes."

"Photon torpedoes ready, sir."

"Warp power to the shields, Captain?"

"Negative, Mr. Sulu. His sensors would pick up our power increase. The more helpless he thinks we are, the closer he'll come. It's as he passes I want warp drive cut in. You'll pivot at Warp Two, Mr. Sulu, to bring all tubes to bear."

"Aye, sir."

"Mr. Chekov, give him the full spread of photon torpedoes."

Scott rushed into the bridge to take his place at his station and Sulu said, "One hundred thousand kilometers, sir."

"Mr. Scott, stand by to cut in warp power."

The engineer looked up from his control. "Fluctuation, Captain. It's the shape of the crystals. I was afraid of that."

"Seventy-five kilometers," Sulu said.

"He'll fire at minimum range, Mr. Sulu."

"Forty," Sulu said.

Scott's worried eyes were on the flickering lights of his board. "It won't steady down, Captain."

The mass of the Klingon ship nearly filled the screen. Kirk said, "Warp in, Scotty. Full power to the shields. Mr. Sulu, warp two. Come to course 147 mark 3."

The Klingon ship fired. The *Enterprise* swerved, began to rotate dizzily in the dazzle of the now familiar auroral blaze reflected from its wounded shields.

"We're still here!" Scott cried, unbelieving.

"Fire photon torpedoes! Full spread!"

They waited. Elaan's hand found Kirk's. Then it came. From far out in space there came the shattering roar of explosion, of tearing metal. Another one detonated.

"Direct hit amidship by photon torpedo!" Sulu yelled.

Spock lifted his head. "Damage to Klingon number three shield, Captain. Number four obliterated. They've lost maneuver power, sir."

Chekov turned. "He's badly damaged. Retreating at reduced speed, sir."

"Secure from general quarters," Kirk said.

Elaan, her eyes shining with proud excitement, looked at him, startled. "You will not pursue and finish him off?"

"No." His eyes met hers. It was a long moment before he was able to say, "Mr. Sulu, resume course to Troyius."

Having said it, he looked away from the dead hope in her face.

In the Transporter Room, Petri had taken his place on the platform. As Elaan entered in her wedding dress, she touched the Troyian necklace she wore and smiled at him. "The two missing stones in this," she said, "saved all our lives, Ambassador Petri." He bowed deeply.

She went to Kirk. "You will beam-down for—the ceremony?"

"No."

She detached the jeweled dagger from her belt. "I wish you to have this as a personal memento. You have taught me that such things are no longer for me." She stooped and kissed his hand. "Remember me," she whispered.

"I have no choice," he said.

"Nor have I. All we've got now is duty and responsibility."

She took her place on the platform, her two guards beside her. "Good-bye, Captain James Kirk." Her voice broke.

"Good-bye," Kirk said. He walked swiftly to Scott at the transporter desk. "Energize," he said. Scott turned the dial and the figure of Elaan began to shimmer. He turned for his last look at her. Her eyes were on his, bright with tears.

McCoy met him excitedly as he walked out of the bridge elevator. "Jim, I've finally isolated the poisonous substance in that woman's tears. I think I've found the antidote."

"There's no need for it, Doctor," Spock said. "The Captain has found his own antidote. The *Enterprise* infected the Captain long before the Dohlman's tears touched him."

Kirk said, "Mr. Sulu, take us out of orbit. Ahead Warp Two."

Was the *Enterprise* the antidote to Elaan? McCoy and Spock seemed very sure it was. He was not so sure. Not now, anyway.